PENGUIN BOOKS

KILLING TIME

Praise for Murray Smith's bestselling novels:

'A first-rate action-adventure that made my palms sweat. With suspense as taut as a trip-mine wire, *The Devil's Juggler* sizzles. I couldn't put it down'
– Stephen Coonts

'A damn good read ... tense, topical and brutally authentic' – Frederick Forsyth

'Terrific, in a word' – *New York Daily News*

'*Stone Dancer* establishes him in the front rank of writers of spy novels' – *Sunday Telegraph*

'Masters like Len Deighton and John le Carré had better look to their laurels; Smith's assault on bestsellerdom seems like a sure thing'
– *Library Journal*

'Compelling and appealing ... Jardine is just what 007 would like to be if he ever grew up'
– *Publishers Weekly*

'I quite literally couldn't put it down ... [*Killing Time* is] his best yet' – Frederick Forsyth

ABOUT THE AUTHOR

Murray Smith, described by the *Independent on Sunday* as one of the most successful writers in British television, is the creator of the top-rated television series, *Strangers*, *Bulman* and *The Paradise Club*. A former paratrooper and Special Forces officer he has had first-hand experience of several of the world's areas of conflict and intrigue. His first novel, *The Devil's Juggler*, was received with great acclaim and has been published in fourteen countries. It was closely followed by *Stone Dancer*, which was another huge international success and was designated a Hero title by W.H. Smith. Both books are published by Penguin.

When not travelling in search of new material, Murray Smith divides his time between his country home, where he raises pedigree sheep, London and New York.

Killing Time

MURRAY SMITH

PENGUIN BOOKS

PENGUIN BOOKS

Published by the Penguin Group
Penguin Books Ltd, 27 Wrights Lane, London W8 5TZ, England
Penguin Books USA Inc., 375 Hudson Street, New York, New York 10014, USA
Penguin Books Australia Ltd, Ringwood, Victoria, Australia
Penguin Books Canada Ltd, 10 Alcorn Avenue, Toronto, Ontario, Canada M4V 3B2
Penguin Books (NZ) Ltd, 182–190 Wairau Road, Auckland 10, New Zealand

Penguin Books Ltd, Registered Offices: Harmondsworth, Middlesex, England

First published by Michael Joseph 1995
Published in Penguin Books 1996
1 3 5 7 9 10 8 6 4 2

Printed in England by Clays Ltd, St Ives plc

'Remorse disappears.'

– *The I Ching*

List of Characters

THE BRITISH

David Jardine: Director of Operations, SIS.
James Gant: A young man of good family, SIS new boy.
Ronnie Szabodo: Clandestine Operations Manager, SIS.
Richard Sykes: Chief of SIS.
Patrick Orde: Foreign Secretary.
Marietta Delice: Director, Counter Terror, Narcotics and Proliferation (CATNAP), SIS.
Kate Howard: Director, Security, SIS.
Stan: Section Head, Clerical 17, SIS.
Angeline: Officer, Clerical 17, SIS.
Eric: Officer, Clerical 17, SIS.
Heather: David Jardine's P/A, SIS.
Fiona Macleod: Intelligence Officer, SIS.
Euan Stevenson: Field Controller, Rome, SIS.
Roly Benedict: Head of Outstation, New York City, SIS.
Constantine Agamemnos: Chief Superintendent of Police, Cyprus Special Branch.
Lady Edith Treffewin: Retired Senior SIS Officer.
Dorothy Jardine: Jardine's wife.
Andrew Jardine: Jardine's son.
Sally Jardine: Jardine's daughter.
Charlotte Gant: Gant's sister.
Rebecca Reed: Gant's fiancée.

THE AMERICANS

Joe Cleary: Sergeant of Detectives, NYPD Homicide Dept.
Al Wiscynsky: Assistant Director, US Diplomatic Security Service.

Sam Vargos: Sergeant of Detectives, NYPD Homicide Dept.
Alan Clair: Director of Operations, CIA.
Harry K. Liebowitz: Assistant Director, Ops, CIA.
Tony Semprino: Intelligence Officer, Ops, CIA.
Frank Grumman: Mortuary Attendant, Bellevue Hospital, NYC.
Mike Curtis: US Ambassador to Cairo, Egypt.
Annabel Curtis: His wife.
Dolores Caltagirone: Restaurant Manageress and sometime hooker.
Johnny Stomparelli: Low-life, pimp and made-man of the Luccheses.
Jack Chisholm: Counterfeiter.
Dr Henry Grace: Scene-of-Crime Pathologist, NYPD.
William S. Clinton: President of the United States.

THE ABU NIDAL GROUP
Zina Farouche: Team Leader, Assassination Squad.
Hanna al-Farah: Commander of the Assassins.
Khaled Niknam: Terrorist.
Zafir Hammuda: Terrorist.
Ben Turabi: Terrorist.
Noor Jalud: Terrorist.
Abdul-Salem Latif: Commander, Station 16 Interrogation Camp, Libya.
Abdel Aziz al-Khaliq: Chairman, Membership Committee.
Sabri al-Banna: Leader of Fatah – the Revolutionary Council. Also called Abu Nidal.

THE IRANIANS
Hashemi Rafsanjani: Prime Minister of Iran.
Ayatollah Khomeini: Spiritual leader of the Islamic Revolution. Died 1991.
Sheik Jamil Shahidi: Vevak. Director-Special Missions.
Javd Assadiyan: Colonel, Special Missions Directorate.
Morteza Azmoudeh: Major, Savama Internal Security.
Mahmoud Dashti: 'Betty Boop'. Savama Illegal – New York Network.

plus sundry whores, diplomats, rollerbladers, bartenders and hit-men.

Key to Abbreviations & Organisations

SIS: British Secret Intelligence Service, also called MI 6.
NYPD: New York Police Department.
CIA: American Central Intelligence Agency.
DSS: American Diplomatic Security Service.
FBI: American Federal Bureau of Investigation.
Sdec: Service Documentaire de l'espionnage et contre-espionnage. France.
Vevak: Iran's Ministry of Intelligence & Security.
Special Missions Directorate: Department of VEVAK controlling clandestine terror and assassination missions abroad.
Savama: Iran's foreign intelligence service.
Pasdaran: Iran's 'Revolutionary Guard'. Controlled by Islamic fundamentalist clergy, to safeguard the 1979 overthrow of the Shah and the establishment of a fundamentalist Islamic state.
PLO: Palestine Liberation Organization. Now opposed to terrorism. Run by Yasser Arafat.
FRC: Fatah – The Revolutionary Council. Renegade Palestinian terror group, run by Abu Nidal.
Special Missions Committee (FRC): Section of Abu Nidal's renegade terror group controlling international clandestine missions esp. bombings, assassinations and hijackings.
Hamas: Palestinian insurgent group. Based in Israeli West Bank, which is mandated to the PLO.
Hezbollah (Party of God): Islamic fundamentalist group. Based in West Beirut, Lebanon.
Islamic Tide: A clandestine terror movement combining

Iranian, Palestinian and other mid-eastern extremist groups, including Hamas, Hezbollah and Abu Nidal's FRC, trained and directed by Iran and its Sudanese partners.

Intel: Abbreviation for Intelligence.

Ops: Abbreviation for Covert Operations.

For Jane

He often wondered, in later years, if things would have worked out differently if he had retained his innocence just a few summers longer. If the first killings had never happened.

Or, if they had to, if that had been part of the disorder of things, why in hell he had been required by his destiny, or by Fate, or Providence, or whatever, to be present . . .

Six in the morning at Rome Airport was kind of a no-man's-land. Tired travellers moved back and forth in that listless, detached way of those who had a journey to make and had been required to haul themselves out of bed in the middle of the night.

The boy, temporarily abandoned to guard his family's luggage, watched through half-closed eyes as, about thirty yards in front of him, some of the passengers were beginning to congregate in the gloom of first light at the three-sided square of El Al check-in desks, and a tannoy system announced in Italian that Flight EA 152 was late in arriving from Amsterdam, *en route* to Tel Aviv.

Knots of itinerant Jews were gradually multiplying. In the half-light, James Gant idly observed plump old women in dull overcoats and headscarves. There were also younger women with small children, and men wearing what James imagined to be Talmudic shawls over black coats, with black felt hats and the dark ringlets of Orthodoxy curling down in front of their ears. Their luggage was kept close to them and some of the older, or the more fatigued, sat on suitcases and bulky travelling bags.

His sister appeared, momentarily, on the periphery of his vision, moving behind him, but, as he turned to attract her attention, his hand rising, she had vanished, intent on joining their mother who he knew would not be too far from the brat.

It had been a good summer. The scuba-diving instructor had complimented him on his calmness and attention to detail, even permitting him to dive in the adult areas where, although the fourteen-year-old youth was proud to be so well-thought-of, he had been scared profoundly. And the Hobie Cat had been brilliant. Sailing that thing alone, with one hull lifted clear of the water, leaning right out over the hissing wavelets, salt water stinging his eyes. That had been something else.

And April Lee Stuart, from White Sulphur Springs, West Virginia, with her apple-fresh, darting tongue . . . easing James from being one of life's apprentices to full membership of the human race.

She had promised to write.

Oh, yes. All in all, a most excellent vacation.

From time to time, and with increasing frequency, uniformed and plain clothes Israeli security guards emerged from behind some screens and questioned the tired travellers intensely, sometimes aggressively, ordering some, it seemed to be at random, to open their baggage and turn out the contents for inspection.

James glanced once more at his tanned forearms, checking for signs of the dreaded peeling skin, when, abruptly, unbelievably, groups of El Al travellers began to collapse where they stood, simultaneously with the terrifying, hammering din of machine-guns.

Oh, Christ, James thought. Although afterwards they said he had screamed it. Oh Christ Oh Christ Oh Christ.

Afterwards, replaying the slow-motion horror over and over in his mind, the boy could not recall any crying out or shouting. One or two of the victims moved about for several endless moments, their progress impeded by relentless bullets, their clothing erupting off them in rags, blood everywhere, spraying obscenely, slippery under foot, stumbling as their legs were shot from under them, arms flung out. Or clutching at appalling wounds.

Two burning slaps on his left cheek forced him to glance away from the horror in time to see, with amazing clarity, another spent 7.62 cartridge case flying, tumbling lazily towards him and, as he ducked, his gaze focused on a handsome woman of about twenty, hunched into an AK-47 assault rifle, her lips parted in a grimace of ... pleasure! ... as she emptied magazine after magazine into the helpless groups of terrified passengers.

It seemed to go on for ever. James Gant tried to move but he could not get his limbs to work. The noise of shooting in that echoing airport hall was dreadful, the smell of cordite all-pervading, the futile movements of old men and infants trying to crawl out of the way pathetic.

The girl, her head half wrapped in a green cotton scarf, eyes bright, appeared to be elated at her work. Then she seemed to trip, dropping heavily onto her knees as if winded, her gun fired twice more and at the same time pieces of hair and the green scarf lifted off the back of her head and James Gant knew she herself, the instrument of death, was being shot. He put his own arms up, instinctively, to shield himself, and yet more firing went on, for there were three more attackers, all men, then, abruptly, total silence, except for the metallic sound of empty cartridge cases rolling around the floor.

He could never quite remember his father hugging him, his mother's tears of relief and guilt at leaving him alone or the accusing looks from the precious Infanta, annoyed that for once her brother was the centre of attention. He could never quite remember the row his father had with the Italian authorities, who had insisted on a witness statement but had settled for a contact address in England. The flight home was a blur, because for every moment of the journey he could see only that vicious face, contorted by a murderous fanaticism that had made so ugly what was otherwise a good-looking young woman, not much older than April Stuart.

And, although all the crowded events of growing up, of family joys and tragedies, of years of study competing with a young man's programme of football, sailing, women and parties, soon healed the memory of that day, no other event would have such an impact on this James Sebastian Gant, whose uncharted future was to carry him relentlessly into a world more dangerous than he had ever dreamed of.

I

A Whisper of Babylon

'It's never nice', the Englishman said, 'to be distrusted by one's oldest allies.'

Alan Clair smiled, as he pushed the rear door of his Buick sedan shut and glanced around. 'I thought', he said, 'the Portuguese were your oldest allies.'

The car had dropped them on M Street, in Georgetown, Washington DC, just a few yards from the corner with Nathan's bar and restaurant. As it moved quietly away from the kerb, the two men began to stroll towards the next intersection.

Old friends, they had first met in Hue, Vietnam, on the eve of the Tet offensive that erupted in the small hours of 31 January 1968. A Cao Dai priest, one of Clair's informers, had given them fourteen hours' warning of the massive Vietcong and NVA attack on over 100 South Vietnamese and US urban installations throughout South Vietnam. It had cost the Communists in excess of forty thousand dead, but so shook the American administration that Tet was generally accepted to be the beginning of the end.

The secret history of that war records that the priest's warning was too late, and probably ignored by military commanders who had less than total faith in the Agency's predictions. But the ensuing days were violent and frightening for the young Englishman, a Secret Intelligence Service field operator by the name of David Jardine, and for Alan Clair, at that time a CIA Intelligence Officer running agents north of the Mekong Delta.

Clair and Jardine had bumped into each other over the years, in clandestine operations from Berlin to Beirut, Moscow and the Far East. Theirs was a friendship that had withstood the shifting sands and unreliable temperatures which sometimes affected the relationship between their respective services.

Jardine was now in his late forties; tall, untidily assembled, with a face that suggested he might at one time have been a fairly unsuccessful boxer. His affection for the other man was unshakeable, but, on the professional front, there were the beginnings of a problem.

The December 1988 Lockerbie bombing of Pan Am Flight 103, headed for New York, had been traced back to Iran, via Syria and Libya, as had the February 1993 New York World Trade Center bomb with its seven deaths and 1,100 casualties. And David Jardine's SIS had worked closely with the Agency, the FBI and the Israeli Mossad to identify the culprits. Although, for many reasons, their evidence was not destined for the criminal law courts.

But, on that sunny April day in Washington DC, as they strolled towards Madeo's, a recently opened Italian restaurant, Jardine was right in discerning an element of distrust in Alan Clair's thoughtful attitude.

'I'll get right to the point,' said the CIA man. 'David, we think you people are running an asset in New York City. Probably, but not exclusively, an Iranian. And this guy, or woman, maybe it's a woman, chador or no chador, knows practically the entire order of battle of our friends in Tehran. Plus what they think and what they are up to right now.'

'Well, that is what we do for a living . . .' Jardine smiled at a good-looking girl roller-skating past, wearing a loose T-shirt, cut off to display a tanned and slender midriff.

'Sure. But we do have one or two rules. Correct me if I'm mistaken.' Clair meant the USA and Britain had a treaty which expressly forbade conducting independent spying operations on each other's sovereign territory. It was a treaty more often abused than officials in the more regular realms of government would have dreamed of. And Jardine had long since forgotten how to blush. 'Well, I wouldn't insult your intelligence, Alan. You're absolutely right . . .'

'That's fine,' replied Clair, neither surprised nor outraged. 'Now we're getting somewhere. So we should wipe the slate clean and share the source. And the cost. I'll just say you guys involved me from the start . . .' The Agency's Director (Operations) smiled. He was quite pleased with this solution.

Jardine paused and gazed into a store window, displaying all kinds of native American artefacts and old Creole stuff from further south.

'I don't think so,' he replied, and there was just a breath of ice in his voice.

Clair stared at Jardine's reflection in the shop window. He contemplated for a minute, then he asked, quietly, 'What's up?'

In the mirrored image, Jardine's eyes met his. The English spy looked tired. He shrugged. 'Don't push us, Alan. I want to be able to level with you. But right now I can't.'

'Is it Ames . . .?'

Clair meant the investigation that the Company was conducting into one of its middle-rank intelligence managers. Aldrich Ames was suspected of selling CIA secrets to the old KGB and the current Russian Foreign Intelligence Service. His motive, they suspected, was not ideology but old-fashioned greed.

David Jardine turned and stared at his friend. He looked like somebody telling his favourite son the dog was dead. 'I'm asking for some time. God knows you don't have to give it . . .'

After a long pause, Alan Clair thrust his hands deep inside his coat pockets and gazed at his feet, turning the toes together. Then he nodded and glanced directly at Jardine. 'David, this is very bad. If we catch you fucking around in NYC we'll burn you. And your fuckin' asset. You dig?'

Jardine inclined his head. 'I do indeed. I truly do.'

As he moved on, Clair said, with a bitter edge to his voice, 'And they used to say we had a special relationship.'

'Yep,' replied the man from SIS, 'I've heard that . . .'

Round about the time that conversation was taking place, James Gant, now twenty-seven, was sitting in a night club, in a basement below a basement, in a war zone. The town was Sarajevo. The country, Bosnia, in what had once been

Yugoslavia. The war was a brutish affair, where relentless shelling, gratuitous mutilation and rape had become the norm.

Gant's unforgiving destiny had thus far taken him through a lacklustre university pass and a job with the British Broadcasting Corporation as a news cameraman and editor, with bonus pay for hazardous assignments, for which he seemed to have found an aptitude.

The disc jockey would have been a beefy guy, before the war. Now his faded denim vest and Ice-T T-shirt hung loose on his skinny frame and the leather pants looked painfully baggy on his ill-nourished legs.

But there was nothing pathetic about the cool energy that radiated from him as he mixed from the Rolling Stones to a black Harlem number by a sassy group called Salt 'n Pepa. It was at the same time hostile and funny and it was called 'Somebody's gettin' on my nerves'. James Gant laughed as the sweating dancers joined in with their own words, in fractured English, including about seven young, bearded and serious-faced Mujahadeen soldiers who danced in a beautifully rhythmic and exclusive ensemble, their steps perfectly in time and learned exactly from the video recording of a live Salt 'n Pepa concert high in the corner of the basement.

'Somebody', the doomed revellers chanted in happy irony, 'is gettin' on my nerves.' And he smiled back at a glowing, scrawny, once beautiful brunette, her shoulder bones too obvious, cheeks too hollow, as she mouthed the words and swigged from a bottle of the local Sarajevo slivovitz, a fiery brew that helped to keep the bombarded, ruined city going.

The lights flickered and the cellar trembled momentarily. A few flakes of remaining plaster fluttered from the cracked ceiling like . . . like what, wondered Gant. Confetti? Or like earth, falling in slow motion, on top of a coffin.

'Who are you working for?' asked the girl about an hour later, sharing a bottle of Kronenbourg from the French Foreign Legion's 2nd Regiment of Parachutists, who were out at the airport. They usually contributed a few cases to the Inferno Club.

James Gant indicated a serious-faced man of about forty-three, sitting on an upturned ammo crate, his flak jacket on the floor beside a makeshift table. The BBC's war chronicler, face familiar to twenty million British homes. On the wall behind him was a giant, torn poster of Jimi Hendrix.

'Him,' he said.

'Are you a cameraman?' She ran a finger along his forearm, and flickered once vamp-like eyes at him. Infinitely exhausted eyes. Way past fear. Beyond grief. 'Sometimes.' He watched the cellar door open and two of the current UN General's bodyguards slid in. For a moment he wondered if, to compound the existing surreality, the everyday madness of the shattered city, the General had just given up his impossible task and decided to get on down and boogie the hellish night away. Like the sane people. Like James and the BBC war reporter and the Disc Jockey and the elegantly surfing Mujahadeen. But it was the bodyguards' four hours off and they looked like they needed a drink.

'And some other times, what?' Stone sober, she offered him the bottle and he took a swig.

'Fuck this war,' he said. By way of a toast.

'Fuck Karadzic,' she responded. Across the cellar, two incredibly drunk Bosnian policemen had started pushing each other. They were soon gently restrained, with infinite patience, by some of the others. Including one of the gravediggers from what had been the Sarajevo soccer stadium, now a mass burial place.

'Sometimes editor,' James said, for her eyes had been waiting for a response. It did not do to leave questions unanswered. Fear might have been exhausted, but suspicion was not.

'And when will you move on? To some other circus . . .' she asked, with weary, Slavonic cynicism.

'It was going to be Monday.'

But then someone had shot down an Italian C-130 transport plane, bringing in medical supplies, and the airport was taking incoming, even as they spoke.

'Would you like to do something for me?' She watched him, almost sultry, even in her gaunt exhaustion.

'What?'

The girl opened her soft leather shoulder bag, a once modish item from one of Sarajevo's chic boutiques, now reduced to shell-blasted rubble, and produced a bundle of about five envelopes, each neatly addressed to someone called R. Bicerkovic, in Tufnell Park, London. 'Would you post these for me?'

It was difficult to get such a simple favour done, for the UN actually searched those leaving the war zone, to confiscate outgoing mail from the besieged population.

James Gant gazed at her. This hellish place was another planet. In a way, you had to dislocate normal feelings of compassion and human sympathy. If you were to survive. Tufnell Park was corner stores and mini-cabs, dull pubs and laundromats. Where comfortable, self-possessed, drab apartment-dwellers watched NYPD Blue and couldn't give a stuff about local politics, let alone disembowel their neighbours and burn their houses on a whim of race, or ethnic loathing.

'Sure,' he said. It was easy enough for someone in a media crew to smuggle out a few letters. And he knew, as she looked at him, that she was grateful enough to let him screw her. And, embarrassed, the young Englishman tried, without success, to disguise his distaste, at the idea of physical contact with one so undernourished. So emaciated.

'Soon as I get to London. I'll post them locally. Cross my very heart.' And Gant met her eyes and smiled into them. With practised sincerity.

Ten days later, James was back in London, on the second floor of the BBC's main building at the Television Centre, Wood Lane. He was busy editing a four-minute slot for the six o'clock news when the phone rang. A quiet voice enquired, 'Mr Gant?'

'That's me,' James replied.

'My name is Estergomy. Frederick, K.'

'Well, top of the morning to you, Frederick K.'

After a slightly foxed pause, for it was 3.10 in the afternoon, the voice called Estergomy said, 'Lady Treffewin suggested I should call you. I hope this is not an inconvenient moment.'

James glanced at his watch. It could not have been more inconvenient, but Edith was his favourite aunt. A doughty dowager of seventy-three, who could pass for one of Oscar Wilde's grander characters, she had started life as, she claimed, an 'actress'. But in fact, she had been one of the high kickers on the chorus line at Murray's Cabaret in London's West End. She still had great legs and her story was something of a legend. Edith's first (-ish) lover, the Earl Treffewin, had saved her, aged eighteen, from the life of a dancer and, when he realized he had fallen in love, the young aristocrat had married her, against his family's wishes. The Earl, aged twenty-six, had died with most of his platoon at Monte Cassino in 1944, fighting against the cream of the German Wehrmacht.

The young widow – their infant son having inherited the title, she became, in accordance with aristocratic law, the Dowager Lady Treffewin – had used her small inheritance and War Widow's pension to put herself through college, where she graduated in Modern Languages, and had spent the rest of her life in some obscure government department, before retiring and becoming an authority on, of all things, rare fleas.

James Gant, like the rest of his family, adored Aunt Edith, and if she wanted him to speak to this mid-European-sounding guy, well, that was all right with him.

'No problem. How can I help you?'

'I have a young relation. She's awfully keen.'

The word 'awfully' just didn't sit right with the strange admixture of old-fashioned Oxbridge and some Balkan or Slav fracturing of words like inconvenient and, indeed, Treffewin.

'Keen on what, Mr Ester-, um . . .?'

'Estergomy. Call me Fred, it's easier. She is keen, James, on editing work. And she badly needs to talk to someone who has beaten the ropes.'

James Gant frowned. 'And Edith said you should get in touch with me . . .?'

'Spot on.'

Spot on; what planet was this guy from? James scratched his head. 'When? When would be a good time?'

There was a slight pause; Gant's gaze focused on the Moviola editing machine, where a distraught Bosnian peasant woman was frozen on a single, lit frame of 16mm colour film, bent over a bundle of rags, in the ruins of a small farmhouse.

The bundle had been all that remained of her youngest child, after a Serbian militia unit had passed that way.

'Tomorrow evening? Just after work?'

No. Rebecca and he were going to the director's cut of *Blade Runner*.

'Tell you what, Fred. Tomorrow's a bitch. How about six-thirty tonight?' And, before any haggling could take place, Gant continued, 'There's a pub called The Scarsdale, in a little square just off High Street Kensington.'

'Yes, I know it.'

'Well, that's the best I can do.' And, just to soften his businesslike tone, 'I'll try to give her good advice, don't worry.'

'That's very kind of you, James Gant.'

'See you at six-thirty.'

'Her name is Amanda.'

'Good.'

'Six-thirty. The Scarsdale.'

'Are you sure you'll find it?'

'We'll be there. Thank you for your kindness.'

Gant smiled. 'I haven't done anything yet.'

The mid-European voice seemed . . . amused. 'See you later.'

Gant replaced the receiver and pressed on with his work.

In the Iranian city of Tehran there is a room in a government building which was once the palace of the Shah of Iran, heir to the Peacock Throne, in the days before the Islamic revolution and the iron rule of the ayatollahs, and their undisputed leader, even in death, the Ayatollah Khomeini.

It is a big room, as befits a palace, and it once clinked to the crystal of a few dozen champagne glasses, mingled with the tinkling of water falling on the rose-petal-covered surface of its now dry fountains, set into marble and gold inlaid walls.

It was a quieter place on that sultry June day, eighteen years later, and the splendour of its ancient rugs and damask wall hangings, crystal chandeliers from France and huge antique mirrors from Venice, had long ago been replaced by rubber-tiled floors, industrial strip-lighting of the sort that glows sodium-cold, and the only things hanging on the marble sides were two plain wood-framed poster-type portraits. One was of Khomeini. The other was of his spiritual successor, the Ayatollah Khamenie, Head of the Shi'ite Islamic fundamentalist clergy, who ruled Iran in tandem with the secular and more worldly President Hashemi Rafsanjani.

Rafsanjani was trying to ease his nation into more normal relations with other countries, for Iran had been shunned by the civilized world, disgusted by the bloody excesses of its Islamic Fundamentalist Mullahs and their Revolutionary Guard, following the overthrow of the Shah in 1979. But the clergy, the Mullahs and the Ayatollahs, wielded the real power, holding millions of fanatical believers in their thrall, not only within Iran's borders but throughout the Islamic universe, from the Philippines to North Africa and from immigrant Europe to New York City, where the World Trade Center had been bombed, with devastating effect, by extreme fundamentalist disciples of the two men whose plain, black and white portraits hung on the sad marble walls.

The drab floor was partly partitioned into four areas, in each of which were two or three desks, where grey and black-garbed officials and computer operators worked quietly, the men bearded and plainly clothed, the women's features cloaked in the traditional grey-and-white chadors which Allah and modesty – and the ayatollahs – required.

One area was larger than the others, and it had two long, plain couches and a priceless Ottoman rug, in addition to a teak desk which had survived the burning and wholesale destruction of the Shah's treasures. Behind this desk sat a lean, spade-bearded man, whose simple robes and collarless white shirt could not disguise a certain nobility of feature, a calm, yet sinister, dignity, and a bearing, even while seated, which had several times been described as chilling.

This was Ayatollah Sheik Jamil Shahidi, Director of the Iranian Clergy's secretive Intelligence Bureau – Foreign Department. His service was independent of Savama, the Iranian Intelligence Agency, and he answered, in theory, to the Ministry of Intelligence and Security, Vevak, where he held the rank of Brigadier. But, in reality, Shahidi answered only to Ayatollah Khamenie and to a secret council of the clergy, led by Sheik Fadlallah. He had agents in Savama,

Vevak, the Iranian Foreign Service, the Secret Police and the Military.

It was Shahidi who had arranged the bombing of the World Trade Center, in New York. And it was Shahidi who was tasked with the execution of the heretic novelist, Salman Rushdie, since the Fatwah, the irrevocable sentence of death, had been pronounced by Ayatollah Khomeini, upon the publication of Rushdie's blasphemous novel, *The Satanic Verses*.

Jamil Shahidi gazed at the stocky Arab sitting, unperturbed, in front of him. The man was clearly over-indulgent, his face, jowls and belly speaking volumes about his enthusiasm for food. And probably Scotch whisky, for many of those Palestinian hoodlums could not get enough of the stuff.

'And how is Sabri al-Banna?' asked Shahidi, in English.

Sabri al-Banna was the real name of a professional international terrorist chieftain, who carried out his butcher's business under the *nom de guerre* Abu Nidal.

'He sends his respects, Sheik Shahidi. And I am to take your message directly to him and no one else.' The Arab was Abdel Aziz al-Khaliq. Abu Nidal's right-hand man. His acts of terror were claimed in his code-name of Abu Awwad.

A West Bank Palestinian, born in 1947, al-Khaliq was controller of the lethally secret Abu Nidal organization's Membership Committee. And therefore one of the very few men the paranoid terror boss almost trusted.

'Tell him this,' went on Shahidi, 'and commit it to memory, for nothing is to be written down in respect of this matter.'

'I am ready . . .' al-Khaliq's memory was formidable – which was why the intelligence services of quite a few nations had entertained the idea of kidnapping him and filling him with Scopolamine, the truth drug.

And Jamil Shahidi proceeded to outline the Iranian clergy's secret proposal, for the Abu Nidal terrorist group to take on the contract for yet another act of terror, against the USA, which was designed to shock the world.

The Scarsdale was one of those traditional London pubs which had actually improved over the years. Untouched by the ravages of plastic and mock Tudor 'improvements', the passage of time had given the place a comfortably worn look, and the small front courtyard was a cheerful riot of hanging baskets of plants and flowers. Inside, it was busy with people on the way home from work, or local residents just back from other parts of the metropolis. The clientele was mostly young, and the hard-pressed bar staff did their best to keep everyone happy.

James Gant closed the door and shut out the buzz of chatter and cheerful laughter from the courtyard. He glanced around, wondering if he would recognize this Fred Estergomy, and his niece who was so 'keen'.

What Fred Estergomy (Ronnie Szabodo) saw was a slender, tallish young man, wearing glasses which were almost rimless, linen trousers – colour dark, maybe blue – a faded cotton shirt with no tie and a shapeless, baggy soft tweed jacket which could either be from the Oxfam second-hand shop or from Armani. He knew it was Gant because, apart from the blurred Sarajevo photograph, he had studied a couple of more detailed close-ups, snatched by London Station's muggers, who worked out of a car re-spray and repair business, located under some railway arches in Brixton.

Szabodo observed James Gant from his table in a corner alcove. To his guarded approval, Gant had not hung around the doorway looking lost, but had moved in casually, checking out the clientele as he squeezed through towards the bar. He was not particularly noticed by the others. Just another guy in a bar.

Thus the potential recruit passed his first hurdle, for in Ronnie Szabodo's arcane lexicon of things to look for, and he had learned the hard way, pausing in a doorway and looking lost, unsure or otherwise vulnerable, was a definite 'No', and, as far as the Hungarian was concerned, end of story. End of recruiting expedition.

If this seems harsh, Szabodo had risked his own life keeping many apprentice spies alive – including the now illustrious, ingrained professional, David Arbuthnot Jardine, Director of Operations no less – and he was, those days, inclined to take on only those men and women with at least the beginnings of a survivor's aptitude.

'That's him, is it?' Amanda Lewis peeled a piece of wafer-thin paper from its little green Rizla packet.

'You're supposed to be a fresh young hopeful. I don't think rolling your own fits the image,' murmured Szabodo. 'Put it away, there's a good girl.'

Amanda Jane Lewis made a face at him and put the cigarette paper back in her purse.

At which moment, James Gant arrived at their table, smiling tentatively.

'Mr, um . . .?'

'Fred Estergomy,' Ronnie Szabodo scrambled untidily to his feet, offering his hand.

It's amazing, thought Gant, how closely this Fred what's'is-name resembles his voice. He had looked for a middle-aged man, with a young woman. The man was more or less what he had imagined – conservatively attired in a sports coat of sage tweed, with an incongruous, button-down shirt of pale blue denim and a Royal Navy tie. Squat in build, with eyes that missed nothing, set in a slab-like Mid-European face with tobacco-stained teeth, except for one of the two front ones, which was too clean and just had to be a denture.

'Cheers, Fred, pleased to meet you.' Gant allowed his gaze to move to the girl, who was still sitting, watching him warily as if, somehow, it was he who had come to her for a favour.

'And this is Amanda . . .' Szabodo grinned and extended his arm, including his young companion.

She's not bad, thought Gant. Hair a bit take-it-or-leave-it, but intelligent eyes and quite classy bone structure. And the mouth had potential, as it smiled coolly.

'Hi,' he said, guessing her to be a couple of years younger than Chas, his sister, who was now twenty-five and doing very well cooking for fat cats in the City, 'can I get you a drink?' and smiled at the man called Estergomy, including him in the offer.

'It's my shout, old man.' Ronnie Szabodo eased past, lifting his half-finished pint glass from the polished table top, defaced with old cigarette burns and faint circles from a hundred glasses and tumblers of many circumferences.

'Mine's a beer. Bass, if you can get it.'

'Draught or bottled?' Szabodo glanced casually into his eyes.

'Draught.'
'Straight glass or handle?'
For God's sake, thought Gant, just get me a bloody drink.
'Straight,' he beamed politely, 'would be absolutely wonderful. Thank you, Fred.' And, dismissing the Hungarian, Gant pulled up a chair and sat down.
'Roll your own, then?' He indicated a tin of tobacco on the table beside her purse.

'He was actually courteous. To Amanda.' Ronnie Szabodo stood relieving himself at the porcelain Armitage Shanks urinal in the men's room on the south-east corner of the seventh floor at Century House. 'He reminded me of a young version of you.'
'Poor sod.' Jardine bent over a washbasin, splashing water on his face. He had been in the main operations room since four in the morning. Overseeing the clandestine lifting of secrets from one of Britain's oldest, but presently lukewarm, allies.
'Who is Amanda,' he enquired, 'when she's at home?'
'The niece, David. Remember?'
'And what particular pie did she jump out of?'
'Intake Forty-Three. She's just finishing at the Farm. First posting is to be Hanoi, I hear from personnel. Good kid. She has balls.'
Jardine paused, pulling the plug from the washbasin and reaching for a towel; his eyes met Ronnie's reflected gaze in the washroom mirror.
'Tell me about him. Worth the beer?'
Szabodo joined Jardine, washing his hands at the next basin. 'Patient. Good listener. Good memory. Discreet. Twenty-seven going on forty. Fancied her, I would say. But never let it show.'
'And did you?'
'One is already committed,' said Szabodo, almost shyly, and David Jardine's mind reeled at the thought of who might have him. Szabodo must have read his thoughts for he grinned, revealing a gap where one front tooth was missing. The cleaner-than-natural denture was only for more formal occasions.

'My condolences to the unlucky woman,' murmured Jardine. 'So what about the Dowager's talent spotting . . .?'

Unknown to any of her relations, James Gant's favourite aunt, Edith Treffewin, had been one of the Firm's most able operators, after her self-financed education, and in fact she had been Jardine's boss, twenty-three years before, when they had run a clandestine circuit in Berlin, operating a black market ring in the Russian sector, dealing in Marks & Spencer's women's underwear, New Zealand butter, prophylactics, Scotch whisky and the wholesale bribery and blackmail of Soviet and East German officials.

It was fairly rare for David Jardine to bother himself with the business of recruiting new blood for the Office. However, Lady Edith had never suggested anyone before, and the man Gant seemed to be made in the right mould, for his name had cropped up, the way these things sometimes do, in recent reports from hardened secret operators in regions of conflict and intrigue. To be specific, Bosnia and Kurdistan.

Ronnie Szabodo dried his hands on the same piece of towel. He frowned. 'He could, actually, have the makings.'

Coming from Ronnie, who had trained Jardine and was unforgiving in the selection of potential recruits to the point of obsession, this was something approaching praise.

David Jardine straightened his tie, and peered at his creased features and his broken nose. 'I'm getting old, Ronnie. This is not my face any more.'

'Follow it through, then?' asked Szabodo.

'Why not?' replied Jardine, with many more vital things on his mind than the maybe/maybe not recruitment of a young man of good family into the brotherhood of the Great Glass Box, and he went out, into the corridors of that castle of secrets, where he and a few colleagues plundered the affairs of nations, for the common good.

Several weeks went by, during which time James Gant, unaware that others were now taking a discreet interest in him, returned to Bosnia, flying in by C-130 transport from Ancona airfield in Italy, assigned as second cameraman to veteran BBC reporter Sam Baldwin.

Worldwide anger had been aroused by the relentless killing

of mainly Muslim Bosnian civilians by the Orthodox Christian Serbs, and international outrage followed the filming by Gant and Baldwin of a Serbian artillery strike on a UN relief convoy and the ferocious machine-gunning of the survivors, sixteen French and British soldiers, as they lay wounded and returning fire.

This episode not only almost got them killed and raised Gant's pulse and adrenaline levels to unprecedented heights, it also highlighted the Catch-22-type anomaly of the UN's half-hearted commitment to its men on the ground. For the TV team's live pictures showed embarrassingly futile low-level runs by two British Royal Navy Harrier fighters and two US Navy F-16s, sweeping close overhead, afterburners roaring impotently, and firing not a shot, dropping not one bomb, because the United Nations Command, safely ensconced in Zagreb, many miles to the north, had refused, yet again, to give the OK for those aircraft to engage.

The news item was replayed several times that evening and sold by the BBC worldwide, with still photographs appearing next day in the international press, and it turned out to be a major factor in persuading the British Foreign Secretary to demand from the British Intelligence Service a series of in-depth plans (the word in his memorandum was 'recommendations') for a clandestine programme aimed at destroying 'most comprehensively' the Belgrade-based Serbian economy.

But SIS had put forward the view that to take the side of the Muslim Bosnians would be tantamount to allowing Tehran-led Islamic extremism into Europe through the Balkans. This view was influenced by a string of quite astonishingly successful espionage operations David Jardine was running inside the Denied Areas of Iran, the international Islamic Extremist movement, Hezbollah and the more radical Palestinian terror groups.

Bosnia was a tragedy, SIS accepted, but the extremist regime of the Ayatollahs and Mullahs of Tehran had seized upon the vicious territorial war to establish a foothold on the European continent.

There was little Jardine did not know about the Iranians' plans and secret liaisons. He believed that the collective mullahs' vision of an Islam-dominated world, imposed by atrocity, conspiracy, terror, revolution and, finally, nuclear-backed military might, was as mad as anything Adolf Hitler had dreamed up.

Long afterwards, when they analysed where things had gone so very wrong, the post-planners at Ryemarsh identified a lunchtime conversation, between the Foreign Secretary and the Director-General of the Intelligence Service, as being a principal, if unwitting, factor in deciding the fate of young James Gant, a man of whose very existence neither was at that time aware. And the politician probably never would be.

'Warren Christopher is fuming,' the Foreign Secretary, Patrick Orde, had said to Richard Sykes, his Intelligence chief, over a light lunch, washed down with a flagon of claret, in the slightly shabby, but exclusively old money, upstairs restaurant of their club, in the upper reaches of St James's Street. 'First because we won't back him over the Americans' desire to bomb the Serbs, deeply satisfying although that would undoubtedly be. And, more germane to your organization, he says we are withholding vital intelligence from the CIA, and he is threatening to order a halt to sharing their Satellite Intelligence with us unless you chaps stop playing silly buggers.'

'I'm afraid it's not quite so simple,' replied Sykes. And he went on to explain that SIS had good reason to suspect the Aldrich Ames affair was perhaps not the only example of bad apples in the American Intelligence community selling secrets for money.

'Remember the Walkers,' he said, referring to a family of all-American navy men who had sold devastatingly damaging secrets to the KGB, ten years earlier.

'Actually, Richard,' the Foreign Minister sipped his wine and gazed coolly at Sykes, 'unless you can be more specific, I imagine the PM would not want you to, ah . . . jeopardize our special relationship on a mere hunch.'

'It's more than a hunch.'

'Really . . .?' Patrick Orde delicately picked an atom of lamb chop from his teeth. 'Am I allowed to know?'

He meant that, as Foreign Secretary, he was nominally the

government minister responsible for the day-to-day supervision of the Secret Intelligence Service.

'To tell you the truth,' said Sykes, slicing a portion of calf's liver and prodding it into some mustard on the side of his plate, 'this is not the place to discuss it.' He glanced up, diffidently, and smiled. Neither was it the place to disabuse the politician of his imaginings about some so-called 'special relationship'. That, as far as Sykes could tell, from his position at the head of the intelligence service, was a dead duck and had been since Margaret Thatcher, having outstayed her welcome, had been mugged by her own side and hung up her handbag.

'Then perhaps you should come back with me to the office.' Orde's eyes had narrowed. 'The Americans are not going to let this drop.'

'Patrick, you know David Jardine, don't you?'

'Of course.'

'Well, maybe', the Chief of SIS chewed carefully, 'I should send him over to brief you. He is, after all, the man running that side of things.'

The Foreign Secretary poured them each some more wine. Not much more, Sykes noted. Nobody drank much these days. Not at lunchtime. And, of course, in Washington it was club soda and de-caff. Maybe the culture difference could never again be bridged.

'Sooner, my dear chap,' remarked Orde, 'rather than later. Mmm . . .?'

'I'll have a word this afternoon.'

'Capital.' Patrick Orde smiled, except for his eyes, for he was truly not amused at this mere spy taking a view in the affairs of nations.

Even the sun's riveting heat, which caused perspiration to run down her face, down her flanks and legs, down her spine, to collect in the small of her back, even such suffocating *chaleur* failed to affect the dank, clammy coldness exuding from the menacing earth walls of Zina Farouche's subterranean cell, the Pit. Her probable tomb.

The roof of this earthen walled cell was of corrugated steel, covered by sandbags, camouflaged with small boulders and stones. There was a gap of about three inches, between the steel and the ground. If she could have stood on tiptoe, Zina might just have been able to reach to within ten inches of the gap. But her hands were manacled to a blessedly cool metal ring, set into the rock-solid, damp earth wall, keeping her at a constant stoop, if she tried to straighten up. If she had had the strength to try.

The floor was warm, though. Warm with her own piss and filth. Even when she had had her two periods, during the six-week incarceration, they had done nothing to help her. The stench was beyond anything she could have imagined and, contrary to her early expectations, it was something she had never gotten used to.

Dirt had caked on her body, blood congealed on her wounds, tears long since dried on her once pretty face. Her hair was matted and awry, like a madwoman's. The long days between interrogations passed in silence, alleviated only by the occasional sound of a vehicle approaching the Administration Block, some hundred yards to the north, a passing airliner, high overhead, taking comfortable travellers from, perhaps, Tunis or Casablanca to Cairo, or Damascus. Or by the more frequent screams of pain and fear, from the Adjustment Block, or from the torture frames, set into the earth about sixty yards to the east.

And, of course, the softer sounds of weeping. Of moaning. If there is a hell, Zina Farouche had often contemplated, it has to be less cruel than this. She had read somewhere, that broken prisoners in her doomed situation tended to look forward to the interrogations. To the silent, methodical beatings. To the rapes and worse.

Well, bullshit, she thought to herself. Not me.

And as this very thought passed through her aching mind, Zina heard the dread sound of the tin roof and its rocks and sandbags being trundled to one side, just enough to leave an opening sufficiently wide for Tahzi, one of the guards, to climb down and unlock her handcuffs.

Zina had become adept at seeming much weaker than she was (which was not difficult because at that stage of her torment, the girl was not all that far from the death for which she prayed every day, to Allah The Merciful) and Tahzi, who was huge and was rumoured to have been the PLO's wrestling champion before his conversion to Abu Nidal, lifted her like a sack of bones and hefted her onto the burning hot ground, where his colleague, Sammy, stood waiting.

Sammy's customary boot in the ribs hurt as much as it had the first time. Only this time, Zina was not fooled by the sympathetic murmur of 'You poor thing . . .', which was the sadistic interrogator's favourite utterance, before the pain. The two men did not drag her by the feet, as had become their custom, across the stones (scorching by day, ice-cold at night), but instead threw her into the back of an old short-wheelbased Land-Rover, and drove over the bumpy ground to the Adjustment Block, within the protected area of Station 16, the Prison and Interrogation Compound.

But on this day they did not march her along the concrete corridor, past the torture rooms where screams competed with the blaring love music of Arab favourites like Fat'mah Balloush or Umm Kalthoum, to her own long seconds and hours of agony and humiliation.

She knew, she was sure, it was the forty-third day, but the date had long since passed from her fevered reckoning. And on this day, Zina Farouche was assisted – roughly, for they knew no other way, but assisted was the word, rather than dragged – up some wooden stairs, with stained, once white-washed walls, to the next floor, across a wide room, where a man she vaguely recognized as having been the getaway driver on a job she had led in Athens typed methodically on an old Remington 70 typewriter, eyes firmly fixed on his work, and through a thick wooden door into a neat and airy office, with an air-conditioning unit humming below the one window.

There was a framed photograph of Sabri al-Banna, Abu Nidal, on the wall, behind a grey metal and plastic desk, at which sat a pale, skinny man of about forty-four, with a greying stubble around his chin and wearing a khaki military shirt, with a black and white kheffiya, the traditional Palestinian scarf, round his shoulders. Abdul-Salem Latif was the Commandant of Station 16 and Zina's heart began to pound wildly, within her scrawny, bruised ribcage. For he was not renowned for his compassion.

Tahzi and Sammy placed her on a chair, removed the handcuffs and left the room. She was, somehow, reluctant to see them go.

In the silence, Abdul-Salem Latif gazed at her with detached indifference. There was a tray on his desk, with a pitcher of clear water on it, the glass frosted with condensation. It must have just recently been in an ice-box. Sprigs of mint and slices of lemon floated on the surface.

Zina's tongue was swollen with lack of moisture. Her lips cracked and dry.

She resolutely gazed directly into Latif's eyes.

Fuck you, was her astonishing message. Perhaps fortunately, it merely came out as an unintelligible croak. The Commandant watched her for several moments, then he spoke.

'You have a visitor,' he said and, rising, lifted his pistol from the desk, turned and opened a door behind him. Standing in the doorway, was a tubby, unprepossessing figure of a man, in a baggy white shirt and grey trousers. Height about five-nine, heavily jowled and somehow, even just standing, short of breath.

'Leave us, please,' he said, in Arabic, with a trace of a cultured, West Bank accent.

Latif stood aside to let the other man enter, then left, without a backward glance. The stranger closed the door gently, and sat behind the desk. He stared at Zina Farouche, taking it all in, nodding slowly to himself. He opened a folder in front of him and read a few random pages. Or maybe not so random.

In her fear, Zina, who was so bravely trying to stop from trembling, lost control of her bladder. And in the long silence, as the heavy-jowled man read on, she recognized him. It was Abdel Aziz al-Khaliq, right-hand man of the Leader, Abu Nidal himself.

Finally al-Khaliq closed the folder. He gazed at her, without expression. His voice, when he spoke, was surprisingly gentle, and surprisingly matter-of-fact.

'It won't take long to put you back together,' he said, not unkindly.

*

There was a particular view, from the seventh-floor room, in the north-west corner of Century House, which was David Jardine's inner office in the days before the great Glass Box was reduced to a pile of rubble and the office moved, lock, stock and barrel, to its present home, a semi-pyramid of bottle-green and sandstone on the banks of the River Thames. It was of the clock of Big Ben, the Great Tower of the House of Lords, the square tower of Saint Margaret's Chapel, the spires of Westminster Abbey and the rooftops of those streets on the far side of the Thames which dated, some of them, back to the time of Samuel Pepys.

The corner room was protected from casual visitors by an outer office manned by Heather, his Personal Assistant, recruited straight from Mar College, in Scotland, about five years earlier.

After a varied, some used the word 'colourful', career, first as a field operative and agent runner of legendary skill, more recently surviving the snakes and ladders of SIS politics, Jardine was currently Director of Operations, and he ran SIS at the sharp end. His job was to supervise clandestine activity on five continents, aware of all the secrets, understanding where all the bodies were buried.

Some whispered that perhaps dear David was too much of an action man; that he was not *au fait* with the machinations of the power-brokers and money-changers who ran the Administration.

But those ignorant souls who whispered thus had no inkling of the spymaster's quiet, but painstaking, years of preparation for his new-found responsibility. And just as there was no one in the Post and Dispatch Room whose name and family problems he did not know and enquire after (and indeed, he seemed to mean it) so there were few mandarins in Whitehall, and senior politicians of all parties, with whom he had not cultivated, if not a rapport, at least a measure of comfortable respect.

Anyway, on the day Richard Sykes had been to lunch with the Foreign Secretary, Jardine stood gazing out of his window, listening to the Chief, who had returned from lunch in a foul mood.

'David,' he was saying, 'I don't like it when Foreign

Secretaries get beyond themselves. They really should be discouraged from interfering with the nuts and bolts of our service.'

Jardine smiled, as he watched three mallard ducks wing their purposeful way across the rooftops, heading for Hyde Park, oblivious to the world's dramas.

'They like to feel we are part of their fiefdom,' said Jardine. 'Children, really.'

'US Secretary of State is leaning hard.' Sykes joined David Jardine at the window; he was not a man who liked to miss anything. 'He does not like the idea of us, quote, withholding intelligence vital to the CIA's successful conduct of its business. Unquote. Plus he is not a happy man that we have not fallen into line over President Clinton's desire to bomb the shit out of the Serbs, while we have fifteen thousand men in blue helmets stuck in the Bosnian snow, with just a few rifles and the odd cannon to back them up.'

'Fairly typical lunch with Patrick, then . . .?'

'Very droll. I told him we were concerned about our cousins' less than watertight security. Plus, I tried to hint that we are perhaps not as close to Uncle Sam as was the case during the heady days of Desert Storm and the Falklands War.'

Jardine turned slowly from the window and gave the Chief what his family called his 'old-fashioned look', which is to say he guessed that was what Richard would have liked to have said to the Foreign Secretary, rather than what he actually did say. But, having conveyed that reservation, he enquired politely, 'And what was his reaction?'

'In a nutshell, David, he says we simply do not withhold vital intelligence on the subject of Iran and the mad mullahs from our closest allies, which of course we would never do, if push came to shove. He reminded me of our treaty obligations and generally came on like a wet hen.'

Sykes tugged a handkerchief from his jacket pocket and stared at two knots he had made on one corner, to remind himself of something, and, as he shook it loose, a bright green, rectangular piece of Lego dropped out, along with a tiny plastic soldier, crouched, holding a gun. His eye caught David Jardine's and the chief grinned, his ill humour forgotten.

'How's the family?' asked Jardine.

Sykes shrugged. 'Terrific. Jonathan's six on Wednesday. They're absolute terrors. Wrecking the place.' He seemed to be happy about that.

Jardine gazed at the Great Tower on the far side of the river and said, 'So how did you leave it?'

Richard Sykes stuffed his knotted handkerchief back into his pocket. 'David, be a sport and have a word. Explain to Patrick about Tehran's place in all of this, would you? Explain that Iran is the coming threat. Not bloody Serbia. It is more dangerous even than Mother Russia under new and alarming management. And explain that we can't compromise our valuable human sources working those territories . . . not even to bolster our *soi-disant* special relationship with the USA.'

'Why don't you tell him yourself?' asked Jardine.

The Chief, soon to become Sir Richard if events moved smoothly, thrust his hands deep into his trouser pockets and ambled into the middle of the room, as if reluctant to deliver a compliment face to face. 'I think Patrick is vaguely in awe of you. You're dangerous; he thinks of you as a proper spy. With me, it would be merely a conversation . . .'

David Jardine watched Sykes carefully. Far from feeling complimented, he had a suspicion he was being used as the fall-guy. The bringer of bad news.

'I'll speak to him,' he said.

'Today? Sooner the better I earnestly believe.'

Jardine spoke into the intercom, on his desk. 'Heather, FCO tomorrow morning, please; ears only briefing for the Minister. Ten minutes will do . . .'

'Ten-Four,' replied Heather, a devotee of television cop shows. 'Don't forget James Gant at two-fifteen.'

David Jardine thanked her and unscrewed a vacuum flask, pouring himself a cup of minestrone soup he had prepared earlier, thinking, we don't all have time for lunches at White's.

'Who is Gant? Anyone interesting?' asked Sykes, taking the hint and heading for the door.

Jardine laid down his plastic beaker and glanced at the Chief. 'I don't know yet.'

2

Joe Cleary and the Freezer Murder

James Gant shared a flat in Chiswick with two sisters, Rebecca and Naomi Reed. Naomi, twenty-three, worked for the London *Evening Standard*, as a researcher and general dogsbody for the literary editor, an able if affected young dandy, all too aware of his power to make or break those authors who relied upon the Metropolis for their acclaim.

Rebecca was two years older than her sister. Petite and vital, she worked as a junior solicitor for D.D. Hengest, a corporate law firm in the City. She had graduated from Manchester University, and before that had been to school with James's sister Charlotte.

The flat was on the third floor of a cramped, white painted terraced house, between two grander houses on Chiswick Mall, which was directly on the banks of the River Thames, not far from the main traffic route out of West London. Chiswick Mall was secluded, and lay so close to the high-water mark that, on the highest of tides, which were not infrequent, the river spilled onto the tarmac road sometimes to quite an alarming degree.

On this particular day, Rebecca was half sitting on the second-hand desk of the study-cum-sitting room she and Naomi shared with James Gant, her sober, charcoal-grey office skirt pushed up around her waist, legs akimbo, arms clutching his shoulders, while the sometime war cameraman, trousers round his knees, pleasured her with a degree of skill and consideration acquired over the years since those first breathless fumblings with April Lee Stuart, in the summer of '85.

Rebecca was one of those young ladies English boarding

schools and quietly privileged families had produced for many years. She was a discreet survivor with a heart of railroad steel and had done all kinds of those courses such young ladies attend, from aikido to flower arranging to, it seemed to James at that particular moment, quite possibly, intimate muscle control, for she was able to dictate the course of their shared enjoyment with the measured skill of a three-day eventer.

Outside, beyond the study windows, against which the gently rocking desk was placed, a police launch held a steady position facing the strong current, while two of its crew assisted a third, cumbersome in diving gear, to climb over the side and descend, by way of a short ladder, into the muddy deep.

The flat had double-glazing, so the tableau was silent, lending a surreal air to the happenings outside.

Afterwards, she looked at him with that look of hers which combined sultry sexuality with a degree of child-like innocence. It was just that combination which had appealed to him from the very start. And now they were engaged, and planning to marry.

'What were you looking at?' she enquired, smoothing her skirt down and twisting to gaze out at the river. Seeing the police launch, and the diver's head bobbing about on the surface near the stern, Rebecca frowned.

'Oh, dear,' she said, 'do you think someone has drowned . . .?'

'I shouldn't imagine', replied Gant, 'they are going to all that trouble because somebody has lost a shoe.'

Rebecca looked thoughtful, slightly lost. 'Just think. We were doing that. And some poor bugger is floating around, just below the surface.'

Later, while a second police launch joined the first, and two more divers got their equipment ready, James and Rebecca sat in the enormous old Edwardian bath, with four eagles' feet resting on four cast-iron orbs, steam deadening sound and shine, sharing a can of Budweiser and perspiring gently.

'Have you thought any more about Barney's idea?' she asked, as he passed the can to her.

Barney was Rebecca and Naomi's cousin and he owned a quietly thriving, small film company that made documentaries and second-unit inserts for other, larger companies, as well as television titles and other graphic sequences. It was one of those specialised areas most people had never heard of, nor ever would, but it made its own quiet way, enjoying a steady reputation in the business it served.

Since the engagement, Barney had offered James a partnership. The deal was that if James Gant left the BBC, and invested £15,000, he would become a 40 per cent partner in the company, earning around £40,000 to £60,000 a year. Plus a rising share in the capital and a big equity profit when they went public in a few years' time.

Gant was half-tempted by the idea, for, although he had saved a few thousand, and earned good money with the BBC, that was only because of his hazardous foreign work, covering wars and famines. And Rebecca had made him promise to settle down, after they got married.

But James didn't feel absolutely thrilled about investing most of his savings in Barney's business, or giving up his rewarding job with the BBC.

'Shall we take a look at a few houses today?' asked Rebecca, tugging a towel from its rail and getting out of the bath. 'I've got a new list from Foxton's.'

'I can't,' said Gant, pulling out the bath plug. 'I'm going to an editors' meeting at the Beeb.'

This was to be the first of many white lies. He was in fact going to see the man Estergomy and somebody called Jardine.

The British Foreign Secretary, Patrick Orde, was in avuncular mood, having just returned from a meeting of the Inner Cabinet where his views on certain aspects of foreign policy had won approval, despite, he recounted to David Jardine with some satisfaction, the best efforts of two career mandarins in his own department to scupper them.

He crossed his long legs, elegantly suited in dark blue worsted, and peered, polishing his reading spectacles on his tie, in friendly fashion at the man he fondly considered to be Director of Operations in *his* Secret Intelligence Service.

'I understand, David,' he said, in that slightly hesitant,

almost diffident way he had, which failed to mask a core of railroad steel, 'you are playing a long game in the Middle East.'

'In Tehran,' replied Jardine, getting straight to the point.

'Richard thinks it puts us in an extremely strong position. No other service, or so we believe . . . has managed to penetrate the Iranian regime quite so . . .' he paused, searching for the word, 'comprehensively.'

'Richard says Warren Christopher is cutting up rough,' Jardine said, determined to avoid Orde's almost oriental talent for circumlocution.

The Foreign Secretary looked pained. For a moment Jardine thought this was because he had leapt so directly into the subject for discussion, but he soon understood it was pain (mild, of course; Patrick rarely reached even the foothills of agitation) at SIS refusing to share all of its delicately filched secrets with its cousins in Washington.

'My American counterpart has expressed his . . . surprise.' Orde raised one hand off the arm of his leather chair, not too far, to illustrate, presumably, the level of the American Secretary of State's surprise. 'He knows you are keeping much of your Iranian product to yourselves. And he's worried, justifiably from his point of view, that this could put American policy, not to mention lives, at a . . . disadvantage, mm?'

David Jardine held Orde's gaze. He allowed more than a few seconds to pass before he asked, 'What is the real problem here . . .?'

Orde stared at him. 'What do you mean?'

'I mean, and you and I go back a long way, Patrick, something has rattled you, in your dealings with Warren Christopher. Warren Christopher has rattled you. And it's not actually my . . .' and here Jardine paused, employing Orde's own device, 'determination, to keep a few secrets back – which is, I'm sure I don't need to remind you, my job, after all . . .'

The Foreign Secretary's intercom buzzed discreetly, on his vast, barren teak desk, of Palladian proportions. Orde ignored it.

A sizeable ormolu clock on the Italian marble mantelpiece gently ticked the hour away. It was, Jardine knew (for clocks were probably his predominant interest, after espionage and lithe, mildly decadent, well-bred young women) a particularly fine example, made during the reign of Louis XIV, with movement by Delunesy and its ornate casing, with fawns and centaurs and Hera the Hunter, created by Jean-Claude Gouthière, the king's own craftsman.

After a long silence, Orde said, 'They really have got it completely wrong, Washington. Sure, they believe Iran is a threat to international stability. But America is distracted by Tehran's desire to become a nuclear power. Trade sanctions, embargoes . . . all that stuff, it's all directed at preventing the mad mullahs from acquiring a nuclear bomb.' He shook his head, quite emphatically. 'Bullshit, David. You know and I know that the real threat from Iran is not nuclear warfare, it's not even war in that sense. We're talking about . . . a disease. Like cancer. The more extreme of the Radical Fundamentalist clergy, and Tehran is the hub of their power, are working to a programme aimed at enforcing its perverted brand of Islam throughout, principally, the Muslim world but eventually the . . . *monde entier*.'

Jardine smiled to himself. Listening to Patrick Orde was like taking a time machine to a bygone age. Why couldn't he just have said it in English?

'And', continued Orde, 'as our good friends in Saudi Arabia and the Gulf – not to mention Russia with its huge Islamic population, and neighbouring states – know only too well, we are not talking about religious zeal here, or even about a desire to propagate a deeply held belief. Radical Islam is about power, and politics. Just like the Roman Church in the Middle Ages. And every whit as ruthless.'

'Control,' agreed Jardine.

'They loathe America. They loathe the West. They abhor Christianity, and the Hebrews. They consider more charitable, more compassionate fellow Muslims to be near-infidels. They despise Buddha and, as for the Hindu, well . . .' Orde glanced around the walls as if one of the priceless oil paintings might illustrate his point. 'They are conducting, your service and other sources convince me, a programme of low-intensity but relentless terror against the West, with a budget of four thousand million allocated at this present time. But can we persuade the men on Capitol Hill, even after the World Trade Center was ripped apart by a car bomb, that this programme, if unchecked, is geared to increase by degrees, until no American or European city is safe? Can we buggery. On the one hand they want sanctions to stop Iran acquiring nuclear clout, and, on the other, they are leaning on us, their oldest allies, to let them arm the Bosnians . . .'

Bosnia was a predominantly Islamic state. Orde and the SIS agreed that the UN had handled the whole Bosnian catastrophe with breathtaking ineptitude, from Day One. He and Jardine, and other British politicians and senior intelligence executives, believed that NATO should have acted promptly, to stop the Serbs in their tracks, as soon as their genocidal campaign to carve out a Greater Serbia from Bosnian and Croatian territory became clear (and in fact SIS had been charting the origins of Serbian ambition since 1947).

But NATO had faltered and the United Nations had blundered into the vacuum, forced there by understandable world-wide outrage at scenes on television of 'ethnic cleansing', mass slaughter of civilians who looked disturbingly like ordinary people from any European or American community, concentration camps, torture and rape.

The Bosnian state, newly recognised and legitimised by the UN, was subjected to an arms embargo, almost fatally limiting its ability to withstand the onslaught from Serbia and, at first, before a treaty was signed, from Croatia as well.

The UN 'peacekeeping' force went in, too little, too late, and, like a chicken with three heads, was unsure which way to move – thanks to a ridiculous command and control hierarchy, the driving seat of which was located in New York City and left empty at weekends, when everybody relaxed in Long Island or Connecticut with their wives or significant others.

Muslim Bosnia cried out for help, desperate, and in its desperation gladly accepted arms and experienced Muslim fighters from the Islamic world. Tehran saw its opportunity and was soon controlling the only sensible aid supplied to the Bosnian people and grateful government.

The irony was that most Bosnian Muslims were descendants of a Christian Orthodox people who had been forcibly converted by the Turks, in the time of the Ottoman Empire.

They were cosmopolitan in outlook, easy going and had been fully integrated with those Croats and Serbs who shared their mixed towns and villages.

But all that had changed.

And any move by the West, urged on by the USA, to lift the arms embargo and provide heavy weapons, tanks and military advisers, would now merely succeed in enabling the Radical Islamic Fundamentalist threat to triumph over Serbia and the Bosnian Serbs and establish a regime as fiercely anti-Western, anti-European, as any in the Middle East.

And this was in former Yugoslavia, which had been, geographically if not politically, a European nation. This was what David Jardine had meant by letting Islamic Fundamentalism into Europe through the back door.

'Well they *are* arming the Bosnians, our friends in Washington. Secretly,' continued Patrick Orde. 'According to you people, along with GCHQ and Defence Intelligence, unmarked C-130s land there, or HALO drop Special Forces people in, seconded to the CIA, not so much to help the poor bloody Bosnians as to check, too late of course, the influence of the Afghans and supplies from Iran, Iraq and Saudi Arabia.'

Afghans was a generic term being used to describe Islamic volunteers from abroad, some of whom had originally gone to Afghanistan to join their Muslim brothers to fight against the Soviet occupation there.

'And you really wonder why I will not share too much with the Cousins . . .?' murmured David Jardine. 'I mean, have I missed something? Some nuance?'

'David, this is a tough old world, as you keep telling me. The show must go on; much wider, more important things are at stake. I do not wish, personally, to contribute to damaging still further our relationship with the USA. Secretary of State Christopher has evidence your service is holding out on his own intelligence machine. What can I tell him?'

'Tell him it's a big boys' game. We won't blow the whistle on clandestine CIA operations to force the UN to lift sanctions against Bosnia, if Alan Clair takes a more relaxed attitude to my service doing its job.'

Patrick Orde, Etonian, economics scholar and author of the definitive biography of William Wilberforce, considered this. In his lap he held a slim Top Secret file Jardine had given him. It detailed Tehran's long history of training camps and facilities for terror groups of all nations, from the Provisional IRA and American 'militia' and survivalist outfits to Palestinian and broad-spectrum radical Islam organisations.

The ormolu clock ticked on while Orde watched the intelligence boss in silence. So many moments passed that Jardine wondered if the man was having a mild stroke of some kind. Then he drummed the fingers of his right hand on the worn arm of his leather chair.

'I presume you have shared with them all this stuff about training camps, um, Beheshita, Manzeria Park, al-Shambat, al-Ma'qil etcetera . . .'

'With their satellites, they could write the book.' Hand it to Patrick, reflected Jardine, he's memorised that file in moments.

'And the players, Ali-Akbar Motashemi, of course; even I know about him. And Ali Fallahian, boss of Intelligence. But this secret intelligence on, um, Jamil Shahidi, Muhammad Shams and Musin Reza'i? Do we share all that with the Cousins?'

Jardine nodded. 'Of course.'

'But you refuse to pass on . . . what?'

'Anything', replied Jardine, 'which might allow a good intelligence service to identify, and therefore compromise, my sources inside the Iranian and general Middle Eastern terror circuit.'

'In other words, you don't trust the Agency.'

The man's timing was impeccable. The question went directly to the nub of the problem. Jardine met his gaze and said, 'They have leaks that go straight to Moscow and Tehran. I would prefer not to sacrifice whole agent networks for the sake of a quiet life.'

Patrick Orde nodded. 'Can you help them find those leaks?'

'It's really their problem. They have one source, a greedy drunk called Aldrich Ames, but we believe there are others. If we get a hint, we will certainly pass it on, that's in everyone's interest. But right now the human assets I am running provide more than any NASA satellite could ever get near. And they trust me to keep them from being skinned alive. Which is not a mere figure of speech.'

To his credit, the Foreign Secretary understood immediately, and he supported Jardine without hesitation. 'OK, I'll fend him off. Thank you, David, for coming over. I get the message. You and Richard don't think we should lambaste the Serbs, whom we all agree are ghastly people, while allowing the spread of Islamic Fundamentalism into Europe through the Bosnian back door. Plus we don't rat on brave agents in place to sustain the, currently somewhat shaky, illusion of intelligence co-operation.'

'Exquisitely put, as one has come to expect from such an erudite and hard-working Foreign Secretary,' said David Jardine, with a deadpan expression.

'Don't be cheeky,' replied Orde, who was, in fact, godfather to Jardine's son Andrew. The two men had been Second Lieutenants in the same company, B Company, of the 1st Battalion, The Parachute Regiment, when they were mere children. Rather hard-assed children, with red berets worn at a raffish angle and a thirst for danger, whether on the field of battle or in the boudoir.

'The Agency will sort itself out,' said Jardine, 'of that I have no doubt. But, like the rest of the USA, they are drifting away, Paddy. To be frank, I can't say I blame them. Maybe it will be healthier to stand on our own two feet . . .' The SIS man rose, his audience at an end.

'How's Dorothy?' enquired Orde, getting to his feet.

'Unstoppable. She's filming in Brazil. Something about the killing of tribesmen to cut down the rainforest.'

'Give her a big kiss.'

'Actually,' said Jardine, 'she asked me to give you one. But I don't think I'll bother.'

'Bugger off,' replied Her Majesty's Foreign Secretary and started to open the door. Then he closed it again and stood there, deep in thought.

'I don't suppose', he said, and Jardine reflected how similar Patrick sometimes looked to a painting he had seen of Cardinal Richelieu, hanging in the Louvre, 'you are aware of anything going on, you people. Anything that might . . . jolt Washington into recognising where the real Islamic danger is coming from? Without, of course, jeopardising your own sources?'

David Jardine held his friend's gaze, saying more with his silence than any words could ever have done. Of course there was something. In this business, there always was.

'Perhaps,' he replied, and Orde detected an uncharacteristic sense of discomfort, foreboding even, in his friend's attitude.

In the background, the intercom buzzed discreetly.

Jardine felt cold tentacles drift over his flesh. 'I don't know if I could live with it, though.'

'I don't want to know.' Orde's eyes were pale, a sniper's eyes, and bleak with the calculation of those who permit others to make ruthless, momentous decisions. 'It's up to you, David. You know we trust your judgement. But I do not want to know a thing.'

The spymaster nodded, suddenly tired, and it was early in the day; when did they ever? When did the politicians ever want to know the shit that went on 'in furtherance of British Foreign Policy by covert means', which was the quaint definition of his service's denied role in the shaping of world history.

Zina felt drained, worse than jet lag, worse even than after giving birth. At twenty-seven, she had experienced more exhaustion, more horrors, than most of the others, recruits or instructors, at the Naji al-Ali terrorist camp of Fatah-The Revolutionary Council, which was Abu Nidal's grandiose title for his tightly controlled groups of murder gangs.

After that first interview with al-Khaliq, she had been taken to the camp infirmary, where a Palestinian doctor had given her a thorough medical examination. She had been found to have three cracked ribs; two split teeth, which required extraction; several damaged finger and toe nails, which needed surgical removal; mild lacerations and contusions; infected wounds; vaginal abrasions; and gonorrhoea. She also had dangerously low blood sugar and low blood pressure, along with skin sores resulting from malnutrition.

After being gently sponged clean, given immediate injections of penicillin and vitamin B-12, Zina had been put on drip feeds of glucose and saline solution. Her wounds had been sutured, her toe and finger nails operated on, under local anaesthetic, her hair treated and rinsed carefully, and cut short, to get rid of the lice. She had then been mildly sedated for a number of days. She was not sure how many.

After some time under sedation – she thought it might have been about a week – the girl had been gently lifted from her infirmary bed, where she had been screened from prying eyes – although who in that hellish camp would have dared even to glance at such a victim of the Station 16 torturers – and laid on a stretcher.

The stretcher had been carried, it was cool and dark, she remembered that, into a Red Crescent ambulance and driven for several hours over the desert towards Tripoli. There Zina had been taken to one of the Abu Nidal safe-houses, a farm, which must have been near the international airport, for she could hear, landing and taking off, airliners just like those which had scored across the sky, so remote and unknowing, all through the unending days of her torment.

The smell of fruit, especially oranges, was pleasant and quite strong.

The room, as she lay indulging her feeling of weakness and lassitude, was clean and comforting. The bed was of tubular metal, with a comfortable mattress and snow-white cotton sheets neatly folded over. A hospital bed, her father used to call it, in the refugee camp at Chatilla. Before the Phalange had moved in, under the averted eyes of the Israeli invaders, and slaughtered hundreds. Her papa and Samih, her eight-month-old baby son, included.

On the table beside her bed was a jug, with water, and a glass, also filled with water. Air conditioning hummed softly. Outside, a few children were playing, some way away. A radio, or a television, played Arab music, quietly.

It seemed to have gone on too long, her short life. Zina felt no real inclination to fight any more, either for her continued existence or for Abu Nidal. Not after that. No way.

The questioning had been quite specific. The suspicion, or alleged suspicion, had been that Zina Farouche – a veteran terrorist killer since the age of fourteen, when she had planted her first grenade, in a café in Jounieh, a resort for the Lebanon's spoiled rich, of whom there were thousands – had allowed herself to be corrupted, and was betraying the organisation to the Americans. To be specific, to a CIA man in Malta. One of the requirements of her interrogators had been that she name this 'contact'.

Well, that was impossible, for she did not know who they meant. Zina would no more have betrayed Abu Nidal and Fatah: The Revolutionary Council than she would have smiled at an Israeli. Unless she meant to lure one to his death.

The door opened and a handsome woman in her early forties came in. She wore a plain skirt and neatly pressed mint-coloured cotton shirt. She stood at the side of the bed and smiled, her eyes meeting Zina's.

'You must not be angry with us,' she said softly. 'The organisation can only survive through our integrity. Believe me, we have all been through the testing. Those of us in the Special Missions Committee. Abu Nidal himself is coming to see you, when you are stronger.' She smiled, and straightened the light oatmeal cotton curtains by the high window. 'And that won't be long . . .'

Zina lay still, absorbing all this. Of course, such tricks would not fool her. She knew the torture could not be long in starting all over again. She was annoyed at the tears which were coursing down her cheeks. That was how damned weak she had become. The woman's touch was cool and fragrant. She gently wiped the tears away, and, leaning over, stroked Zina's cheek.

'You are wrong, child,' she said. 'There will be no more interrogation. You have passed the test. You are one of us now.' And, leaning close to the almost broken girl's ear, she whispered, '*Marhabbah.*' Which meant, 'Welcome.'

The moment James Gant set eyes on David Jardine, he knew the man was some kind of spook. For Gant had been around the block a few times since that day in Rome airport, with the bullets and all that blood. Beirut and Peshawar and the former Yugoslavia, where he had worked on news assignments, were all places where intelligence men and women of several nationalities moved like ghosts, affable or driven ones, according to their temperament and training.

From the moment this Frederick K. Estergomy – a real name? surely not, thought Gant – had phoned with that nonsense about his so-called niece, the young cameraman/editor had been mildly interested to see just what the score was. And some kind of snooping had never been very far from the agenda.

He met Jardine's gaze as the older man indicated a leather chair, high-backed, like a dining-room seat, a carver, with dark rosewood arms, at the same time settling himself down on a scuffed leather two-seater couch and saying, 'Please, Mister Gant, make yourself comfortable.'

The room was in a small Georgian terrace house of three floors and an attic, in one of those ancient narrow streets between Scotland Yard and Parliament Square. The ground-floor hall had seemed like the lobby of a private surgery, or an expensive old-money solicitor's office. A young man, maybe the same age as James, had been sitting behind a desk and a door behind him had led into an office room, where two women had been typing quietly. The place had had a comfortable, slightly hushed atmosphere, where one might expect to encounter an historian, or a curator of rare manuscripts. The walls were plain cream, or magnolia, as Rebecca called it when planning the décor of their apartment-to-be, with attractive, slightly primitive paintings of eighteenth-century farmyard animals and sailing boats. A quietly self-possessed girl had led him upstairs, making small talk about the Oxford and Cambridge boat race, which was due to take place that weekend.

Gant sat on the leather seat and stretched his legs.

'Thanks for coming over,' said Jardine, glancing at his wristwatch, as if to say this won't take long.

Gant's gaze moved to the closed door, then returned to Jardine.

'Where's Fred?' he asked.

'He'll be along shortly.' Jardine let the silence prolong itself, then asked, 'Would you like something . . .?'

James felt like saying yes, two Chinese acrobats and a monkey on a one-wheeled bike, which is what his sister said she often felt like replying when somebody asked her that. But he replied, more prosaically, 'I'd kill for a cup of tea.'

'Me too.' Jardine lifted a phone and spoke quietly into it.

Everything about him – the well-cut but slightly crumpled fawn Prince of Wales double-breasted suit, the cream shirt that Gant recognised as one the man had probably ironed himself, the elegant, sober silk tie, the old, polished hand-made boots – spoke somehow of quiet power. Of amiable but lethal self-assurance.

'Fred won't be long.' Jardine replaced the receiver. 'But I should probably make a start.'

Gant wondered what the hell this was all about. If David Jardine was indeed some sort of security creature, and clearly quite senior, what had he himself done to come to the man's attention? The only thing James could imagine was something he had unwittingly said, or seen, or even filmed, while abroad. In Bosnia probably. Well, too bad. It was a free country.

But where on earth did dear old Edith fit in?

'Some weeks ago, Mister Gant, you posted these letters, to an address in Tufnell Park.'

Ah . . . those bloody letters.

Jardine produced three envelopes addressed to R. Bicerkovic, which the too-thin, once beautiful girl had given to James Gant in the Inferno Club, in Sarajevo. He glanced, pleasantly enough, at the younger man.

'Yes. I posted them,' replied Gant. So bloody what, was his exact feeling at that moment, and it showed.

Jardine smiled. 'Good. Will you be just as frank in answering my next question?'

Gant's heart suddenly quickened. This guy was not slow in putting the arm on. He forced himself to remain relaxed. 'Try me.'

'Did you read the contents?'

'I don't understand Serbo-Croat. I can't read Cyrillic script. Not the handwriting anyway.' He shrugged.

Jardine nodded. He did not seem displeased. 'So you did open them.'

Gant returned his gaze. 'I was curious. I am in the information game.'

Jardine let the envelopes drop back onto the couch.

'Well, so am I,' he said. Then, matter of fact, 'They say

you did quite a good job of it. Hard – well, quite difficult – to detect.'

'Thank you.'

'Did your aunt teach you how to do that?'

James Gant gazed at Jardine, expressionless. 'Which aunt would that be?'

'Edith Treffewin.' David Jardine got up and crossed to a hatch, from where a trundling noise could be heard. 'Dumb waiter,' he murmured, apologetically, adding a touch of the surreal to Gant's perception of this strange meeting, and, opening the hatch, he leaned into a dark space in the wall, then emerged, like a magician, with a large tray on which was a silver teapot, three Delft china cups and saucers and a tray of chocolate-chip cookies.

'She was my boss', Jardine continued, 'in Berlin. When I started out in this game. A thousand and ten years ago.'

Well, strike me pink, thought Gant. He rested an elbow on one arm of the chair, keeping his expression politely interested. 'Which game is that, Mister Jardine?'

'Oh, a sort of offshoot of the Foreign and Commonwealth Office. Research. That sort of thing.'

'I thought she was with the Board of Trade.'

Jardine nodded, lifting his cup and sipping the tea. 'I hope you don't mind Lapsang.'

James lifted his cup and saucer and sniffed at the aroma.

'I got spoiled in India,' he replied.

The older man nodded, contemplating this obtuse statement.

'Assam is actually my favourite,' Gant went on. 'PG Tips rather put me off, with all those monkeys.' He was referring to a television commercial.

'So, James,' Jardine laid his cup down, this nonsense of the tea discarded, 'let me be quite level with you. You have a good job, and you have travelled extensively in . . . difficult areas. Areas of conflict. I've seen quite a few of your team's reports. Quite a bit of, quite a lot of film. In terms of physical length. Of the actual celluloid.'

'Footage,' said Gant. 'It's called footage.'

'How very succinct.'

'And celluloid went out with *Gone With the Wind*. It's

highly inflammable. We use an acetate stock. If it's film. Sometimes we use video cassettes. Much simpler.'

Jardine gazed at Gant. 'But you don't get that wonderful grainy quality of a Grierson documentary. Is that the correct term?'

Gant met his host's innocent gaze. 'I'm sorry, I can be a bit pompous.'

'Can't we all?' David Jardine put his hands together, as if in prayer. 'James, how would you like to be . . . considered, for employment?'

The cameraman put his cup and saucer on the desk beside him. He glanced at the letters and envelopes on the couch, beside Jardine.

'I can't actually help wondering if I already have been.'

Jardine nodded, thoughtful. There was still no sign of Szabodo. 'The next step, if there is to be one, and that's up to you, would involve your participation . . .'

'Perhaps you could explain the job,' said Gant, unable to decide if he felt flattered or annoyed at his future being considered by complete strangers. 'Is this a temporary thing? Or something you want me to fit in with my day job? I take it – please correct me if I'm barking up the wrong tree, Mister Jardine – I'm inclined to assume we're talking about some form of . . . snooping here. I mean, what is this? MI 5? The Security Service?'

David Jardine conveyed the impression of being mildly insulted. 'Good Lord, no. We are not the nation's prefects. More, um . . .' his eyes smiled, 'more like its pirates. We travel a lot. Behave badly, in a quiet sort of way.'

So Aunt Edith had been a spy. And nobody in the family had ever guessed.

'SIS, then,' said Gant. No longer confused.

'That's the one. How would you feel about a career with us?' Jardine made it sound as everyday as a job in advertising.

Wait till I tell Charlie, thought Gant, but in the same moment guessed he would be asked not to tell anyone.

'Would it mean leaving the BBC?' he asked.

Jardine smiled. 'Of course it would. I'm talking about a full-time job. Subject to you successfully completing a board and one or two other, administrative, requirements.'

'You know my mother was an American?' enquired Gant.

Jardine nodded. 'Some of our best friends are Americans,' he said, 'even these days.'

James Gant was seldom astonished. His life since that autumn of '85 had produced more than most people's share of surprises. But here he was, sitting in the secret office of some senior spook, being offered a career, no less, with MI 6. Which was what the press called the Secret Intelligence Service.

After a long pause, during which David Jardine collected the cups and put them back on the tray, Gant said, 'Would you mind giving me a clue what I would be doing . . . I don't actually read spy books. I'm sorry.'

This question pleased Jardine, very much in the same way that Gant's casual, unflustered way of walking into the Scarsdale pub without looking as if he was looking for someone had gone down well with Ronnie Szabodo. For the last thing SIS was looking for was some starry-eyed innocent who had OD-ed on a diet of Tom Clancy and John le Carré.

So he told the boy that the job involved acquiring, by unorthodox, sometimes not entirely legal, means, the most precious economic, political and military secrets of their nation's enemies, potential enemies and, on occasion, even their friends, in order to be able to provide the United Kingdom's democratically elected government with the best possible, most up-to-the-minute information, in order to allow it to plan for the future – and to deal with current problems. How it meant recruiting agents, citizens of those countries – target countries – and running them to produce the best results for what the spymaster termed 'UK Limited'.

James Gant nodded, watching Jardine's back, for the big man had delivered the last part of this monologue from one of the room's two Georgian windows. Maybe he really was wondering where Fred Estergomy had got to.

'Well, that describes very clearly what your . . . department does. Where would I fit in?'

David Jardine glanced back at him. 'Assuming you're interested.'

'Assuming that,' agreed the foundling, which was what Jardine's colleague, the Director of Personnel, called the various waifs and strays who finished up in SIS via routes less orthodox than the talent spotters at the better universities, the armed forces and the City.

'I expect,' said Jardine, 'providing you passed our Board and one or two fairly simple tests, that we would want to train you in all the skills necessary to be a good officer in the Service. Then you would probably be assigned to an experienced Field Officer, somewhere abroad, using a cover occupation, where you would learn how that individual ran his agents and generally acquired the sort of information we're paid to fish out. Then maybe a spell back to learn more specific skills, depending on your aptitude, and, more than likely, a posting possibly to an embassy, where you would work under diplomatic cover, probably as Third Secretary in the Commercial or Press offices. Something like that.'

'Why me?' asked Gant.

David Jardine glanced at his watch and crossed to his desk, seemingly looking for something, pushing his papers around. 'Fred really should have been here.' He smiled to Gant. 'He's not usually so late.'

At which instant James Gant, who had indeed the makings of a most excellent spy, one day – for he had that essential attribute, almost feline perception – had a mental picture of the squat Hungarian rifling through the drawers of his desk in the flat at Chiswick Mall, empty, of course, while Rebecca and Naomi were at work.

'Your aunt . . .' Jardine had just said.

Two minutes in here and I'm already paranoid, thought Gant.

'. . . She thinks you would be good here.' Jardine gave the younger man a fairly friendly look. 'And she's never suggested anyone else. As far as I know.'

Gant frowned. This bloke seemed just too used to getting it all his own bloody way. 'It's a bit unexpected.'

'Apologies,' lied Jardine, without a blush.

'I don't suppose you can offer a few days' job experience?'

If this was a joke, it went down like a concrete turkey.

Jardine smiled coldly. 'No.'

'Well, I would like to think about it. Ah. Silly question, really, but what about the, um . . .'

'Twenty-three thousand a year. To start with. Plus insurance. Medical, housing, all that sort of thing.'

'Promotion prospects?'

'We would want to promote you as far as you could go.'

Jardine found what he was looking for – a rectangular printed card, about half A4 size. He turned to face Gant. 'I started more or less like you. Worked for Reuters, in East Germany at the time. Now I'm clearing a hundred thousand. Will you sign this? It's just an extract from the Official Secrets Act. Obliging you not to repeat this conversation or the fact of this visit or, rather dramatically, my actual existence. Do you mind?'

James Gant laughed spontaneously. 'And if I don't, what happens, do I just disappear?'

To which David Jardine replied merely, 'Dear-dear.' But the look in his eye, even as he grinned politely, made our young man wish he hadn't asked.

Joe Cleary's wife was exactly nine months pregnant, which is to say he was about to become a father at any second, and which is also to say this was no time for him to be caught eleven floors up on the outside of a building on 44th Street with his fuckin' coat pocket caught on a nail and a ginger tomcat doing its level best to scratch out his eyes, while he hung out over the street, with two hundred and twenty-three feet of clear air beneath him, grabbing onto the rusty fire-escape step with one hand, while the other, bleeding from a half dozen swipes from the big feline, tried in vain to grab the goddam creature by the scruff of its neck.

Apart from which he had no head for heights.

Noise from the traffic, way below, drifted up, the deep bellow of truck horns, some engine noise, a faint, even this far away slightly nasal, yell of 'Eddie, Eddie, don't forget the . . .' and the rest drowned out by the distant whoop of an ambulance siren. Then Cleary became aware of a woman's voice nearer, but somehow not so immediately distinct.

'Mister cop, Mister cop,' the voice was calling.

'Yeah?' replied Sergeant Joe Cleary, unwilling to take his eyes off the cat, which was now spitting and making like a black and ginger porcupine with its spiky fur, balanced precariously on a rusty pipe rod, just out of reach, its outraged stare completely focused on him, ready to spring.

'Telephone . . .'

'Say what?' Still watching the tomcat.

'It's for you.'

Cleary realised he had let himself get almost to the point of no return, hanging out from the goddam fire escape. Very carefully, he eased his weight back, gripping the cast-iron step tightly, still watching the cat, which seemed just about to launch itself at Joe's face.

What the hell, he thought, enough with the Tom and Jerry already, and, as he swung himself back up onto the step, grabbing at the rail with his right hand, twisting his back towards the animal, he heard an unholy banshee shriek, right at his ear, and he swore later that at least one set of claws just missed his head – he was aware of the swishing – before the shriek rapidly diminished as the doomed tomcat discovered that it couldn't fly.

Sweating, his coat pocket ripped nearly clean off, heart pounding, Sergeant of Detectives Joe Cleary, of NYPD's Homicide Division, found himself on his hands and knees on the fire escape, facing an open window, where, inside, the little old Italian lady that he had arrived to interview, when she had asked him to help her Arthur, who was stuck on the underneath of the fire-escape, stood holding a phone receiver.

'Thanks,' said Cleary, somewhat embarrassed, and took the phone, as she hurried to the window. 'Yeah? Cleary here.'

He was half expecting to hear 'Congratulations, you're a father.'

'Joe,' it was Detective Annie Rossi, 'we got a Ten-Nineteen in the kitchen of a restaurant on West Broadway.' A 1019 was a plain-clothes cop, or similar, dead of gunshot wounds or otherwise illegally killed.

'Where?' Cleary watched as the little old lady leaned out of her window, peering around the now empty fire-escape and calling 'Arthur' in that Tweetie Pie voice such ladies use for their lethal pets.

'It's called Bartello, way downtown, number two-o-one-eight. Got a sunken garden. Great zucchini.'

'I know the place; who's on the scene?'

'Sergeant Wharton. He figures the stiff is a Fed.'

'When did this happen?'

'Uh . . .' she was checking, 'victim found at ten-o-five.'

Cleary checked his watch. It was 10.52. 'I'll be right there.'

He hung up, and, as he touched his scratched face, the old woman turned and stared at him. 'Where is my Arthur?' she demanded.

'He's, uh, he's free. He jumped clear.' Joe Cleary shrugged and smiled, trying to look casual, as if dealing with homicidal cats was no big deal. He could feel the blood trickling down his neck, onto his collar. The woman took one last look outside, and when she turned back she was smiling. 'What a hero you are.'

He spread his hands, feeling awkward. 'No big deal.'

She turned to rummage in a dusty old vase, with scenes from Venice on the side. 'Let me give you something for your trouble . . .'

'Absolutely not. I don't deserve it,' said Cleary truthfully. 'I gotta go. Emergency.'

As he headed for the door she said, Mrs Ferrari was her name, 'What about the kids I saw?' She meant the two teenage crack-sellers who had gunned down a rival using a MAC-10 on the rooftop across the street.

'I'll be back for a statement,' replied Joe Cleary, over his shoulder as he fled, heading for the street eleven floors below, his brown Ford sedan and a nice simple homicide.

He thought.

Bartello is a spacious, clean-looking place with an art-deco feel to it. As you go in off the street, there is a polished bar-counter, ahead and to your right. The cash desk and reception is to the left of the bar, then there are a couple of steps down to the start of the dining area, which has comfortable deep banquettes for the tables around the walls, and the other tables are well apart from each other. At the far end of the dining room, a glass wall leads out to a narrow terrace, where other, more intimate tables are set, and steep stairs at either end take you down into a sunken garden, with trees and more tables. In the evening, Chinese lanterns hang from the trees and the entire garden is surrounded by the usual high brownstone so common in downtown Manhattan.

Joe Cleary knew the place. He had taken a few girls there, including the one who finally caused his financially crippling divorce. Before he met Lauren. But at eleven-thirty in the morning, with orange and white police tapes everywhere, to keep the crime scene clear and the rubberneckers at bay, there was nothing romantic or seductive or fashionable about the place.

A broad-hipped uniformed cop, Charlie Benwell, held one such piece of tape up, as Cleary ducked underneath.

'Wha's up?' said the cop, as much a statement as a question.

'Hi Charlie.' Joe Cleary glanced around and checked out the stretcher on its rubber-rimmed aluminium wheels, waiting near the kitchen entrance. A couple of detectives from the local precinct, the 16th, were taking notes from three members of the staff: two cooks and the somewhat dishy early-shift manager, a tall, fair-haired girl in her very early twenties. She must've been about six feet, and slim, but not skinny, no way. Joe remembered her from a couple of months earlier, when he had brought Dinah Brewer from Fingerprints for a plate of spaghetti and a few bottles of Bud. Boy, had that been a saga: she wrote four letters in five days, the last one starting, 'I don't know why you won't take my calls, don't you know what that night meant to me?'

Answer, no, considered the detective as he pushed open the double doors to the kitchen, nodding to the kid in police uniform standing guard, and went inside.

Sergeant Eugene Wharton, being the uniformed Patrol Supervisor who had reached the reported murder and established that there was indeed a cadaver and that the circumstances were assuredly suspicious, had become at that moment Crime Scene Supervisor, which, from his expression, was not precisely how he had planned on spending this Wednesday morn.

He glanced up at Cleary. 'What happened to your kisser?'

Cleary shrugged. 'Line of duty – fuckin' pussycat. I don't see any corpse.'

At which Wharton almost brightened. He held up a finger and, his eyes glinting, announced, 'Wait.'

He led Joe Cleary round the ovens and racks of kitchen pots and pans to a big wall-freezer, the door of which, hanging open, obscured its contents. Wharton stepped round and extended his arm, like a master chef. '*Voilà*.'

The body was encrusted with frost, from the refrigerated closet where a few legs and sides of meat hung. It was upside-down, a meat hook through the left ankle. Blood had run down, which is to say up, the trouser leg, before freezing. So the victim was alive at that point, for dead men don't bleed.

Because the skewered ankle was about five feet from the floor, the head and shoulders of the body rested at an odd angle on the ice-covered bottom of the freezer closet. The hair was spiky with icicles and frost, but there was no mistaking the lack of ears or nose.

Cleary's gaze automatically flicked to check the corpse's fingers. He was not surprised to see four lying some way from their original and more natural locations.

But he did not recognise the mutilated face.

'Annie said a ten-one-nine,' he announced, as if ready to write that off as a mistake.

'Sure. J.D. was carrying a Glock in a Fed-issue holster. Also a State Department pin was in his jacket lining.' Wharton indicated a jacket of blue wool, lying across a solid wood butcher's table, its pockets turned inside out, lining slit.

'They missed it?' It was clear as day to the Homicide sergeant that the victim had been tortured and searched. Probably the other way round.

Wharton raised his shoulders. 'You're the detective, Joe.'

'Yeah, fuck you, too.' Joe Cleary smiled. He and Wharton went way back.

Eugene Wharton handed him a small plastic evidence-sachet. Inside was a round enamel pin, with the US State Department emblem, the bald eagle clutching arrows and olive branches. The scroll around it said United States Department of State. It was worn smooth and some of the enamel had come off.

A noise in the background announced the pathologist had

arrived. Cleary smiled, he could smell the bourbon even at the range of fifteen feet.

'Whaddaya say, Doc?' he said, without turning round, still contemplating the stiff.

Henry Grace, the pathologist, was a short, stocky man in his fifties, with graying hair and round, gold-rimmed granny glasses. He stepped past Cleary and peered at the cadaver, pushing his glasses up as they slipped on the bridge of his nose.

'Once had a case the nose had been shot off. Before that, same case, some guy had bitten it off. It had been sutured back on. Good take.' He leaned into the freezer closet, to get a better look.

'Some people have no luck with noses, I guess,' replied Joe Cleary, to be sociable.

Silence greeted this. He wondered if the tall blonde Sicilian chick was still outside.

'Henry, I'll be in the restaurant if you want me.'

But Grace was too engrossed in his examination to hear.

Outside, in the reception/bar area, Homicide Sergeant Cleary checked the statements of the two early-shift cooks who had found the corpse. The tall girl sat on a bar stool, looking cool and just a smidgen uncomfortable.

'You don't like cops, huh?' asked Cleary, as he sat on the next stool and took a pack of Camel Lites from his good coat pocket.

'Have you been in a fight?' asked Dolores, for that was the name on the witness sheet.

'Yeah, with a goddam cat. On a fire escape, would you believe?'

'I can believe anything,' said the girl, in an attempt to be worldly. Mind you, good-looking Sicilian chicks who looked like Nordic ice-maidens, no, Valkyries, she was so fair and tall, were probably real worldly by the time they reached twenty-two, which was what the witness sheet stated to be her age.

'Tore my pocket, look.'

'Some cat.' Dolores looked bored already.

'Who's the man in the fridge?'

She raised her shoulders, shook her head slowly, and, to

Cleary's mild surprise, said, 'I think his name is Maclean. He ate here last night. Nice guy.'

'Who with?'

'Alone. If that is his jacket in the kitchen.' She was suddenly a kid after all and she shuddered as she said, 'I didn't, I couldn't – I didn't look too close. You know?'

Sure. Joe Cleary knew. Maybe even in the dim recesses of his mind he could remember once not being able to look too close at a mutilated piece of human meat. He laid a hand on her arm, it was trembling.

'Sure, I know. Listen, kid, if you want to take a walk, a cuppa coffee or something . . .' He offered her a cigarette. She shook her pretty head.

'I'm fine, I'll be fine,' she said. 'He paid by Diners Club – you want to see the check?'

Did he ever.

'Take your time. When did he leave?'

'I don't know. Round about midnight.'

'Still alone?'

'Yeah.'

'OK,' Cleary lit his cigarette, 'I want you to think hard, Dolores.'

'You shouldn't smoke so much.'

'What's so much? We just met.'

'Two left in the pack.'

'Maybe I bought it last week.'

'The pack's too new.'

'Hey, who's the detective around here?'

She smiled. That was better.

'So, lemme get this straight. Mister Maclean comes in. What time?'

'Nine-thirty.'

'Good. He has booked?'

'No.'

'In off the street.'

She nodded.

'He talks to anyone? Sits at the bar first?'

Dolores frowned. 'I don't know; we were busy. I work at the desk there, so he could have been at the bar first. Ask Jerry.'

'That's fine. He talks to anybody when he's in the dining room?'

She shrugged. 'I don't think so. Just the waiter. He looked over at me a few times. Kind of smiled.'

And who would blame him, thought Joe.

'OK. Dolores, just as soon as you get that check for me, you can go.'

Dolores nodded obediently. It occurred to Joe Cleary she might have been busted for something. Like possession, or cheque theft. Or prostitution. She was that kind of girl, and this was that kind of town.

And when Dolores Caltagirone opened her desk and extracted the Diners Club slip and a carbon copy of the check, the detective said maybe it would be a good idea if he took all the records of last night's diners. The girl hesitated for a moment but Cleary had switched from easy-going to the-cop-who-might-mean-trouble, and his hunch that she felt uncomfortable with the law around paid off.

'Thanks, kid. Why don't you split and go home. I'll need a statement, so if you want to come over to the 15th Precinct and ask for me,' he gave her his business card, 'I'll treat you to a particularly bad plastic cup of coffee.'

She glanced at him. Her eyes were the palest blue. 'You know how to tempt a girl.'

'Yeah,' he said, 'so I've been told.' What the hell are you doing, he asked himself, even now Laurie could be in labour. Jeezus. Us men, what rats. He smiled and took the keys of the reception desk from her. 'Say about four o'clock.'

'Today?'

No, next Mardi Gras.

'Sure, today.'

Dolores nodded, the kid was still shaken up. 'All right.' Like she was agreeing to a date.

And she walked out.

A half hour later, back at the freezer closet, Joe Cleary stood watching as Doctor Henry Grace knelt with a hair drier, playing it on the dead man's frozen fingers, the four that lay together, stuck to the ice on the bottom of the fridge.

'He had blackened grouper for supper. Followed by lemon cheesecake,' announced the cop.

It took a great deal to amaze the Homicide Division's most experienced pathologist, but he turned and gaped at Cleary, astonished. 'But I haven't even opened the stomach.'

Joe Cleary smiled and held up the dead man's dinner bill. 'It's on his check, Henry.'

At which point Officer Benwell ambled in, grinning like a fool. He fumbled in the top pocket of his blue uniform tunic and produced a long King Edward cigar, which he waggled at the Homicide Sergeant.

Cleary dropped his last cigarette and ground it with his heel, the relief enormous. 'What is it?'

'Congratulations, Joe, you just became the daddy of an eight-pound baby boy.'

Everybody around the kitchen and the thawing cadaver whooped and hollered and crowded round the lean little Irishman, clapping him on the back and saying all right and wow and congratulations, except for Doctor Henry Grace, who was scrabbling on his hands and knees protesting, 'Don't step on the goddam fingers . . .'

The Secret Intelligence Service takes recruiting extremely seriously. After all, those men and women who come in from Wonderland are the operators, agent-runners, desk officers, analysts and, above all, colleagues of the future. Their selection and training has been honed over many years of experience, and the fledgeling Intelligence Officers (Probationer) will have received, by the time they complete Selection, Induction, Preliminary Training, Special Skills and Operational Experience – a process which takes five months – arguably the best grounding in the world for effective employ in the second oldest profession. And by the time they pass out from the final course, more than 40 per cent of the original intake (usually about nine souls) will have been dropped from the programme.

That figure would be very much higher if, like the military's special units, recruits were taken from those who volunteered their services. However, one sure way to avoid being employed by the British Intelligence Service is to make the mistake of actually putting yourself forward. For, to the arcane minds of those who run the offensive espionage networks, anyone who imagines they would make a good spy is probably a crackpot dreamer or a dangerous fool, steeped in an overdose of movies and pulp fiction.

Thus, potential career officers are discreetly talent-spotted, sometimes tested without their ever realising, and approached in a fairly matter-of-fact way, with the offer of an opportunity to serve the nation and enjoy a worthwhile career at the same time.

Sometimes those approached are already working for the government, in the armed forces or the Treasury or the Ministry of Defence. It is not done to poach from what the Firm calls the 'straight' Foreign Office. But of course it happens. Sometimes without the Foreign Office ever becoming aware of the new arrangement.

All of this background information was given, with a leavening of humour and self-deprecation, to James Gant in the perhaps appropriate setting of the Terrace of the House of Lords, in Westminster, over a plate of cucumber sandwiches and a pot of Darjeeling tea. His counsellor was the Dowager Countess Treffewin – Aunt Edith.

At seventy-three, she was less tall than in those wartime days when she graced the chorus line of high-kickers in Murray's Cabaret Club, or when she ran Operation Ransack as an SIS network boss in East Berlin. But Edith was still upright and graceful, if a touch wrinkled these days, with the imperious gaze of someone who was used to fighting and winning her personal battles. She also had a definite twinkle in her eyes, particularly when talking to her favourite nephew.

'This chap Jardine said it was your idea, for them to approach me,' remarked Gant, reaching for his fourth thin-cut, slightly soggy crustless quarter of cucumber sandwich.

'What nonsense,' replied the Dowager. And studied her Delft china teacup.

'Aunt Edith,' said Gant, 'You would not, by any chance, be lying to me?'

'Of course I am,' she replied, without a blush.

James shrugged. 'What makes you think I want a change?'

The Terrace overhung the impressively murky, dangerously

tide-swirling broad River Thames and Edith glanced up at a tugboat shoving a very long barge through the choppy wavelets.

'I shouldn't imagine you do, James. You seem perfectly fulfilled with the BBC. Going to all those wars and things.'

'Then I don't get it.'

Edith Treffewin laid down her cup and saucer. Gant felt that, if the old darling had had a lorgnette, she would have trained it on him.

'Sometimes one has to consider what one can do for others, my dear young man. I think you and SIS are probably made for each other. You're just bloody lucky I still have a few connections.'

Gant gazed at the tugboat. Somebody was walking back from the bow, without a care in the world. He found himself thinking, what would the suffering individuals in those 'wars and things' give for such everyday boredom. Such ordinariness. And, in that moment, he began to understand what Edith – and probably David Jardine – were trying to offer him.

Still watching the boat, Edith said quietly, 'Instead of recording life's woes, Jimmy, you might just get a chance to make a difference.'

Sunlight suddenly brightened the surface of the water, glinting on the waves, and the tugboat sounded four brief blasts – 'I am going straight ahead.'

Gant was not a particularly superstitious man, but he felt a strange resolve spread through him, as if he finally knew what direction his life should take. And, more practically, it did not involve putting his hard-earned savings into Rebecca's bloody cousin's film company.

But what would he tell Rebecca? After all, it was her future, too. James Gant became aware his aunt was watching him quietly, as if she was aware what was going through his mind.

To hell with it, he had signed that absurd card, binding him not to mention his interview with Jardine (this conversation with Edith seemed not to count, for was she not part of Jardine's world?), so he would not say a word. Anyway, they might not have him, at the end of their pompous-sounding

Boards and tests. But he had a feeling, he knew, that they certainly would. For it was meant. Somehow, he had always known it.

He smiled and turned to Edith. 'It would be fine, it would be something, wouldn't it? To make a difference.'

3

Leather Face at the Ostrich

Three months had passed. Now it was summer, hottest in Tripoli, just about as hot in New York City – but more humid – and not much cooler in London, where Wimbledon Centre Court sweltered in one hundred degrees.

Joe Cleary's wife, Lauren, had been delivered, that day of the freezer murder, of a plump baby boy who was christened Patrick Cheyenne MacMonagle Cleary, taking into account the fact that Lauren was a direct descendant of Cheyenne medicine men from way before the Pilgrims (she was also part German, a fearsome mixture), and that Joe's mother was a MacMonagle from Skibbereen in County Cork.

The stiff in the freezer was no nearer to being identified, save for the certain knowledge that (State Department pin and standard Federal-issue handgun notwithstanding) the guy's fingerprints proved beyond doubt that he was not, nor ever had been, any kind of agent or employee of the United States Government. Nor had he ever committed a felony or been held as a suspect or been in any of the several situations where his fingerprints would have been held on record.

So the murdered man remained on file as a John Doe, which was NYPD parlance for an unidentified stiff and, frankly, there had been so many more homicides in NYPD's areas of responsibility that, unless something like a small airplane towing the relevant information buzzed low (and several times at that) over Number One Police Plaza, there was fat chance of the victim's name ever becoming known.

As for suspects, you have to be kidding.

*

And Zina Farouche was in Paris; she had driven three in a small BMW convertible 325i she had bought second-hand in Vienna. She was not at all like that emaciated victim of the jailers and interrogators at Station 16 of the Naji al-Ali terrorist camp, in the Libyan desert, 170 miles south-west of Tripoli.

And neither did she bear much resemblance to the weak and exhausted patient, recuperating at the Abu Nidal safe house, the orange and vegetable farm near Tripoli Airport, where she had been tenderly nursed back to health by none other than Hanna al-Farah, 'Commander of the Assassins' and older sister of the feared 'Doctor' Kamal, the Abu Nidal group's Intelligence Chief.

This Zina Farouche was a slender and elegant young woman, with the glowing fitness of an athlete. Indeed, she could on occasion be seen at the select Les Peupliers tennis courts in the Bois de Boulogne, playing sets with certain members of the Banque de la Méditerranée and one or two diplomats from the Tunisian and Syrian embassies.

She had accreditation with the Tunisian embassy, as a junior member of their Security Staff doubling as interpreter of French, English, German and Italian, and her diplomatic credentials indicated she was on temporary secondment from the Tunisian Foreign Ministry.

The deft infiltration of a stateless child of the Palestinian refugee camps (and a secret terrorist operative since the age of fourteen) into the unsuspecting diplomatic service of a sovereign Arab nation had been accomplished by way of a most clandestine agreement between certain Arab rulers, brokered by Syria, Jordan and Saudi Arabia, for full nationality to be granted by most Arab states to those Palestinians who qualified, under strict guidelines. They had to be sponsored by the recognised Palestine authorities, which is to say the Legal Department of the Palestine Liberation Organisation – the PLO. They were required to undertake allegiance to the country issuing them with a passport, and they were obliged to respect the laws and customs of that country.

Once granted nationality, in this case of the North African state of Tunisia, the individual was to all intents and purposes a citizen of that country, with full rights, including the right to apply for government work.

Because the PLO's covert Al Fatah directorate ran all intelligence and security matters, this facility was in effect a licence to acquire bona fide foreign nationality for its members. It was a gift, in terms of presenting its operatives with twenty-four-carat-gold cover, for the documentation involved would be genuine and not forged.

The well-funded Abu Nidal Group, which was a violent, breakaway, independent, indeed renegade, terrorist organisation (it had condemned PLO chief Yasser Arafat to death, for his move away from random violence towards diplomacy), had infiltrated Al Fatah's system for acquiring such foreign citizenship and thus Zina Farouche had been a genuine Tunisian national since the age of sixteen.

And her employment by the Tunisian Foreign Ministry had been finagled by officials in the pay of Abu Nidal, handsomely bribed and certain of death should they fail in their discretion. Any examination of the records would reveal, most convincingly, that the young woman had been in the job for two years and four months, with pay drawn, assignments recorded, confidential personnel reports on her work and occasional travel details. Although Paris was, apparently, her first foreign assignment.

Zina shopped at chic boutiques in the Champs Élysées and ate, sometimes alone, sometimes with colleagues, in a number of small cafés and restaurants in the neighbourhood of Saint Germain des Prés.

It had been five weeks since her arrival in France, and the DST, the French Security Service, had taken a discreet look at her, tapping the phone of her tiny apartment in the Rue Napoléon, and intercepting her mail, which on the face of it consisted of: two letters from her mother, a doctor in Tunis's main hospital; four from her boyfriend, Tariq, a wealthy Tunisian money broker based in Zurich, Switzerland; and three invitations from the *Reader's Digest*'s Rome office to take advantage of the fact that, out of millions, her name had been chosen by the computer etcetera etcetera.

A note on her unremarkable file at DST Headquarters in Fontainebleau concluded that Mademoiselle Farouche was, as far as could be established, precisely what she seemed to be.

Which was not quite accurate. For the letters were the

careful product of Abu Nidal's Committee for Special Missions and Zina was working skilfully and clandestinely (with such care and expertise that even David Jardine of the SIS would have given grudging approval) to bring her team together, in order to carry out successfully the Abu Nidal Group's contract, awarded three months earlier, in the old Shah's Winter Palace, in north Tehran, by Ayatollah Jamil Shahidi of the Iran clergy's Foreign Intelligence Department – Special Operations.

It was a contract written on no paper, conveyed by the merest whisper from Shahidi's lips, placed close to the intent ear of the overweight, profusely sweating terrorist emissary Abdel Aziz al-Khaliq. Who in turn had flown to Libya and consulted with his master, Abu Nidal, who had graciously accepted the contract (and the twenty-million-dollar down payment that arrived with it). Al Khaliq had then travelled immediately to the Naji al-Ali training camp, where he had collected Zina Farouche from her cesspit and her rapacious interrogators and initiated the process of transforming her from abused victim to ruthless terrorist cell leader.

For it was Zina Farouche whom Nidal had chosen to arrange and run the Iranian contract, although, because his organisation operated on the need-to-know principle, she had not been told of Tehran's involvement.

The contract was for the simultaneous slaughter of eighteen men, women and children in the comfortable State of Connecticut, on the East Coast of the United States of America . . . The Great Satan.

The same three months had seen James Gant meet once more with David Jardine, just three days after their first encounter, and, receiving honest answers to his several queries and misgivings, accept SIS's invitation to appear before its Board, as an applicant for entry into the Service.

The Board had been held in one of the small conference rooms on the second floor of the Firm's new headquarters, the towering post-modernist Gothic-Bauhaus edifice on the south bank of the River Thames, almost facing the staid and mildly disapproving Tate Gallery on the other side.

'A touch of Gotham City, bit like Batman's Castle,' Jardine

had murmured apologetically, as he had collected James from the janitors at reception, duly photographed by a magic video device which had produced his mugshot, neatly enveloped in a plastic visitor's pass, complete with family name and a pale-blue striped band marked 2-ESCORT ONLY.

In the conference room, three men and two women made up the examining board. They seemed of equal status and it had been impossible to decide who was in the chair, although Gant's money went on either David Jardine or a tough, forty-something, chain-smoking woman, thick set, with jet-black hair streaked with steel grey. Her eyes were ceaselessly examining, yet somehow full of humour, and her hands had been just a bit too strong for her gender. The woman's name, James Gant was to learn in time, was Marietta Delice, pronounced Delichi, and she was Director/Counter Terror, Narcotics and Proliferation, as in nuclear proliferation. The office acronym for this division was Catnap, for obvious reasons.

The man Gant knew as Frederick K. Estergomy was also on the Board, along with one Tony Allardyce, the Director of Personnel. Allardyce was a slight, tanned man of about thirty-eight, wearing a conventional dark suit, a startling yellow waistcoat and a Garrick Club necktie – broad swathes of salmon pink and mint green.

The fifth member had been a young woman, with expensively cut shoulder-length hair, composed yet restless hands, elegant wrists, spectacles that kept slipping slightly askew, and a crisp cotton blouse beneath a roomy grey wool cardigan, none of which succeeded in hiding the fact that she had the potential, given different circumstances, to be disturbingly attractive. This was Kate Howard, youngest Director of Security for SIS since 1946.

The forty-seven minutes James Gant had spent there (and which, were he to be frank, he had been quietly dreading, for he lacked, he felt, the essential glibness he imagined necessary for success in oral examinations) had been surprisingly civilised and, if not exactly pleasant, certainly not the pompous ordeal he had anticipated.

He had been questioned, closely and with disconcerting perception, about his life to date, his attitude to events and people, his relationship with his family to an intrusive degree, his philosophy and his personal ethics with regard to his then employment, recording international strife and human misery. They had thrown several hypotheses at him – the what would you do if such and such happened, if you had to decide between this and that sort of problems, some of which had been designed to make him contradict earlier responses.

His knowledge of foreign languages – French, German and Arabic – had been tested by several of the Board members, who seemed fluent to the point of being accentlessly bilingual. They had quietly, he felt, skilfully, tried at times to make him angry, offended, on his guard or reluctant to give a full, possibly self-compromising, answer.

Jardine had then escorted him from the building, pleasantly reminded him of his obligation of non-disclosure, comforted him that, even if the Board turned him down, he had been considered most carefully, a privilege granted to only a few, and then he was out on the street with a long walk to the nearest bus stop. Cameramen engaged to be married could not afford to take taxis.

James had sat on the bus back to Chiswick quietly fuming. He had never asked for a bloody job with those damned spooks. Who the hell did they think they were? Privileged indeed. That dumb Board with its motley crew who looked in the cold light of day, away from the charmed atmosphere on the second floor of the Office, as they liked to call it, like nothing more than a collection of self-congratulatory members of some eclectic television panel game. Of course they would turn him down. I mean, who wanted to be part of all that? Sign this, don't breathe a word of that, one fine day, if you're really lucky, I might tell you my real name? Give us a bloody break. Lead story in the *Nine o'clock News* and eight minutes of film in *Panorama* will do me just fine, thank you very much.

And when James Gant had arrived home, still coldly angry and feeling conned and made somehow ridiculous, Rebecca had phoned from her corporate bank in the City to say she had seen a two-bedroomed flat advertised in Clapham, and her parents were going to give the mortgage deposit as a wedding present.

Well, that was just super, James had replied, and, sure,

why not have a plate of spaghetti at the Bersaglieri in the King's Road later, and talk to her cousin Barney about sinking his few thousand into Barney's film-editing company.

Welcome back to the real world, Gant had thought to himself, and the moment he replaced the receiver the phone had rung again.

He had lifted it, not feeling friendly towards the world.

'Yep?' he had ungraciously enquired.

'James?'

'That's me.'

'James, David Jardine here. Well done, old man. You're in.'

Silence.

A broad grin had started to spread across James Gant's face. 'I'm sorry?' he had replied, just wanting to hear it again.

'They like you. We want you to start as soon as you can.'

Silence.

'James . . .?'

The grin had become so huge he felt like an imbecile.

'Oh. That's, um, well . . .'

'Presumably you need to give notice.'

The response was rapid and, James hoped, did not completely betray his absolute delight. 'Oh, yes. That's terrific. Christ. Wonderful. Notice. Yes. About two weeks, I think I can get away with two weeks. Maybe sooner.'

Jardine sounded gently amused. 'Two weeks will be fine. James, will it be OK if one of my young men comes round and has a quick word with you about, um, how to handle this? Obviously you will need some sort of thing to tell your family and present employers. You know what I mean.'

Well, of course Gant had no idea precisely what the man from the netherworld meant, but there was only one way to find out.

'Of course. There's a pub near here. The Boatman's Tavern. Six o'clock?'

'Good man. I think you'll get on fine with our chap. His name is Malcolm Strong. Good luck.'

'Thanks very much.'

And that was how James Gant became a spy.

*

Those three months had passed quickly, but not without straining his relationship with Rebecca and testing his ability at performing, as a matter of routine, something James was not in the habit of doing – lying.

For when Gant had strolled from his flat that first night of his new apprenticeship, along Chiswick Mall, with water from the high tide lapping at the edge of the road, and families of ducks debating whether to establish themselves in the sparse bushes and hedges there, and had waited in the Boatman's with a pint of Murphy's Irish stout in his hand, Malcolm Strong, the man David Jardine had sent round 'for a quick word', had quietly explained to our young man the rudiments of presenting a cast-iron cover story to his nearest and dearest, his colleagues at work and to casual acquaintances and old friends, sufficient to convince them totally and arouse zero suspicions as to the real nature of his new career.

The cover story Strong had chosen for Gant was this:

Great Aunt Edith, the Dowager Lady Treffewin, had heard from a friend in the Foreign Office that their Press and Public Relations Department was looking for someone with his film and tape-editing and photography skills, university educated, well travelled and with a grasp of languages, to work on a project with them, with a view to being taken onto the permanent staff as an executive officer, visiting embassies abroad and co-ordinating media events.

James was to reveal that he had quietly and without fuss – which was quite typical of him, being very much an understated, un-showy individual – attended an interview, a few weeks back then; and just today, he had been to a more formal affair, a Selection Board, and had been offered the job. And, although the starting salary was about half of his present one from the BBC, future prospects were good and the idea of joining the Diplomatic Service appealed to him. So he had decided to take the offer. After all, if he did not like it, he could always leave and go back to the news desk.

'What', Gant had asked, concerned, 'if the real Press and Public Relations Department gets to hear of me, and this . . . fiction?'

Strong had smiled and, upon returning with two more pints of Murphy's, assured the foundling that the Office was most professional and all of James's recruiting would from this moment – well, some days beforehand, actually – be handled by that very department of the 'straight' Foreign and Commonwealth Office. For that was the nature of the way the Firm worked, buried within the bureaucracy of government.

Well. Rebecca's reaction to this surprising news of Gant's was less than sanguine. The subsequent scenes, the rows, the tears and tantrums, the slamming doors and heart-rending pillow-sobbings, the cold silences and pendulum swings between sighing hurt and shrew-like fury, all added up to one unavoidable conclusion: Rebecca was not absolutely thrilled by her fiancé's sudden change of direction. Why, hadn't cousin Barney (you remember, the nice Etonian whose father was a minor Admiral?) made a considerable sacrifice by preparing a place for James as a partner in his going-places film-effects and documentaries company?

Suffice it to say, at the moment when we rejoin James Gant, in his twelfth week as an SIS trainee, strolling through the small French port of Banyuls in the foothills of the Pyrenees, being discreetly assessed for personal anonymity, coolness and tradecraft, as he made his way to the old harbour, on the lookout – without appearing to be – for his 'contact', from whom he was to take a brush pass (that is, the transfer of an innocent item, say a book of matches, containing 'coded information', without anyone noticing), the former cameraman was free and unencumbered, a veritable bachelor, which was a healthy state for an apprentice spy aged twenty-seven.

'What happened between you and Rebecca?' enquired his trainer that evening, as he assessed his protégé's efforts earlier in the day. The book of matches had slipped and fluttered off the harbour wall, to float away on the wake of a passing fishing smack.

'Well, Ronnie,' the absurdly named Frederick Estergomy had turned out to be called Ronnie, second name as yet unknown, 'Rebecca was a near-perfect fiancée, as fiancées go. And as fiancées go, she went . . .'

And James Gant had met Szabodo's gaze and lifted his shoulders.

'Oh, my dear chap,' said the Hungarian, in what he really imagined to be the upper-class cadences of Oxford, where the

Firm had sent him, after several hair-raising years working for the British in Hungary, just after the 1956 uprising, when Ronnie was a mere youth in his teens, 'are you very hurt?'

And James Gant had looked at him coolly, in a way that both chilled Szabodo and gladdened his ruffian's heart.

Later, Ronnie Szabodo had spoken to Jardine – whom he had also trained, several thousand years before – and, when asked about the new intake of four trainee spies, had replied, 'That chap with the camera . . . heart of bloody ice. Cold as flint.'

And in his flat in Tite Street, in London's Chelsea, David Jardine had moved his malt whisky gently around its tumbler and murmured, 'Oh, excellent. I guessed he might just do.'

The Banyuls training exercise and assessment resulted in James Gant being graded ACCB in various arcane skills, peculiar to espionage at street level. Tradecraft was the term used by Szabodo, and that was apt enough. For the business of moving among others, mere mortals in the innocent world – Wonderland was the Hungarian's word for it – without being noticed, like an unremarkable ghost (observing, following, avoiding being followed, avoiding being observed, listening, merging, assimilating, communicating and, above all, remembering to the last detail, whether among beggars or princes) all of that was vital stuff in the business of operating successfully in that most ancient of the secret trades.

Then it was back to England for a second course of instruction at Myg Trefwny, the Honey Farm, down in Wales, a hundred acres of discreetly guarded land, deep in the hinterland, surrounded by mountainous hills and forests, supposedly a sewage farm belonging to the South Wales Water Board.

There, the days of the six surviving novices on Induction Course 44 were filled with lectures and indoctrination briefings, informing them of the real SIS and what it did, how it did it, and some of its successes and failures. And endless written and oral questions on why they had succeeded, or failed. There was also, of course, the fitness training – runs at six in the morning and six in the evening. They had started, during the first three-week period there – two days after their engagement by SIS – with one mile, then, after three days, two, and three days later, three miles. Now, on their second visit, the runs were five miles, morning and evening, and the lectures and seminars were interspersed with street fighting, unarmed combat, and circuit work.

Earlier, starting on Week 5, Course 44 had attended explosives and demolition training, which was in essence the study of blowing up bridges and factories, and making and defusing booby-trap bombs. There was also close-quarter pistol work and foreign-weapons familiarisation, run at a secret location on the North Sea coast, not far from Scarborough. The instructors were senior non-coms from the 22nd Special Air Service Regiment and each one of them had personally put his expertise to the test, often to the accompaniment of extremely noisy and fast-flying enemy lead.

There was counterfeiting, impersonation, wire-tapping, burglary and subtle and not-so-subtle ways of altering one's appearance. And, of course, there were specialist language groups, where Gant found much of his instruction and examination taking place in rapid and unrepeated French and Arabic. The French he felt relaxed with, for it really was his other language, but he had immediately regretted claiming fluency in Arabic, for which he was not surprised to learn he had been graded D – 'As in agricultural, my dear chap,' Ronnie explained, obtusely.

Each recruit had been given a codename and none was to know for some months the real names of his or her colleagues. Gant was Impetuous. Upon which later, of course, the wiseacres at Ryemarsh, the examiners of entrails, were not slow to remark.

Anyway, one night, round about when Zina Farouche was busy in Paris, conducting her clandestine business (in precisely the manner in which the trainers of SIS were coaching James Gant, but with a degree of experience and lethal skill which, assuming he were to survive, the new recruit would be lucky to have acquired in the same time that it had taken the slender Palestinian – thirteen years), James Gant was rudely awakened in the small hours, blinded by a strong flashlight, and told to get dressed in his issue linen trousers and shirt. Before he could reach, squinting in the glare, for his boots, a black hood was placed over his head, and he was bundled into the back of a van, which James recognised by smell and sound as the green Ford Transit with darkened windows which the directing staff sometimes used to drop off their few recruits for an exercise, let's say, in the Welsh hills or in some big town within fifty or sixty miles of the Farm.

The drive, via winding country roads and over the slightly swaying Severn Bridge, then onto the M5 motorway, he guessed, took about two hours. Then the freshness and scent of high-octane fuel told him they had disembarked at an airfield. The smells reminded him of Sarajevo.

The fact that nobody bothered to remove the hood suggested it must be a military air base, probably in some remote corner, where any service personnel present would doubtless be security cleared and accustomed to such shenanigans. The 'funny people', they called SIS, the SAS and other, even more secret, outfits.

James Gant was assisted up some steps, into a spartan fuselage, and strapped into a seat set along the side-wall of the fuselage. By this time he was thirsty and dying for a pee, but no one spoke to him, although he was aware of routine muttered voices nearby. Then the engines started up and he heard and felt the rear ramp lifting. It was a C-130, Hercules Transport, the reliable workhorse of the Royal Air Force's Transport Command.

Now, one of James Gant's deepest personal secrets was that flying, by any means, terrified him. He knew it was irrational, but every single time he sat in an aircraft, taking off, landing or just, in fact, flying steadily, he remained in a state of near panic, heart pounding, until the wheels were all firmly back on terra firma. But he had been told, on one of several hair-raising flights into Sarajevo, when the aircraft was required to dive steeply then level out at the last moment before landing, in order to avoid the flak, that the C-130 was the safest large plane in the world, and the RAF the world's most accident-free 'airline'.

The take-off was more alarming than ever, James Gant discovered, when he couldn't see. And, as he settled into the flight, he realised this was what the previous three months had been leading up to. For the surviving students of Course

44 had been warned that something disorientating, alarming, and unconventional was planned for each of them. The object was to test them and, if they made the grade, using their wits and remembering all they had learned, they would enter directly into the last phase of the Training Programme, Operational Experience, where they would find themselves assigned to a seasoned agent runner, in some foreign station.

Sitting, uncomfortable, bladder full, and hooded, Gant carefully rehearsed all the lectures, all the discussions, all the casual conversations of the past three-and-a-half months, for he had not forgotten a remark by one of the visiting staff, who came down from Vauxhall, or Century House, to help their future colleagues with insights into the business, words of personal advice, and general . . . conversations about operational conduct. In other words, how to behave in hostile territory – Denied Areas was the term, meaning places where one's illegal activities on behalf of the British Government could quite easily result in the removal of one's finger and toe nails, one's balls, one's eyes and one's life, although not, except for the last of these, necessarily in that order.

It was the sharp-eyed, chain-smoking Marietta Delice who had mentioned, almost too innocently, in that gravel voice of hers, that the whole business of surviving in this dangerous game was not remembering the obviously important things heard or seen. It was the seemingly casual, off-the-cuff, thrown-away piece of information which might just, at the end of the day, save your bloody skin. To quote La Belle Dame Sans Merci, as Course 44 had christened Marietta.

So Gant began to try to remember such snippets, in case they might be of help in whatever form this ordeal was going to take.

And, of course, his mind went virtually blank.

About an hour into the flight, some member of the crew, or one of his guards, had, in the nick of time, led him to the aircraft's cramped WC, where he was locked in and allowed to remove his hood and have a blissful pee. But the moment he ran some water from the trickling faucet, to refresh himself, the door was opened by one of the instructors, known to the intake as Jungle Jim Who Never Smiles, who led him back to his uncomfortable seat near the rear of the plane. And, without expression, Jungle Jim put the hood back on, fixing it securely over Gant's head.

Back to darkness.

Apprehension should perhaps have eased with the temporary removal of the hood, and a glance round the cavernous cargo hold of the C-130, smelling faintly of burnt fuel and warm plastic. Recognising Jungle Jim. Seeing the two RAF Air Dispatchers dozing on a pile of hessian nets. But it did not. And he sat there, trying to get some sleep, which he knew he was doubtless going to need.

An hour later, the C-130 began its descent, and this time the destination was not Sarajevo. For it was able to land in the normal way, still stomach-churning for Gant, but smoothly and effortlessly, without that terrifying dive from the sky.

When the aircraft had taxied to a halt and the rear cargo ramp was lowered, he felt wafts of hot, humid air and heard voices speaking in Italian. Hands firmly took Gant's elbows and he was guided down the ramp and off the plane, onto warm tarmac. Then he was walked to a vehicle, another van of some kind, and assisted inside, through the rear opening. The doors were slammed shut and he heard them being locked.

After a few minutes, somebody climbed into the front cab, the engine was started and the van moved off. Not giving a damn if he was being escorted or not, James Gant pushed off the suffocating hood and found he was alone in the back of a blacked-out van. Probably, he guessed, a Peugeot.

After about forty minutes, the vehicle seemed to be in a busy, winding city, or large town. Exhaust fumes made the inside of the van uncomfortable. Finally it stopped. The engine was turned off. One person got out. He heard the cab door being locked. Then the driver seemed to stroll away, whistling tunelessly.

Now, James asked himself, do we wait for forty or fifty minutes, which might be prudent in some circumstances. Or is this one of the times when the bastards have put some kind of small device, maybe a smoke bomb or something, set to go off and cause the local cops to find me, without shoes, papers or money, locked inside this van?

He decided to get out immediately and, after examining the

lock, searched around and found an apology for a tool kit (two wrenches and a rusty screwdriver). Then, quite professionally Gant felt, he unlocked the back doors and stepped out, examining the door hinges, as if he had been doing some repair, something ordinary and everyday.

He found the van was parked in a narrow street, but nearby he could hear the car horns and cheerful rumble of a busy thoroughfare. There were one or two passers-by, but only a beggar, ambling along on the far side of the street, glanced at him, then wandered on, mumbling to himself.

Gant tried the doors of the front cab. Locked. But, thanks to the strange assortment of experts who had been his mentors in recent weeks, within twelve seconds James Gant, Impetuous, Course 44, was sitting in the driver's seat and reaching underneath the dashboard, selecting just the right wires needed to breathe life into the starter motor.

Eight seconds later, the engine purred into life, its ignition wires linked the way he had been taught by somebody called Frank, who had also taught them how to drive a car in a manner that would ensure a sizeable jail sentence in the wrong circumstances. But his effort had been useless for of petrol there was virtually none. The needle was way below empty.

James shrugged. So it was not going to be that easy. Patiently, beginning to enjoy the game, he checked out the street for watchers. So far it seemed clear. But he knew the organisers of this exercise were not beyond phoning an anonymous warning to the local Polizia, that this was a stolen car.

So, next question. Do I stay with this van or just leg it and take pot luck, with nothing but what I stand up in? Namely my socks.

Always use what you know you have available, he remembered someone dinning into him. The instructor with only one eye and two fingers missing from his right hand. Whose advice had *he* not listened to?

So James searched the vehicle, systematically and thoroughly. And he won a prize. Under the front passenger seat, he found, inside a paper bag, a battered pair of size-ten sneakers, his size, and he slipped them on.

A further rummage among the discarded candy papers and

cigarette stubs revealed three books of matches, some old Italian newspapers, including two Rome evening editions, and a crumpled McDonald's 'Big Mac' wrapper upon which was written something in French. One word, '*Autruche*'. Which meant 'Ostrich'. Of all things.

Deciding not to hang around the vehicle, Gant checked that his rust-coloured shirt and tan linen trousers were not so crushed or stained they might draw unwanted attention to himself. He felt his unshaven jaw, but decided that, since this was clearly Italy, probably Rome, no one would pay much attention to a touch of stubble.

After a last, fruitless, search of the van, in the faint hope that they might have hidden a few lire, to let him function in a busy city, Gant climbed out and sauntered away. The shoes fitted perfectly. And the tramp, who he had suspected might be some kind of boringly predictable Course 44 instructor playing silly buggers, was no place to be seen.

Turning a corner, past a neat little restaurant, with pavement tables and contented lunchtime patrons, called 'Piccolo Mondo', James walked down a slight incline, to the busy thoroughfare. It was a broad avenue, with impressive buildings on the far side, which sloped downwards, to the right. The Via Veneto, stated a street sign, obligingly.

Which confirmed for James Gant that he was in Rome, for the Firm's foundling was a movie buff, and he had seen the street in a dozen Italian classics, like *La Dolce Vita*.

The Sweet Life.

Maybe later, thought Gant to himself, squinting in the sunlight and wondering what the hell 'Ostrich' had to do with anything. And if, indeed, it was a clue to his next move.

For since some of the intake had been given code names relating to birds, maybe it referred to a fellow recruit, although he could not remember anyone called that. There had been Blackbird, Peacock, Parakeet. But Ostrich did not ring any bells. It might, just as easily, be a horse backed by the absentee van driver. Whoever he was . . .

The day was pleasantly hot and James strolled, hands in pockets, along the Veneto, past the Excelsior Hotel, casually checking out the pretty women and their men as they sat at pavement tables, enjoying an aperitif – it was close to lunchtime – or discussing business, their love lives or whatever, in that animated fashion Romans so enjoy.

Problem number one, James, old son, he told himself, is to get some cash. Number two, a jacket. Maybe even a necktie, in case things got more formal.

Over the previous three months and a few days, James Gant had been well coached in the business of clandestine existence in foreign territory. The illegal acquisition of protected information, when push came to shove, involved deceit, bribery, blackmail, burglary, impersonation, safe-cracking, hot-wiring, self-defence and . . . theft.

The men's room of the Excelsior proved too busy for Gant to practise his new-found skills. But a couple of blocks further down, not far, ironically, from the British Embassy, a bustling branch of Giorgio Armani saw the young Englishman slip into a booth to try on a designer number, only to emerge moments later, returning it to a bored, overworked assistant.

Gant gestured in the hubbub that it was too tight, and he sauntered out into the street, heart pounding, carrying oh-so-casually an oatmeal wool jacket he had lifted from a counter, dropped there by a pompous, arrogant man just a tad larger than James, who was at that moment intent on admiring himself in a mirror in the far corner of the store.

The jacket itself would fit OK, but it was the comforting bulge in the inside pocket that had attracted the recruit from Intake 44.

James turned the jacket inside out and walked deceptively quickly, seeming in no special hurry, until he had put a few blocks between himself and the designer clothes store.

In an alley, first checking he was unobserved, Gant slipped a hand inside the jacket pocket and withdrew a slim but promisingly heavy leather wallet. He checked the other pockets and found only some breath-fresheners, a nail-manicure file and a key ring with a BMW key and a couple of door keys for some apartment.

A quick glance in the wallet revealed credit cards, business cards, an ID with a photo of an executive of FAO, the Food and Agriculture Organisation of the UN, and, joy of joys, several thousand lire. The equivalent of about two hundred English pounds, or three hundred dollars.

There was no future in wandering around Rome wearing the jacket of a doubtless furious minor official and, with a degree of regret, for it was a very comfortable-looking and stylish garment, James abandoned it under a pile of rubbish and strolled back into the street.

I should be feeling a total shit, he thought to himself. Theft is degrading. It is also immoral and, more to the point, illegal. He doubted if, should he be caught, any explanation about being on a British Government training exercise would carry much weight.

And yet, James Gant felt . . . elated.

For here he was. He'd broken the law. Something really cheap and shoddy. But fifteen minutes earlier he had been alone and penniless, in a foreign country, and now he was merely alone.

Gant smiled. A lady passing smiled back. Gant inclined his head to her before striding on, jauntily.

The sun was warm. Luck was with him. No one had found him out. Yet.

This had to be one of the better situations, for a spy. That much even this novice understood.

He felt terrific.

Using the pompous man's gold Amex card had been so simple James Gant was almost shocked. An hour after abandoning the man's oatmeal coat in a Rome alley off the Via Veneto, he had fitted himself out in a pair of cotton chinos, of elegant cut, a navy blue polo shirt with a Ralph Lauren design on the pocket, and a second-hand leather zip-up windcheater he had (shame on him) lifted from one of the crowded stalls at the flea market in Trastevere, not far from the Piazza di Santa Cecilia.

He kept the beat-up but comfortable sneakers he had found in the van, out of superstition. These were his pickpocket's shoes, his lawbreaker's shoes. And he was beginning to like them.

Sitting at a table outside a bar in a tiny square, a tiny *piazza*, in Trastevere, the artists' quarter of Rome, at about three that afternoon, James Gant took stock of his situation and forced himself again to rehearse every lecture, every casual conversation, he could remember, from the Farm, from the Fort, from the debriefings and from the days immediately before he had been hauled from his bed (God, was that only yesterday?).

Ostrich, ostrich, ostrich . . .

Of course. Marietta Delice. The day she had come down to the Farm to talk to them. It is not the obvious things that people say, she had told them. It's the seemingly insignificant, the throw-away lines, that might just help you to survive.

Ostrich . . . casual remarks. Ostrich . . . Rome. Italy.

Yes.

It had been a breezy, surprisingly warm day. About three weeks before. Five of Course 44 had been sitting on a hillside, overlooking the place at Scarborough, watching a pleasure steamer and a few sailboats, tiny on the dancing waters below them. The Poet had been instructing them on booby traps and recognition signals. Two more disparate subjects James had found it hard to imagine.

They called him The Poet, this instructor, because he always carried a book of Yeats in the multi-pocketed bush jacket he never seemed to take off.

Recognition signals was essentially the business of how two spies on the same side, who had never met, made themselves known to each other. And The Poet – real name Jeff Andrews – had told them a very funny story about how that had always gone wrong for him in Rome, of all places. And how, to console himself, he had repaired to a bar called Lo Struzzo. The Ostrich.

Where, where . . . Gant could not remember. He could not even recall if Jeff had said exactly where. But it had certainly been in Rome.

Unless the bastard was lying.

But it was all he had.

By ten that evening, after thumbing through phone directories, enquiring of hotel doormen, and several taxi drivers, and even visiting the Tourist Information Office (closed), James Gant finally struck lucky.

For the first policeman he had tentatively asked had immediately taken out a pen from an immaculately pressed shirt pocket and had written down the address of the Struzzo bar.

It was in an hotel off the Via della Technica, in EUR, the modern suburb Mussolini had built for the Rome International Exposition, before the Second World War.

James had taken a taxi and, cruising past the hotel, called disingenuously L'Imperatore, he had cased the joint, not only for Course 44 instructors and thugs, but for outraged owners of jackets, wallets and credit cards.

Noticing nothing which jangled his nerves, Gant strolled into the modern marble-and-glass entrance and, inside the pleasantly air-conditioned lobby, crossed to a wide corridor, just inside which a discreet sign with a painted ostrich on it announced 'Bar'.

Inside the bar, James settled into a corner seat and ordered a glass of beer, although by this time he felt more like a very large whisky.

There were five other people in the bar. Two couples, one in their twenties, the other middle-aged, and a slender, wiry man of medium height, with his hair brushed perhaps too flat, lazy eyes and a face which, while lacking much expression, was deeply tanned and might have been made of leather. He was about forty and, as soon as the white-jacketed waiter had left James Gant with his beer, this hair-brushed-flat, leather-faced, lazy-eyed man had slid from his bar stool and wandered over to James's corner table.

A cop, thought Gant. He's a bloody cop. And I was doing OK.

The man laid his tumbler, clinking with ice and some amber liquid, on the thick antique glass table top and gazed at Gant with eyes that had seen it all before.

'My dear boy,' he said, with just the sofest hint of an educated Scots accent, 'where in the name of God have you been? I'm actually bored shitless.'

And he watched Gant balefully, examining him mercilessly.

'I don't know you, I'm sorry,' replied Gant lamely, immediately regretting having answered in English, for he had harboured a bizarre intention to conduct this Rome test in French, his fairly fluent alternative language.

'Oh, don't be bloody silly. Surely it hasn't taken you since ten this morning to figure out what ostrich meant?'

Gant's delight at operating so seamlessly, he had imagined, in a foreign environment, evaporated under his companion's withering gaze.

'Look, um, I really don't know what you're talking about,' he contributed, hating each thoughtless word as it bumbled out.

'Impetuous, right? You are Impetuous. I notice you're still wearing the shoes we left in that noisy van. Did you smell the fumes? Exhaust pipe's leaking. Listen, youth, I was the tramp, OK? All you actually had to do was follow me. Couldn't be simpler. Anyway,' the man drained his glass and stood up, 'let's get out of here and do some work.'

And, as they passed through the lobby, he glanced at Gant and said, 'I see you're not wearing the same bloody clothes you started out in. Hope you didn't nick 'em. Relations with our hosts are pretty dicky at the best of times . . .'

Which is how, within moments of meeting his first operational boss, young James Gant wished the ground would open up and swallow him.

It was a chastening experience. And one which was to save his life, the way such things sometimes do.

The murdered man, the cadaver in the freezer cabinet at Barolo, remained on ice, in a sliding drawer in the morgue at Bellevue Hospital, on East 28th, not far from the Hudson River.

The morgue attendant on duty was a lanky, former gas-station jock from Nebraska, name of Grumman, first name Frank. Frank Grumman had come to New York in 1990, the year the bank had foreclosed on his old man's small farmstead, and he was studying nights, to get a degree in the dramatic arts. It was a course they ran at NYU and he had hopes of using his degree to get a place teaching drama back in the Mid-West.

On the same day that James Gant was in Rome, still wondering what the hell he was supposed to do next, round about twenty after five in the morning, Frank the morgue attendant was sitting in a white-tiled room next to the rooms where the dead were stored in refrigerated containers that slid neatly into the walls. He was immersed in William Shakespeare's *Julius Ceasar*, a play by an author he had decided to check out, mainly because Miss Holly Mansel, a right-on PC oh-so-pleased-with-herself lecturer at NYU night classes, had forbidden her students to have any truck with Dead White Playwrights, and had scribbled on the blackboard a list of those thus proscribed.

The list had included Oscar Wilde, Aristophanes, some guy called Cyril Tourneur, Ben Jonson, William Shakespeare and Anton Chekhov.

Well, Frank, although he was discreetly but uninhibitedly gay, had not taken to Ms Mansel's strident proselytising of her blinkered view of the world and he had been quite disappointed to learn he had only been accepted for her classes – which were considered a stepping stone to certain ambitious sections of SoHo's literary, artistic set – because of his orientation, which, number one, he felt was his own business and, two, he did not feel should exclude him from the rest of humanity. Frank Grumman did not wish, or need, to be labelled.

So he had gone directly to a couple of bookstores and purchased as many of the banned authors as he could find. He had already read Aristophanes' *The Frogs*, Chekhov's *Uncle Vanya*, Wilde's *A Woman of no Importance* and Shakespeare's *A Midsummer Night's Dream*.

Now it was the turn of *Julius Caesar* and, Lord, how boring he was finding it. This olde English dude would never have sold his stuff to any stage manager on Broadway.

The man who interrupted Frank Grumman's studies was about five-ten, with a dull straight's suit straight off the peg from Brookes Brothers and an intense yet slightly shy way of looking directly into your eyes. Frank wondered for a moment if this was maybe a bereaved relative, a smidgen deranged with grief.

But his visitor was from the CIA.

'Mister Grumman, my name is Harry Liebowitz; I work for the Government.' The man handed over a business card, which stated Harold K. Liebowitz, Room 441, Government Offices, Langley, Virginia. There was a small, round gilt crest on the top left-hand corner.

Frank Grumman examined the card and offered it back.

'Keep it,' said Liebowitz, 'you might want to get in touch.'

There was something about this guy that did not inspire contentment. Frank wondered if this was some kind of shakedown concerning his timid sorties into certain leather and bondage clubs in SoHo. He had been amused at the time of his photo being taken wearing just a Hell's Angel's motorcycle cap and several yards of chain. What the hell, it was only a Polaroid and, anyway, he kept it on top of his clothes closet in the cramped studio room he rented in a brownstone off Bleeker.

But that was the kind of uneasy feeling of guilt this Harry Liebowitz gave you.

'So, what can I do for you, Harry?' asked Frank Grumman. Like, if it's not to do with the stone-cold dead, you're fresh out of luck, he thought to himself. This ain't no branch of Brookes Brothers.

Liebowitz pulled up a black plastic chair and lowered himself into it. In retrospect, Grumman could not remember the man taking his eyes off him for a moment.

'This is government business, Frank,' said Liebowitz conversationally, 'and you are not to talk about it; don't discuss it. With anybody. That's important. You got that?'

Maybe I need to see some ID right about here, decided Frank Grumman, who was not taking to this *soi-disant* 'government agent'.

'Mister, I need to check you out,' said Frank, and reached for the telephone.

Liebowitz sat patiently while Frank phoned his supervisor. But there was no reply. It just rang and rang. So Frank tried the operator. Same thing. Endless ringing.

'Can we get on with this?' Harry Liebowitz took a leather wallet from his jacket pocket and slid it across the grey table top, past the log book of cadavers in and out. Frank was not a lot surprised to find, on opening the wallet, that he was looking at the credentials of a CIA officer.

'Have you fixed the phone?' he asked, laconically, having seen all the movies.

'Jesus, no. This is hardly Watergate,' replied Liebowitz, and he loosened his necktie, even though this was the coolest place in the hospital.

'OK,' Frank Grumman checked his wristwatch, 'I got reports to write up.'

'Frank, you have a cadaver, a John Doe, brought in from Barolo, an Italian place, right?'

'Barolo?' Frank shrugged. 'You have a tag number?'

'Sure.' Liebowitz fished around his pockets and produced a slip of paper. It was a carbon of an NYPD Crime Scene report. 'Let's see here . . . six-one-nine-nine. Male. Caucasian. Missing fingers.'

'Aw, missing fingers, sure, you should've said.' And Frank took a bunch of keys from his desk and stood up. 'Sure. You want to see him?'

'That would be great.'

And the two men went through, into one of the morgue rooms off the main admin room.

Frank slid open one of the dozens of drawer-cabinets which were set in the wall. Well, they were really metal coffins, kept very cold, to stop the longer-term guests from becoming anti-social.

Liebowitz stared at the corpse. He walked round the head of the container and examined the face.

'We got an imprint of his teeth,' volunteered Frank, relaxed now that he was sure this spooky visitor was not interested in him.

'Yeah, these can be faked . . .' murmured Liebowitz, and he stooped slightly to peer even closer at the face.

'Can we get the eyes open?' he enquired.

'I guess so.' And Frank Grumman took a pair of tweezers from his tunic and twisted them under the right eyelid of the three-month-dead man. There was a stickiness, a resistance, as the lid gently peeled back.

Lacking all moisture, eyeballs adhere to the inside of the eyelids. They also, even with generous regular doses of chemical preservatives, like formaldehyde, deteriorate more rapidly than skin, which takes on a waxen texture.

Frank, of course, was aware of this, and he experienced a mild satisfaction as Liebowitz failed to mask his horror. For a moment the morgue attendant thought the CIA man might throw up all over the cadaver.

'They go like that. I'm sorry,' he said mildly.

But Liebowitz continued, to give him credit, to examine the dead man's facial features. Then, satisfied, he straightened up.

'OK.' He indicated Frank could close the container.

'You look kinda pale,' said Frank Grumman, sliding the drawer back into the wall.

Hanna al-Farah knew London well. She had lived there off and on since the seventies. She had assisted her brother Ali, Head of Abu Nidal's Libyan-based Intelligence Directorate, to establish four teams of sleepers in the city, between 1987 and 1991. In the way of that clandestine world, not all the sleepers knew they were being run by Abu Nidal. Having been recruited, and taking an oath of secrecy, unto death, sworn on the Koran in the name of Allah the Merciful, some believed they were working for the Popular Front for the Liberation of Palestine (General Command), an extremist group sponsored by Syria and Iran, and based in more recent years in the Sudan, which had become virtually an Iranian sub-state.

Others thought they were faithful soldiers of Hezbollah, the Party of God, an Iranian controlled extremist faction of, predominantly, Shi'ite Islamic Fundamentalists, whose roots were in the Lebanon's Bekaa Valley and the teeming streets of West Beirut. But in truth they were creatures of Abu Nidal's, and his deception had at one time set him at loggerheads with the distinctly humourless intelligence and terror directors of Vevak, who had sent out orders from Tehran, condemning Nidal to death.

There were no more ruthless or canny survivors in the Middle East terror industry, however, than Sabri al-Banna – Abu Nidal – and he had visited Khartoum, the Sudanese capital, in person and took part in a series of secret meetings with the late Sheik Abbas al-Mussawi, the Iranian Government's trusted co-ordinator of Hezbollah terrorist tasks, and with Ahmad Jibril, leader of the PFLP (General Command), who had transferred his allegiance, after the Gulf War, from the defeated Iraq to Iran.

Abu Nidal squared his differences with the Hezbollah/Iran axis and, upon agreeing to co-ordinate his activities with

Tehran (and to carry out occasional special tasks), he received further massive funding from the Iranians and their sleeping partners in international terror, the Syrian Intelligence Service.

All of this passed through the mind of Hanna al-Farah as she drove her silver-grey Audi 100 coupé up Prince's Gate, in London's Kensington district, and paused at the red lights, smiling as a gaggle of tiny, adorable little girls in bright blue blazers, light cotton dresses and straw hats were ushered across the junction by two pretty young teachers.

The sun was strong for England, the radio had said ninety degrees Fahrenheit, and there was a sultriness about the day.

Four minutes and twenty seconds later, al-Farah was turning right, off High Street Kensington, and a red and white security barrier loomed closer. There was a dusty, dark green coloured guards' cubicle on the left and a uniformed security man, neatly turned-out in the well-pressed black trousers and crisp (as crisp as ninety degrees would allow) white shirt, with the black and gold epaulettes of the Corps of Commissionaires, an ex-servicemen's organisation, waited patiently as she smiled up at him from the open car window.

'I'm picking up my sister, flat twenty-six.' She nodded towards a stone apartment block, next to the red brick building that was the Israeli Embassy. 'I'll only be a minute.'

'Got a nice day for it,' replied the perspiring uniformed man, and he raised the barrier to allow the car through.

The Metropolitan Police Special Branch had received warnings from the Middle East that, with the Palestine Liberation Organisation and Israel signing a peace accord, shaking hands on the White House lawn and moving into a new era of uneasy but well-intentioned trust and co-operation, 'certain extremist elements' might attempt to register their contempt by some act of terror. Similar warnings had flashed around Europe and indeed around much of the world. A massive car bomb in Buenos Aires, capital of Argentina, had killed eighty people. A small airliner taking off from a Panama airport, with many Jews on board, had blown up and fallen out of the sky.

But Scotland Yard had lived for twenty-five years with the constant threat and fact of IRA urban terrorism, and the feeling at the Monday morning meeting with the Commanders of Special Branch, the Anti-Terrorist Branch and the Diplomatic Protection Group, chaired by the Assistant Commissioner in charge of Specialist Operations, was that the city was already very much on the alert for such deeds, and that the specific threat to Israeli and Jewish targets, and, indeed, to the offices of the PLO, while noted, did not require more than an enhanced level of watchfulness and an increase in overt mobile patrols, to deter any possible attempts.

Thus, Constable Gerry Harmer, with twelve years' experience in the Diplomatic Protection Group, was taking no more than a reasonably close interest as the Audi nosed into Kensington Palace Gardens, past the raised security barrier.

In addition to the Israeli embassy, the private road housed the Russian and other foreign embassies and, about four hundred yards up, Kensington Palace itself, one of the homes of the Prince of Wales. There was also a grey stone terraced house sandwiched between one of the embassies and a block of expensive residential apartments. Compass House was owned by the Crown, and it was occupied by an outstation of London Station of the Secret Intelligence Service, along with a number of colleagues from the GCHQ, the British Government's top secret electronic eavesdropping outfit.

On the third floor of this building, as chance would have it, on this particular day, David Jardine sat on the front edge of a somewhat worn old yew wood desk, in a small room, sparsely furnished with two leather chairs and a bookcase, plus a wall lined with filing cabinets and a painting above the defunct fireplace of a cricket match in 1888, at Lord's cricket ground.

It was an agreeable part of his duties to keep in regular touch with covert activities like those at Compass House, and at 12.07 that day he was listening to a young woman of about thirty, slim and with a way of pushing her spectacles straight every few minutes which both endeared her to him and reminded him of someone else. Someone in fact he found himself thinking about rather a lot these days. Another young woman, another colleague, who had with quite remarkable single-mindedness graduated from one of the most interesting jobs in Personnel – the selection and clearing of deep-cover operatives, known as black operators, whose existence and tasks were totally deniable – to Operations, an area almost impossible for females to participate in, and thence to her current appointment as Director (Security).

And, increasingly, the tall, scarfaced Director of Operations was finding it difficult to get out of his mind the one day the pair of them had spent in her delicious bed, three years before, during an operation to plant a black operator deep inside the Colombian cocaine Cartel. It had been the day he had, so pleased with himself, found himself staring into the top shelf of a mirrored wall cabinet in the delectable Kate Howard's bathroom, and finding there a pair of unmistakable gold cufflinks belonging to the then Chief of SIS, Sir Steven McCrae, KCMG.

David Jardine smiled as he watched the young London Station officer, Fiona Macleod, read extracts from her monthly report. Oh, yes, Kate Howard had left no stone unturned on her relentless way to the top.

'What?' asked Fiona, glancing up at him and adjusting her glasses.

'Oh, nothing. Just day-dreaming . . .'

Constable Harmer had been joined by a member of the Israeli Embassy's own security team, a thirty-three-year-old former paratrooper called Raoul Levy. Both men were experienced and they watched with growing impatience as the red-headed woman in the Audi slowly manoeuvred her car into a space by the green fence inside the courtyard to the apartment block, directly beside the Embassy building. The proximity of the fence was a source of concern to successive Israeli Security attachés, but it was more or less typical of the problems attached to any foreign city.

A 'No Parking' sign was prominent on the apartment-block side of the fence.

'Silly cow,' murmured Gerry Harmer, uncomfortable in his bullet-proof vest, in the heat and humidity of the hottest London day since 1983. He instinctively straightened his peaked cap and fingered, momentarily, the .357 Smith & Wesson revolver in its holster on the right of his belt, which also carried his radio battery, in a black pouch, and his handcuffs.

Together with Israeli security man Levy, he moved out from the embassy yard and towards the newly parked car, as the driver, who was wearing huge sun-glasses, making her look a bit like a Mediterranean-complexioned rodent, climbed out and locked the car, using an electronic bleeper on her keyring.

'You can't leave it there, Madam,' said Harmer.

The woman glanced round and made a typically helpless female-in-a-hurry raise of her shoulders – she was wearing an expensive blue suit – and, as her arms spread, he noticed she was carrying a dark green plastic bag, with a Harrod's logo on the side.

'I'm just popping this in to my sister's,' she smiled, with orange-lipsticked mouth. 'I'll be right back.' The voice was international wealthy, with a trace of foreign accent. And, with that, she turned and walked away, towards an entrance porch at the side of the apartment block. The side furthest away from the embassy.

If it had not been so hot, if she had not seemed such a dumb, middle-aged woman so typical of local residents, Gerry Harmer would probably have hurried after her.

As it was, he turned to Levy, who was looking thoughtful.

'I'm not happy . . .' said the Israeli, listening to his earpiece, where the Security Control Room inside the bowels of the embassy was bitching about the fact that somebody on duty thought he had recognised the woman. Which would turn out, as it happened, to be bullshit, but timely bullshit.

'Right, then.' Harmer ducked his head and spoke into his personal radio, clipped to the shoulder strap of his kapok-armoured vest.

'Delta-four-one. Receiving, over?'

'Proceed Delta.'

'Can I have a VC on kilo-eight-four-niner, delta-hotel-tango, over?'

'Wait one.'

Levy had moved nearer the Audi and Harmer caught up with him. He was about to offer to have it towed away when to his confusion he was lying flat on his back enveloped in a huge roaring thunderclap of enormous noise; it really hurt in the micro-second before his ear-drums ruptured and, the ground shuddering under his shoulders, the sky went black with the explosion of thirty-one pounds of RDX military explosive.

The RDX had been supplied to Hanna al-Farah's Number 3 Sleeper Cell by the VEVAK deputy at the Iranian Embassy just around the corner, complete with detonator and electronic timer with a delay programme of anything from zero to nineteen hours. Hanna had set it to eleven seconds, a fellow member of the unit having previously timed the casual walk from where the Audi was parked to the safety of the entrance lobby.

The blast had catapulted David Jardine off the front of the desk and flattened him against the facing wall, before he crumpled onto his knees and instinctively hugged the floor, rolled into a tight ball, hands over his head. Glass scythed across the room and embedded itself in the underside of Fiona's chair, which had been tipped backwards in the first rush of huge, expanding energy.

As the noise stopped, to be replaced at first with total, uncanny silence, then by the sound of glass and debris returning to obey the laws of gravity, Jardine took his arms from his head and moved carefully, exploring his limbs for injury, across to Fiona, who was just lying there, eyes wide open.

Oh, Christ, she's dead, thought Jardine, who had no doubt about what had happened. Then the girl moved a bloody arm to touch her face and, still staring at the ceiling, mumbled, as if mildly surprised, 'I've got glass in my mouth . . .'

So had he. He gingerly picked out a few lumps from the spaces between his teeth and his cheeks and gums.

Watching him, like a trusting child, Fiona did the same.

'Can you move your arms? Here, let me help.' And very gently, the big man eased her legs off the overturned chair. Her skirt was torn and Jardine began to check her ankles and knees.

'Was it a bomb?'

'Oh, yes, quite big. And quite near. Very bloody near.' She had a longish, mercifully shallow, cut on her thigh, at the back, stopping on her left buttock, which Jardine forced himself not to admire. Admirable though it was. A most admirable left buttock. As indeed was its companion.

'Is it bad . . .?' Fiona asked, her heart thumping now, as adrenaline coursed through her veins.

'Not in the least. We'll get you a couple of stitches and you'll be skiing in no time.'

The young woman glanced up at him, even in slight shock reading his eyes, searching for what he really meant. It was a habit this Fiona Macleod had. Which was one reason why she was considered a natural for the Firm.

'David, I can't ski.'

'You see?' Jardine replied. 'Something good has come out of it already.'

And she managed a slight grin.

Outside, while the neighbourhood was still caught in a frozen moment of silence, of confusion that would soon give way to near panic, Hanna al-Farah stepped into the deserted entrance lobby of the apartment block, tugged off the dreadful hennaed wig, removed the sunglasses and the expensive blue Karl Lagerfeld jacket and stuffed them into the Harrod's carrier bag. She took the service stairs to the first floor where, on the landing, a cleaning woman, of Middle-Eastern appearance, was waiting with a laundry basket. Into the basket went the Harrod's bag. Off came the navy blue skirt and a cream silk blouse. The cleaning woman handed Hanna a pair of faded blue jeans, which the now close-cropped, fair-haired, attractive woman pulled on. Then a faded, plum-coloured T-shirt with a Planet Earth motif and a pair of Reebok trainers, well worn.

Within three minutes and eight seconds of the car bomb exploding, the red-haired female in the expensive blue suit, with huge sunglasses, had ceased to exist.

It was a further twenty-one hours before a photofit of the non-existent suspect was distributed by the Metropolitan Police to the media and a full-scale and time-consuming hunt for her began.

In that time Hanna al-Farah had flown from London Heathrow on Air France Flight AF 104 to Paris Orly, using an Italian passport forged immaculately by the Documents Section of Abu Nidal's Special Missions Committee, which had recently moved from its safe-house in Hamra Street, Tripoli, in Libya, to a sprawling villa in its own walled grounds in Khartoum.

Two days later, while in London David Jardine worked with colleagues in the Firm's Intelligence Directorate, together with officers from the Security Service and an impressively switched-on Mossad team sent from Tel Aviv, to identify and trace the perpetrators of the two London explosions, Hanna al-Farah strolled in the Quai Anatole France, on the banks of the Seine, close to the Ministry of Foreign Affairs in the heart of Paris's government district, deep in conversation with a slender, attractive young woman employed at the Tunisian Embassy's Security Section.

Zina Farouche, unaware of her companion's murderous activity in London, brought the Abu Nidal Group's 'Commander of the Assassins' up to date on her progress so far.

She had chosen, from the nine men and women she had met clandestinely, in Paris, Vienna, Amsterdam and Munich, four of her proposed team of five, which she had decided was the size of the team she required to accomplish her mission in Connecticut, during United Nations week in New York. And she was at that moment outlining how she planned to infiltrate the murder squad into the killing zone, minimising to the utmost degree their chances of arousing suspicion or of being caught, before or after the successful completion of their mission.

When Zina had finished, they strolled on in silence. A large pleasure boat rumbled past, half full with sightseers and tourists, and Hanna al-Farah seemed more interested in that than in the Palestinian girl's briefing.

Zina Farouche, fit and tanned, the memory of her ordeal in the pit at Station 16, of the interrogations and sexual abuse, fading but never far from her consciousness, affected unconcern. But her pulse quickened with the certain knowledge that the elegant woman beside her had it in her power to send the young terrorist team leader back to the desert, with all that entailed, any time she chose. By nightfall, even.

Finally, Hanna al-Farah, still gazing at the pleasure boat, said, in Arabic, 'Well, that is truly excellent . . .'

Ah, Allah be praised.

'. . . you have rewarded the faith we have in you, child. It is a good plan. Ingenious, yet not too complex, like all the best

. . . stratagems. I like the . . . insolence of it.' She went on, 'You will need help with the arrangements, I suppose. Placing your operatives in their cover roles.'

Zina agreed. That would be necessary.

'Well, I think I can make a case for the Committee to assist you.' They strolled past a pair of teenagers, embracing. 'After all, what are brothers and lovers for?' And she turned and smiled, into Zina's almond-shaped, liquid brown eyes. Zina Farouche smiled back. And the older woman gently touched her hand. Zina, the survivor, responded, by closing her fingers round it. Al-Farah stroked gently, with her thumb.

'What about the fifth soldier?' she asked, her voice slightly hoarse now.

'I'm taking a train to Rome, tonight,' replied Zina, glancing back as the Commander of the Assassins looked at her again. 'There is a good man there. Expert with phosphorus grenades. Also in wet work and the neutralisation of close escorts.'

Close escorts was the professionals' term for bodyguards.

'Tonight?'

'Time is passing. I need to train them, for the specific operation.'

Hanna al-Farah considered this. In the weeks of recovery, of nursing and the restoration of Zina to health, she had cared for the young terrorist, bathing her with infinite gentleness and sitting with her, reassuring her. Hanna had become Zina's friend and confidante.

But being an attractive, some said even beautiful, woman, Zina Farouche had become aware of her new friend and leader's own needs, and preferences. And while al-Farah had never once put a foot wrong, Zina Farouche knew the sister of 'Doctor' Kamal, Abu Nidal's Intelligence chief, had become seriously attracted to her. Perhaps, lusted after her would be more accurate. And, being a survivor, the twenty-seven-year-old Palestinian smiled and said, modestly, 'I'm going back to my apartment first. Would you like to come with me?'

The older woman hesitated. 'Are you sure you mean it'. . .

Zina nodded. After Sammi, the PLO wrestling champion and the stinking Tahzi, her two tormentors, it could not be too bad. And there was always a first time for everything.

'If you want . . .'

Hanna al-Farah shuddered slightly, in anticipation. Zina was amazed that one woman could feel like that about another. And in her heart, she was more curious than revolted.

4

Stop Don't Walk

David Jardine shared a maisonette apartment in Chelsea's Tite Street with his sister Jessica. She was four years his junior and made a reasonable living painting racehorses for wealthy patrons. At present she was in California with her latest beau, a well-heeled 'wine doctor', who earned a good living travelling from Australia to Bolivia to the States, as visiting consultant on the lucrative and specialist skills of soil, sun, chalk, moisture and bird-shit balance in the husbandry of vineyards, the fermenting of grapes and the production of good wines.

The Sunday papers, that next weekend, confidently informed their readers of the identity of the mystery woman responsible for the Israeli Embassy car bomb. Apparently she was a Palestinian whose husband and brother had been killed in the Lebanon by the Israelis. Well, of course Hanna al-Farah was not such a person, but no one in the media had the slightest idea of the woman's true identity.

And there were maps and diagrams and assertive disclosures as to who had ordered the explosion and why. In that respect, at least, they were not far from the mark, for, although often wrong in the detail, the political editors had correctly understood the growing threat from the dangerous power of Iran's extremist clergy and their murderous ambition to wipe all infidels and traces of the Great Satan from the face of the earth.

Reading through the press that Sunday, Jardine devoutly wished that his Chief, and indeed the Foreign Secretary, could bring their very considerably better-informed political forecasts into line with those of the press who, while constantly getting the details wrong, were bang on target with their gut feelings, when they pointed the finger at Tehran. Probably the breathtaking dimensions of Iran's long-term strategy made sober civil servants sceptical, but many recent disastrous military adventures, for both the West and the Russian Federation, from Somalia to Bosnia, had seen the cold hand of the Mullahs at work.

Being the firm's Director of Operations, Jardine was in a unique position to watch, day by day, week by week, as Vevak and the Pasdaran, Iran's Revolutionary Guards, controlled by Ayatollah Khamenie and Sheik Fadlallah, organised cells of the Palestinian West Bank guerrilla group Hamas and lesser known clandestine terror groups, of which the perhaps prophetically named Islamic Tide, directed from Tehran and its stooges in Khartoum, was possibly the most lethal, the best funded and by far the most professionally led.

With 'brigades' trained and infiltrated into the USA, Europe and the Far East, able to integrate completely into western societies and to live and function without drawing the slightest attention to themselves, Islamic Tide had thus far succeeded in staying out of the spotlight, and Jardine was not aware of any of the so-called 'well-informed' media experts having heard as much as a whisper of the organisation.

He had, however, no doubt that the Israeli Embassy bomb, and a second one twelve hours later, in London's Golder's Green district, which was predominantly Jewish, were the work of the Islamic Tide's Europe Brigade. He also had privileged information, from the agent whose very existence he was battling to keep from the CIA, placed deep inside the Iran/Palestinian extremist coalition. This person's codename was Urchin, and Urchin told him that a covert sleeper-unit of the Abu Nidal terrorist group had been sub-contracted by Islamic Tide to support the London 'operation'.

The unit consisted of five terrorists holding Jordanian passports – much in the same way that Zina Farouche was a bona fide Tunisian citizen – who had merged quietly into the London scene, drawing no attention to themselves, with jobs and unremarkable social lives. Their identities were, however, well-known to David Jardine. In fact he had a headful of

Top Secret intelligence that would have made those so all-knowing, always half-wrong journalists swoon. For SIS had lifted the Iranian stone and, under it, they had uncovered all manner of foul and putrid things; plans and furtive, murderous schemes on a global basis. None of which boded well for suffering humanity.

The phone rang. Jardine lifted the receiver from his big table, strewn with Sunday papers, piles of books, and a half-finished model of the *Flamingo*, a three-masted tea clipper which had held the East India record, from Calcutta to Glasgow for eighteen months in the 1870s. His mother's great-grandfather had been, at the age of twenty-eight, the ship's captain, a fact of which the family were rightly proud.

'Hello?'

'Yo, Dad, what's up?'

Andrew. His son. Age, nineteen.

'Not a lot. Just getting ready for work. Few notes, you know . . . How about you?'

Andrew was just back from Argentina, where he had been working on a ranch, and was immensely proud he had hog-tied and branded over a hundred cattle. Jardine loved the boy and he was pleased his son had thought of phoning him.

'No sweat. Safe.' This was the way the boy spoke. He and a few of his friends had started up a band at their school in Dorset. The music had been predominantly black American urban and they all spoke like refugees from 'The Boyz In The 'Hood'.

'So, what's up?' God, he was doing it now.

'I've got an interview at Bristol.'

'University?'

'No, McDonald's.'

'You're joking.' It was not often David Jardine sounded genuinely appalled.

Silence.

'Andrew?'

Muffled chuckle. 'Jesus, you really are a casualty of the class war.'

Bloody hell. Well, don't panic, David.

'McDonald's, eh? Well, um, better than being on the dole, eh?'

'Dad, it is actually the University, I was pulling your pisser.'

Relief. Jardine's eyes un-narrowed. 'I knew that.'

'Yeah, yeah, of course you did.'

And they both laughed. Maybe Andrew more than his father.

'Well, an interview, that's great. What subject?' While mentally praising the boy's initiative, Jardine felt more than somewhat discomforted. He would have liked just a tiny input into his beloved son's education.

'Guess.'

Guess. Jesus. Two Bs and a C. English, History and French. Andrew's sister Sally was, on the other hand, brilliant. Medicine at Cambridge. It was important not to shove that down the kid's throat. 'French.'

'Film.'

'Film?'

'It's a three-year course.'

'You can get a degree in film?'

'What do you think?'

No hesitation now, for which Andrew would always admire him. 'Is that what you want?'

'If it's OK with you.'

Silence. He realised the boy was apprehensive. Even though his son was sixty-odd miles away, down in the Jardines' old farmhouse in Wiltshire, David Jardine felt very close to him.

'You going to work at it? Do yourself proud . . .?'

'Believe it, man. Sorted.'

'Is that close to an affirmative?'

'Yeah. Yes, Dad. It's what I want to do.'

'Well, good luck. Don't be too disappointed if it, you know, the interview . . . if it doesn't work. If they have no bloody taste.'

'It'll work. You got a number for Mum?'

Dorothy, Jardine's wife, was a Producer in the BBC's Current Affairs department, working on a documentary in Brazil. Once a considerable beauty, later an alcoholic, and now a tough professional with the build of a rugby prop forward, there was no one in the world he had ever loved more.

'Sure. What you doing?'

'Just had some lunch. Walked the dog.'

Pause.

'You all right down there? Want to come up for a few days? Doss down in Jessica's room?'

'The interview's on Tuesday.'

Christ, the child's racing towards manhood far too fast, thought Jardine, caught with remorse for lost time together.

'Come up tomorrow, then. Maybe I can give you a few tips. For the interview.'

'Times have changed, man. I'll be cool.'

Silence. This bloody job. I should be with him; it's a big moment in his life. Jardine frowned. 'Andy, I could drive down tonight.'

'No way, you have notes to get ready. Affairs of state. It's cool.'

Jardine checked his watch: 4.43.

'I'll be down about seven. We can sink a few tubes and I'll make risotto.'

'You don't have to.'

'Aw, bless you, I'm your dad. It's no sweat. I wouldn't forgive myself; sod the work. Let's get you off to a good start, man.'

Slight pause.

'I meant, you don't have to cook risotto. Please. I'm on my knees. Not the risotto. Jesus, what did I do to deserve that?'

Jardine smiled. 'Be there about seven.'

And he was pleased, because he had understood what the boy had wanted. Why he had phoned. It was time for David Jardine the father to take over from the spy.

Down in Wiltshire, Andrew Jardine put the phone down, thoughtfully, and turned to a rather gorgeous seventeen-year-old girl, curled up on the sofa, wearing just a T-shirt.

'I'll drive you to the station,' he said, ruefully. 'Dad's coming down. He means well, bless him.'

At about the same time that David Jardine was driving down to Wiltshire in his pride and joy, a dark-blue fifteen-year-old Aston Martin coupé, which cost him an arm and a leg to run,

Zina Farouche was walking along a narrow Rome street, towards the Piazza del Popolo, where she had a rendezvous with a man she had worked with before, a professional killer who had been through the same extremes of testing, at the hands of Abu Nidal's torturers in the Libyan desert camp as she herself had suffered and survived so recently. His name was Zafir Hammuda. He was forty-five years old and he had killed sixty-seven men and women targets, not counting the random victims of his activities.

There is a restaurant in the piazza, called Serafimo, which specialises in fish dishes. Zina, having been brought up in Beirut, enjoyed fish, and the spacious little place reminded her of the Lebanese port of Jounieh, where she and her husband had met, while planning the car-bomb explosion of June 1985, which had killed a Druze militia boss and thirty-one other people in the crowded street around his office base near the harbour.

A waiter guided her to a table and she accepted it, noting that it was placed between the main door and a door to the kitchen. Most kitchens had access to the street, or to a back alley, and Zina Farouche was trained to give herself options, when it came to planning an exit. Rest-room doors did not often provide means of escape, as more than a few had learned too late. She would, ideally, have chosen the table directly opposite, for it gave a more commanding view of the square outside, and was nearer to the kitchen. But that was occupied by a man in his forties, with a tanned, leathery face and oiled hair, who was reading the local paper and toying with a plate of spaghetti vongole.

The Palestinian girl lit a cigarette and smiled at the waiter who had brought her a menu.

'*Grazie.*'

He asked if she would like a drink and she requested mineral water.

Sitting there, with a few minutes to pass until Hammuda was due to arrive, she savoured the almost too-strong tobacco of her Marlboro and contemplated that afternoon, only the day before, in her Paris apartment.

Zina had never been made love to before by a woman, and her emotions were difficult to resolve. Hanna al-Farah had been as shy as she, it seemed, but clearly experienced. The older woman had been tender and patient and, after initial tenseness and shyness, mixed with distaste, the young terrorist had found the experience not as unpleasant as she had anticipated. Hanna had a slim and fragrant body, in perfect condition, and she had seemed gently concerned to relax Zina Farouche and to give pleasure more than to exact it.

The man at the opposite table seemed oblivious to her as she smiled slightly, at the memory of her surprise at just how successful the other woman had been.

Well, Zina was sure she would not make a habit of it, but at least she did not feel used, or abused, which was what she had been resigned to. Plus, the fondness the Commander of the Assassins had demonstrated for her eased the girl's mind about her future with the Abu Nidal faction.

In fact, Zina had the feeling, if she accomplished this task to perfection – and she had no doubt that the killing of two entire families relaxing at a house by the sea in Connecticut, the epitome of the sanctity of the United States of America, was going to be a major, perhaps *the* major, act of international terrorism since the Lockerbie bombing of Pan Am Flight 103 – that her place, her own safety and well-being, within the organisation would be secured. Who could tell? Perhaps she might even find herself with a senior role in the Special Missions Committee.

At that moment, Zafir Hammuda strolled in. He looked fit and at ease with himself. Six-foot-two and muscular, with a slim waist and flat belly, broad shoulders that moved in harmony with his loping walk, the Arab was a good-looking man. His brown eyes, set deep, twinkled, and a thick, black moustache drooped, Zapata-like, downwards. High cheekbones and a swarthy, lean jaw contributed further to the look of a fellow who was strong, reliable and who could look after himself. But Zina Farouche had studied his file, and she knew he was afraid of the dark.

'How are things?' asked Zafir, glancing around casually as he sat down.

'Progressing.'

The waiter arrived and the Arab ordered a Coke. Most of the tables were occupied and that pleased Zina Farouche, because her conversation would be lost in the general hubbub.

'I have a project,' she continued, as the waiter moved away. 'It will occupy us full-time between now and October.'

United Nations Week in New York City was the last week in September.

'Subject?' Hammuda meant target.

'Major,' replied the girl.

He nodded sagely. 'Assuming he's still Prime Minister . . .'

Zina frowned, then shook her head, amused. 'I mean, the subject is a major . . . event.'

He glanced across at her, searching for a hint she had been making fun of him.

The waiter appeared with a glass of Coke. '*Pronto ordinare*?' he asked. Were they ready to order?

'Not just yet.' Zina smiled and the man nodded, melting away.

'As big as anything you or I have ever taken on,' she said, and stubbed out her cigarette.

'Where?'

'Let's wait till I decide if you're in or out.' The look Zina Farouche laid on him was cold. Merciless. And she was not acting. Zafir Hammuda knew she meant that, if he was allowed to know too much before becoming part of the team, and then was not chosen, his life expectancy would be minimal.

'I have my own fish to fry,' he said.

At which the Palestinian girl picked up her menu, not bothering to reply, and studied the courses. Minutes passed. Hammuda took one of her cigarettes, doubtless to indicate he was not fazed by her, and used her gold Dunhill lighter. Only then did he turn to his own menu and peruse it.

What an asshole, thought Zina to herself. And she reached for another cigarette. One of these days she was going to stop, she kept telling herself. But deep at the back of her mind, the young terrorist-cell leader knew that the undoubted long-term hazards from tobacco were academic. She was pretty certain it would be a miracle if she reached her fortieth birthday.

A pleasant guy of about the same age, she guessed, as herself, approached the restaurant from the piazza and stepped inside. About six feet tall, slim and agile looking, he glanced around casually, and for some reason his gaze settled on her for the merest moment, before he saw who he was looking for and sauntered across to join the leather-faced man at the best table in the place, for those interested in a quick and unorthodox exit.

The two men seemed to know each other and soon they were laughing and talking together. At no time did the good-looking young man pay any further attention to her, and Zina Farouche shrugged, sure that his passing interest was a natural one for a healthy and self-confident male to express in an attractive girl. For Hanna al-Farah had left Zina in no doubt that she was desirable, particularly to the sensualist in man or woman.

She laid the menu down and nodded to the waiter. When he came over she said, 'I'll have the carpaccio, followed by grilled sea bass.'

'*Signore*?' enquired the waiter, and Zafir said he would start with spaghetti and have lobster to follow.

'Anything to drink?'

'No thanks, just more mineral water,' said Zina, and as the waiter disappeared, she met Zafir's eye and waited.

'What are you looking for?' he asked petulantly. 'Why did you arrange this rendezvous? I am involved with serious people. They too have . . . major projects.'

I was right, she thought. He's an asshole. 'You are here because you were ordered to be here. If you had not come, our Committee would have disciplined you. So cut the macho bullshit and settle down. In this relationship, I give the orders and you obey. Tell me you understand. Tell me now, Zafir, or we are going to get off to a very, very bad start.'

Zina Farouche said all of this very quietly, occasionally smiling for the benefit of any interested party.

The tall Arab slowly stubbed out his cigarette. When he glanced back at her, there was respect in his eyes. Either that, thought Zina, or he knows what's good for him.

'I heard they had put you through Number Sixteen,' he said. He was referring to the interrogation unit at Abu Nidal's Naji al-Ali camp, in the Libyan desert.

'I heard you went through the same. In eighty-eight.'

He nodded. All survivors of the relentless abuse and torture of the Station 16 interrogators were sworn never to mention their ordeal, on pain of death. So both of them were deliberately saying, in effect, fuck them. We have something very special in common.

It was cool of Zafir to clear the air like that, after such a bad start. Zina Farouche inclined her head to one side, holding his gaze and smiling just a little.

'Sure,' he replied. 'Four months.'

'And we are stronger people for it . . .' she said, allowing the statement to be almost a question.

'In all kinds of ways.' Zafir nodded. And, after a moment, he lifted his glass and raised it to her. 'Zina, I salute you.'

Praise be to Allah, she thought, relieved, for the meeting had taken on all the signs of a disaster. 'And I salute you, comrade.'

They sipped, watching each other.

Finally, Hammuda murmured, 'Where you lead, I will follow. Unto death. And without question.'

She examined his eyes, and was satisfied that he meant it.

'Babylon Two,' she said. And Zafir smiled. Babylon One was the Nidal Group's codename for Washington DC. Babylon Two was New York.

'Around eighteen subjects. Controlled environment.'

'Precious?' He meant, will they be well guarded?

'More than.'

'And our sales team?'

Zina considered. Part of her brain told her that Zafir Hammuda was kind of a loose cannon. Because he was so good at multiple killing, and because his tasks had all been accomplished well, if sometimes more than necessarily bloody, the man was something of a prima donna. On the other hand, she needed his particular skill. Plus his very presence on the team would give the other four the deadly *élan*, the unit confidence, needed to make the job a success.

'We will be six in all.'

'Travelling together?' Hammuda frowned.

'Of course not. This is a maximum-support venture.' She meant the entire resources of Abu Nidal and his contacts into certain Arab diplomatic conduits were at her disposal. Money, false documents, weapons and supporting cells, unaware of the team's mission, would all be made available.

'OK, I'm in,' declared the terrorist.

'Good. Now drop the subject and enjoy your meal. I want to see you in Madrid on the seventeenth. You'll learn where later.'

Madrid, in the confusing lexicon of their particular trade-speak, was Vienna. By the seventeenth, she meant seventeen days from the date of this rendezvous.

'Major . . .' he said, stroking his moustache. Then he grinned. 'That could have been awkward.'

And Zina Farouche was almost amused.

Now, when they explored the history of all this, when they dissected it, it was considered that James Gant's momentary interest in the undoubtedly attractive, probably desirable, olive-skinned girl sitting at the table close to the kitchen swing-door, which, of course, was what he had been looking for, noticing her only in passing, was perhaps part and parcel of the foundling's innate prescience, his essential sixth sense, his instinct for survival, which was to become so proven in the weeks and months to come.

However, at the time, sitting across the table from Euan Stevenson, the man with the lined, leathery face, young Gant had no such conscious thoughts. The girl on the far side of the room was completely forgotten, ignored, as he listened to his very first SIS boss, on the fourteenth day of his attachment to the secret, illegal cell 'Marigold', working out of an air-freight office near the Coliseum.

Marigold's current pre-occupation was the infiltration of the extreme right in the Italian administration, which included the Government, the Civil Service, the Trades Unions, the banks, the Intelligence and security services, the police, the Mafia and the Vatican.

'It's a tall order, old son,' Stevenson had remarked, the very evening he had led James out of the Struzzo bar at the Hotel Imperatore and back to his attic apartment in the artists' quarter of Trastevere, on the 'other' side of the River Tiber, 'plus you are something of a guinea pig. We have never before attempted to filter an absolute beginner into a working operation, it's some brainwave of the folk upstairs. Not your fault, though. And the best we can do is go through the motions. As the man who couldn't swim said. When he fell into the sewer.'

So during the next fourteen days, the former BBC cameraman had found himself thrown in at the deep end, in matters clandestine, given unstinting help when needed, advice when he slipped up, encouragement most frugally, and support when he was, rarely at first, permitted to make a decision. It had been an intoxicating experience and James had been allowed to attend agent meetings and service dead-drops, observe how real professionals sanitized a location for a brush contact, and to write up reports on various tasks he had been given, some of which he suspected were merely exercises to make him feel part of the cell, others quite risky, which demonstrated a degree of confidence in his untried tradecraft on the part of his minders which he wished he could share.

But the other members of Marigold he had met, two men and a woman of about twenty-nine, whose cover was PA and general factotum with Achille Air Freight Services, had accepted him without reserve, discussing the most closely guarded of the Firm's business with him and opening up their Pandora's box of agent identities and penetrated areas to him as if he were a fully-fledged and paid-up intelligence officer with SIS.

Which he supposed he had just recently become.

'What fun . . .' he had just remarked to Euan Stevenson, over a plate of linguini and a glass of Vino Nobile di Montepulciano.

And Stevenson made a grimace and waved his fork at the boy.

'Fun? Fun? 'Never, ever let them hear you say that, laddie. They don't like the notion of any bugger enjoying themselves in Accounts Section. Bunch of torn-faced old bastards. Goes for Personnel as well. Oh, no. This is hell, sonny boy. Absolute hell. Impossible hours, stressful responsibility, grim participation in the monitoring of the shittier side of world affairs. We hate it. But we do it for Queen and country.

Don't you bloody well forget it.' He shook his head sadly, 'Fun? Oh, dear me, no. Dear, dear.'

Maybe it was always thus, thought James Gant. But he had begun to love this carnaptious lean Scot. He nodded, and busied himself with his pasta. Behind him, the olive-skinned girl and her tall, Middle-Eastern-looking companion left, the man holding the door for her. But Gant did not notice, her presence forgotten.

Euan Stevenson, on the other hand, being not quite as open as our young man imagined, kept his counsel and later that day, about eight in the evening, sent a coded message round to the SIS Station working out of the British Embassy. It informed them that one Zina Farouche, known agent of Abu Nidal's, had been seen munching with the terrorist psychopath Zafir Hammuda, last seen in Khartoum with an Iranian intelligence operator. Three days later, that intelligence had found its way to an office at Vauxhall Cross, where a mosaic was gradually being built up, concerning the assembly of Zina Farouche's team.

'They're putting something quite special together,' David Jardine remarked to Marietta Delice, his Director/Catnap.

Marietta had booked fifteen minutes with him, that Tuesday morning, to present her Division's analysis of reports that had been coming in for a number of weeks, from sources in Europe and the Middle East, which had been quietly tracking Zina Farouche's commendably professional covert contacts with a number of very dangerous Palestinian terrorists, known to be secret members of the Abu Nidal organisation – or gang, as Marietta preferred to call it. She had brought up three Top Secret 3.5″ computer discs and Jardine had fed them into his computer. Information appeared on the screen while, at the same time, she projected surveillance photographs onto a white part of his office wall, from a rotating slide carousel.

There was Zina strolling along the Quai Anatole France, deep in conversation with Hanna al-Farah. Zina in Munich, window-shopping in an elegant street, in the company of one Abd al-Hadi al-Turabi, more commonly known as Ben Turabi.

'Ben Turabi, remember him?' murmured Marietta.

Jardine nodded. 'The grenade man.' During a terrorist attack by pro-Palestinian extremists in Austria, Ben Turabi had herded a group of Soviet Jews, on their way to Israel, into a railway station waiting-room, by the simple expedient of firing his AKS automatic assault rifle around them, then, when they were all cowered in the one place, from which there was no other exit, he had opened up on them with his automatic rifle and with hand-grenades, which he kept producing from a canvas satchel hung round his neck.

The casualties had been eight dead and five grievously wounded. Al-Turabi had been arrested, after a shoot-out with the Austrian security police. And three weeks later, following the threat of bombs and assassinations throughout Vienna, by the Hammadi brothers, of Hezbollah, based in Beirut, the killer had been quietly released, into the custody of two representatives of the Sudan Intelligence Service. And two days after that, Ben Turabi was in the Bekaa Valley, in the Lebanon, celebrating his freedom and the 'successful' operation in the company of his comrades and a number of prostitutes shipped in from Nicosia, in Cyprus. For Ben liked English girls and the night-clubs and brothels of Cyprus always had a few 'dancers' and hostesses from Birmingham and London's suburbs, lured there by advertisements in *The Stage*, offering a start in show business.

'I also have a sighting of Zina with the lesser spotted Mustafa,' said Marietta.

At that time, the Firm was aware of around twenty terrorists with the name Mustafa. The four most active had each acquired an identifying sobriquet. Two of those suffered from bad skin, and the 'lesser-spotted' one was Mustafa Sharik, aged thirty-two and an expert in surveillance and planning. He was particularly skilled in arranging exfiltration after a hit. In fact, unknown to Zina Farouche (and only suspected by Marietta Delice), it was Mustafa Sharik who had planned the complete disappearance of Hanna al-Farah from Kensington Palace Gardens after the Israeli embassy bomb.

'He's the planner, right?' Jardine swung round in his seat and punched a rapid instruction on his keyboard. Details of the most recent known movements of Sharik appeared on the computer screen. Last seen in the village of Wardaniyya, in the Lebanon's Shuf mountains, in the company of the two Iranian operators suspected of planting a car bomb in Buenos Aires, Argentina, just ten days before the London explosion.

'Interesting . . .' David Jardine scratched his nose, annoyed at a fly that refused to stop bothering him. 'Do we think these people are involved in the London bomb?'

Marietta raised her shoulders, gazing at the screen. On the wall, she had projected a surveillance photo of Mustafa, taken in Beirut, in the souk. He was slightly built, with magpie-bright eyes and a thin, sallow face, fringed in a jet black beard. His two front teeth were yellowing and quite prominent.

'I don't know,' she replied. 'The girl Farouche had dropped out of sight for a while. They're all Fatah Revolutionary Council.' She meant Abu Nidal's creatures. 'She has been doing most of the travelling around but maybe she's just a runner for Hanna.'

Jardine, deep in thought, tapped his pen on the desk, again and again, relentlessly, until his colleague felt like ripping it from his fingers and breaking it in two. Fortunately for harmonious interpersonal relations, at that moment he abruptly stopped and, scratching his nose with the offending instrument, enquired, 'So what's your view, Marietta? What's all this about?'

Marietta stretched her legs out in front of her and wiggled her feet. 'God, I'm getting old and stiff.'

'Tell me about it,' smiled Jardine. 'Will I get some coffee?'

'I thought you only had fifteen minutes.'

'For my mates, dearest Marietta, time stands still.'

She glanced at him and grinned. Rumour had it that Marietta Delice had been a stunningly beautiful girl, when the world was young, before the Jack Daniels and a million cigarettes had etched their lines and broadened the corpus. And rumour had it that David Arbuthnot Jardine, CMG, and the young Marietta, when she had joined fresh from the Royal Navy, of all places, and they had been on the same induction course, had once been more than just a little close. Quite a lot more than once, actually.

But that was just the rumour.

'Cut the bullshit, David, and order the coffee. Plus a dark

chocolate digestive. My spies tell me you keep them in your desk. Third drawer.'

Jardine lifted the phone and asked Heather for coffee. He slid open the third drawer down on the left of his desk and took out a packet of biscuits, placing them near his colleague.

'And what do your spies tell you about all this?' he asked, indicating the computer screen and the projected transparency on the wall.

'Just what we've seen. My view, and young Bernard's,' (Bernard was Catnap's senior analyst) 'is that Hanna is gathering a team together. Using the Farouche girl as her go-between. Her cut-out. Since indicators point to a Tehran connection – but what doesn't, these days? – I think we are talking about some excitement being planned using quite particular skills.'

'Ben Turabi is a mass murderer. Car bombs are not interesting to him,' said Jardine. 'Zafir Hammuda ditto. These are operators who like to eyeball their victims, before, during and after doing the business.'

'And the lesser-spotted Mustafa, David. They want a plan which will get them out safely.'

'Well, that's not because they're a caring organization, the old Abu Nidals. That's because they badly do not wish to leave any clue behind. God bless you, child.' This last to Heather, who had just come in, carrying a tray with a white ceramic pot and two cups with saucers. 'And may his angels guard your sacred throne.' He smiled to Marietta. 'When did you stop taking sugar?'

'Eight years ago,' she replied, giving him a jaundiced look. 'You always ask that.'

'Dear me. So where and when is the sixty-four-thousand-dollar question.'

Heather left, as quietly as she had entered.

'Bernard thinks an airport,' said Marietta.

'Does he now?'

'He thinks maybe Athens again. Maybe something really outrageous, like Amman.' She meant the capital city of Jordan, which had just signed a peace accord with Israel. 'Or maybe Eilat, the Riviera of the Red Sea.'

'Well, good for Bernard,' remarked Jardine, studying his

coffee. And, privately, he was thinking, so far so good. For he alone, within SIS – well, he and Ronnie Szabodo, which was to all intents and purposes the same thing – knew the grim and bloody target with which Zina Farouche had been tasked. And he would be more than content if the Bernards of this world continued to furnish him with predictions so very wide of the mark.

'Keep me posted,' said the Director of Operations to his expert in Counter Terrorism. 'And I', he lied, 'will of course do the same for you.'

Marietta Delice sipped her coffee and let her gaze examine his expression.

The charming bastard's got something cooking, she thought to herself.

'Wonderful coffee,' she said. 'Heather really is a treasure . . .'

It was by complete chance that Sergeant of Detectives Joe Cleary decided to take the 1046 (Homicide With Perpetrator On Premises) that came over his car radio as he headed back to Queens and a shower and some quality time with Lauren and Patrick Cheyenne. His new son was still at the sleep-most-of-the-time stage, but with a most winning smile when awake, and the bluest of blue eyes that seemed to hold the wisdom of centuries when his daddy gazed into them for long, quiet moments, the way daddies do.

'Ten-forty-six, Martina's Tavern, Christopher and Weehawken, perp armed and suicidal, exercise extreme caution.'

Cleary flicked a switch and spoke at the pin-head microphone fitted just beside the sun visor above the unmarked Ford's windshield.

'Five-eighteen, three minutes.'

He switched on his hidden strobe lights, flashing electric blue along where the dash and windshield met, also along his rear window shelf, and hit the gas.

Joe was not surprised somebody had gotten killed in Martina's. The place was very heavy with queen bitch pimps muscling in on each other's territory, for Martina's was a colourful gay bar with the emphasis on heavy metal, from the raucous rock music to the chain-studded leather underpants and mini skirts on too broad behinds.

Martina was not a woman but a thirty-six-year-old former dope pusher and ex-stevedore called Martin Thomas, and the gay Wall Street brokers and Mid-Town lawyers and surgeons who paraded there to get their kicks had no idea their pretty but rough pick-ups were run by a mafia of ruthless 'madames', one of whom had already done seven years in NY Pen. for blackmail and extortion.

So it was just a question of when.

And today was the day.

Cleary was in Dominick, near the Holland Tunnel entrance, and he made a right into Hudson, left into West Houston and headed uptown on West Street about five blocks to the junction with Christopher Street, which was two-way there. He waited as two ESU vans, sirens howling, all red and blue flashing strobes, cut across in front of him, coming down West Street from uptown, and, by the time he had pulled up at the kerb on Weehawken Street, there were guys in all kinds of bullet-proof vests and dark overalls, with black baseball caps, brandishing enough ordnance to retake the Winter Palace, running tactical from this doorway to that corner to behind this automobile and like that.

Customers from Martina's thronged the seedy intersection in semi-hysterical but still-preening disarray, and the place was a riot of Harley Davidson leathers and feather boas.

Joe Cleary got out and pushed his car-door shut. He took an Owl Special from its pack and bit the end off. Spitting that onto the sidewalk he patted his jacket for the Zippo he kept mislaying. Finally he found a book of matches from the Precinct prisoners' property box and cupped the tentative flame protectively as he sucked on the tobacco.

'I can't hear shooting,' he remarked to an adrenaline-wracked Lieutenant wearing some kinda lightweight bomb disposal outfit that made him look like a baseball-catcher from hell.

'Maybe the guy has a silencer,' the Lieutenant replied, and Joe had to look to see if he was kidding.

A local precinct Detective joined them, a young guy name of Tony something. He had just made Detective and he was taking his job real serious. Joe seemed to remember the kid had worked for a time in a pasta place on Waverley called Popolino's, paying his way through college for a Bachelor's in Law, and now here he was, a cop. Word was Tony Gelardi had been a uniformed cop first, then student, then cop again, this time having won his detective's badge on account of hard work and his law degree. How was that for dedication? If the kid's father had been from Donegal he could have saved a bit of time.

'What's up, Tony?'

'Sergeant Cleary. The victim is just inside the door. Shot a few times, that's a quote, from a twelve-gauge.'

'A twelve-gauge?' That was the weapon for a heist, an armoured truck robbery or a motorcycle gang feud. Greenwich Village was .45 Colts, Smith & Wesson .38s, cheap grease-guns, and Ingram MAC-10s. Twelve-gauges were powerful shotguns and he could understand why somebody shot 'a few times' with one was beyond the help of paramedics.

'The perp?' he asked, ignoring the fact that a whole Lieutenant in Samurai kit was standing right beside him and was technically the man in charge.

'Somebody called Henrietta. Transvestite, six-four, two-twenty. Dressed like Tina Turner.'

'Jesus Christ . . .' said the Lieutenant.

'Where?'

Tony shrugged. Somewhere inside was what he meant.

Joe Cleary thought about this. 'Tell you what,' he said to the Samurai, 'gimme a couple of minutes before you storm the building.'

'Hell, man, I don't plan on storming nowhere. Some low-life in there wasting its own kind? I ain't risking our boys for that.'

Cleary exhaled and nodded, as if he understood what in God's name was going on in this diminutive Demolition Man's mind.

'So, uh, what's all the pizazz . . .?' he enquired politely.

The Lieutenant hunched his shoulders. All that gear and body armour was probably weighing him down. 'Two things. One, to protect innocent bystanders. Two, things are slack on

TV news today.' Even as he spoke, a dirty-white WXNY Television News truck appeared at the West 10th intersection, at the far end of the street. 'And the Mayor's office likes a reassuring response – you heard his speech the other day . . .'

It was true. The Mayor had appeared in person at a Bronx eatery, where a hold-up had been foiled by an off-duty subway cop, bringing with him a whole battery of New York's press corps. This is what we do for you, he had told the cameras. No crime is too small for the full weight of New York's Finest. You have my word, things are changing. The streets are going to be safe again.

Again? What planet had this guy been living on?

'So you won't rake the place with gunfire if I go inside and see what's what?'

He had to ask this because the cop in charge at an ongoing crime incident ran the show. Homicide, in theory, should take over after the event.

'Be my guest,' replied the Lieutenant.

Joe Cleary considered this for a moment, then dropped his cigar and walked towards the crime scene.

Inside, there was a bar counter, on the left of the door, running away from the entrance into the darker part of the room. Two tables lay on their sides. Broken glass crunched underfoot. The place was gloomy, in a midnight-blue-and-purple sort of way. Neon islands of pink, green and white created shapes and words. A sombrero here, a Michelob sign there. This was not a gay joint, Cleary thought to himself, as he stepped away from the heavy curtain draped around the street entrance, to keep the light out. This was sad.

The jukebox was still playing Chris Montez, a sound from the '60s, doing the more I see you the more I want you.

Cleary waited, letting his eyes get used to the gloom. He could smell stale beer and gin and tobacco. It was like his brother's apartment after an all-night poker game.

Was it more important, he considered, weighing his 9mm Glock 17 in his right hand, to try and find the switch for the goddam jukebox, or to keep to the shadows and locate the killer of the wrecked cadaver he had just stepped over, touching something of a damp and squishy texture splattered on the counter. Yeah, yeah, probably his brains, Cleary thought to himself, for at moments like these you had to say to yourself, I am a real tough guy, bad as Beelzebub, quicker than Arnie Schwarzenegger, more ruthless than Hilary Clinton and no fuckin' low-life such as a six-foot-four, two-hundred-pound queen with a pissy little twelve-gauge is going to survive *my* attention.

Sweat trickled down the hollow in the small of his back.

'Blam! Blam!!!' Joe nearly jumped clean out of his socks and, 'Blam!', he dived to his right as daylight flooded in from a shattered black window and, 'Blam!', the flash from a twelve-gauge is brilliant and even in the new, lesser gloom, the cop had no trouble firing back, one-handed, none of that special tactics shit for him, and, after six rapid, he struggled to his knees to get a better hit and continued to squeeze off round after round, his left hand steadying his wrist after about round eleven and he kept on firing until the slide stayed jutting back, his extended clip of nineteen slugs empty.

No more 'Blam! Blam!' That was good.

Cleary got to his feet, curling his right toes under the foot the way his judo instructor had taught him when he was a novice. A simple thing, but it gets you up easily, without wobbling. And, as he rose, he let the clip drop out to the floor and slid a fresh one into the butt, springing the slide forward to ram a sweeter than sweet copper-jacketed bullet into the chamber.

In the half light he could see the crumpled figure of a big guy, in wispy clothing, with fishnet tights and lime-green high heels, slouched motionless in a way so awkward no living person had ever tried, a long, auburn wig at a rakish angle, half covering a face bloody on one side and grey with five-o'clock shadow on the other. There was blood on the wall behind the dead man and the twelve-gauge pump-action Remington shotgun, with a polished wood stock, lay across his legs, both of which had clearly been broken by the fusillade of Joe Cleary's returned fire.

You gotta be brutal, thought Cleary. But he felt no joy.

Poor bastard. What purgatory had this goddam Henrietta gone through to end up the lifeless star of a crime scene?

Somebody was sobbing. Snuffling and saying 'Oh, God' over and over again.

Cleary tugged the Remington out of the dead man's grasp. It was an automatic action. His ingrained, on-the-job training.

Then he stepped round and peered behind the bar counter, pistol ready. But all that was there was a huddled figure, a pale-skinned guy in leather vest, Nazi motorcycle boots and a Marlon Brando-type leather motorcycle cap, with chains and Hell's Angel badges. No trousers. No underwear. The guy looked so pathetic.

He started as the cop moved towards him, screwing up his tear-stained face and flinching, protecting his head with trembling arms.

'It's OK, pal. I'm a cop . . .' Joe Cleary had long ago lost the capacity to be surprised or shocked, whatever that was. Examining his real emotions, he would have guessed he was relieved to find somebody alive in that charnel house.

At this moment, the Samurai Lieutenant and his black-clothed SWAT team burst in through the doorway and spread all over the place, smashing windows to let more light in.

The survivor instantly returned to his foetal huddle and began to hyperventilate.

'Hey, Joe,' called out the Lieutenant, examining the dead transvestite, 'I thought you was gonna talk to the guy . . .'

Joe Cleary straightened up and gazed at the Lieutenant.

He raised his shoulders and spread his hands, 'Yeah, yeah, yeah . . . Somebody get this guy a blanket and keep those goddam cameras outa here, have some respect for the fuckin' dead.'

The bodies of the murdered man and his killer, who harboured dreams of being mistaken for Tina Turner in a darkened bar, were photographed, examined by the police surgeon, pronounced dead and taken to the morgue at Bellevue Hospital.

Which was a minor coincidence.

'OK, name?' demanded Homicide Sergeant Joe Cleary of the man he had found sobbing behind the bar and who was now sitting across the desk from him in a borrowed space in the bustling detectives' room on the third floor of the 6th Precinct House in Greenwich Village. A material witness.

'Grumman,' the man muttered. He wore a pair of cotton hospital trousers one of the ambulance team had produced and Cleary had lent him an old gray sweater from the trunk of his car.

'First name.'

'Francis Paul.'

Joe scribbled and glanced up, conversational. 'Would that be Frank?'

Frank Grumman nodded. For a minute Cleary wondered if he was going to burst into tears again.

'Occupation?'

'I work at Bellevue. Um, hospital. Hospital technician.'

'Doing what, Frank?'

Grumman, for the first time, looked him in the eye. 'I work in the morgue,' he said, and, without a trace of irony, added, 'with the stiffs.'

'The one man I really want,' said Zina Farouche, 'is Kosroshahi.'

'No Iranians,' murmured Hanna al-Farah.

They were strolling in the Rue du Bac, a narrow, pleasant Paris street, with small boulangeries, boutiques and smart wine shops. Hanna had arrived the night before. They had dined quietly in a Vietnamese restaurant in the Rue de l'Université called Tan Din. Hanna had stayed at Zina's apartment. It had been quite pleasant and she had not insisted on sex, even though they had shared the one large bed. Zina was amused to discover she was not sure if she had been relieved or . . . disappointed.

'I don't care if the organisation doesn't trust Tehran,' she replied.

For a long time Abu Nidal had given the impression that his Fatah Revolutionary Council was at daggers drawn with the Iranians. The disinformation suited both him and his occasional clients in the dead Shah's Winter Palace. And here was an experienced terrorist, getting close to the hub of the group, who actually believed the myth.

Zina went on, 'He knows New York. He is a professional intelligence man who knows the way things work there, and he will be . . . invaluable.' She was too much of a survivor to say essential, which was probably what she thought.

Hanna smiled and touched the younger woman's arm, gently. 'To tell you the truth,' she said, pausing to admire a window display of handmade leather shoulder purses, 'Mahmud Kosroshahi has not been seen around for some time.'

Zina was puzzled. She assumed the organisation was all-knowing, all-powerful, for that had been the point of her ordeal, and it had been pretty damned effective.

'Where is he?'

Hanna al-Farah shook her head. 'Let's just say, he is no longer available.' She used the glass of the *vitrine*, the shop window, to survey the street around them. The matter was not for discussion.

Ah, Zina nodded wisely. Mahmud was dead. If he was lucky.

She shuddered.

'Cold?' asked Hanna.

'Hungry,' replied Zina Farouche brightly, and, turning her olive-skinned survivor's face to the warmth of the July sun, she said, 'In that case, I have selected my team. We will move separately into New York, provided the Committee can arrange the necessary credentials.'

Hanna al-Farah lost interest in the window's reflections, satisfied they were not under surveillance. 'That will be no trouble.'

'And materials?' Zina meant guns, transport, grenades, night-vision devices, phone-tapping equipment, silencers, ski-masks. All the paraphernalia of surprising, awful, merciless slaughter.

'We have sleepers in the United States. New York is a facility just waiting for your list of requirements.'

The Palestinian girl contemplated this. She was completely up to date with the general organisation of the international terror business. Which depended on a whole kaleidoscope of mutually supporting, although sometimes rival, factions, and the sponsorship of different Middle Eastern governments.

Abu Nidal was powerful, but it was becoming clear his group was able to call on other resources for the American job.

'Who will get the credit for this?' she asked. 'When it is done.'

Hanna al-Farah paused on the kerb, waiting to cross the street, her hand on Zina's elbow, tighter than seemed necessary. 'Don't ask questions that do not concern you.'

There was no need for her to explain the alternative.

'Child, you *are* cold,' she said, 'like ice.'

And, as they crossed the Rue du Bac, Zina Farouche pictured in her mind a tiny broken body of an infant child. Its face and arm protruding from the bulldozed rubble of Chatilla refugee camp, in Beirut. Her son, Sami. Blue eyes wide open, he looked like a broken doll.

And, just yards away, her father's leg, in its neat gray trouser, and on his foot one of the pair of shoes Zina had bought for him in the Rue Hammra bazaar.

The Israelis had guarded the place, the abattoir, with tanks, and sent flares over the night-time massacre, to help their Phalangist Lebanese stooges kill over eight hundred old men, women and babies with machine-guns, grenades and hatchets. They had kept hysterical relatives and local residents outside and they had looked the other way. One young paratroop sergeant she had seen crying. Tears running down his handsome, haggard Jewish face.

Just the one.

And still she was not completely trusted by the Committees. In the name of Allah The Merciful, what more was she required to sacrifice?

During the next few weeks, Zina Farouche worked quietly in Paris, drawing no attention to herself, and travelled to Vienna, Geneva, Hamburg and Milan, assessing and briefing her team, for the American contract.

She had chosen five seasoned killers from the Abu Nidal Organisation's secret files, which she consulted on her computer inside the Tunisian Embassy, using a single 3.5″ disc kept in her private safe in the Security Officer's room. The coded access passwords were serial numbers known only to herself and kept in her memory. They were not numbers she was likely to forget for they were the birth dates of her dead son and father.

Working on the need-to-know principle, she only told each member of the team as much as he or she required to prepare for the job. The location and the identities of the intended victims were not imparted. And they were not even aware of each other's names.

Meanwhile, in London's Brixton district, David Jardine got out of the office Ford Sierra which had dropped him off, and made his way, under a thundering iron bridge, and through a narrow alley, to some rubble-strewn, almost derelict yards, and a row of railway arches at the back. The arches had wooden or corrugated-iron doors and they had been turned into workshops for three or four car re-spray and repair outfits. All of which were owned by a co-operative whose accounts and records, such as they were, would reveal a lamentable disregard for tax or pension laws or indeed any other fiscal consideration.

This was the Directorate of Operations' clandestine, deep-cover and innocently named London Facilities Section, and from its scruffy, unremarkable premises, Ronnie Szabodo ran all manner of quite illegal activities, from burglars in Moscow to wire-tappers and letter-intercepts in New York City.

Given modern global satellite communications, and the squat Hungarian's awesome collection of black-book personal contacts throughout the civilised and not-so-civilised world, there was very little that Ronnie could not accomplish in surprisingly quick time, be it springing someone from prison, or . . . best not to think of it.

Very few people inside the Green Palace were even aware of its existence. And certainly no politicians or government administrators.

'What's green and red and goes like a bomb?' he asked, not looking round as Jardine stepped into his catastrophically untidy inner office. Jardine watched as Szabodo painstakingly applied a soldering-iron to the workings of a condenser coil.

'I don't know,' he said.

There was a puff of acrid smoke, and, satisfied, Szabodo

lifted the soldering-iron clear. 'A toad in a toashter,' he announced triumphantly, in his bizarre linguistic mix of educated English and Magyar.

David Jardine stared at him, bemused.

'That can't be right.' He studied a calendar with a semi-naked blonde astride a Harley Davidson motorcycle. 'Ronnie, Hindsight is dead.'

'Ah . . .' Ronnie Szabodo turned round and pointed at a battered filing cabinet. Jardine crossed to it and, after a struggle, opened a drawer. Inside was a bottle of Canadian Club bourbon. The spymaster, a malt-whisky man, grimaced.

'I thought he might be,' went on the Hungarian. 'Either that or stuck in some dungeon', he said dun-ji-on, 'in Tehran or Shiraz. And I'll wager, dear boy, it wasn't quick.'

'Apparently not.' Jardine turned on a tap over a big, once white, industrial sink, and rinsed out two coffee cups before pouring some whiskey into each one. 'He turned up in a freezer. Hanging by the heels. Nose and fingers cut off before his candle flickered out.'

Szabodo reached out, his eyes met Jardine's, and he raised the cup. David Jardine met his gaze, but only just.

Both of them could well imagine what Major Muar Abbas, an SIS operative deep inside the Iranian Intelligence Service, had gone through before death's merciful intrusion.

'Where?' asked Szabodo.

'New York. Downtown Manhattan. Harry Liebowitz made the ID.'

'When?'

'Our man died four months ago. Harry found him twenty-seven days ago.'

'He didn't rush to tell us, then.'

Jardine shrugged. 'I'm not sure if even now he knows Abbas was one of ours. Alan Clair never approved of us running our own people in New York.'

'You think they did it?'

David Jardine rubbed his chin. Szabodo thought he looked tired. 'No. It had all the hallmarks of his own kind.'

'And did he talk?'

Jardine sipped his whiskey and turned away, pacing the

arched cellar like a big cat. Then he stopped, and gazed at his feet. 'Ah, Ronnie. If only we knew . . .'

So the question is, they were to ask themselves at Ryemarsh in years to come, poring over the entrails of an enterprise which by that time was sailing so perilously close to the wind that the great ship of state had come within mere inches, maybe less, of certain dark and razor-sharp rocks, all the way across the Atlantic, where relations with Her Britannic Majesty's Government were already stretched to breaking-point, the question is, just what, precisely, was David Jardine, Director of Operations in that Government's most secret of its several deeply secret departments, playing at?

What in the name of hell, as Timothy Runder, one of the Firm's 'Trustees', one of that handful of former, unsung, more intelligent heroes of the espionage game, was to enquire of his fellows, was Jardine's intention in keeping so much devastating knowledge concerning the planned murder of around eighteen souls to himself?

It was a question that only the man himself knew the answer to. And it was the burning question that swelled within his conscience as he knelt before the carved crucifix in the small chapel of Saint Luke, adjoining the Seamen's Refuge in Limehouse, near Narrow Street, in London E14. Jardine had gone there directly from his meeting with Ronnie in the railway arches workshop that was London Facilities.

There were times in the affairs of SIS, when the gathering and distribution to Subscribers of what was quaintly termed Product, became side-lined by the operational plans of the service's chieftains and their hidden agendas, generally in cognizance of certain unwritten but clearly understood aims of Government. Essentially this meant that, on occasion, the outfit would take it upon itself to act directly on secret intelligence gleaned from its agent networks, and such information would never leave the confines of the Green Palace. Any steps which the Chief and his Director of Operations considered necessary would be taken, would be implemented, by the service itself. If that action required a degree of clandestine muscle, then a small team would be recruited from the tight-lipped ranks of the 22nd SAS Regiment, based in Hereford, a regiment more used to operating in casual civilian clothes than in uniform.

And the results, it was devoutly to be wished, would never be laid at the door of Her Majesty's Government.

That was the theory. It was a remarkable tribute to the total efficiency and discretion of the new, streamlined, able and grown-up SIS that not one breath of its activities in the field of Direct Action (or Implementation, as it was known, only to a few) had ever leaked out.

Even to sister services.

But that evening, as David Jardine knelt in front of the half life-size delicately painted carving of Jesus on the Cross, which leaned out from the wall of the nave at a slight angle, and as he placed his wavering, flickering candle, it was not Direct Action which troubled him.

It was Direct Inaction.

For with his private and most secret line into the heart of Abu Nidal's innermost councils he knew as much, if not more, about the plans of Zina Farouche than she herself.

While a tiny number of his operatives and executives, in the nature of things, was each privy to a blurred piece of the whole scenario, Jardine had ensured – as with certain other operations – that only he had the complete picture, in perfect focus. And he had not breathed a word of what he could see so clearly to anyone.

Oh, Lord, he prayed – for he had long since lost that insouciance which had led him to think of God as a Sport, as his Chum, which had characterised his early, quite joyful approach to his conversion from the ranks of atheism – Oh, Lord, please help this poor sinner to use his secret knowledge for the good of all. And not just for the immediate salvation of a few innocents.

Am I, Dear Lord, doing right?

Bullshit, David, he told himself. Try again.

Dear Lord (this was such a big issue, he wondered if he should perhaps address himself to the Holy Trinity and assembled choirs of angels), I know it is wrong to deny those people, about to assemble in Connecticut for a few days of happiness and respite, and their protectors, the opportunity to save their lives. But all the evils of Islam's most cruel and power-hungry faction, the ayatollahs of Iran, can, I believe, be grievously damaged by my silence.

Please help me, Lord.

And Jardine raised his head and stared, past the flickering, wavering air, lit by a dozen candles, at the carving of Christ.

In the silence, he could hear muttering from the cramped confessional, at the other end of the chapel. Somewhere outside, a motorcycle growled past, its noise soon rasping away to a lonely echo. The wooden statue of the man on the Cross seemed to have no inclination to comment on the spymaster's dilemma.

Jardine said a number of Hail Marys and Glory Bes, climbed stiffly to his feet and inclined his head, then turned and walked towards the arched doorway, deep in thought.

And, as he opened the door, on a warm but draughty August evening, the flickering flame of his thirty-pence candle blew out.

5

Blood Favours

'This is Angeline.'

'Hello.' James Gant smiled politely. At each stage of his new career he felt like a boy on his first day at school.

'Far bloody cry from sweet sixteen,' went on Stan, a former Sergeant in the Intelligence Corps who had astounded his betters by buying himself out of the army and taking a Double First in Modern History and Philosophy at Manchester University and, allowing himself to be recruited into the outfit, had taken upon himself the role of office wit.

Gant had no idea what he was talking about. Sweet sixteen. But he had an idea it was in some way salacious. Maybe they had this kind of office banter going on.

In fact Stan, in those first few moments of acquaintance, was one of the last people with whom the former cameraman would have chosen to share this spacious but slightly shabby room, on the first floor of the Foreign and Commonwealth Office, facing the inner courtyard, between King Charles Street and Horse Guards Parade.

'I am actually thirty-four, which is a damn sight nearer sixteen than you.' Angeline smiled coolly and eyed Gant as if he were a houri in a Turkish brothel.

She was short, maybe just five feet, with a general chubbiness and that glow of the congenitally overweight which reminded James of Alan Bennett's wonderful description of three pigs which had been groomed and manicured for one of his stage plays; 'like plump, pink, naked land-ladies in high-heeled shoes'.

'That's your desk, Jimmy,' said Stan. 'There's a kettle in

the loo just down the corridor, past the daguerreotype of Gordon of Khartoum.'

The desk thus designated was, surprise, surprise, in the least attractive corner of the room, hemmed in by a row of olive-drab filing cabinets on one side and a long trestle table with two shredders, a photocopier, a fresh-drinking-water dispenser and a cardboard box of paper cups.

'So I'm the tea boy?' enquired Gant mildly, thinking, only last week I was handling a brush pass in Saint Peter's Square under the eyes of two mafia hoods and a reputed closet queen from the Italian secret service.

'We take turns,' said Angeline, in a voice so seductive he found himself wondering if she were a nymphomaniac.

'This is Eric.' Stan moved past Angeline and extended an arm towards a quiet, slender man working at a desk by the tall window. 'Or,' and here Gant knew exactly what was coming, 'little by little.'

'Hi.' Gant inclined his head.

'You'll find this a trifle tedious after Euan's Italian cut-purses,' nodded Eric, a Peterson pipe clenched in his teeth, eyes meeting Gant's and, thank God, twinkling with normal, everyday, good nature.

'You know Euan?' asked Gant, pleased to hear the merest suggestion of continuing contact with what he had come to accept as the real SIS.

'We all know Marigold,' said Stan and he smiled at Gant's frown of disapproval.

'The very name Marigold is classified Top Secret,' Euan Stevenson had instructed his protégé, and it was certainly not for bandying around this dusty bureaucratic outpost of the thrillingly named Clerical 17.

'Relax,' said Stan, closing the heavy, high door to the corridor with Gordon's portrait, 'we are all cleared and indoctrinated to Cosmic and Atomall.' He meant security classifications way beyond Top Secret. 'Including yourself, Jimmy. Now, listen in . . .' Stan sat himself on a desk set at an angle in one corner. There was a framed photo of the Ayatollah Khomeini on the wall above his seat. The glass was badly cracked and the wood singed, its black veneer blistered in places. There was also a framed photo on his desk of a smiling, dark-haired woman and two little boys of about six and eight. Judging by the sunlight, and the colour, if he had been using standard 400 a.s.a. it had been taken in a Mediterranean location, probably with ozone and mild smoke pollution.

'Jimmy has been, as we all know, working for the last three months with Marigold in Rome.'

Eric pushed his chair back and removed the pipe from his mouth, watching and listening, relaxed and, somehow, relaxing, which was the hallmark, Gant was learning, of the good operator.

'He has been on the indoctrination course, learning what it is we do here, and acquiring what Monsignor Jardine likes to call the "overview" of all SIS methods and current operations. Also the grammar of the firm's network runners and the three hundred and sixteen codenames for our operations worldwide, the what the where and the who of those operations and their earlier codenames going back three generations.'

'And he passed?' asked Eric, approvingly.

'Scraped through,' replied Gant.

'In the best of all possible worlds,' went on Stan, 'James would now be apprenticed to one of us, probably each of us in turn, to learn the trade and become as profoundly meticulous as the delectable Angeline, as disturbingly intuitive as Eric and as awkwardly . . . questioning as myself.'

'But Georgie's gone . . .' interposed Angeline, still examining Gant as if he were at a cattle auction.

'So we're a man down. Plus the bloody Treasury cuts. So, Jim, you will spend this week reading everything that Angeline and Eric and I pass on from our desks, anything we send back to our own office, our reasons why, and you will acquire a contact list of desk officers at Vauxhall with whom we have secure telephone access in the case of queries and borderline cases. Then, next week, starting on Monday, you will process your own line of product. If you have problems, discuss them with Angeline and no one else. Not me. Not Eric. And, although you have access for this week only to the lines of all three of us, you do not cross-fertilise. We try to operate on a need-to-know basis.'

'Except we all hear each other on the phones,' remarked Angeline, finally giving up her examination of the new boy.

'Yeah, well. I'm sure you get the point. Any questions?'

Gant raised his shoulders and moved towards his desk. 'Not yet.'

Stan gazed at him shrewdly. 'You're not a happy camper, Jimbo, what is it?'

'His name, Stan, is not Jim, or Jimmy. Or even Jimbo, which sounds like something out of *The Jungle Book*. It is James . . .' said Eric so gently that, in another environment, it might have been chilling. He eased his chair on its legs to meet Gant's eye. 'Am I right?'

James Gant smiled. 'Yep.' He glanced at Stan. 'Only my parents and one great-aunt call me Jimmy. Or the occasional lover.'

Stan frowned. Shook his head slowly.

'Shit,' he said, 'I don't suppose I qualify, then.'

'No,' said Gant. 'But I promise not to call you Stanley.'

This was the Probationer Intelligence Officer's introduction to the more mundane and – contrary to the impressions given by the espionage genre of popular fiction – more usual side to intelligence work.

Clerical 17 was an office set up by SIS within the Foreign and Commonwealth Office's illustrious main building off Whitehall, at the heart of Britain's power and influence. Its corridors and staircases were vast and impressive, ornate in a style that would not have disgraced the French Empire at its zenith, and the walls hung with huge murals and oil paintings depicting historic epics from British history – the Battle of the Nile, the establishment of Hong Kong harbour, the dash by HMS *Amethyst* down the Yangtse River under fire from Communist Chinese guns – and portraits of august ministers and senior diplomats down the centuries, some famous, many long forgotten.

In recent decades, the most jingoistic and triumphal of the huge, heroic canvases had been quietly replaced with less abrasive – and less well painted – works on subjects like irrigation in the Nile Delta and the building of the Hubert Murray Highway and Suspension Bridge, in Papua New Guinea. For a few brief years, works of art celebrating the work of missionaries in Africa, the North West Frontier and

China had remained on display, until complaints by the women's section of one of the Civil Service unions, backed by the Minorities Groups Committee, that such overt proselytising of Christianity was grossly offensive to Muslims, atheists and those immigrants from pagan regions who might find themselves working for the Foreign Service, persuaded the administrators of those grand staircases and corridors to consign any pictorial reference to things Christian to the basement.

The purpose of Clerical 17 was surprisingly sensible. It was to act as a last check before distributing Product from the Intelligence Service at its Vauxhall Cross and Century House offices to its many subscribers throughout the Foreign Office and the Diplomatic Service.

The job of the four officers in that room overlooking the inner yard was to scrutinise every classified document, every memorandum, every supplementary note, originating from every SIS Desk, Division, Section and individual for any inadvertent clue which might identify a secret source – say, an agent working inside a foreign service – or espionage network or operational method or codename or indeed anything else which the Secret Intelligence Service required, for its security and probity, to keep to itself.

Now the originating offices in Century and Vauxhall were already well-versed and proficient at maintaining the security of intelligence for onward dissemination. But following a couple of potentially dangerous lapses, Clerical 17 had been established as a last filter, to protect the integrity of the Green Palace's myriad secrets. And, while the job was potentially boring, it was made less so by the intriguing fragments of skulduggery and international power games discussed in the constant flow of documents passing across the desks of Stan, Angeline, Eric and now James.

It was a demanding and responsible job, and the foundling officer was once again surprised at being flung right into the thick of Top Secret work, with complete access – essential in the nature of this particular job – to the Firm's operations and agent identities right across the spectrum of its global commitment.

The first week had been instructive. The work needed a

whole lot of concentration, and, in a way, thought James, you needed a mind like a magpie, able to spot the glint of some hidden lapse among the hundreds of pages of immaculately secure intelligence analyses and recommendations.

It had also been educational in coming to terms with his three colleagues.

Stan, it turned out, was a weekend orienteer, running around wooded mountainsides chasing map references and clocking times in competition with others of the same persuasion. The wife and two boys in the framed photo on his desk had been killed by a car bomb in a Belfast street, on their way to buy a school uniform for young Garry, for his first week in primary school, an event about which the child had been much excited. Stan didn't talk about it and the information had come from Eric, who had introduced Gant to a small pub off Birdcage Walk, where they drank a glass or two of beer and enjoyed a sandwich in their lunch break.

Angeline was a strange mixture of bright and breezy, and shy and introverted. Her habit of looking at Gant as if entertaining thoughts of lust had not diminished and he had decided she was probably near-sighted and wore uncomfortable contact lenses.

She was, of the three experienced staff of Clerical 17, the ablest and most thorough. Her career with the Office had been spent in the backrooms of clandestine administration and intelligence analysis. On occasion, a car would arrive and sweep her off to Vauxhall or one of the London outstations, for Angeline was possessed of a true photographic memory, for words, photographs or faces, and she would be able to assist, in just a few moments, in solving puzzles that had been perplexing her more senior colleagues for days. Sometimes weeks.

She was quite droll company, and, if she had a fault, it was an inclination towards office gossip. The BBC had been full of such characters, and Gant had generally been content to get on with his work, in the News and Current Affairs editing suites or abroad on assignment, without participating. However, if he were to be 100 per cent honest, there was no doubting the fact that this chubby, pink, super-efficient but scurrilous-tongued sugar-plum fairy was able to fill in many gaps in his understanding of the personalities and operating procedures of his new profession.

For instance, it was Angeline who confirmed his suspicion that Eric had indeed been a courageous and able field officer, experienced in clandestine operations in a dozen Denied Areas, before alcohol and a nervous breakdown had resulted in four months' convalescence at a private nursing home funded at arm's length by the Service. On his recovery, James Gant was impressed to learn, the Firm had rehabilitated Eric and found a place for him with Clerical 17.

Something the Induction Course and Operational Training had never formally mentioned, but which was becoming apparent to Gant, was a certain spirit of mutual respect and camaraderie inside the outfit which bound them all together in a way that he had never dreamed of when working in Wonderland. The Office looked after its own. It was forgiving and indeed compassionate towards those within its ranks and to its friends. And ruthless, to an extent which chilled the blood, to its enemies.

By the end of the third week of this first real posting, Gant was working eight hours a day processing and clearing 97 per cent of the papers passing across his desk, and querying or sending back for further sanitisation the rest. He was becoming au fait with secret intelligence operations in regions as disparate as China and the Arabian Gulf, Moscow and Latin America. It was fascinating to observe how some quite dramatic and dangerous episodes in far-flung Denied Areas, under the noses of alert and vicious internal security apparats, became translated into dry and objective Special Intelligence Reports for circulation to various subscribers in the straight Foreign and Commonwealth Office.

A similar set-up existed at the Cabinet Office, the Ministry of Defence, the Home Office and the Treasury – Clericals 16, 14, 15 and 18 respectively.

While a small fraction of the information passing across James Gant's desk was dramatic – on rare occasions momentous – much of it was, frankly, dry as dust. Indeed, extremely boring.

It was not how he had envisaged a life in the secret world, but James accepted, philosophically, this period in his personal odyssey when he was merely, as he put it to his sister Charlotte one evening, 'Treading the backwaters, in a kind of Foreign Office limbo. Quite peaceful and stress-free, actually. Lots of time to catch up on movies I've missed. Books to read. Girls to . . . um –'

'I have no wish', said Charlotte primly, 'to hear about that.' Then, after a pause, she had looked at him shrewdly and asked, 'No regrets about Rebecca?'

Gant considered. Then shook his head, 'Uh-uh. I wasn't ready for ... all that grown-up stuff.'

'You are such a bad boy, Jimmy. I don't actually think you ever will be . . .'

And they had smiled, as relaxed and close as brother and sister should be, easy in each other's company.

This was in Charlotte's flat, on the top floor of a mansion block in Prince of Wales Drive in Battersea, on the south side of the River Thames and not in fact very far from David Jardine's place in Tite Street, just over Albert Bridge.

It was a cramped but pleasant little apartment, which she shared with a barrister called Hugo, who had been a Harrier jet fighter pilot with a promising career before being shot down over Iraq during Desert Storm, and had lost an eye and damaged his hearing. He had adapted well to civilian life and Gant liked his sister's boyfriend quite a lot.

Since parting with Rebecca, his former fiancée, James had been staying in a two-bedroom apartment in Beaufort Street, just down from the MGM Cinema in the Fulham Road. It belonged to the BBC correspondent he had worked with in Sarajevo and Kurdistan, and Martin had rented it to Gant for £150 per week, which was more than generous. Martin was happily living with a stunning blonde in Geneva, when not roaming the world's trouble spots, and he said he was happy to have someone keeping his London place warm.

Charlotte sat curled up on the sagging, comfortable sofa, a Peruvian wool rug thrown casually over it and scattered with big, Afghan cushions.

She had changed quite a lot since they were kids, thought Gant. Never an academic star at school, Charlie had done the usual cordon bleu course in cooking, then she had gone to the

Perigord region of France to live with a family who owned a restaurant and a vineyard. To everyone's surprise, young Charlotte turned out to be a natural. She had gone from Perigord to Biarritz for a year and, upon returning to England, had found a job as sous-chef with a catering outfit that served in the Board rooms of several top merchant bank houses in the City.

The constant contact with wonderful food had not affected James's younger sister's trim figure. Just five foot two, she compensated for her lack of height with a vigorous work-out programme and spent much of her summers swimming and water-skiing, and her winters cooking and skiing in the French Alps.

About five years after the terrifying massacre at Rome airport, James's and Charlotte's mother, a kind and able woman, born in North Carolina, of Scottish stock, had been driving home from Oxford, where she had spent a happy evening at Tudor Hall, the girls' boarding school, attending a concert where Charlie had been playing the clarinet in a Mozart and Vivaldi selection.

The police said later that the driver of the juggernaut had suffered a stroke just milliseconds before. Whatever, the huge articulated vehicle, carrying nine new Ford Escorts, had suddenly ploughed across the central safety barrier and tumbled over on its side, destroying Mary Gant's Volkswagen Passat and killing her instantly.

James had been in his first year at St Edmund Hall, in Oxford University, and his father had phoned him with the news. The young student, devastated and in that numb limbo which keeps grief and shock at bay, had collected Charlie from Tudor Hall and driven her to their home in London's Phillimore Gardens.

James Gant Senior was a leading surgeon and Professor of Neurology at Saint Bartholomew's Hospital. He had written the standard work on micro-surgery of the human brain and regularly travelled to the USA and to Europe, to lecture and attend conferences. His wife's sudden and unplanned-for death radically altered him from a warm and caring parent to an increasingly remote man, difficult to approach and taking on more and more work, in order to distance himself – the fifteen-year-old Charlotte gravely reasoned – from the unbearable pain of bereavement.

After the funeral, the confused James and Charlie had found themselves thrown together in their grief and bewildered at the emotional void between them and their once-devoted father, which seemed to increase daily.

The result was that James Gant took upon himself the role of carer and loving closest friend of a sister who, until then, had been merely a younger sibling and a bit of a nuisance. That closeness had developed into affection and the sort of love that allows two people to spend hours in each other's company without ever having to exchange a word.

James would take Charlie on holiday with him. At first they travelled to new places – Brittany, Florida, Morocco – but later they found themselves spending her school breaks revisiting places where they had been happiest with their mother and father, before the accident. Places like North Carolina and New York City, where they had stayed at least a couple of weeks every year, spending Christmas with their grandparents, who had owned a pleasant town house in one of those streets between Madison and Lexington. Both grandparents had passed away, probably mercifully, just a year before the juggernaut. James and Charlotte were both born mimics and they could each have passed for streetwise New Yorkers, the way they so easily assimilated the language and mannerisms.

If James Gant Senior – professor, neurologist and widower – had perhaps been able to bear his pain better, and if he, essentially a wise and kind and worldly man, had taken time to observe what was taking place, he might well have been able to divert, gently, his two children from the increasing inevitability of what was happening to them.

And one half-term break, eighteen months later, as Charlotte approached her seventeenth birthday, James and she flew to Venice and booked into two rooms in the same small hotel on the island of Burano. Charlotte's room, with its view from the open third-floor window, across the Laguna to the spires and roofs and the poplars of San Francesco del Deserto, was the room the two of them had slept in, aged nine and thirteen, when they had first stayed there, with their parents across the corridor.

Standing in that same room, gazing out past the open window across the lagoon, in the sultry warmth of a weekend somewhere between Easter and summer, arms round each other's shoulders, they had talked about their mother, and the good times they had spent together.

Charlie had stared to cry, softly, and James too had found himself suddenly sobbing.

Perhaps if it had been in the night time, when they would have been undressed for bed, their natural sense of propriety would have signalled a warning. But it was the afternoon. Nothing was less likely.

And they had gently consoled each other.

And afterwards, lying together, they had sworn undying love, as brother and sister, and had, guiltily, but less ashamed than perhaps they should have been, agreed that what had happened was understandable and was never to happen again.

And they would never speak about it, ever.

And they had agreed all that, most solemnly.

And they had spent the rest of that day together. In the room with its view across the lagoon.

And it was their secret.

Now, watching Charlie curled up on the couch, facing him, gossiping about Hugo and the Merchant Bankers she cooked for, James felt more comfortable and content than he had felt since before SIS, since before getting engaged to Rebecca.

'So it's pretty boring, then, this Foreign Office?' asked Charlotte, pulling her slender legs under her and sipping from a big mug of coffee.

'Has its moments.'

Charlie grinned, and glanced at him, holding his gaze. 'You know, for a while we all wondered if you had gone off to be some kind of spy.'

James smiled. 'Dear Charlie, will you ever grow up?'

Charlotte lifted her coffee mug to her face, hiding all but her eyes as she drank from it.

'Do you want me to?' she asked.

After a long pause, James Gant said, softly, 'I think we really should.'

Charlie gently laid her cup down and slowly stood up.

'But not just yet,' she said, quietly.

James Gant looked at her for several moments. Then he glanced at his watch. 'When', he asked, 'is Hugo due back?'

'This', said the guy from State, 'is Ramses Ibrahim Selim, the Egyptian Ambassador. During UN Week he'll be staying at the Plaza Parthenon on West Sixty-four. He has taken the whole fifteenth floor. Staff of three diplomats from the Washington Embassy plus a Political Officer from Cairo. Also a security team from the DC Embassy.'

Assistant Director Al Wiscynsky was addressing a team from the Joint Task Force of NYPD cops, US secret servicemen, FBI agents and special agents from the State Department's Diplomatic Security Service, in Number 3 Briefing Room in the DSS Field Office high in the World Trade Center, which overlooked the Merrill Lynch Building and the Hudson River.

United Nations Week in Manhattan meant cancelling all law-enforcement leave and involving hundreds of Government agents and police officers in the protection of visiting politicians, Government ministers and diplomats from every country that was represented at the United Nations Headquarters on the banks of the East River, between 42nd and 46th Streets.

Senior American statesmen were, as always, in the care of the United States Secret Service, a department of the Treasury. Visiting foreign ministers and their ambassadors to the United Nations were protected by the Diplomatic Security Service, Department of Protective Services, which was run by State. The FBI, as the US Government's senior counter-terrorist agency, was required to provide up-to-the-minute intelligence on known or suspected or potential threats by any one of the plethora of groups of disaffected foreign nationals residing legally or illegally in the USA, who might have cause to make attempts on the lives of those dignitaries from all around the world who had descended on New York City for a week or ten days of intensive UN diplomacy, socialising, shopping, visiting the theatres and galleries and etcetera.

Every good hotel from 86th Street down had its share of protected guests and they all expected to be able to travel around town on UN or private business and, for those considered by the DSS to be even remotely at risk, each journey was accomplished by saturation protection; the sealing-off of leaving and destination points, helicopter surveillance and motorcades with security teams, sirens whooping, red and blue lights strobing and armed agents leaping out to secure intersections and sometimes entire blocks, so that, several times an hour, the city would become gridlocked.

It was a nightmare. And it was only three weeks away.

And because all the aforesaid secret agencies were stretched to the seams, they were obliged to fill the ranks of their footsoldiers with honest-to-goodness ordinary detectives and plainclothes cops from New York's finest.

Thus, Sergeant of Detectives (Homicide) Joe Cleary, proud father of four-month-old Patrick Cheyenne, found himself in that section of the DSS Field Office Commissary temporarily designated Briefing Room 3, gazing at a big black and white slide projection on the wall behind Al Wiscynsky of a handsome, sixty-something kind of tired-looking man, of sallow, more or less noble, middle-east physiognomy, with dark, intelligent eyes and a nose that seemed more reminiscent of Ancient Rome than downtown Cairo.

Not that Joe had ever been near Cairo, but in earlier days on the Force he had run in more than a few taxi drivers from that part of the world. Even in Manhattan their lunatic driving stood out. Plus there was an Egyptian detective in the 18th Precinct who had just transferred to Homicide from Narcotics. Sammy Abdallah. Short and serious. Good cop. But none of them had the noble schnozz of this Ambassador.

'Of course,' went on Wiscynsky, 'the Egyptian Foreign Minister will be staying there too. But that is not something we want to spread around, OK?'

The assembled agents and cops gazed back, unmoved. They had all done this before, it was no big deal.

As he watched photos of the Egyptian Foreign Minister,

the various members of Egyptian staff and their own security personnel, plus plans of the Plaza Parthenon hotel and listened to big Al Wiscynsky's overview of The Threat from Islamic Fundamentalist terror groups in Egypt, along with mugshots of a number of known Islamic Jihad activists in the New York area, Joe Cleary found himself wondering about what that mortuary queen Frank what's'isname had told him.

The thing was, about certain types of gays like – what was his name? Yeah, Grumman, Frank Grumman, they were so scared you were going to . . . despise them, that when you just ignored where they were coming from and treated them more or less like any other witness, or victim, or even suspect, they were so fuckin' grateful it was like saving a Chinaman's life. You couldn't get rid of them.

Anyway, Frank Grumman had phoned – after Joe had taken his witness statement, eliminating him from any suspicion of being involved in the Martina's Bar killing, and let him go – grateful for his decent treatment and, in his gratitude, he had told Cleary about some spook from the CIA coming all the way from Washington DC to look at the body of 'this John Doe', as Grumman had called it.

Well, Joe Cleary had been less than wild with interest till the morgue attendant had mentioned the cadaver had been found dead in a freezer cabinet at Bartello, on West Broadway, minus its nasal organ and with four fingers missing.

That was *his* John Doe.

And if some fancy fuckin' secret agent from DC thought he could keep any knowledge he might have – he obviously did have – from the investigating officer with NYPD Homicide, i.e. Sergeant Joseph MacMonagle Cleary, he had another think coming.

So it had paid to treat Grumman like a human being, thought Cleary to himself, as yet another slide of some Islamic Holy War fanatic flashed onto the far wall.

'The Protective Detail will be split into three shifts. Shift Team Controllers will overlap, for continuity, and two DSS Organisers will work twelve hours on twelve off. Ten NYPD officers will be under Sergeant Cleary, most of you know Joe, he's with Homicide covering the Tenth and Sixth, with frequent overlaps into Mid-Towns North and South, not to mention the rest of Manhattan, which he knows like the back of his, uh . . .' Wiscynsky paused.

'Say hand, Al. There's ladies present and one of them is on Hillary's detail,' Sid Graham, a Secret Service agent from Washington growled, in his gravel voice and continued, 'You don't want to finish up in Haiti.'

Nearly everyone laughed. Even Hillary Clinton's lady bodyguard, on temporary assignment.

Cleary grinned. Washington chit-chat bored him. 'OK, don't look. Who can really, without looking, describe the back of his hand?'

They all glanced down at their hands.

'A philosopher, already,' said Wiscynsky. 'Joe, get together with Martin and slot your guys into the roster.' He meant Martin O'Connor, the DSS Special Agent In Charge, who was running the Egyptian protection detail.

'Sure,' said Cleary.

'Well, that just about does it.' Wiscynsky clicked off the slide carousel and arched his aching back. 'FBI, how do you rate the threat?'

The FBI woman present, a good-looking thirty-three, with promising legs and the palest of grey-green eyes, stood up, not bothering to glance at the file she held and had been scanning just prior to Al's question.

'We have eight major problems this year. Israel is at the top of the list, closely followed by Chairman Arafat of the PLO. The South Korean Foreign Minister is high, so is the Saudi delegation. As far as Egypt is concerned, there is a general major level of threat from their extreme Islamic radicals, who undoubtedly have contacts with the crazies who bombed this place' she meant the World Trade Center, 'just two years ago, causing over one thousand casualties.'

She glanced around, to make absolutely sure she was getting her message across. 'At this time we have no specific intelligence to suggest that Ambassador Selim is in any specific danger.'

'And their Foreign Minister?' somebody asked. 'How about him?'

Helen Sorensen raised her shoulders. 'Nothing specific.

But this is a high-risk assignment. These people need us, it is not cosmetic, believe me.'

'There we go,' said Wiscynsky. 'So let's keep everyone alive.'

'Starting with ourselves,' murmured Sid Graham.

'Amen,' said Joe Cleary. And he fingered the scar on his ear, where that goddam cat had got him, as it plunged earthwards, the day of the freezer murder.

There is a creek near the shore in Essex County, Connecticut, meandering, shallow from the height of the summer to the advent of autumn, swamp-like in the spring thaw, with banks of wild rice and a couple of docks, to the sprawling properties of some very old WASP money.

One of those properties – the one nearest Hudson Sound and the Essex River delta, with its peaceful, New England townships and wedding-cake churches, was called Beauregard, and its quietly impressive architecture was more suited to the white-and-gray-wood colonial piles of plantation land, way south of the Mason-Dixon Line, than to the Yankee Baptist settler pepper-box homes in that carefully preserved region.

Beauregard was set in twenty-two acres of rolling meadow and woodland, sloping down to the winding creek, with its own private dock, which was kind of a grand name for an L-shaped wood pier.

It belonged to Annabel Curtis, née Longstreet, who had inherited the place from her father, Senator Jed Longstreet, who had inherited Beauregard from his own parents. And the house had originally stood a few hundred miles to the south, in confederate country. In 1880, Major-General Jed Longstreet had been so taken with the pleasing lines of the big, understated mansion, with its servants' annex and conservatory, that, after the first battle of Manassas, where he had distinguished himself by second-guessing and outmanoeuvring J.E.B. Stuart's fast-moving and capable Rebel cavalry skirmishers, the General had moved into Beauregard and staked his claim to it – the entire male family being killed in the battle and the womenfolk and coloured servants having fled.

After the peace, the General had purchased legal title to the property, for the princely sum of $600, and he had arranged for it to be dismantled in its entirety and transported all the way north to his family farmstead on the banks of that creek, winding into the Essex delta. There, Beauregard was restored to its former glory, and it was in the old servants' annex, now as tastefully decorated and furnished in simple (but expensive) American colonial style as the rest of the house, that Annabel Curtis was to be found, on the same day as Joe Cleary attended the UN Week briefing at the World Trade Center, busy with her two Colombian housemaids, getting the place ready for an influx of guests.

Her husband, Mike Curtis, was US Ambassador to Egypt, where together they spent most of their year in a splendid villa not far from the American Embassy, in the Gezira district of Cairo.

In the four years that they had been posted there, they had become very friendly with Ramses Selim, the Egyptian Ambassador to the United States, meeting him on visits back to Washington, or when Selim returned to Cairo for consultations with his Foreign Secretary. The two men had hit it off, almost at once, and, more important, Annabel and Nabila Selim instinctively liked each other.

The second year of Mike Curtis's tour, the two families had taken some time off from the hectic bustle of United Nations Week in New York City, to rest up in the family home in Connecticut, Beauregard.

The Curtises' three children had been there, two daughters and a son. Harriet, the oldest girl, was married to a young doctor practising in Boston, and her sister, Lauren, had at that time been engaged to a book publisher from California. And Sam Curtis, twenty-six, was a history teacher at Harvard.

Harriet had twins, aged four, and a six-month-old baby boy.

The next year, the first time having been a quiet success, Ramses and Nabila Selim had come accompanied by their grown-up son and daughter.

And now, this year, towards the end of UN Week, the Selims were due to arrive with their son Nass'r, daughter

Abir and the son's pretty French wife Jacqueline. Abir was also bringing her best friend Fatimah, whose father was a senior Egyptian judge.

All in all, Annabel worked out, as her two maids unfolded crisp bed-linen and made up the rooms, there would be about eighteen souls enjoying Beauregard.

Well, it would be fine to see the house almost full, that's what it was there for. There would be barbecues by the dock, and beach tennis. The men would play chess, and there were wonderful walks and a ton of books to read.

Lauren, the Curtises' younger girl, liked to paint and she would sit all day, sometimes, at her portable easel, which she liked to move around, from day to day.

Grace, the Curtises' Filipino cook, and her husband were right at that moment working on menus and buying in fresh produce from the local farm store.

Then there were the . . . what Annabel called 'the attachments'; the Selims' security people, which State insisted on, because of the current unstable political situation in Cairo. In fact, it was because of the tension and the killings by Islamic radicals in Egypt that the two families so enjoyed those annual get-togethers in the tranquillity and easy grace of Beauregard and its remote rural environment.

Ah, bliss, Annabel Curtis stretched her arms and smiled as a ray of sunlight spilled into the second-best guest bedroom, across the polished wood floor over the 1790s rocking chair and onto the delicate pastel patchwork coverlet the maids had just laid over the bed, with its iron and brass head and foot boards which they had found in that antique shop in Essex; run by a delightful but quite eccentric girl who never stopped talking and was married to some millionaire.

It was going to be an oasis of peace in an otherwise hectic and often anxious life.

What heaven. Annabel just couldn't wait . . .

Biarritz is a sleepy town nestling in a comfortable curve of the Atlantic Ocean, just a few miles from the border between France and Spain. It is Basque country, where those proud and ancient people inhabit the foothills of the Pyrenees and indeed the very heights of the forbidding mountain range that, more effectively than any border, divides the two nations.

It is remote from the rest of France, from the rest of Europe, with its elegant promenade, old port and narrow streets sloping down from the higher ground surrounding the sweeping bay, dominated by the enormous Palace built by Napoleon III for his Empress Eugénie – now an hotel with many stars – and it is very much a resort for the French themselves, who like to escape there from the horrors of the tourist seasons.

For centuries the Spanish Basques have struggled for independence from Metropolitan Spain, and their resistance movements (terrorists or freedom fighters, depending on one's viewpoint) have received shelter from cousins over the border in France.

In recent years, the French authorities have clamped down on this safe haven, and undercover agents of the Gendarmerie Nationale, along with the DST, France's Internal Security Service, have conducted a relentless and sometimes bloody campaign against the secret cells of ETA, the Basque Nationalist group, and other, smaller but quite lethal outfits.

It was to Biarritz that a number of middle-class Basques, of mixed French and Spanish nationality, had brought their families to rest from the rigours of urban and rural guerrilla warfare. The Gardeazabals, the Orués and the Maguregi lived quietly and were careful not to draw attention to themselves. For four of their menfolk and two of the women were the prime movers behind a faction of ETA, which they chose to call ETA-Negro. Black ETA. And they had been responsible that summer for a number of bombs in Barcelona and Madrid.

The house they had rented was a big walled mansion at the top of the Rue Hugo, above the bustling, covered market of Les Halles and not far from the Protestant church, which was further down the hill.

Tony Gardeazabal and Pepe Orué were in the third-floor games-room playing table tennis, that Tuesday morning. They had spent the earlier part of the day planning a car-bombing of the Chief of Police in Santander, just across the border. The reconnaissance had been carried out two weeks earlier by Marta, Tony's thirty-six-year-old wife, and Christina, the twenty-one-year-old mistress of the group's leader, Ángel Guerrero Maguregi, a forty-six-year-old schoolteacher from Bilbao.

Marta was on the ground floor, in the kitchen, preparing lunch for all eight occupants, including her sixteen-year-old son, Miguel, and Christina Uribe's brother, Luís, twenty-seven, who would be driving the car bomb into position. He had performed this function twice before, in Madrid and in Barcelona, with devastating results. Big successes as far as ETA-Negro was concerned.

Christina had just returned from Les Halles, where she had bought a leg of lamb, two kilos of merguéz, spicy North African sausages, and fresh vegetables.

Young Miguél and Christina's brother Luís were in the garden, cleaning the swimming pool with a net and a pool-vacuum.

Ángel Guerrero Maguregi was in the garage, working on the engine of his big Citroën DS 21, an immaculately maintained 1982 model. Its distinctive deep leaf-green colour was well known to police on both sides of the border, as were Maguregi's good works with children of the poor throughout the Basque region. The fact that such charitable journeys provided excellent cover for Maguregi's terrorist activities seemed to have passed unnoticed.

Pepe Orué's forty-year-old wife, Denise, a French national from St Jean Pied-de-Port, a village in the foothills of the Pyrenees, was in the first-floor bathroom, shampooing her hair – it was thick, luxurious and auburn, almost russet – and looking forward to that evening, when they all planned to visit the Bar des Halles, where they had reserved two tables for dinner cooked by the patron's wife, whose simple Basque fare was among the tastiest in town.

So, although Marta was busy preparing lunch, Denise decided to eat lightly, so that she would be able to do the evening meal justice.

When Luís Uribe fell into the pool, tripping, it seemed, on the edge, Miguél Gardeazabal burst out laughing, as the older man went right under, still clutching the vacuum-pole. He was still laughing as the left side of his head disintegrated and his throat exploded, torn apart by a 7.62 dum-dum bullet.

Hearing the splashes and brief laughter, cut off so abruptly, Ángel Maguregi straightened up from the engine with its hood propped open, small monkey-wrench in his left hand, and glanced towards the open garage door and frowned, confused by the ski-masked figure in dark overalls, crouched facing him. In the split second before he died, Ángel Maguregi's whole system was hit by a thunderbolt of wild fear. An entire magazine of thirty 9mm slugs from a silenced French MAT-49 sub-machine gun hammered his jerking frame four feet backwards, destroying his mid and upper torso comprehensively and spraying the immaculate Citroën with ribbons of blood and scraps of Maguregi's flesh.

In the kitchen, Marta Gardeazabal had just reached for the paprika jar, on a shelf beside the cooker with its big pot of coq au vin simmering gently, at the same time stirring the stew with her left hand, when she heard the back door to the garden opening and said, 'Whoever that is, would you set the table.'

But whoever it was grinned silently, beneath the black Balaclava, and shot her eight times in the back and in the head. Two slugs from the .45 Colt, silenced (like all the weapons used that day), passed clean through the woman and penetrated the big, copper pot, causing broth from the coq au vin to pour out in streams, onto the floor and the bleeding corpse of the murdered cook, whose nervous system kept the body twitching violently for almost two minutes.

This was the sight that greeted Christina as she came into the kitchen from the hall leading to the front door, laden with plastic bags with the lamb and merguéz and fresh vegetables from Les Halles.

It had been sheer chance that had allowed the silent attackers to kill four of their victims so easily, but the shrieks and screams of Christina destroyed their run of luck.

She dropped the bags and just stood there in hysterics, rooted to the spot as in a nightmare, for all of four long seconds, while the hooded figure drew a short broad-bladed machete from its scabbard strapped to his leg, strode across the tiled floor, slippery with Marta's blood and coq au vin gravy, and with one sweeping slash, slit her throat, almost beheading the just-recently pretty girl.

Tony Gardeazabal and Pepe, up in the top of the house, heard the shrieks and ran to the windows. Pepe could just glimpse a section of the swimming pool, where the body of Miguel lay floating, face down, with dark red spreading in the water around him.

Tony lifted a Moroccan rug and prised open a piece of floorboard. He passed a Spas-Franchi twelve-gauge combat shotgun to Pepe, and threw him a cardboard box of twenty-five shells. For himself he chose two loaded handguns – a British 9mm Browning Hi-Power, a gift from some friends in the Provisional IRA, and a Smith & Wesson .357 revolver, the Highway Patrolman.

As the two men, adrenaline surging through their veins, hearts hammering, emerged from the table-tennis room, moving tactically, as they had trained and indeed practised so many times, covering each other, a second series of horrific screams came from the first floor.

From the bathroom.

'Denise!!' yelled Pepe Orué, and he went down the stairs five at a time, passing the second-floor landing and glimpsing too late the slight figure in the navy boiler suit and slit-eyed black hood who lurked in a bedroom doorway, silenced Skorpion 7.65 machine-pistol hugged to its hip.

Orué's big combat shotgun boomed off three shots in rapid succession even as bullets from the Skorpion thudded remorselessly into his slight frame and shattered pictures and plaster on the wall behind him.

'Blam! Blam! Boom!' Firing his pistol and revolver Tony slowly advanced down the stairs, deliberately aiming at the slender, hooded boyish shape who continued to shoot Pepe as the Basque somersaulted, grievously wounded, to end in a crumpled, bloody heap on the half-landing between floors. And the slender killer, splinters of wooden door-frame and plaster erupting all around, would have died in seconds, if a fusillade of slugs from two sub-machine guns had not turned Tony Gardeazabal into a Frankenstein-like, still-standing cadaver, which continued to empty the Browning and the Highway Patrolman until death stilled its trigger fingers.

Ignoring the body of Gardeazabal, as it collapsed untidily down the staircase, the killer calmly took aim at the still groaning, huddled form of Pepe Orué, on the landing below, and emptied a burst at his head.

The groaning stopped.

Silence.

'Check every fucking room,' said the slight figure, speaking in French. And her four hooded, boiler-suited colleagues obeyed.

Three minutes later they reported back to the downstairs hallway.

'Clear,' said one.

'Clear,' announced the others.

Their leader paused, listening, sensing.

Nothing.

No police sirens.

Silence, apart from the comfortable ticking of an old clock. And, in the distance, a rumble of thunder, heralding yet another of Biarritz's autumn *orages*, the wild, cataclysmic storms of the region.

'*Allons*,' she said. Let's go.

And as they left, alert and ready to defend themselves, a telephone started to ring, in the front-hall lobby.

It was only when the covered Peugeot van had moved quietly away from the back yard of that house in the Rue Hugo, joining the light traffic heading sedately for the old port, that Zina Farouche tugged off the black hood and pushed a hand through her sweat-streaked hair.

'Zafir,' she said, 'we'll have to move faster than that.'

'Quite a party,' said David Jardine.

'Started off very professional,' remarked Szabodo, 'then got messy. Maybe a team who have not worked together before . . .'

They were in the squat Hungarian's untidy office at the back of his machine-room in the bowels of his London Facilities Section's undercover workshops beneath the railway arches in Brixton. And they were studying photos of the carnage at the house on the Rue Hugo. The kitchen had taken on the look, in those black and white prints, of stills from a movie by Quentin Tarantino.

'Sdec swear they didn't do it,' said Jardine. And the office's contacts inside the French service had confirmed just that. 'Likewise the DST.' Jardine removed his reading glasses, yet another unwelcome sign that he was no longer young, and polished them on his tie. 'And if the Spanish are clean . . . who else would?'

Ronnie Szabodo leafed through a file sent by fax from the Biarritz office of the French foreign intelligence service, the DGSE. 'A rival Basque group? ETA-B?'

Jardine considered this. 'We would have heard from Maverick.' Maverick was Madrid Station's man inside the Basque Separatist movement.

Szabodo lifted his pipe from a jacket pocket and sniffed at the bowl, like a labrador at a lamppost. He patted his clothing as if, like a conjuror's trick, a lurking stash of Balkan Sobranie might emerge.

'About five years ago,' he volunteered, 'the Provisionals rubbed out nine ETA-B people, to protect their security in Spain.'

Jardine dismissed this. 'PIRA's keeping its head down. It'll all go sour one fine day. But they wouldn't risk the embarrassment of this sort of thing. Not right now.' He pushed the photos around.

Ronnie wandered over to a filing cabinet and produced two bottles of Dos Equis beer, flipping the tops off on a ragged edge of one drawer.

David Jardine rubbed the back of his neck. Something lurked at the back of his mind.

'Why did the French send all this to us?' he wondered aloud.

Szabodo glanced at him, as he handed over one bottle. 'Perhaps they think you know something they don't . . .'

'Well, I do sincerely hope so.' Jardine grinned and met his old friend's gaze.

'I mean, you are becoming the guru on, um, Tehran. Aren't you . . .? Which is the one option nobody's mentioned.'

They both knew that, as so often in their arcane world, it was the unsaid which was beginning to intrude upon events. And, in this affair, the dead breath of Radical Islam was somehow, indefinably, lingering on the window pane.

'See if you can get hold of their ballistics reports. Ask for all calibres, just to fudge the issue, Ronnie.'

In fact it would be forensic details of the spent 7.65 mm bullets which could confirm this dawning suspicion, for SIS had arranged for a consignment of Skorpion machine-pistols, destined for Abu Nidal, to be proofed, secretly, at the Libyan armoury which supplied them, so that the firm could keep track of their users. The 7.65 was a comparatively rare calibre, since both NATO and the former Warsaw Pact had standardised at 7.62 mm.

'Apart from running out of suspects, David, why should this be something to do with the Tide of Islam?'

Jardine touched one of the photographs. 'Look at this. Cutting the throat. And what they did in the bathroom . . .' He spread out three photos of Denise, butchered and mutilated beyond the needs of mere assassination. 'Where did we last see this?'

Ronnie Szabodo stuck his hands deep inside jacket pockets and studied the grisly detail. 'Geneva,' he announced, finally. A former senior aide of Abu Nidal's, who had defected to Nidal's arch enemy, Abu Iyad (Chief of PLO Intelligence), had been slaughtered in a rented house on the shore of Lake Geneva, along with his three bodyguards, his wife and two teenage daughters.

The particular form of mutilation performed on the women then was too similar to the butchering of Denise Orué to be mere coincidence.

'Zafir Hammuda,' said Jardine. 'Footsoldier of Abu Nidal and a particularly sadistic member of our flawed species.'

'He uses a machete, honed to slice off the wings of a . . . butterfly,' contributed the Hungarian. Rather poetically, he thought.

'But why? Why the Basques? Why would Abu Nidal send a team to take out an ETA sub-culture?'

'Maybe he was loaned out. Maybe Hammuda has gone private.' Szabodo sipped his beer.

David Jardine glanced at him, then started to shuffle the photos into a neat pile. Ronnie had known him for many years, and he understood this meant the subject was suddenly not for discussion.

'Just a second,' said Ronnie. 'Just a tick . . .' He frowned, head sunk into his bull-like neck. 'Yes. Zina Farouche. Remember? Euan saw them together in Rome. Zafir Hammuda has been recruited, we thought, into this team the lovely Zina is putting together.'

'We never really got a handle on that,' lied Jardine, placing the photos back in their box.

'So maybe this was the job she was planning.' Szabodo relaxed. As if satisfied with his theory.

'Jolly good,' said Jardine. 'Ronnie, I have to see the Foreign Office in half an hour.'

'Unless', went on the squat Magyar, unmoved by his boss's clear signals, 'she was just trying out her new toy . . .'

'Meaning?' asked David Jardine warily.

'Like . . . a training exercise. On-the-job training. To see if it would work on a bigger, or more important, target.'

'A pretty bloody training exercise,' said Jardine, almost too casually.

'They are, actually, pretty bloody people, old sport,' replied Szabodo. Watching for a reaction.

After a long silence, David Jardine tapped the lip of the bottle against his chin, shrugged and said, 'Forget it.'

Ronnie nodded; but it irked the Hungarian to be shut out from something he felt he should be helping with.

'Quite a girl, this Ma'moiselle Farouche,' he ploughed on, and the Director of Operations glanced at him sharply. Szabodo held up his hands.

'Consider it forgot.'

'That would be helpful, Ronnie,' said Jardine, and he walked out of the office, already thinking about the next item in his crowded day.

Well, not quite.

The dreadful image of the slaughtered Denise Orué and the carnage in that kitchen remained stuck in his mind. And he wondered if in all truth he could really consign two entirely innocent families to a similar fate, three thousand miles and just three weeks away, in Connecticut, USA.

Just to secure a strategic advantage. Which, in the final analysis, he reminded himself, would save countless lives.

And he saw in his mind's eye that carved figure of Christ on the Cross, in the Limehouse mission.

The decision is yours, it had seemed to convey. And whatever you decide, I'll see you later . . .

Or sooner.

'This is Colonel Khallif, Ambassador Selim's Head of Security.' Al Wiscynsky had gone down to the lobby of the DSS New York Field Office to greet the Egyptian and bring him back up to Briefing Room 3. This was two days after the initial briefing and admin meeting of all the Protective Detail people involved.

Just the three senior men on the detail were in the room on this occasion: Special Agent In Charge Martin O'Connor, Special Agent Helen Sorensen and Homicide Sergeant Joe Cleary, on secondment from NYPD.

'Pleased to meet you,' said Helen.

'Colonel. Always a pleasure,' said Marty O'Connor, quick to establish he and the Egyptian security chief were almost old pals.

The Colonel's amused, dark-brown eyes flicked to Cleary, whose unshaped woven oatmeal jacket and tie worn loose, top shirt button undone, marked him as an unlikely Federal agent.

'How ya doin'.' Joe nodded, meeting Khallif's gaze.

Khallif held the eye contact, then he smiled. And without replying, turned to Wiscynsky. 'Al, let me take you through the itinerary of the Foreign Minister.' He put his attaché case on a table and unlocked it. Cleary noted that it was handcuffed to the Colonel's wrist.

After seven minutes of rehearsing the Egyptian Foreign Minister's schedule of journeys to and from the United Nations Plaza, between 42nd and 48th, his planned luncheons and dinner dates, his visits to other foreign diplomatic receptions and so on and so forth, Marty O'Connor discreetly cleared his throat.

'What is it, Marty?' asked Wiscynsky.

'Where is Ambassador Selim during all this time?' Helen Sorensen enquired, and O'Connor nodded, temporarily silenced by a fit of coughing brought on by his having recently given up smoking.

'Uh, he'll be with the Minister, right, Colonel?' said Wiscynsky.

Khallif glanced round at the State Department official. He shook his head. 'Ambassador Selim will spend the first couple of days with the Minister. Thereafter, he is visiting Mike Curtis in Connecticut.'

'Mike who?' asked Wiscynsky.

'He's our Ambassador', contributed Helen, 'to Egypt.'

She ignored Joe Cleary's amused look of approval.

'In Connecticut.' Al Wiscynsky was unmoved by his own lack of knowledge. 'And just how does he get there?'

'I have arranged for our own security staff to organize that,' said Colonel Khallif.

Slight pause.

'No kidding,' said Wiscynsky, straightening up and arching his stiff back, the way Cleary had seen him do when he started to get mad.

I love it, thought the detective, when they fall out. He glanced at his wristwatch. Laurie would be feeding Patrick Cheyenne about now. He caught the FBI woman looking at him. She had a certain something, no doubt about it. Some of them just love small, rat-like guys, he admitted to himself, like me. He winked back and she gazed at him as cold as if he were a sign on a doorway.

Cleary shrugged. What the hell.

'. . . of that for us, would you, Joe?' Al Wiscynsky and the Colonel were gazing at him, waiting politely for an answer.

'Take care of what for you?' asked the Homicide cop.

'A detail to look after Ramses Selim,' said Colonel Khallif. 'In transit from Manhattan to Connecticut.'

'I ain't familiar wid the place. North of Pelham Bay I need a seeing-eye dog.'

Al Wiscynsky laughed, but it was not a sign of mirth.

'Joe, Marty will assign an agent detail on the Connecticut home of Mike Curtis.' Al made it sound like Mike and him were old buddies, although two seconds ago he didn't know who the guy was.

'So run over it for me again, Chief,' said Cleary, deadpan, as if he had been listening the first time.

And that was how Sergeant Joe Cleary of NYPD Homicide, on temporary attachment to the Diplomatic Security Service, was tasked with arranging the safe journeys of Egyptian Ambassador Ramses Selim from the Plaza Parthenon hotel on West 64th Street to Essex County Connecticut and Beauregard, the old colonial home of Michael Ulysses Grant Curtis III, United States Ambassador to Cairo.

It was a commonsense move by Wiscynsky, to put the journey through New York City in the hands of a local cop, rather than one of his own Special Agents. For, apart from Marty O'Connor and a couple of junior men, most of his DSS team were from out of town.

'. . . once you get him safely to Beauregard,' finished Wiscynsky, 'and hand over to the live-in detail, your mission is completed. For the return trip, it's the same.'

'Al, I have four of my security people who will be with Ambassador Selim twenty-four hours.' Colonel Khallif spread his hands, eloquently. 'If you are stretched here, I'm sure we could liaise with the local police. We do not want our Ambassador's social plans to deplete your resources.'

Wiscynsky arched his back so far Cleary thought it might break in two.

'It's no problem,' he said. 'The United States Government is responsible for every one of your diplomats' security, on our soil. Believe me. We have no problems with that.'

Khallif smiled politely and thanked Assistant Director Wiscynsky. More detailed planning took another four hours.

And Marty O'Connor and Joe Cleary had to work all that evening, with just four Buds and a plate of pastrami on rye, plus a pack of Camel Lites, to completely reshuffle a duty schedule that had not taken into account one of its two protectees spending some quality time in the boondocks.

In Paris, on the Avenue Foch, near the Bois de Boulogne, there is a large house which, at one time, during the Second World War, had been occupied by the Gestapo, and where events every bit as inhuman as the tortures in Abu Nidal's Naji al-Ali terror camp in the Libyan desert had been a daily (and nightly) occurrence.

Now it was owned by a wealthy international financier and arms dealer, a Saudi by the name of al-Wahid, and the place was spacious and luxuriously furnished, but at the same time spartan, in the style of the Middle East, with just a few Louis XIV pieces and one or two decorative baubles from the Palaces of Napoleon III to lend a cosmopolitan touch.

Al-Wahid had put the third floor of this house, with offices and an apartment, at the disposal of a Syrian business colleague, in settlement of some shortfall in a 1993 contract to supply US-built Surface-to-Air missiles to the Syrian Army.

The Syrian in his turn had passed the apartment over to his Intelligence Service and they had rented the place to a Swiss investment broker who was in fact an administrative agent of Abu Nidal's Fatah – The Revolutionary Council.

Thus it had become the Paris base of Abu Nidal's Special Missions Committee of his Intelligence Directorate and Hanna al-Farah, Commander of the Assassins, was using it as her safe house.

'How did the rehearsal go?' she enquired.

'So-so,' replied Zina Farouche. She gazed at an original Canaletto of the Grand Canal, Venice, and wrinkled her nose. 'It started like clockwork. We took out two by the pool and one, the leader, inside the garage, working on his car. Just like I told you we would. Then, inside the house, Ben does OK in the kitchen. Negotiates a woman by the stove and a girl who strayed in. Girl gets very noisy. The two men in the attic games-room have time to arm themselves and come down the stairs shooting like Butch Cassidy and the Sunday Kid.'

'Sundance,' said Hanna. 'It's the Sundance Kid.'

'It was unforgivable. I just happened to be clearing the second-floor bedrooms and nailed the first one as he went past. The next one nearly got me . . .' Zina touched a livid red graze on her upper right arm. She was wearing a simple blue dress with shoulder straps.

'Who should have been covering the attic?' asked al-Farah, her face grim.

'Zafir,' replied Zina, quietly. As if she really had not wanted to get him into trouble.

'So where was he?'

Zina raised her shoulders. She glanced away and mumbled something.

'What . . .?' asked the older woman, in disbelief.

'He raped Pepe Orué's wife, while he was cutting her up.'

'Cutting her up? When speed was of the essence? Quick kills were surely your orders . . .'

'In Connecticut, if I understand my mission correctly,' Zina Farouche felt her stomach begin to knot, all too aware that her life and death, and much worse, were in this elegant, strangely attractive woman's hands, 'there should be an element of . . . horror.' She shrugged diffidently, like a schoolgirl answering a potentially difficult teacher. 'That is my understanding. If there's time . . .'

In the silence that followed, Hanna al-Farah shook her head, trying to evaluate what Zina had just said. Finally, her voice taut with anger, she said, 'Horror or no horror, he raped a target and fucked up the timing of your entire operation. In the name of Allah the Merciful, did he think we arranged this for his entertainment?'

'I couldn't believe it myself . . .'

Hanna al-Farah crossed to a telephone and reached for the receiver.

'Wait,' said Zina.

Hanna paused.

'He got there with the bullets in time to get me out of the shit.'

Hanna stared at the girl. 'He has to die. Such a breach of discipline can't be permitted.'

Eventually, Zina Farouche met her gaze. 'He will not make any more mistakes.'

In the silence that followed, Hanna al-Farah thought hard. She knew how able Zafir Hammuda was in a fast, brutal exchange of prolonged gunfire. How cool he was in backing up with lead and in getting the mission completed. He also had powers of leadership, should anything happen to the team leader.

She nodded, reluctantly. 'If you say so, Zina.'

Zina watched her, calmly. She knew the Biarritz trial run had gone well. Eight leading Basque terrorists killed in their home territory, a faultless exfiltration and no one in the press or, from what she had heard from Hanna, in the French or other secret services, had the merest notion as to who had committed the massacre.

'The question is, have you learned from it?'

Zina said she had. They all had. And she had altered her plan for the Beauregard assignment accordingly.

'Now run over your schedule for placing the team in New York. Will they all be entering the USA under diplomatic cover?'

Zina said no. Two would be going on visitors' visas, which belonged to two regular Lebanese travellers to the United States, who had been persuaded to allow their passports to be used. After the Connecticut Contract, these two unfortunates were to be terminated. At present they were guests of Abu Nidal's at the Naji al-Ali camp, in Libya.

The others would enter America as members of Arab delegations to United Nations Week. Zafir Hammuda as a driver with the Algerian Delegation; Noor Jalud as a secretary with the Kuwaitis – but everyone knew she was in fact the mistress of the Kuwaiti Minister's favourite son; Ben Turabi, the grenade man, was entering as a cook with the Moroccans; and, of course, Zina Farouche was on the security staff of the Tunisian Delegation.

'And as such', she informed Hanna al-Farah with a degree of quiet pride, 'I shall be attending security briefings with the American Diplomatic Security Service and the FBI.'

Hanna settled into a comfortable couch and smiled. 'You know, child, you could rise far after this . . .'

'I'll be glad when it's over,' said Zina. In the silence which followed, she became aware of a change in the atmosphere. It was a change which she was quietly surprised to discover engendered a slight *frisson*, a hint of a thrill, in the pit of her stomach. She glanced away from the older woman's appraising gaze, to the sideboard, on which stood a tall, filigree silver jug, on an electric hot-plate, and a number of tumblers, in similar silver holders, with delicate handles.

'Shall I bring you some mint tea?' she asked.

'That would be nice, thank you, Zina.'

And Zina Farouche, aged twenty-seven, a political killer since the age of fourteen, meekly crossed to the sideboard and poured from the warm silver jug two tumblers of sweet mint tea.

Beside the jug was a slim remote-control wand for an expensive Bang & Olufsen sound system. She selected CD channel number four, which was a collection of love songs in Arabic by Fat'mah Baloush. Whenever she heard it, Zina was reminded of the Chatilla Camp, when the radio had played Fat'mah Baloush night and day. Before the Israelis. Before the massacres.

She took the tumblers across the softly lit room and handed one to Hanna, then sat beside her, on the soft leather couch.

For a moment or two, they both sipped, without speaking.

Then Hanna quietly laid her mint tea down, on an inlaid teak and ivory coffee table. And, as the young terrorist's pulse quickened, Hanna al-Farah gently slipped the straps of Zina's blue dress over her tanned, lithe shoulders and with infinite tenderness undid the zip at the back.

'Oh, child,' she murmured, gazing at the angry red weal, where a 9mm slug from the doomed Pepe Orué had only just missed its mark, 'how close we came to losing you.'

And the Lebanese girl arced her slender neck as Hanna let her gossamer tongue trace lightly over the graze. Zina could feel al-Farah's soft breath, aromatic from the mint tea, on her shoulder.

Zina Farouche put her own tumbler down and stood up, allowing the light, linen dress to slide to the floor. It was all she had been wearing, apart from her shoes.

Hanna explored this child of violence with her eyes, as Zina slowly stepped over the discarded clothing and stood facing her, trembling like a racehorse. Then the Commander of Assassins shuddered and reached out a manicured hand to stroke the desirable skin of her latest conquest.

'My God, child,' she breathed, close now to the fine, golden down covering the girl's belly, 'you are so ready.'

Zina Farouche let her hooded eyes settle on the woman in front of her. She lifted her left foot and placed it further astride, feeling more deliciously exposed, more wanton, than she could ever remember.

'Oh, yes,' she whispered, 'oh, yes . . .'

And in Arabic, the voice of Fat'mah Baloush sang, 'If our love is doomed, then that's the way it has to be. It is fate. It is the will of Allah.'

6

Dangerous Times

While the Abu Nidal team prepared to infiltrate the city of New York using their various covers, and Joe Cleary worked with the Diplomatic Security Service to cover every eventuality in the course of United Nations Week that might pose a threat to their assignment, to keep the Egyptian Foreign Minister and his Ambassador to the USA from harm, and while David Arbuthnot Jardine wrestled with his dilemma of whether or not to sound the alarm over the Iranian Service's contract for multiple homicide on the Connecticut coast, young James Gant settled in to the relative monotony of his work with Clerical 17, in that drab SIS office overlooking the Foreign Office quadrangle.

Stan, Angeline and Eric had given generously of their time, during his first couple of weeks, but now James had a desk of his own and he was expected to keep his head down and get on with it, pulling his weight and processing a full quarter of the volume of intelligence assessments and memos flowing every hour of the working day from SIS Headquarters in the rococo Green Palace at Vauxhall Bridge for distribution to 'subscribers' within the Foreign and Commonwealth Office machine at home and abroad.

It was a tall order, and the information he was rapidly becoming privy to was very frequently quite dramatic, particularly when even careful screening and deliberate obfuscation could not hide the fact that men and women had taken incredible risks to acquire and pass on the most closely guarded secrets certain nations and organisations within them possessed.

The recipients of this secret intelligence were mostly Heads of Departments, senior foreign policy advisors and decision takers, right up to the Permanent Secretary, the Secretary of the Cabinet Office and, through his closest aide, a Permanent Under Secretary, to Patrick Orde, the Foreign Secretary

All in all, James Gant was satisfied with his new career. He had been invited to Personnel, shortly after his posting to Whitehall, and there Malcolm Strong, the SIS officer who had joined him in the Boatman's Tavern behind Chiswick Mall, had congratulated him on passing out of Euan Stevenson's Operation Marigold with what Strong had described in his understated way as 'a very acceptable confidential report' from old leather-face himself.

'A propitious beginning,' said Strong. He advised Gant to work on bringing his main languages up to serious bilingual standard, and to cultivate his already sharp awareness of everything going on around him, however seemingly insignificant, both within the Office environment and in his life generally – in other words, Peripheral Events – 'in order to achieve the calibre required to assign you to Field Operations'.

James must have seemed fairly pissed off at this condescending verdict, for Malcolm Strong had appeared quietly amused and had wandered off, made two cups of real coffee, Colombian, and had told him about his own first assignment; infiltrating the cocaine Cartel of Colombian war-lord Pablo Escobar, posing as a Peruvian drug smuggler.

Strong had been tasked to replace another SIS man who had been killed in mysterious circumstances, in a graveyard in Bogotá. And the job Strong had landed with Escobar? His go-between with the Colombian Government, to negotiate a brief prison term which Malcolm Strong had gone on to serve along with Don Pablo, before they had all escaped and lived a nerve-wracking life on the run, until one by one all Escobar's henchmen had been gunned down, and finally the big fish himself, '*El Padrino*', had died in a hail of bullets, directed there by Strong, via a satellite communications link to SIS in England and back to the Colombian Secret Police in Bogotá.

'So you see', concluded Strong gently, 'why we really do insist on, and I know it sounds precious, profound excellence.

With perhaps a couple of areas for improvement, provided we think you will improve without getting us all compromised.'

Well, bless my soul, thought Gant to himself, we do take ourselves seriously.

And the very next day, working quietly in Clerical 17, our young man found himself processing a note from the Directorate of Operations to Sir Derek Prideau, Permanent Under-Secretary, and the Foreign Secretary's closest advisor and confidant.

In the note, using the generic codename 'Dante', was a comment from the chief of D/OPS, referred to as DAJ (for David Arbuthnot Jardine), that the attached list of names was in all probability a team of terrorists assembled over the last few months by a Tunisian national, originally a Palestinian refugee, gender female, name of Zina Farouche.

She was on the files as a member of Abu Nidal's Fatah Revolutionary Council, and, while Farouche's gang was suspected of carrying out the Biarritz multiple killing, SIS did not assess that had been their principal task. According to Jardine, a reliable source continued to insist the woman had been tasked with a far greater international incident, much bigger than Biarritz, which, although a dramatic piece of terrorist theatre, was still a mere sideshow in global terms.

'Sadly,' someone with the initials MLD – Marietta, maybe Lucretia, Delice? – had neatly handwritten in the margin of this Top Secret memorandum, 'our asset with primary access is no longer active, and we have no indication of Dante's ultimate target.'

James Gant read and re-read this document. Then, out of mere, idle curiosity, he accessed on his computer screen the Top Secret internal SIS directory, checking for Marietta's middle name – it was Lydia. Gant was cleared to retrieve such information, but he was required to log his reason for doing so. In this instance, he noted it was to obtain Catnap's fax number. The very ease with which he had strayed into that protected computer file was not immediately significant to Gant, and if the entire Dante traffic had not been destined to become something akin to an obsession, that small act of casual electronic burglary would probably have been immaterial.

But during the morning, certain phrases from that note stuck in his mind, including Marietta's neat scribble in the margin – 'our asset with primary access is no longer active'. Why? Had she meant asset simply retired from the clandestine life? Gant thought not. And he began to wonder precisely what was to be the 'greater international incident.'

What fresh atrocity did this murderous bunch have on their agenda? And even as he contemplated, he was transported back, in his mind's eye, to that dreadful morning in Rome Airport, with the grimly smiling girl, not much older than April Lee Stuart, pumping bullets into an hysterical crowd of Israeli passengers.

Old men and women butchered. Infants with parts of their bodies hammered into the air.

'You all right, sport?' asked Eric quietly, as he left for his mid-morning stroll in St James's Park, and a smoke of his pipe, recently banned from the office by Angeline and Stan.

'Fine,' replied Gant, 'I'm just fine.'

'Sweating, though,' observed Eric.

'Touch of the flu coming on . . .' smiled James Gant, wanly.

'Well don't try to kiss me till it's over,' replied Eric, the former hero, and he went out.

Gant shrugged off the awful memory and returned to study the memo.

'Zina Farouche', he read, and he knew it was one of those names that was going to stick in his mind, like snatches of a tune, or some radio catchphrase.

The Beaufort Street apartment Gant had rented from his former BBC colleague, war correspondent Martin Chimes, was on the top, actually the attic, floor of a converted private house, just a few doors down from Tulley's, the Chelsea furniture store, where for the last sixty years young couples had shopped for comfortable, reasonably priced sofas, chairs and tables.

It was convenient for local delicatessens, laundromats, bars, bistros – which London chic had decided to call brasseries – bookshops, video libraries and the MGM Cinema with its four screens.

Free of his engagement to marry Rebecca, Gant spent his evenings and weekends visiting the cinema, eating with friends, reading, listening to jazz and avoiding Charlotte and Hugh. For he felt very bad about his involvement with Charlie. Every time (and there had not, in truth, been many) he had vowed to himself that would be the last.

And each time he had talked about it with her, and she had agreed.

There was not the slightest question in the young man's mind about the profound stupidity of what they had become involved in. More than the immorality of the situation, more than the mutually destructive course they had embraced, more than the illegality of their liaison, James was appalled at himself for the complete senselessness of his actions.

And yet, no two lives on this planet are the same, he told himself, and the naturalness of that first coupling in the hotel room, overlooking the Laguna and the island of San Francesco del Deserto, had lingered on.

It was not as if Gant was either sexually naive, or lacking in opportunity for more acceptable liaisons. Before Rebecca, apart from pleasant dalliances of little consequence, there had been three other serious relationships. One at Oxford, one with a stunning, slender, copper-haired doctor he had met in Kurdistan and, of course, the gorgeous Roisin Clancy, a restorer of fine art who worked at the Royal Academy and whose father was a renowned Belfast newspaper editor.

If anyone could have saved James Gant from his flawed hunger, it had been Roisin. Only in her arms had he felt anything approaching the same all-enveloping, utterly inflaming and complete harmony of mutual arousal that afterwards, lying together, peacefully spent and slick with sweat, made him so close to being . . . home, wherever that was.

And with Roisin, as with Charlotte, it had always seemed, somehow, illicit. Too much pleasure to be permitted to ordinary people, as Charlie had once remarked.

Like all stolen pleasures it couldn't last and Roisin had told him, one matter-of-fact day, as she stepped back into her pale-green slip, that Joe Flannigan, the bloodstock dealer from Newmarket, had proposed to her and she had the ring in the glove compartment of her old Renault parked outside.

So that was the end of that. A lifebelt to more conventional pleasures abruptly withdrawn.

But James knew his and Charlie's lust for each other could easily end in disaster. For a start, discovery would lead to the end of his career with the Firm, for broad-minded though they had turned out to be – quite impressively so – Gant was sure they drew the line at incest.

So, after their latest transgression, in Charlie's flat, which as usual had taken him by surprise, James avoided his innocently decadent sister, and her fiancé, and went about his life quietly, working hard at Clerical 17, and spending his leisure hours as described.

He was experiencing, in what the Ryemarsh people later described as his 'limbo phase', a certain feeling of anti-climax, of unreality, which was not just because of his solitary day-to-day existence.

The thrill of being recruited, the training and his Rome assignment had not prepared James Gant for the flatness of being dropped back into cold, mundane reality. And working in London, his familiar home territory, bumping into former friends and acquaintances from Wonderland, added to, rather than assuaged, a disquieting feeling of detachment. Gant felt like a character in one of those Star Trek episodes, who had been beamed down to a near-facsimile of a city once familiar but, at the same time, quite alien.

It is perhaps inevitable that servants of the clandestine professions tend to keep themselves to themselves. Fairly soon their circles of friends from earlier days reduce in direct relation to their progress through the secret journey. It can really become very easy for a spook to relax only with other spooks, for it is only in their company that he or she feels truly comfortable.

Add to that the fact that one experienced espionage operator can very often recognise another, of whatever service or nationality – seafarers and police officers, paederasts and, it is said, pickpockets, acquire the same empathy – and we have the makings of events ranging from the absurd to the tragic. So, quite sensibly, the training and conditioning of the very best intelligence services specifically includes advice on how to avoid falling into such obvious pitfalls.

For the sense of being different from others, of being in a kind of state of secret grace, is a dead give-away and must be resisted twenty-four hours a day.

James Gant had been warned of this, and he had been counselled to maintain an easy-going social life with the best of his friends and acquaintances from his life pre-SIS. But it required something of an effort. Old chums' conversation seemed banal after the undercover life with Marigold and compared to those documents marked Top Secret which crossed his desk every hour of his new working life, each one allowing just a flicker of light, just a glimpse, into some dark corner of the deadly game that civilised nations earnestly deny, and, indeed, condemn with solemn mendacity.

Gant had experienced similar emotions when he had begun to take his cameras to war and to countries laid desolate by famine. Each return to London's pubs and bars, with their cosy coteries of the would-be worldly and cynical, had made him feel alienated and remote. Then, Edith Treffewin, of all people, had spotted her favourite nephew's problem attitude and she had asked him to do her a 'tiny favour, darling' and help her with a project she had in the East End of London, locating runaway youngsters and abandoned children, living rough on the streets and thieving or prostituting themselves to stay alive.

'Don't imagine, dear Jimmy,' she had said in that wonderful *grande dame* way of hers, 'one has to run away to bloody Bosnia, or Timbuktu, to find horror, or to "see life", whatever that means. Just get your sweet arse down here if you want a taste of reality, darling.'

James Gant smiled at the memory. He was sitting in his flat, nursing a large gin and water, a taste he had acquired in the British general's sandbagged headquarters in Sarajevo. Edith was, quite simply, wonderful. Edith would understand about Charlie and him. Dear boy, she would murmur, you two really are just *too* naughty and you do know, Jim, it's got to stop . . .

James nodded, her imagined voice as real as if she had been standing at his shoulder. He was playing a UB-40 compact disc, a mellow track called 'Don't Let It Pass You By'.

That's me, he thought, never prepared to let anything pass me by. No experience, no incident, no . . . adventure.

Bloody Peter Pan, he considered. One day, boy, you are going to have to grow up. Join the dull people. At which moment the music ended and the track changed to one called 'Don't Break My Heart . . .'

Gant stared at his tumbler of gin and sighed. What a fix, dear old Edith, he reflected; super career, thanks to you, world my oyster, as you would say, and here I am, in love with the one girl on earth who's forbidden.

He smiled ruefully, aware this was the first time he had dared to admit the blindingly obvious, shrugged and drained the gin.

The next morning, nursing a mild hangover, James Gant worked his way through the pile of classified documents in his IN tray, initialling most of them for immediate distribution to subscribers within the Foreign and Commonwealth Office and its various related departments. A couple he referred back to their sources, mildly querying if they really wished to mention this or that source or operational method.

At 11.09, just as Stan deposited a mug of tea – 'standard NATO', i.e. milk and one sugar – and a chocolate digestive biscuit on his desk, Gant lifted the next file for his attention and began to read:

TOP SECRET – DANTE EYES ONLY

From D/CATNAP

File 6/3009/18

For PUS/2b

DANTE 30/8

1. BIARRITZ incident now confirmed to DANTE. Source A-1. Team leader confirmed to have been ZF.

2. This multiple killing was undertaken as a favour to PIRA Chief of Operations. The ETA-Negro victims had failed to pay for 300lbs SEMTEX explosive, 14 × AKS automatic assault rifles and, the principal transgression, 3 × STINGER ground-to-air

missiles. PIRA had been trying to obtain payment ($475,000) for four years.

3. Because of current temporary cease-fire, PIRA were not able to carry out punishment op. themselves. ABU NIDAL undertook contract on their behalf.

4. One theory being considered is that BIARRITZ was undertaken by DANTE as opposed to any other ABU NIDAL unit, as a form of operational training, a rehearsal, if you like, for the main item on their agenda.

5. Acting on this assumption, we consider it prudent to continue to seek identification of their final target.

The document was signed MLD, and she had written neatly in the margin, beside the reference to PIRA (the Provisional IRA) the name of the current IRA Chief of Staff, who featured daily on television making portentous noises about peace in our time.

Gant scanned the message for any breaches of SIS disclosure policy. Of course, there were none. Not where Marietta was the author, he was learning. And as he sipped his standard NATO brew, he read the message again.

'Team leader ZF' . . . in other words, Zina Farouche.

He wondered what this woman looked like. Was she some middle-aged harridan, swarthy and mannish, as some Arab nationals became, from the fierce sun and the cruel hardship? Or was she young? Did she look, he knew he was really asking, like that girl in the Rome Airport thing? Cool, attractive, and full of hate.

The Dante traffic which passed across James Gant's desk in the next few days began to present to his trained editor's eye a picture, where the gaps were sometimes more eloquent than the released information, of a fanatical, ruthless and resourceful murder gang of proven efficiency.

Just after lunch on the Tuesday, a secure fax was dropped on his desk by Angeline. 'You're on Dante, I think,' she had whispered provocatively, dropping the flimsy paper onto his desk, like a billet doux.

The fax was from Marietta's office and it read:

TOP SECRET – DANTE EYES ONLY
NO FOREIGN

Facsimile 18/24417/3017

From D/CATNAP

File 6/3009/23

For PUS/2b

DANTE 8/8

Information on passport/visa details and diplomatic credentials of the following would be helpful:

FAROUCHE, Zina	Tunisian Foreign Service.
f/27	Paris Embassy
HAMMUDA, Zafir	Algerian Foreign Ministry
m/34	Algiers
JALUD, Noor	Kuwaiti Foreign Ministry Staff
f/23	United Nations New York USA
TURABI, Ben	Moroccan Foreign Service
m/32	Damascus Embassy

Also any details on passport/visa movements of:
al SHARIK, Mustafa m/29 PWB

James Gant's pulse quickened. This was the hit team: 'f/27' indicated that the female, Zina Farouche, was twenty-seven years old. The same age as Gant himself.

He found himself wondering just how the Firm was planning to stop this murder gang in its tracks. And he began to think about the unknown victims. Who? Where? Somewhere obvious, like Jerusalem? Or maybe London again. Paris? He also wondered what had happened to the documents between serials 6/3009/18 and 6/3009/23, and shouldn't they have been processed through him?

It took another thirty-six hours for James Gant to twig that not all secret intelligence regarding Dante was being shared with any foreign service. Not even the Americans, who were virtually partners in a substantial proportion of SIS's work.

A note from David Jardine to Derek Prideau in the Secretary of State's office was unambiguous:

. . . in answer to Patrick's request to supply all DANTE intelligence to our Cousins in Grosvenor Square, please be advised that protection of assets is considered vital, repeat, vital, in this matter.

I have already lost one deep-penetration agent, of irreplaceable value, in part due to our Cousins' size fourteen boots.

Please rest assured that this service is working round the clock to ascertain the target of DANTE, and as soon as I can, I shall share that with my opposite number at Langley, as well as, of course, with your good self.

D.A.J. Director/Operations SIS

Now, precisely how James Gant suspected from this somewhat testy memo that Jardine was lying, by suggesting he had no idea who was Dante's target, was hard to quantify. But that was his gut feeling.

Derek Prideau, the Permanent Under-Secretary, who was a wise bird, alert to every dodge in both the 'straight' Foreign Office and the Firm, it is assumed read and filed the memo, taking it at face value. So why did Gant not? Is it precisely because he was a relatively new boy, not yet fully detached from Wonderland?

Either way, Gant felt in his bones that the Director of Operations knew one hell of a lot more about Zina Farouche and her Dante team's target than he was prepared to disclose. And, while he had no illusions about the world he had been happy to enter, aware that all kinds of ruthless, even cruel, decisions were made every day, yet he was intrigued – no more at that stage – to witness even the shadows of such things unfolding.

In his suspicions, James was in harmony with Marietta Delice. But Marietta, being a survivor from way back, was content, for the moment, to keep her powder dry.

He read and re-read Jardine's note, 'I have already lost one deep-penetration agent, of irreplaceable value . . .'

That seemed to be driving the rest of the message, '. . . Please rest assured', and, '. . . of course . . .'.

In a pig's ear, thought Gant. This is one highly pissed-off

senior spook and he is not going to risk another priceless agent if he can help it.

So, the sixty-four-thousand dollar question; does David Jardine actually know not only who, but the where and the when of Dante's planned massacre?

Assuming the information on Dante was accurate – and on Jardine's own admission it came from an 'irreplaceable' source – it was bound to be something on the international stage. For the Iranian Special Missions Directorate would not have contracted out to Abu Nidal anything less than a global atrocity on the scale of the Pan Am airliner bomb over Lockerbie, in Scotland, on 23 December 1988.

But this time, the expertise assigned to the terrorists' task was not the placing of time-bombs on passenger aircraft. Judging by the collection of psychopaths the Farouche woman had assembled, it was to be face-to-face, eye contact and murder by gun and cold steel.

By the Thursday of that week, James Gant had processed nine Top Secret Dante communications, from D/OPS and Catnap. He was interested, no more at that stage, not yet really worried, in identifying hints that David Jardine was keeping vital information to himself. And indeed he was still confident of finding clues about what active measures were being taken to head off the terrorists.

Would they be 'neutralised' before they could accomplish their awful assignment? Would they be arrested as they congregated, wherever it was their target was located? Or would the intended victims either be moved out of harm's way, or be so obviously super-protected that the game would cease to be worth the candle? Both were standard moves in the protection business, which James had learned about from the Poet, in the SIS training school near Scarborough, on the north-east coast.

By that Thursday morning, Gant's interest in this gathering drama had become, although he resisted the realisation, close to preoccupation.

He knew from long conversations into the small hours with Euan Stevenson and the others in Rome, that, contrary to protestations, even at ministerial level, seriously violent skulduggery was from time to time employed by the office.

Sometimes using clandestine units seconded from the Special Air Service, sometimes even more shadowy characters from the murky world of free-lance operators and mercenaries. It's a tough old world, Euan had remarked, and the taxpayer expects us to get our jackets off, should the situation require it.

So at that time, James Gant told himself, he needed have few worries about the Dante terror group actually succeeding in its horrific purpose. He was merely fascinated, he rationalised, to be able to watch the clandestine system in action.

Until, just before noon that day, he found himself processing a classified reply to Bill Greenfield, the CIA Station Chief in London, in answer to a routine enquiry faxed by the American Embassy-based office to D/OPS in the green palace at Vauxhall Cross.

A copy of the CIA man's original note was pinned to the reply. It was basically a list of foreign diplomats and politicians scheduled to attend UN Week in New York, along with a request for any secret intelligence which might indicate a particular threat to any of those listed.

Beside one or two such names, Greenfield had scribbled comments or specific queries.

For instance, beside the details of the PLO delegation, including Yasser Arafat, Greenfield had noted that the CIA itself had arranged for a special team from its Langley Virginia headquarters, along with thirty men and women from the Diplomatic Security Service, to be specially assigned to protect them, and that a request from the Israelis to slip one or two secret agents in with the US protection team had been firmly rejected.

And beside the name of Ramses Selim, the Egyptian Ambassador to the USA, he had written:

> Selim is ducking out of the UN thing to spend a couple of days with Mike Curtis, our man in Cairo. Curtis married money and the two families are getting together at his wife's place in Connecticut. It will be an additional headache for DSS getting them in and out of NYC plus protection for them in the boondocks. Any special info on Islamic Tide or other Tehran-inspired threats which might be a problem here? We have

unconfirmed rumors about Abu Nidal playing footsy with the ayatollahs.

I'll bloody say so, thought James Gant, and there is no way D/OPS can duck out of this. But, as his eye flicked over the various, in some cases detailed, replies, he was astonished to read:

> Ambassador Selim. While Tehran and Hezbollah continue to be behind various hostile moves and acts of terror, this office has no specific indication that the Egyptian delegation is in more danger than usual. There are indeed indications that a unit of the Abu Nidal faction has been tasked by Tehran with acts of terror, but those have thus far been confined to Europe. See our report F/91167/k Spain. It is not improbable that the Biarritz excitement will see a lull in this group's activities. Please info if you can add more on this.

And it was signed D.A.J.

Oh, you bastard, thought Gant, and there was no longer any doubt in his mind that, if not directly lying to his American colleagues, David Jardine was at the very least being, in that immortal phrase, 'economical with the truth'.

Over the next week, when cooking for himself in the Beaufort Street apartment, or drinking with friends from the BBC Current Affairs unit, going to the movies or just shlepping around Fulham Road buying garbage disposal bags, electric light bulbs and stuff for the refrigerator, James Gant became increasingly haunted by his knowledge of the Dante team and their allegedly unknown target.

He found himself wondering over and over about the identity of those unsuspecting future victims. Would there be women? Children? And he finally understood that the trauma of Rome had never really gone away. It had just remained submerged. Like a submarine . . .

On two occasions he woke up about four in the morning, heart pounding and bathed in sweat, the screams of the dying and the clatter of machine-gun fire still clamouring from his dreadful dreams.

And each day, Gant had found himself waiting with a sense

of mounting foreboding for every new development in the Dante material crossing his desk.

By the following Wednesday, his preoccupation had become close to an obsession, and James volunteered to remain in the office over the lunch break, to man the telephones.

Quite what he intended to accomplish he was not sure, and he still had a suspicion that he was making a monumental fool of himself, that this was precisely the sort of thing he was bound to encounter with increasing frequency, the closer he came to the hub of the Firm's business.

However, James Gant had long ago promised himself that he would not be one of the pliable masses when push came to shove. He knew from his own work with the BBC in Bosnia, Kurdistan and Cambodia that the world was full of horrors. In a way, he supposed, he had subconsciously sought out such experiences in order to cauterise the pain of the Rome thing.

And even as a cameraman, Gant had acquired a reputation for getting involved. It was James who had arranged for starving orphans in Bosnia to be taken by British soldiers on UN duty to the comparative safety of a hospice in Sarajevo. And it had been James who had steadfastly refused to stop filming when Turkish commandos on the Iraq border had wanted to gun down eighteen Kurd irregulars, thereby saving their lives (for the time being), by putting his own on the line.

But on every previous occasion, he had always been an observer, remote from involvement, hiding behind the viewfinder of a camera.

But not this time. Now he was among the players.

As soon as he had the place to himself, Gant extracted from his pile of files one marked REFER, which held classified data relating to material being dealt with by one of his colleagues.

This provided him with a reason to be at one of the other desks, in the event of someone returning unexpectedly.

Feeling extremely guilty, with one eye on the door, which he had considered locking, the young intelligence officer unlocked the deep secure drawers in Stan's desk and lifted out the folders of documents Stan was working on, together with his 3.5″ computer discs.

Gant took a deep breath and, as calmly as if he had every right to be pirating his colleague's secret work, searched rapidly through the material, looking for any mention of the United Nations Week in New York City, or of the Egyptian delegation there, or of Abu Nidal, the Iranians or the Dante group.

Finding nothing, he replaced everything exactly as he had found it and moved across to Angeline's desk, repeating the exercise.

Here he had more luck, and he learned that Angeline was handling Top Secret Intelligence data concerning the British delegation's visit. James could not control a flush of apprehension at reading details of meetings scheduled to be held, informally and in conditions of covert security, with various unlikely bedfellows of Her Majesty's Government, some of whom were, on the face of it, outside diplomatic contact and indeed some of whom were at daggers drawn with each other.

However, there was not a word about Abu Nidal, or the threat from Tehran, or Dante, or anything suggesting a cover-up, or withholding of intelligence on the subject.

This is none of my business, Gant realised, and he replaced the files and locked the drawer.

As he rose from Eric's desk, the door opened and Gant's heart almost stopped. Bathos followed promptly as the enormous backside of Jeanette the tea lady waddled in, the good woman tugging her trolley of tea and coffee urns.

'Ah, excellent . . .' pronounced Gant lamely.

'How yo, massa?' muttered Jeanette, whose black slippers almost disappeared beneath her sagging tree trunks of ankles.

James could not help feeling a twinge of humour.

'Jeanette,' he said, 'I happen to know you were born in Stoke Newington, not a million miles from here. Your father was, I remember hearing you tell Angeline, an Arsenal supporter before you were born, so, please, what's with the Swannee River stuff?'

Jeanette straightened up and puffed out her cheeks, giving

James a steely glance. 'Just 'aving a larf,' she declared. 'Tea or coffee?'

'Coffee would be great. Thanks.'

So four precious minutes went by, while Jeanette poured coffee and they exchanged a couple of words about nothing in particular.

And when she had gone, James went back to Stan's desk and had one last quick look through the other drawers, which held felt-tip pens, paper clips, a Mars bar, a small bottle of Lucozade, some Tippex, a half-empty packet of throat lozenges and, of all things, a packet of condoms – pack of three, unopened. Gant frowned and could not help wondering about Stan and the either over-heated or short sighted (he still had not figured out which) Angeline.

And at the very back of the drawer was a slim, worn, black 1993 diary. It was filled with unremarkable entries about birthdays and vacation schedules, squash games and endless weekends of orienteering and cross-country running. On the last few pages were phone numbers and addresses, and on the third last page was a series of numerics and letters which James Gant instantly recognised as his own secure computer access codes and exit formulae.

On the pages before that, in older, different colours of ink, were three other access codes, each carefully written in Stan's neat hand.

Gant glanced at his watch. 1.42 p.m. No one usually came back from lunch until 2 o'clock on the dot. Sometimes later. He quickly copied the words and numbers onto a slip of paper, replaced the black diary exactly as he had found it and returned to his desk.

Aware of his heart thumping and feeling perspiration trickle down his neck, James Gant opened up his own computer access path until he arrived at the query:

PLEASE ENTER PERSONAL ACCESS CODE
THIS IS A ONE-TIME ONLY SESAME

Which meant get it wrong and the system shuts down.

He paused and contemplated. Each of the three codes he had copied (stolen, he knew, was more accurate) would be specific either to Angeline, Eric or Stan. There was no way of knowing which was which, and the only Personal Ident cipher he knew was Angeline's, for he sat near her and over the weeks had more or less automatically, thanks to his recent training, memorised it.

James knew that one mistake would not only shut down his venture into computer hacking. It would also identify the electronic signature of his own personal keyboard, for the Firm's Security Section had devised an additional security measure whereby only certain keyboards could gain entry to specific, protected SIS directories. And in the event of a stranger trying to use it, such a keyboard would silently shout HELP and shut itself off. Which would leave James Gant with the equivalent of a huge cartoon arrow pointing down at him, like Jehovah's accusing finger, and a whole lot of explaining to do.

Why in God's name am I doing this? he asked himself. Why shouldn't I just take the pay cheque and watch from the sidelines, like a good little spy?

Well, James Gant knew the answer to that. At Rome Airport he had been a helpless kid. And now he was not. It was just that simple.

He sighed, took a deep breath, contemplated the three access lists and decided that the one written in purple was Angeline's. He entered the first digits, typing rapidly, committed to succeed or fail.

Zina Farouche was worried. She gazed down at Long Island Sound as the Air France Concorde settled into its final approach. Sitting beside her was Azouz Ben Larbi, the Tunisian Foreign Ministry's senior Economic and Press Counsellor, who was also in the Tunisian Delegation's advance party and who would have been dismayed if he had suspected his colleague was in fact an international terrorist.

Preparations for the Delegation's visit to New York had thus far gone like clockwork, and the clandestine assembling of her team of killers was working smoothly. No cause for concern on those fronts.

She was worried about Hanna al-Farah. On reflection, she could think of no way she could have avoided accepting a sexual liaison with the older woman. Hanna's lust for her had been transparent, and when they had made that first rendezvous in Paris, it had become clear to Zina it was only a matter of time. By making the first move, she had hoped, in that survivor's way of hers, to ingratiate herself with the woman who held her fate in her hands.

Unfortunately, the pretty Palestinian told herself, it had not stopped at mere lust. That was a hunger she had long since learned to use to her advantage. No, Hanna al-Farah, 'Commander of the Assassins', was beginning to get fond of her. And with fondness would come possessiveness, Zina Farouche knew that much.

And with possessiveness . . .?

Zina did not like the idea of that. Even in the darkest days of the struggle, even during her ordeal in the pit, at the hands of her tormentors at Station 16, nobody had truly possessed her, for the more she had longed for death's merciful release, the further she had moved away from their power.

But Hanna al-Farah was an intelligent and ruthless woman. Someone Zina was required to work with on a regular basis. And she knew it was going to require all of her instinct for survival to control the developing relationship. The sex was fine; the young Palestinian felt her cheeks burn at the recollection of their last encounter, at her . . . abandon. But a love affair?

No way.

'If our love is doomed,' the Arab singer Fat'mah Baloush had sung, as they made love together, 'that's the way it has to be. It is the will of Allah.'

Zina Farouche prayed, as the tyres of the Concorde hovered those last inches of flight, above the tarmac of JFK, that their lust would not turn to love.

For that could only lead to disaster.

The Tunisian delegation would be staying at the Essex House Hotel, on Central Park South. They had arranged to share the sixteenth floor with the Moroccan delegation, the Tunisians occupying everything to the west (the right) of the elevators and the Moroccans the entire premises to the east.

Zina had been seconded from the Paris Embassy to the

Tunisian Delegation and she was one of three Security Attachés responsible for liaison with the American authorities to ensure the physical protection of the Tunisian Foreign Minister and his senior cohorts.

She had arrived on 5 September, three weeks ahead of United Nations Week, to meet with the US Diplomatic Security Service in their New York Field Office, apprise herself of their risk assessment and the overview of their comprehensive Main Plan to ensure the smooth running of moving over two hundred foreign dignitaries around Manhattan in conditions of maximum security.

She would meet and strike a rapport with the particular individuals assigned to her Delegation and she would conduct a comprehensive floor-by-floor, corridor-by-corridor, elevator-by-elevator, reconnaissance of the hotel. She would prepare a plan of those and devise escape routes using staff stairways and elevators, both upwards, to the roof – she intended to inspect the roof in detail – and down to street level and below.

She was to familiarise herself with surrounding buildings, and routes and streets in the immediate vicinity and outwards; where the nearest medical facilities were, the fastest route to the 18th Precinct, which is what the New York Police Department called their Mid-Town North division's headquarters building; and many things like that.

In addition to the Department of State's Diplomatic Security Service, Zina Farouche was expected to make contact, both formal and informal, with officers of other US agencies involved in UN Week security – the US Secret Service, protecting America's own senior diplomats, and, of course, the President himself; FBI agents assigned to the UN Week Task Force; cops assigned to NYPD's Intelligence Division, for updates on local information on the terrorist threat; and, although they tended to be elusive, officers from the CIA's UN Station, based in Manhattan not far from the UN Building on East 46th.

This was the routine work of a Security Attaché and it was what was called an 'advance'. And in that first week in September, New York City was busy with scores of foreign security officers touching base with their US hosts, attending briefings and having quiet lunchtime gatherings, in order to net into and become part of one of the most massive security operations anywhere in the world.

And it happened every year.

The ketch, bobbing at anchor in Limassol harbour, was just about perfect, not unlike the yacht of David Jardine's dreams, which he sometimes drew on the margins of documents during boring meetings. His father had always managed to own a boat of some description, whenever he had been in funds, which was every few years. The lean ones had often been enlivened by Runyonesque episodes as the old boy, a racehorse breeder and trainer, embarked upon extravagant and imaginative ways to recoup his floundering fortunes.

The craft of Jardine's youth had ranged from a dipping gaff cutter, built in Largs, Scotland, in 1893, with open cockpit and two cramped berths under the fo'c's'le cover, to a rather attractive German motorised yawl, liberated by 'Colonel' Jardine (a rank he had temporarily and locally held in the Royal Marines, for three weeks at the end of the Second World War) from a Kiel canal dock in 1962, 'since nobody seemed to know within whose provenance it lay', which is to say he paid the dock supervisor a few thousand Marks to allow the slightly shabby, but basically sound, vessel to be towed away, out of sight, out of mind.

Jardine Senior had taken the yawl, originally *Die Fledermaus*, to Denmark, where friends of his owned a boatyard. Three months later, the seventeen-year-old David had driven his ageing MG TC two-seater to Dover, onto the ferry, and across France and northern Europe to Denmark, where his father had found an enthusiast willing to pay £540 for the car, which was more than twice what young Jardine had paid for it.

David Jardine and his father then sailed the newly named *Lucky Strike* back to Scotland. She had been lovingly restored, with great taste and with no expense spared, for hadn't the Colonel trained the winners of the Sandown Gold Cup (Blue Moth) and the Irish Derby (Fly's Eye) that year, and once again money had been no object.

Ever since then, David Jardine had gone sailing whenever

he could get the chance. Andrew and Sally had no great love of boats, and Dorothy positively hated them, so he had generally gone with colleagues from the office, or from kindred services. In fact some of his best sailing had been with Alan Clair who knew the Kennedys and Nantucket Sound in just about equal measure.

And this little ketch was a beauty. White hull, pale blue below the waterline, lowish freeboard, varnished mahogany superstructure and teak decks. Gold leaf scrolling on the bow, rope and teak rubbing-strake and her name in white on a mahogany board, above the square wheelhouse door – *Pyramus*.

'I have put a man on board,' said Constantine, and, sure enough, a lean, fit-looking young chap of about thirty lounged on deck, sitting on the hatch forrard of the wheelhouse, wearing faded jeans and a dark T-shirt, worn loose to cover his pistol. 'And I have spoken to the Inspector in charge of the Harbour Police. He is my wife's cousin.'

Would it were so simple in England, wished Jardine.

'Thanks, Connie,' he said.

'Also the Customs people have been told to do nothing until I release the craft. But we will have to do that later today.'

'Connie, you're a brick,' murmured Jardine, as the cutter's engine died and the white hull of *Pyramus* loomed suddenly large before them.

The cutter lost way exactly as its starboard gunwale seemed about to touch the clean white paint and the short boarding-ladder attached to the other boat's hull.

Jardine climbed up onto the ketch's deck and waited for Constantine, a Chief Superintendent of Police with Cyprus's Special Branch, to join him. Constantine Agamemnos was a stocky, short man in his mid-forties, with a mop of thick, black hair and a deceptively gentle demeanour. He smiled readily and his eyes were alert, like a sparrow's, missing nothing.

Connie had been on the Firm's payroll since before the Turkish invasion and the partitioning of his precious island. The jewel of the Mediterranean, he called it. And since Cyprus had become the offshore gathering-place for Middle

Eastern terrorists and warring Lebanese, Egyptian and Algerian political and religious groups, the Cypriot detective had earned his money, which worked out at around $1,900 each month, paid in cash out of Nicosia Station's slush fund.

The fact that he also sold information and administrative favours to the American DEA, the CIA, the French DGSE and the Mossad did not really bother Jardine. Perhaps a younger man would have been annoyed, shocked even, but the Englishman had been around the block a few times and he understood the entrepreneurial Third World culture of his paid agents in places like Cyprus, Peking and South America.

The teak deck had been kept scrubbed clean. Spotless, apart from the bloodied footprints.

'Bare feet,' he remarked.

'Yes. We think they swam out.'

They nodded to the young man, who had got to his feet and gone aft, to unlock the wheelhouse door.

In his telephone call to Jardine's Tite Street flat, at nine the previous night, Connie had mentioned frogmen, probably two.

'This is Demetrius,' said Connie. And Jardine nodded. The more Greeks he met on those occasions, the more he felt as if he had entered a time capsule, for his first encounter with the Demetriuses and Agamemnons of the region had been as a schoolboy studying the Peloponnesian War.

Demetrius slid back the door and the faint odour, the faint, sick-sweet, rotten fungus odour which had been a mere suggestion before, roared out from the sun-hot wheelhouse and the dark saloon cabin below like a horde of surprise phantasms.

Oh, yes, thought Jardine, even as he gagged on the putrid stench.

Hello again.

The floor of the wheelhouse was sticky with clotted blood. A crimson hand-print on the windscreen glass reminded him of an infant's painting class – Sally had brought home ragged-edged cardboard sheets with her palm prints in yellow and red and green – and two swathes of gore descended towards the floor indicating where someone had slid, or stumbled.

Jardine stepped down delicately into the cabin, where the

bright sunlight was dimmed by its drawn curtains, across the six portholes, three on each side.

As he stood there, squinting in the gloom, breathing through his mouth to limit the smell, his feet flexing alternately against the movement of the sea beneath and all around, the sight which met his gaze was so absolute in its horror that his senses, as they do at such moments, seemed to become instantly anaesthetised, and his emotional drive went into neutral.

'I have asked for the initial post-mortems to be carried out on board,' said Constantine, quietly, as if he were in a church.

Yes, thought Jardine, I can see why. As his eyes became accustomed to the gloom, he examined the cabin in detail. It was as if a hand grenade had exploded. Except there was no damage to the wood or fabric. And the severed limbs were too neatly cut off for an explosion.

'Did anyone hear it?' he asked, finding that, even at this late stage in a lifetime of such sights, he could still feel amazed – yes, and angry – at the human animal's capacity for cruelty.

'If they had,' replied Connie, 'they would probably have thought it was an outboard motor.'

'Of course,' said Jardine. They had been talking about the noise of a chainsaw.

'When I notified you of their arrival, what . . . sixteen days ago? . . . I kept a discreet eye on them.'

Oh, well done, Connie, thought Jardine, you've only gone and killed them.

'Nothing obvious, please understand. But I have much business in the harbour and a ketch at anchor is quite easy to observe without anyone noticing.'

'And what did you see?'

The Cypriot shrugged. 'They lived their cover. Early-morning clean up of the boat. One or both would come ashore in their rubber Zodiac. Buy fruit and things for the next voyage. They said they were sailing to Junieh.'

'Did you ever speak to them?'

Connie shook his head. 'My sister runs the harbour bar. They sometimes took coffee there, sometimes a meal in the evening.'

'So she spoke to them.'

'Sure.'

There were no flies, yet. But in this heat, the maggots would soon mature and become fat and grey, too bloated to use their wings. As he looked around the cabin, it became clear the boat had been ransacked.

'Did they say anything of note?'

Connie looked puzzled. 'Are you asking, did they sing . . .?'

Jardine smiled, beginning to feel quite faint in the sticky foetid air of the cramped saloon. 'Did they say anything interesting, Connie?'

'Just what you would expect. They were dispossessed Persians, he had been an administrator in the Shah's court. The yacht was all they had been able to take with them, and a few thousand dollars in a Beirut bank.'

Yes, remembered Jardine, that had been the legend with which Vevak had furnished them. He had been impressed by their thoroughness at the time. Seven years ago. It had become apparent that their cover as husband and wife had brought them a little happiness. His eyes strayed to a severed head. The nose had been cut off, doubtless early in their longest night.

'So was I right?' enquired the detective. 'I felt it in my water. Are they two of ours?'

David Jardine turned and looked his occasional agent straight in the eye. He loved the 'ours' bit. That was rich.

'Absolutely not,' he said.

Connie nodded slowly. The policeman in him receiving conflicting signals. 'So I can call in the cavalry? Cops, Customs, try for an ID?'

'Why not?' Jardine gazed around the stinking charnel house one last time, then turned to leave.

'Press?'

'It's your show now, Connie. Thanks for giving me first refusal.' He climbed agilely into the wheelhouse and out onto the deck, where he rejoiced in the light breeze and sea air.

'I just had a feeling you would be interested.'

'I know. And I'm grateful. Don't ever feel shy about doing it again. We are particularly interested in the Iranians these days. You were absolutely right to get in touch. You have a remarkable . . . instinct. Which is why we love you.'

Connie beamed. He knew David Jardine was a legendary agent runner, and he was pleased to be patronised by the best in the business.

'My lady wife would esteem it, if you can join us at home this evening. A little light supper, some Mavrodaphne . . .?'

'Thanks, Connie; I'd better look in on the office while I'm here. First flight out in the morning.'

The policeman smiled as brightly as ever. They had the same conversation each time. 'No problem.'

And he waited as Jardine swung down into the cutter. 'I'll just wait here,' he said. 'Time to get the circus started.'

'Sure.' Jardine grinned. Now that he had passed, on Connie's scoop, the Cypriot would no doubt be offering it to his other patrons. Probably a profitable day's work, since he was paid on a bonus system.

'Oversight is dead,' Jardine said. 'Murdered by chainsaw. Interrogated first. Also his wife. Killer unknown but modus suggests Vevak. Wrap that up in a signal and send it to Ronnie at London Facilities.'

Fiona Macleod glanced up from her shorthand pad. She had been posted to Nicosia on recovering from the Kensington car bomb. 'Copy to Catnap?'

Jardine gazed at her. The young woman had learned a lot in her three years with the firm. He nodded. 'Why not . . .?'

They were in the SIS office on the third floor of the British High Commission overlooking Metaxas Square, in Nicosia, the capital of Cyprus. Shafts of sunlight filtered into the big room through wooden slatted blinds.

There were three old cedar-wood desks, with faded green leather tops. An ancient, comfortable leather couch, a generous three-seater, was against one wall, under a map of the Mediterranean. And there were framed prints of racehorses and cricket matches on lazy English village greens.

Fiona scribbled and closed her pad. 'Anything else?'

The way she looked at him, pushing her silky hair where it had dropped over one eye, reminded him of earlier times, when Kate Howard had sent similarly confusing signals, in the months before their brief but intense affair. If you could call seven hours in Kate's delicious bed, in the daytime, an affair.

'How are you settling in?' he asked, gently.

'I love it. The climate's bliss after London. Everyone is brilliant. Really helpful. Work's . . . interesting. Actually, it's a dream posting.'

Jardine smiled, what a pleasant metamorphosis from that terrified kid lying in the shattered room at Compass House in Kensington Gate, after the car bomb, only a few months ago.

'Nice to see you in, um, such good form.'

In the silence, they could hear the traffic cruising around Metaxas Square. An occasional car or truck sounding its horn.

Fiona grinned. 'It was nice of you to visit me in hospital. My mother was amazed at all those flowers. And Dad drank most of the malt whisky.'

'Did he, now . . .'

Silence. Was he imagining it or was this child sending out some very grown-up signals? That's enough of that, Jardine, he told himself. Silly old goat. 'Be a good girl,' he said, 'and send that to Ronnie and Marietta's office.'

Fiona stood up and nodded. She walked round her desk and there was something about the way her slender hips moved that made Jardine long, not in a predatory way – more, wistfully – for the comfort of a lithe body and the reassuring affection of an intelligent young woman.

For a man of his standing in the Establishment, a man of his required gravitas, it was the sort of human frailty he should probably long since have drummed out of himself with a regime of self-denial, hard work and some vigorous sporting activity like squash. But women had always liked David Jardine and, over the years, he had acquired more experience of lithe and slender bodies than perhaps the uncharitable might consider to be his fair share.

Jardine turned and gazed out of the window, for he had no wish to seem a sad case of middle-aged . . . something.

'Um, classification, David?'

He glanced back. 'Eyes Only, I think.'

'I'm on the case.' She pulled a message pad from her pending tray and, opening a drawer, lifted out a code book and a one-time cipher pad, which was a booklet with page after page of groups of five numbers chosen at random by computer, thousands upon thousands of them. Each page was itself numbered and the only other copy of that booklet was kept under secure conditions in the SIS Cipher Room at Vauxhall Cross. Fiona would choose a page and her opening signal would tell Vauxhall its number. The encoded message would then be converted into five-figure groups and enciphered using the chosen page.

Upon receipt of the signal, transmitted by a secure radio burst of a fraction of a second, via satellite, Vauxhall would acknowledge its arrival and both parties would immediately destroy that page. About forty years old, the basic system was virtually unchanged, for nobody had come up with a safer way of sending secret messages.

'David . . .' said Fiona, chewing the end of her pencil as she thumbed through the book.

'Mmm?' he replied, examining a lithograph of W.G. Grace striking out at a rising cricket ball.

'Are you going to eat with Quentin?' She meant the Head of Station, who was that afternoon up at the Communications Complex, for Cyprus was a major Intelligence eavesdropping post, listening in on targets from Bosnia to South Yemen in the Arabian Gulf.

'I don't actually want to be seen with him; not the same day as Oversight's murder. I don't think it would be a good idea to send out signals suggesting we are particularly excited by that . . . event.'

Silence. She jotted down some figures. 'So, um, seeing friends, then?'

He chuckled and shook his head. 'Early night. Early plane back to Heathrow. Is that new?' He had noticed an old-fashioned barometric machine, a roll of paper with a pen nib arranged to touch it, the other end attached to a tiny meteorological engine. The lot enclosed in an oblong glass case.

'I don't know. Would you like me to cook something for you? I've got hummus and some fresh lamb. Or fresh sardines – I got them this morning.'

Well, if you say yes, Jardine told himself firmly, you behave like the irreproachable father figure she clearly thinks you are, and leave the child with a good impression of her Director. A perfect gentleman.

'That would be lovely,' he said. 'What a treat . . .'

And she smiled and carried on writing.

'So,' said the tanned, dark-eyed guy approaching through the crowded hubbub, and examining her plastic ID tag, 'you must be Zina Farouche.'

Zina had been feeling comfortably ignored in the sea of Middle-Eastern security people who had gathered for an introductory coffee-and-cookies get-together with their US State Department hosts in Conference Suite K on the eighth floor of the vast, anonymous and kind of tawdry Manhattan Hilton, on the Avenue of the Americas, eight blocks and a nine-minute walk downtown from the Essex House hotel.

She smiled and gripped his offered right hand, balancing a cup of tepid coffee at the same time. 'Mister Wiscynsky?'

He pushed an untidy lock of black hair off his forehead and grinned. He had nice eyes, but they missed nothing.

'Please, call me Al.'

'Al.' Zina let go and lifted the cup from its saucer. 'Is this your show . . .?'

He lifted his shoulders. 'For my sins. More coffee?'

'Not right now.'

After a slight pause, while he glanced around the room, Al Wiscynsky met her gaze. 'I thought we would get everyone into the next room in a few minutes. Give the usual opening pep talk. Then pass around some paperwork, which gives essential information about phone numbers, local knowledge, you know. Like that.'

'Is there still a lot of . . . mugging?' asked Zina.

Wiscynsky smiled, perplexed, and arched his back slightly. 'I guess we can get mugged in any big city, Ma'am. Even in downtown Tunis, if you find yourself in the wrong place.'

'I don't think so,' said Zina. 'We tend to cut off their hands.'

'Oh, Jeez,' replied Wiscynsky, looking forlorn, 'I wish the hell we could do that here . . .' And he looked her in the eye and she just couldn't tell if he was serious or not.

At that moment a wiry little guy, with unruly, wavy black

hair and a wool sports coat, necktie not quite pulled tight and his top shirt-button undone, appeared at Wiscynsky's side.

'Al . . .' he started, then, as he noticed the olive-complexioned Middle-Eastern girl his automatic charm button got pressed. 'Ma'am. Where's my manners. Excuse me.'

'It's all right,' said Zina.

'No. No, it's not all right, what was I thinking of? Listen, don't let me interrupt. I'll see you later, Al.'

Zina Farouche was amused. Cleary exuded sex appeal and he was confident about it without being pushy.

'I'm Zina Farouche,' she said, smiling. 'I'm with the Tunisians.'

'Only thing I know about Tunisia is the Miles Davies number.' He stretched his neck, as if even with the button loose he hated wearing a tie.

Zina looked to Wiscynsky for help.

Al sighed and spread his hands. 'It's a jazz tune. "A Night In Tunisia". Zina, this is Sergeant Joe Cleary, NYPD.'

'Will you be looking after us, Mister Cleary?'

Cleary gazed at her, liking what he saw. Then he shrugged and said, sadly, 'I wish. But I gotta stay with the Egyptians.'

Zina Farouche nodded, her pulse quickening. She had a sudden intuitive flash which involved gunfire and screaming. She checked out his face and body outline as she shrugged and replied, 'That's too bad. Maybe next year.'

'Amen to that, Ma'am.' Joe Cleary turned to Wiscynsky. 'Al, catch you later,' and with a nod that all but invited her for cocktails the cop turned and melted into the throng.

Zina watched him go, ensuring she would recognise that rear outline again, and the way he moved, lightly, able to look after himself.

'Crazy guy,' remarked Wiscynsky.

'Really?' Zina Farouche shrugged. 'I liked him.'

7

Damascus

David Jardine studied a photograph of the Palestinian girl, taken as she moved through JFK from the Concorde Arrivals Lobby. One of Ronnie Szabodo's New York watchers had been sent to ensure that a minor Tunisian diplomat travelling under the name of Farouche was one and the same as the Zina Farouche Jardine and his colleagues in Catnap had become so interested in.

'Good looking girl,' commented Marietta Delice, twisting one of the six 8″ × 10″ black and white photographs on his desk to study it more closely.

The terrorist team leader was wearing a loose-fitting, well-cut suit in some plain material, probably by Chanel, the top of a black-body all-in-one peeked under the V of the jacket's neck and her shoes were elegant and simple.

'That's those shoes,' remarked Marietta.

'What shoes?' asked Jardine, immediately visited by the pleasant memory of a couple of evenings earlier, when he had gently removed Fiona Macleod's shoes, one by one, after the demure Scots girl had initiated the course the evening was to take, by inviting him to inspect the wonderful job the surgeon had made of suturing the long gash along the back of her tanned thigh to that firm and delectable buttock.

'Last time Hanna al-Farah was in London. She bought them in Manolo Blahnik. It's a chic little shop in Chelsea; they must have the same size of feet.'

'When was that? July? The Israeli Embassy bomb?' He thought of Fiona, not among the glass and splintered wood, but more recently, eyes bright, searching his, jaw slack with lust . . . her quiet little gasps of pleasure. And that soft, low chuckle afterwards.

'She came back once after that,' Marietta replied.

'Unnoticed?'

'Well, hardly, David. I have her on video. Catnap has nothing to do with falling asleep, you know.'

'Anything overt? Was she questioned at point of entry? Picked up by Special Branch?'

'Mm-mm.' Marietta shook her head. 'The Security Service were on the phone as soon as she landed at Heathrow. Simon Crawford wanted to know if we had anything that might make it worth while arresting her under the Prevention of Terrorism Act.'

'But you preferred to let her run . . .?'

The only sound was of Jardine's Thomas Mudge carriage clock ticking gently on the bookcase behind him.

'Somehow,' Marietta said, in that low, whisky voice of hers, 'I thought that's what you would have wanted.'

Jardine removed his reading-glasses and met her gaze. He was a good-looking man, she reflected, with his thick, untidy hair, the merest hint of a broken nose and a trace of a scar which ran from beside his left eye to just above his mouth.

'Now why would you think that?' he asked, quietly.

She knew that voice, the honeyed voice of cold steel, as Kate Howard had described it. She reached into her briefcase, propped against her chair, and withdrew more photographs.

'You've shown me yours, David,' she said, 'now let me show you mine . . .'

And like a poker player with a winning hand, she fanned out a number of 5″ × 4″ colour photographs, onto the desk, half obscuring the larger black and white surveillance shots of Zina Farouche.

David Jardine studied the photos. They were of a corn-blonde woman in her middle forties, tall, rangy, hair tied back in a ponytail. Faded blue jeans and a long sweatshirt with Nile Delta Polo Club printed in a circle on the front, over a man on a galloping horse, swinging a polo stick.

Beside the woman – this photo had been snatched as they came out from a small-town general store – was a smaller, rounder female, with the tanned, swarthy features of South

America. Further south than Mexico, considered Jardine, for he had not too long ago run West 8, the office's South American espionage networks. She could be from Ecuador, or Colombia, for there might just be a hint of Tolima Indian about her.

There were a couple of dozen photographs, and it was clear from the angles, the lengths of focus and the poor quality that they had all been taken clandestinely. The fair woman and her companion, probably a servant, had been caught on celluloid buying food, loading up a Jeep Cherokee, talking to someone they had met in the tiny square of the small town, and so on. Its architecture suggested the place to be somewhere in New England.

Then there were other surveillance shots, this time in New York, of a big-framed, earnest-looking man, six feet and a couple of inches tall, crossing from a yellow taxi to the Harvard Club, on West 44th. And, in completely different light, three photographs of a distinguished-looking man, shorter than average, with a strikingly prominent, but aristocratic, nose. He wore a gray suit that looked expensive and the photographs had been taken in the inner courtyard of a group of buildings which were reminiscent of the Austro-Hungarian Empire style of architecture found from Zagreb to Constantinople. The sunlight was very strong and the shadows it created dark and well-defined.

David Jardine felt as if the weight of the world's suffering humanity, inhumanity, was on his shoulders. He knew, of course he knew, precisely who the people in those snatched photographs were. But there was no possibility, not at this delicate stage in his bleak and agonizing deliberations, that he might share his special knowledge with anyone, not even Marietta.

He glanced up at her and touched one of the photos. 'New England, am I right? A comfortably off American woman, with her South American housekeeper or maid or something. A man on the sidewalk, West Forty-Fourth Street, going into the Harvard Club, where one has spent many a pleasant hour chewing the fat. A Levantine . . . um, banker? Cabinet minister? Surgeon? In some hot Middle Eastern town. I wondered about Beirut but I think further south. Could it be Egypt?'

And all the while Marietta Delice had been watching him, reading Jardine's features for just a momentary glimpse of the real meaning of this rubbish he was spouting.

'The woman is Annabel Curtis. The wife of this man,' Marietta tapped the Harvard Club photos, 'Michael Curtis, who is US Ambassador to Egypt. This is the Foreign Ministry yard in Cairo, in the Gezira district. The man with the schnozzle is Ramses Ibrahim Selim, he's their Ambassador to Washington.'

Jardine nodded. 'I thought that might be Selim.' He smiled wanly. God, thought Marietta, he looks tired. 'And just what is the common denominator here?'

Marietta's sympathy for her colleague's apparent fatigue evaporated as she moved in for the kill.

'These turned up during a covert search of Zina Farouche's Paris apartment, in the Rue Napoléon.'

In the silence which followed, Jardine slid the photographs around, like cards in a game of patience.

'Before or after she left for New York?' he asked.

'Two nights ago. She had gone to the Abu Nidal safe house on the Avenue Foch. That usually occupies her for at least two hours.' She glanced at Jardine, waiting for him to ask who she had gone to see, or what occupied her for two hours in a busy schedule, but his expression did not suggest . . . anything at all. Which was unlike him.

She continued. 'My team decided to take a chance and turn the place over. These were in colour negative, hidden in a three-point-five-inch computer disc. It's a method used by the Vietnamese Intelligence Service and we know they have two advisors at the al-Shambat camp in the Sudan, which is where Zina trained, year before last.'

Apart from a desire to hurt the West, in revenge for the past, David Jardine could never figure out why the Vietnamese should bother to help Islamic terrorism. And, in truth, he was disappointed, for he had always felt a sneaking regard for any small nation who had seen off the might of two great powers.

'I know your people are like ghosts in the night,' he murmured, 'what was it Maupassant wrote? "*Au pas de loup, avec l'air du complice* . . ." But can we be sure this is not a, um, deliberate thing? To confuse us. A false, um . . . trail.'

'David, it is my belief these people are targets of the Dante team. I mean, have you thought about it, United Nations Week is being held in New York in three weeks' time. That's what darling Zina is doing there, officially. Security, would you please, with the unsuspecting Tunisian delegation. I got hold of a list of the Egyptian players from Bill Greenfield at Grosvenor Square. Guess who is included in the Foreign Minister's party . . .'

'Ramses Selim?' Jardine eased his back against his chair, still gazing at the Egyptian's surveillance photo, and moved his head from side to side, trying to ease some of the tension.

'And I know you have seen the American fax about Selim taking a few days off in the boondocks. To use Bill's expression. Because I checked the file. He and his family, David, are getting together with Ambassador Curtis and *his* family. Very cosy.' She lifted a pack of Winstons from her jacket pocket and dropped one cigarette into her hand, tapped away the loose tobacco and put it between her lips, flicking open her slim Zippo and lighting up. As she exhaled, Marietta murmured, 'And viewed from Tehran, a perfect target.'

Jardine nodded, without speaking. There was no way this conversation could end without push having finally come to shove, in the context of David Jardine's secret and privileged knowledge.

In the profound silence, Marietta waited patiently. She knew that she had played her way to the high-stakes table, with this particular hand. She knew that her Director of Operations and once, a hundred and ten years ago, lover, was contemplating taking her into a desolate maze of real secrecy. Where conscience and legality could shrivel and become mislaid. It was a dangerous place and she began to wonder if perhaps she really wanted to be there.

Finally, David Jardine made up his mind. He looked Marietta in the eye, and, after a considerable silence, said, 'You're right, of course. Something is going on. It was naive of me to imagine you might not . . . zero in on it. Catnap never has had much to do with sleeping.'

He swivelled out of his chair with surprising agility and crossed to one of the two windows, looking out across the river. He stood there for a while. A gust of wind moaned around the outside. Then, without looking round, he said – asked, really – 'Marietta, will you please trust me, for a while longer?'

'Well, I have always done that. But maybe you need some help with this, David.' She flicked some ash into an ashtray on his desk. 'To tell you the truth, I have never actually seen you so . . . burdened.'

Jardine smiled, ruefully. As usual, Marietta Delice was on the ball. And her offer of counsel was terribly tempting. After all, he had received precious little consolation from the man on the carved cross, in that little chapel in Limehouse.

'Is this about protecting a source?' she asked, gently.

Jardine turned and gazed down at the photographs, damning not because of their subjects, or even the clandestine way they had been taken. They were damning because of where they had been found. And whose apartment they had been found in.

'If only, my dear Marietta, it were that simple . . .' He met her cool, searching gaze. 'You should continue to pursue this. For I have no right to tell you to stop.'

She allowed blue cigarette smoke to wreathe from her mouth, forming delicate skeins in the still, silent air. 'But you have the authority. You can say back off, and I'll have to do it.'

He frowned, then really smiled. 'You just do your own thing. It might help me to make the right decision.'

Might force him, Marietta realised was more probably what David Jardine meant.

'Classy joint,' remarked Joe Cleary, as he turned his '83 Pontiac off the road from the Essex cable ferry into the dirt trail leading up a quarter mile to the sprawling mansion house. The stone pillars at the gateway looked even older and Joe guessed they had probably come from one of those big old town houses in Upper East Side, built in the early part of the century with antique stone accessories shipped over from Europe by an enterprising Irish architect called Foley.

His companion was Sergeant Sam Vargos, a fellow Homicide detective seconded to the UN Week Task Force from the 14th Precinct, and, like Cleary, for him the old-money rural gentility of Essex County was unfamiliar territory.

'It looks like it should be way down south in Dixie,' commented Vargos, revealing a hidden depth of architectural prescience.

'Gentlemen, hi, come inside, can I offer you something? A beer, coffee?' Annabel Curtis ushered them into a big room, scattered with couches and easy chairs, tables and rugs over an old wooden floor. American wool rugs in natural colours were casually draped over chairs and couches and the walls were lined with old, yellowing cherrywood bookshelves.

'Coffee would be great, Ma'am,' said Cleary.

'This security thing must be a real nuisance for you policemen,' smiled Annabel as she crossed over to a recess beside one bookcase, where a coffee percolator sat warm on its hob.

'Makes a change from fingerprinting stiffs,' replied Joe Cleary as he gazed around the vast and tastefully furnished room approvingly. There was nothing that was not authentic early-settler in colour and design. It was like being inside a three-dimensional Grandma Moses painting.

'And you,' said the wife of Ambassador Curtis, as she handed them mugs decorated with Algonquin Indian symbols, 'are going to keep us safe, while we entertain our Egyptian friends . . .'

'As a matter of fact, thank you, Ma'am, as a matter of fact our job is to get the Egyptian Ambassador here safely, and back to New York after his visit.'

Annabel Curtis smiled and indicated a couple of big chairs. Joe thought the wool rugs bore an Arapaho pattern. 'And I'm sure that's the kind of job you can do in your sleep, Sergeant Cleary.'

'Ma'am, with respect, it's the kinda job we can do in our sleep that tends to turn right around and bite us in the ass,' replied Cleary, and, as he said it, he had a strange feeling, like a cold wind breathing right down his spine.

'Well, I'm sure this will pass just fine,' said Annabel, but Cleary was not really listening. For such a big room, he was thinking, really the size of two big rooms knocked into one, it was surprising there were so few ways to get out of it.

'How do you get to the back of your house, Ma'am?' he

asked. And when she replied you had to go back into the front hall and through the library, the detective nodded.

'Does that give you problems?' she asked, sensing his preoccupation.

Joe Cleary looked at her, and, after a pause, said, 'I sure hope not . . .'

Round about the time when Jardine and Marietta Delice had begun their meeting, James Gant sat staring at his computer screen feeling satisfied, apprehensive and slightly drained. For he had guessed right, the day before. The entry code he had chosen then had indeed been Angeline's. And the material she had been processing included EYES ONLY SUBJECT: DANTE, for the Permanent Secretary and no one else.

He had spent the twelve minutes left to him that lunchtime more or less ransacking her files. They had been flagged with cryptic symbols which meant that, immediately after reading, the message had to be shredded by the recipient's own hand and the time of that act to be noted.

There were seven such messages and, although they were lost forever to Gant, who could only peruse the records of their scrutiny by Angeline, they were enough to confirm to him that the entire Dante business was being cloaked in the deepest secrecy, even within the secret environment of SIS/Foreign Office communications.

Then the others had come back from lunch and he had extracted himself from the computer directory. It had taken all his patience to wait almost twenty-three hours until now, when once again he had volunteered to work the lunchtime shift.

As soon as he had the office to himself, James had once again accessed Angeline's secure files and, after some minutes, sifting through files of no interest to him, he came across background information in response to that Catnap signal he had processed ten days before, on 8 August, requesting passport and visa details on Zina Farouche and four others, whom Gant had recognised as known Palestinian terrorists, probably with Fatah – The Revolutionary Council, which was the highfalutin' name Abu Nidal had adopted for his terror gang.

Normally replies to such requests would be sent from the Foreign Office to SIS at its Vauxhall headquarters, but this one had been routed back via Angeline in Clerical 17 to D/Catnap, in conditions of maximum secrecy. But Clerical 17 was, strictly speaking, a one-way system.

So this little outpost was not precisely what it seemed, or what James Gant had been led to believe. 'We have no secrets among ourselves, Jimmy' – Stan's words on his first day there. Well, that should have rung alarm bells for a start.

The revelation in itself left him fairly unmoved. It was the content of those secret replies, passed back through his office, that was more damning than anything he had expected to find.

Every one of the names on the Catnap list, except for Mustafa Sharik, had been issued with special visas and diplomatic credentials to enter the USA and work with the Tunisian, Algerian, Kuwaiti and Moroccan delegations to the United Nations during and in the period leading up to UN Week in New York City. Which was to say, during the month of September. And this was 2 September, so some of them might already be in place.

Only Mustafa Sharik was not on the list and the Under-Secretary's department had no information about him, other than a note that he was wanted for questioning about terrorist offences in Britain, Germany and the Lebanon. Interpol, the UK Security Service and the FBI all had issued his photograph and other details to the authorities of fifty-eight countries worldwide.

And these five people, considered Gant, are believed by Catnap to be members of the hit-team responsible for the Biarritz massacre. According to D/OPS's 'irreplaceable source', now deceased, this same gang has been tasked by Abu Nidal to carry out a sub-contract on behalf of a secret faction of the Iranian intelligence service for an act of global terror to surpass the 1988 Lockerbie Pan Am bombing of a 747 passenger jet.

And yet, David Jardine has flatly denied to the CIA Station Chief in London that we have intelligence forewarning of any specific threat from the direction of Tehran.

So what bloody game are you playing, D.A.J.?

At that moment, Stan and Eric breezed into the office, deep in conversation about the England soccer team manager's garish taste in neckties.

James tapped a rapid series of keys and had extracted himself from Angeline's dedicated computer directory by the time his colleagues had shut the door and strolled to their desks.

'That's what I like to see, Jimbo,' said Stan, dropping his jacket over the back of his chair. 'A man at work.'

Gant grinned. 'Nobody phoned, Stanley. Not even a fax. I think I'll just grab a sandwich.' He shut down his computer and climbed to his feet, stretching.

'Hey, Jim,' said Stan, and Gant paused at the door.

'Yes?'

'Angeline . . .'

'What about her?'

'Are you giving her one?'

Gant chuckled. 'Certainly not.'

'So why have you left a packet of Johnnies on her desk?'

Gant's heart stopped. He stared at Angeline's desk.

Stan roared with laughter.

'Just kidding,' he chortled. 'But, by Christ, Eric, did he not look guilty!'

Eric smiled, and glanced to James as if to say, what a trial, in an otherwise civilised office.

'Very bloody funny,' replied Gant. 'If I hadn't been wearing a truss I'd've ruptured myself laughing.' And he turned to leave, bumping into Angeline who had just arrived.

'Did I miss something?' she breathed, gazing up at him and flattening herself against the door frame, fluttering her eyelashes demurely.

'Just Stan being his usual side-splitting self.'

'We should try and get our lunchtimes to coincide, James,' murmured the plump, pink vampette.

'Why don't we do that?' James replied, and peeled himself away from her appraising gaze, heading for the inner quad and King Charles Street.

By 2.20 he was ravenous, but a smoked ham and lettuce sandwich, washed down with a plastic bottle of apple juice, failed to take his mind off the Pandora's Box he had opened.

Surely to God the System, They, the Firm, did not really intend to keep the Americans in the dark about Zina Farouche and her Dante assignment.

James had of course no proof, nothing that would have impressed his first operational boss and mentor Euan Stevenson. He just could not get that note out of his mind. Maybe Curtis and the Connecticut get-together were not Dante's target. But some group of luckless human beings certainly were. And there could be no doubt now that the atrocity was to take place in the USA. And during the next three weeks.

By this time, Gant was sitting on a bench just inside St James's Park, throwing bits of his sandwich to some Muscovy ducks. The distant chatter of machine-gun fire and the screams of grievously hurt Jewish travellers in that blood-spattered airport hall wandered through his brain like snatches of some tune he could never quite get out of his mind.

He stood up. Glanced at his watch. Felt in his pockets for change and headed for the pay-phones in Broadway, just a couple of hundred yards away, through Queen Anne's Gate.

'If you ever', David Jardine had said to him, upon his return from Marigold and Rome, when Aunt Edith had taken them both to lunch at the Basil Street Hotel, 'need a Dutch Uncle, some friendly advice or a shoulder to cry on, don't hesitate, James. Just give me a shout. Forget I'm D/Ops and remember I had to start the same way as you. Times will get tough, or, worse, confusing. Or you might fuck up and feel totally lost. Just call me. I won't let you down.'

So when the private number Jardine had given him rang, and when a pleasant, youngish, Scottish woman answered, James Gant asked if he could speak to David Jardine, please. And it was James Gant calling.

Seconds later, Jardine's deep, always approachable voice asked James how it was going, as if they were old friends, and when Gant said he needed to see him urgently, there had been a pause and David Jardine had enquired, 'How urgently?'

'Really, um, it's urgent, sir.'

And without a moment's pause the Director of Operations said, 'Come over. I'm in that ghastly green place today; when shall we expect you?'

Gant checked his watch. 'Fifteen minutes.'

And now, twenty-five minutes later, Heather was showing him into the inner office of the legendary spymaster and controller of each and every operation, including those which would always be denied even at the cost of careers, reputations and life itself, which Her Majesty's Secret Intelligence Service had running at that particular time.

James Gant had met Marietta Delice in the outer office, as he had waited to go in. The boss of Catnap had glanced at him and nodded as she left. She had seemed pre-occupied.

'Come in, James. Settling in to life at King Charles Street? They can be very pleased with themselves, the straight people.'

As Gant made some predictable and polite response, he noticed a scattering of photographs on Jardine's desk. Some were in colour, and others, beneath those, printed larger, on 10″ × 8″ matt paper, in black and white. And somehow he knew, with that prescience which his trainers had noted, that the good-looking girl in the chic and expensive suit, with its tailored jacket and miniskirt, was the terrorist Zina Farouche.

'Not a bad looking girl,' said Jardine, as he watched Gant stare at the photos. 'Do those photographs', he asked with perhaps a degree of indifference, 'suggest anything to you?'

James Gant turned to face him, and his determination to start off cool and objective was suddenly gone. 'If her name is Zina Farouche, she is twenty-seven years old. Height five feet and six inches, weight about one twenty-nine. She is a Palestinian-born naturalized Tunisian, at present in New York working as Security Attaché with the Tunisian Delegation to United Nations Week in Manhattan. She is a member of Fatah – The Revolutionary Council, Abu Nidal's terrorist faction, and she is the leader of a team of killers who have been tasked by Nidal, under the terms of a secret agreement with the Iranian Service, to carry out an atrocity at least equal in terms of world spectacular to the Lockerbie disaster. Three of her team also have diplomatic cover and the fourth is at large, no doubt using some other method of entering and functioning in the United States.'

Jesus and your hosts of attending angels, was David

Jardine's first reaction. Is there nobody in SIS, not even the tea-boy, who is not in on this particular act? But outwardly, the man his South American networks had christened *El Malabarista*, The Juggler, produced a slow, appreciative grin.

'Well, they do say a picture speaks a thousand words. Would I be correct in assuming that impressive catalogue of intelligent guesswork has something to do with this unexpected visit?'

One day, pal, I'll be as smooth as you, thought Gant, but, for the moment, blunter instruments suit me just fine. 'Sir, I have been processing much of the Dante material, both from Marietta Delice's Counter Terror desk and from yourself.'

'I know you have,' replied Jardine, which was not strictly speaking true, but he realized some of his more anodyne signals and notes to FCO would have been routed through the Clerical 17 office.

'And, well, it's impossible not to draw one's own conclusions, even from the scraps that pass across my desk.'

'Please, sit down,' said Jardine, flicking a switch on his desk intercom which would ensure Heather kept them undisturbed. Marietta had got to the heart of the matter just the day before, but this ingénu was clearly shooting in the dark, and that's exactly where he would remain.

Gant sat on the chair still warm from Marietta's meeting with David Jardine.

Jardine wandered over to a long bookcase and seemed to be browsing, as if he had forgotten his agitated visitor.

For several moments – twenty-seven seconds; James Gant was counting – there was silence, except for the comfortable ticking of an antique clock on the spymaster's bookcase.

'Mmm, hmm . . .' mused Jardine. And he turned to gaze back into the room. 'I don't quite get the point of all this. So you have been able to read between the lines and get a general idea of an intelligence operation against a specific terrorist enterprise. I mean, James, so what? This is what we do for a living.'

And here James Gant found himself in difficult waters. For if he revealed all he knew, a brief investigation would show he must have illegally accessed a protected computer file.

'It's more serious than that.' And, braving the look of

growing disapproval on Jardine's face, he went on, 'Why are we not telling the Americans what we know? Surely we are not going to allow a massacre to take place, against a dozen or so innocent people, on the territory of a close, our closest, ally?'

Do you ever have one of those days – Dorothy Jardine had recently enquired of her husband, back in the Wiltshire farmhouse, while he was preparing a recipe for coq au vin he had come across in a book he was reading, by Guy de Maupassant – do you ever have one of those days when you wish you had never gotten out of bed? She used words like 'gotten' in their correct context, did Dorothy, who had achieved a rare starred first in English at Oxford, many years ago, when the world had seemed simpler.

Well, this was indeed one of those days.

Give me, dear Lord, he had prayed in St Luke's and elsewhere, every day since this business had begun, a sign. Help me with this terrible burden.

Quite possibly, considered Jardine, Marietta and the puppy Gant were signs from on high. If so, it was a pity for Gant, for, whatever the outcome of all this, there was no place for arrogant 'concerned' whippersnappers, their cheeks still damp from nurse's milk, to step in and offer their three-pennyworth of wide-eyed bleating.

'James, dear boy, I will not offer you a cup of something' (hemlock came to mind) 'because you will not be staying long.' David Jardine pulled his seat back and sat down at his desk, ignoring the damning photographs spread in front of him. 'Each and every piece of intelligence you work with is privileged and protected by the Official Secrets Act. But you know that. Discussion with anyone not cleared, and in the case of operations like Dante, that means almost everyone, is an offence under Section One of the Act. Tell me you understand.'

Controlling his rising temper at the attitude of this patronizing bastard, Gant nodded.

'Good. You are in a very sensitive office because you have a high security clearance, both from the Vetting Office and from other sponsors. Any indiscretion on your part, however well intentioned, would result in immediate withdrawal of those clearances and the resulting loss of your job with SIS, for we have no slots for non PV-ed people. Do you continue to get my drift?'

'Of course I do,' James Gant almost snarled.

'That's fine. Now I appreciate you coming over here, in the middle of what must be a busy day.' The Director of Operations' total sarcasm was undisguised. 'James, you will come across tons of stuff like this in your current posting and even more so when we put you into the field as an operations officer. This is not the Third Reich or the Soviet Union. It is not even a banana republic or the United States in the McCarthy era. You must always speak your mind and you must stand up and be counted if you think something unacceptable or contrary to our own standards of decency and rectitude is going down.' Jardine paused, softening his thunderous expression. 'But this is the shitty end of democracy's long stick. We work in conditions of considerable secrecy not so we can hide our mistakes or abuse our admittedly terrifying powers. We are the *secret* intelligence service because our free country wants one. Knows it needs one. You know as well as I do we are not permitted to do half the things the man on the Clapham omnibus imagines we get up to. And that's just as well. But it doesn't hurt to allow him, or more importantly, our enemies, to believe our arm is long, our hearts are of tungsten and our souls without mercy. Are you sure you won't have that cup of coffee?' he asked, disconcertingly.

'So, I'm to mind my own business and get back to work?' enquired James Gant.

Jardine scratched his forehead, checked his fingernails. 'What if I say to you, I am not able to discuss this with you? That I hear what you say, I applaud, without reservation, your courage in coming storming in here. And your concern. What if I tell you, this conversation never took place, you have become privy, which is inevitable in our line of work, even as a probationer, to affairs of the highest sensitivity, and what if I remind you that your first duty, as is mine, is to the country and the monarch you have sworn an oath of allegiance to.'

'Sir, I understand all that. I came to lean on your shoulder.

That stuff you said about a Dutch Uncle. You know, forget your high rank and remember you were once as raw and . . . untutored as me.'

Further down the river, Big Ben chimed the half hour. Jardine gazed at this James Gant. What was it Ronnie Szabodo had started his initial report by saying? 'A young man of good family'. Jardine remembered Edith Treffewin in the early days, when she ran the Berlin thing. The Dowager with nine balls, they had called her. Edith took no bullshit from anyone and it looked as if her nephew was a chip off the old Countess.

'Well, you came to the right place.' He was gratified to note the relief on Gant's face. 'But this is the job, James. If all goes well and you prosper here, you too are going to suffer the same ordeals that involvement in the world of espionage inevitably brings in its harlot's wake. Agent networks rounded up. Close friends tortured and their families, even infants. You are going to see traitors to this country and our allies rise to positions of power and influence. You are going to have to make decisions that will break your heart and it will not heal, I promise you. This is a very lonely profession sometimes, and you will, if you are anything like me, wake up shouting and in a lather of guilty memories. And you will not be able to discuss that with your wife, when you eventually choose one, or, sometimes, with anyone at all. Are you religious?'

Gant shook his head.

Jardine watched him closely, the man was not that much older than Andrew. 'Well, I suppose you have seen more than your share of horrors. That was a dreadful experience you had as a young boy, at, um, Rome Airport, wasn't it? And Bosnia. Cambodia. Personally, I need someone I can share my . . . darkest knowledge with. But then I'm a Christian. A Catholic. Although for many years I was an atheist, at least in the daylight.'

'I can't stand still and watch it happen,' said Gant with simple honesty.

'I don't think I can either,' David Jardine was surprised to hear himself saying. 'But that is not your concern. If you can't stand the heat, chum, then maybe you should ask yourself if this career is right for you. Perhaps you would be happier in the Diplomatic Service. Or the British Council. We can easily smooth a transfer for you . . .'

The man's eyes are like flint, thought Gant. Not in the metaphorical sense but really. They were really like two chips of flint. Well, there had not been much possibility of this Quixotic visit to the lion's den turning out any differently. But the photographs had been an unexpected bonus.

James got to his feet. 'I don't know what I was thinking of,' he lied. 'Sheer arrogance thinking I could throw my weight around. You have let me off quite lightly. Of course I can take the heat, I enjoy being part of the Office, it's like family to me. Probably a bit sensitive because of, um, Rome. You're quite right . . .'

David Jardine was out of his seat and crossing towards the door. He rested a hand on the handle and smiled, for the first time in those difficult few minutes. 'I think you're made for the outfit. Just grit your teeth and prove what you're made of in your present job. Clerical Seventeen is not the most glamorous slot but we have our eye on you, James, and Malcolm feels you will make a great Field Operator.' He opened the door. 'Probably what you've done today proves it.'

James Gant gripped the older man's hand and stepped out, past Heather who mentioned she was sending some files down to the Foreign Office by car and would he like a ride back to Whitehall. He was escorted out of the building by Albert, one of the janitors, who informed him he was going to Torremolinos in a couple of weeks to see his married daughter.

In the dark blue Ford Scorpio sedan, driven by a quiet woman who offered no smalltalk and received none, James Gant felt coldly excited. He knew Jardine had been put on the spot, he believed he had lulled the man into thinking he would toe the line, and, most important, those coloured photos on Jardine's desk, shuffled among the black and white shots of a woman who might be Zina Farouche, could possibly provide him with conclusive details of the Dante group's target.

He had a shrewd idea of the identities of the people in the

surveillance photographs but he intended to make sure, before deciding what to do next. It would mean staying on for a few minutes after the others had gone, but it was not unusual for one or the other of them to work late, to clear any urgent backlog before close of play.

Back in the office, no one remarked on his extended lunch break and Gant settled down to concentrate on the pile of documents which had accumulated on his desk.

It seemed an aeon till 5.30 came, and the others were locking up their systems and signing files back into the care of the Security Clerk, who locked them into a wire barrow, like a caged supermarket trolley. Stan shrugged into his worn, faded blue anorak – Angeline called it his train-spotter's coat – and peered at James, still engrossed in his work.

'Got no home to go to?' he enquired, as Angeline brushed past him. There was certainly something going on between those two.

Gant smiled apologetically and said he still had some work to catch up on.

'Don't forget *Crocodile Shoes* . . .' said Eric quietly, as he opened the door to leave.

James wondered for a moment if that was a code-word, then he remembered it was the title of a television serial he had mentioned he enjoyed.

'On tonight, is it?' he enquired.

'Nine-thirty,' replied Stan and ushered his sugar plum fairy into the doorway, as she unwrapped a transparent plastic raincoat in a manner which could only be described as voluptuous.

And suddenly they were all gone. Time, thought Gant, for a look at Circe, one of the office's latest toys.

Circe was a protected, classified SECRET computer programme which was able to identify known individuals from composite facial features, fed into its memory rather in the manner of those identikit pictures built up by police witnesses and reproduced in newspapers and on television.

Because David Jardine had not actually confirmed the girl in the photos was Zina Farouche, Gant decided to identify her, before proceeding to the others. He keyed in the features, indexed separately as:

EYES > EYEBROWS > FOREHEAD > HAIRLINE > HAIR-STYLE > EARS > CHEEKS > NOSE > MOUTH > CHIN > FACIAL-SHAPE > DISTINGUISHING-MARKS > NECK >

and when he was satisfied that the result was as close as possible to the photo of the girl on David Jardine's desk, he asked Circe to identify the owner of what, he had to admit, was a not unattractive young face.

WAIT instructed the screen.

Then, ENTER PASSWORD.

Gant frowned, then took a flyer and typed DANTE. The screen instantly shifted, keeping the composite on the left half and dividing the right sector into two. On top was a full-face photograph of the same girl, her hair cut slightly shorter, and, on the bottom quarter, the information:

FAROUCHE – ZINA. Palestinian origin b. Chatilla Camp Beirut 14.6.67 Tunisian naturalized 09.11.83 American University Beirut '84–'88 BA Intntl Law Tunisian Foreign Ministry 1989 current Tun. Emb Paris 3rd Sec Sy.

RED-RED BLACK-BLACK NFWA REPALL URG

So there it was. SY. was the office abbreviation for Security. RED-RED BLACK-BLACK meant the subject was of special interest and was considered hostile and dangerous.

NFWA meant No further interrogation (of the computer) without authority, and REPALL URG was an instruction to report all new sightings or other intelligence concerning the person as a matter of urgency.

Thus encouraged, Gant attempted the same process with composites of the tall American woman and the businessman on West 44th Street. But this time the code word Dante failed to convince the computer. Fortunately these were not 'one time sesames' and he was able to attempt several pass-words before he succeeded using BLUE EAGLE, which was the Firm's code-word for the US State Department. Sure enough, there on the screen appeared photographs and potted biographies of Annabel Curtis and her husband, Mike, American Ambassador to Egypt.

The other face was more difficult, even with the prominent nose.

After drawing a blank with the Dante password, and the generic password for faces of that description, for there were over six thousand middle-aged men listed as having large noses, and 1,173 with unusually big 'Roman' noses, he decided to concentrate on the courtyard with its deep, clean-cut shadows and its particular arrangement of windows and tall double doorways. Also the stone shield with an imperial eagle carved above the smaller of the two doors.

With docile swiftness, the screen split into three, and there was the courtyard Gant had reproduced from memory, almost precisely the same. And the legend in the lower right quarter announced it was a northern aspect of the secondary courtyard of the Egyptian Ministry of Foreign Affairs in Cairo. Gezira district. It was used by diplomatic service officials who were allowed to park there provided they were in possession of the necessary permit, displayed on the left upper part of their windshield.

'Got you,' breathed Gant, and he asked the computer to provide him with a positive ID photograph of Monsieur Ramses Selim, Egyptian Ambassador to the USA.

And there it was; Imperial Roman nose and all. A more formal photo, taken as Selim presented his credentials in a minor reception at the Department of State's Protocol Office, in Washington DC. The very same man in the photo Gant had seen on Jardine's desk.

James Gant closed down his video terminal. He rang for the Security Clerk and signed in his files. Then he left the office and strolled out from King Charles Street, into Horse Guards Parade, across St James's Park and made his way to a pub in Petty France called the Buckingham Arms.

Gant liked the place. Stan and Eric sometimes used it at lunchtime but there seemed to be few regulars. He knew nobody there and nobody there knew him. Plus it served an excellent pint of Young's Special.

The first was downed inside a minute. The second was pulled for him by a cheery barman, unbowed by the noisy press of anonymous Home Office clerks, local office workers and detectives from New Scotland Yard which was just at the end of the street, round the corner in Broadway.

The young intelligence officer took his second pint and

folded quietly into a corner seat, where he pretended to read the *Evening Standard* while he thought hard about the day's events.

The noise of laughter and cheerful conversation receded as he tried hard to put other, less damning interpretations on the facts he had become aware of. But the more he analysed it, the clearer it seemed that certain people at the top of SIS (surely not only Jardine, powerful though the man was) were, at the very least, contemplating allowing the massacre to happen. By the sin of omission, he reflected, and he knew from his work in Clerical 17 that was not an uncommon tactic in the world of secret diplomacy. 'Masterly inactivity' was the delicate phrase he had heard used.

Gant understood, from his years in current affairs, that such a horrific act – even to be planning it – was a potential catastrophe for the blinkered mullahs of Tehran.

Just a few years after their now universally known responsibility for the Pan Am Flight 103 mid-air explosion over Lockerbie, the sheer political miscalculation of commissioning another such deed could easily backfire on Iran. Their promising attempts at restoring international trade and political relations would be kicked out into the wilderness for four or five, or ten years to come.

A dread coldness breathed through his soul as James Gant comprehended the desolate logic which could persuade intelligence chieftains that the 'net saving' of human lives would probably be far greater by allowing Tehran to go ahead and turn itself into an international pariah. But to *know*, and to do nothing? What sort of people could live with themselves after that?

It was, he considered, precisely the same as planning or undertaking the massacre itself.

And a cold resolve settled on him, as James Gant understood the inevitability of what was to come.

'I say,' said a familiar voice, 'James, my dear chap . . .' Pushing through the throng appeared the smiling face of one Dosser Thackery, who had been in River House with James, at school.

'Dosser. Have a drink.' James stood up. 'What you up to?'

'City, my dear. Trading commodities. On the third Porsche and loving it still with the BBC?'

'Foreign Office these days.'

'Ah-ha. A diplomat.'

'Not quite. I'm with their PR department.'

'Is that bitter or special? Let me do it.'

'Special, just the half.'

'Quite exciting, though? Get to travel?'

'I think I'm just about to,' replied Gant and, draining his glass, handed it to this apparition from the days of his youth.

Joe Cleary sat in Bartello, on one of the leather benches on the right of the front door, waiting for the tall, corn-blonde Sicilian chick to finish her stint at the reception desk. It was ten after nine in the evening.

The bar on his left, facing the street window, was medium busy. He recognized Johnny Stomparelli from the Brooklyn numbers game; the hood was a collector and enjoyed a rep for making you remember never to pay late again. He was also reputed to be enforcer for a vice ring that ran a string of high-class call-girls. He wore a white shirt, gold chain, curly hair dyed straw-coloured. Gray silk suit, five o'clock shadow masquerading as designer stubble. Big rings, like knuckledusters.

When Dolores was through, she glanced over to see if Cleary was still there. He smiled cheerily and raised his hand, waggling his fingers in a desultory wave.

Dolores disappeared into the staff room. Joe became aware of Johnny Stomparelli's menacing stare.

Ten whole minutes later, just as Cleary was beginning to wonder if she had left by another exit, the kid emerged. She wore a simple black wool dress with a square neckline and she looked terrific. Her long hair had been cut since the freezer murder and it suited her. She strode over – no way with striders like these could you call it mere walking – and stood facing him. Although it was warm outside, a gray wool cardigan peeked out from the straw basket she held loosely in her left hand.

'OK?' asked Cleary, still seated, gazing up at her.

She nodded. Maybe a touch apprehensive.

He rose. 'So let's go.'

And as they moved to the door, surprise, surprise, Johnny Stomparelli moved to block their way.

'Aw, Johnny, cut it out,' said Dolores.

Joe Cleary said nothing. But he was watching the upstart hoodlum warily.

'Where the hell you going?' demanded Stomparelli.

'Mind your own, I gotta life,' replied the girl.

'Yeah, so let's keep it that way. Park the bag and come over to the bar.' All this time it was like Joe Cleary did not exist.

But now Joe spoke up. 'Leave it, pal,' he said, 'the lady is with me.'

It was one of those moments when everybody, all those guys and women talking and laughing, had stopped talking and laughing and there was silence. So they all heard him say that and J. Stomparelli knew they had heard it and that was bad for his reputation.

'There must be some mistake,' said Stomparelli. 'I think you are confusing me with somebody who don't cut the balls off monkeys in blue coats.'

No prizes for guessing what colour of coat our detective was wearing.

Cleary wished people would start talking again, so that he could converse with this low-life without it becoming a situation. But by now they were hooked, amused at the wiry little guy's predicament. Glad it was not them.

'Johnny, I –'

The hoodlum's hand snaked out and gripped her throat between finger and thumb, shutting her voice box.

'When I let go, walk to the bar and sit there.' His eyes were too bright, a trace of a smile flickering on his face.

Tears appeared on Dolores's cheeks. There was total silence until, after just a tad too long, Stomparelli opened his fingers. She drew in air and glanced at Cleary, who had not made any move to intervene.

'Go on,' he said. And nodded towards the bar.

Dolores walked, slowly, subdued, to a stool some fat guy had rapidly vacated.

Johnny Stomparelli watched, then turned to examine Cleary.

'You know, wise guy, I would never let anyone do that to a woman. Not even a *puta* like her.'

He smiled a cold, chilling, soul-less smile he had seen in

Reservoir Dogs and practised in mirrors, ten, twenty times a day.

The speed with which Joe Cleary clapped both hands, held open, palms inwards, against Johnny's ears was only matched by the merciless force of the assault.

Stomparelli stood absolutely still for about three seconds, then he tenderly raised his hands to his ears and slowly sank to his knees, where he began to wail and keen, like a hound dog that has lost its mate. Blood trickling out, between his fingers.

Cleary stepped over the injured man and opened the door.

'Neither would I, pal,' he said. And held out a hand for Dolores who, after a moment's hesitation, left the bar stool and walked out of the place.

On the sidewalk, as they walked to his '83 Pontiac, the kid was very quiet. Cleary unlocked the car and they got in. She sat, thoughtful.

'Does that make problems for you?' he asked, as he headed uptown.

Dolores shrugged.

'Kid, it ain't none of my business but I can figure out what kind of a hold he got on you.'

She gazed out at the passing street, and tugged the gray cardigan out of her straw bag.

Cleary's gut instinct had been right – that day of the freezer murder – about the beautiful, tall, fair-haired Sicilian girl. She had a tiny record; two counts of prostitution and possession of a couple of lines. The whoring had been up-market stuff, working for the Eve Escort Agency which took $700 a time and supplied diplomats and the Wall Street boys.

And that was the outfit Johnny worked for. It was run by one of the five families. And real efficient; they never made waves, never had any complaints.

But when Joe had said it was none of his business he meant it. Tonight, he had other things on his mind. All the pizzazz with the State Department and the UN Week Task Force had not side-tracked him from a matter that had begun to . . . annoy him. Most of the time there was so much shit going down on the Homicide scene, crack gangs, mafia wars, muggings, shootings, knifings, fatal rapes, violent robberies and so on and so forth, that they slipped by so fast you could never really expect to get a handle on every one. And the freezer murder had been like that, just slipping by. Slip-slidin' away. And as time passed, the detective's work-load of homicide investigations just began to bury the Bartello-freezer John Doe under more pressing business.

Until Frank the morgue attendant, grateful for Cleary's treatment in the wake of the Martina's-bar slaying, had passed him the information that some spook from the CIA had flown in from DC, checked out the cadaver, made an ID, Frank Grumman had felt, sworn Grumman to secrecy and gone back to wherever he came from.

Well, that had been five months ago. Joe Cleary had waited patiently, knowing how slow the wheels of bureaucracy turned. But not a word. He had even sent out on the wire an all-agencies request, through NYPD's Intel Division – which used to be known as BOSI – with details of the murder victim, in case that might jog some Agency clerk into co-operating.

But the result was zip. And brushing shoulders with so many security and Intel agents on the UN Task Force had reminded Cleary how pissed off he was becoming at such high-handed arrogance. What Federal law allowed some spook to ignore the criminal justice system and the hard-working Homicide Division of New York Police Department?

This was why, on his return from checking out the idle rich at Beauregard, and liaising with the various County Police Departments, Highway Patrol and the State Police, Sergeant Joe Cleary had phoned the slender Sicilian babe and asked her to have a drink with him after work. For if the victim had been tortured and killed in the course of some goddam secret enterprise, that cut no ice with the Irish detective. His personal pride demanded all leads would be followed up. And Mr Harold K. Liebowitz of Room 441, Government Offices, Langley, Virginia, was just another lead to him. No more, and no less. But first, he had other avenues to explore.

He swung into the right-hand lane as they approached Columbus Circle, on the south-west corner of Central Park.

'Where we going?' Dolores enquired, without much interest.

The kid is used to being treated like a piece of baggage, Cleary realized.

'How about a drink?' he suggested. 'I know this bar on Central Park South.'

She pouted a response that might have meant sure, or who gives a shit?

Joe Cleary parked outside the Ritz Carlton hotel and left his NYPD Sports Club member's card on the dash. He nodded to Francis the doorman and ushered Dolores into the old Jockey Club cocktail bar, by the side of the main entrance. It was part of the hotel and once had been one of the nicest and most civilized bars in Manhattan. But a couple of years back, the management had suffered from a desire to spend on refurbishment. The result was that the wood panels, the long bar and the clubby oil paintings of Clumber Spaniel dogs, racehorses and saddleback pigs had gone, to be replaced by expensive pink marble and a rich Italian look.

There was nothing wrong with it. It just was not the Jockey Club any more. Except for Norman the barman. Norman was a forty-something New Yorker, originally from Rockaway Beach, but now moved uptown, who was a more or less constant fixture of the place, except for Yom Kippur and other religious holidays. He was a friend of Joe's, for Joe's first precinct, when he had been a brand new uniformed cop, had been at Rockaway Beach, and they had played pool in the same bar on Edgemere Street.

Always turned out in bartender's black, complete with apron, white shirt and black tie, Norman had a droll line in throwaway, deadpan wisecracks and the best memory for faces of any guy in New York.

He glanced up, for a half of a second, from mixing a couple of Gin Slings and met Joe's gaze, before continuing with some conversation he was having with three rich dames out on the town and hell bent on having a good laugh.

Joe found a table for two, in the raised alcove by the street door and they sat down. He watched the slender girl as she slipped her cashmere cardigan off her tanned and lithe shoulders and folded it over the side of the chair. The kid was at home in such classy surroundings, noted Cleary, and he figured she would never have gotten the job at Bartello if she had not been confident and reasonably cosmopolitan. And the Eve Agency would not have been interested either. Poor babe. Her looks and pretence at *savoir-faire* would probably be her undoing.

'So,' he went on, as if they had not just spent twenty minutes in more or less silence, 'am I right? You're one of Johnny the Stomp's girls.'

'Maybe I used to be.' She meant, sure she used to work for Johnny Stomparelli, and there was no maybe about it.

'Till when? Tonight?'

She took a long, slim, green cigarette from a thin, gold cigarette case, and it waved impotently between her fingers as her street-wise sophistication faltered. She looked at Cleary and said, 'Listen, uh, Mister – whadda I call you? I don't know what to call you . . .' And her moist eyes were earnest as they searched his face.

'Call me Joe, kid. Like I said. This ain't official. It's, um . . .'

'A date?' She smiled suddenly. Amused.

There was just the off-chance, mused Joe Cleary, that this Dolores Caltagirone, given even half a break, might be able to relax and enjoy herself.

He spread his hands as Norman the barman approached. 'Sure. First date, though. And I'm a good Catholic boy, Dolores, so you can relax.'

She was still gazing at him, for the first time interested, maybe thoughtful, as Norman arrived beside them.

'I don't serve table any more,' he announced, and he and Cleary gripped hands and grinned, happy to see each other.

'Norman, this is a friend of mine. Dolores, meet Norman. The worst pool player in the Rockaways.'

'With friends like him who needs them?' said Norman, and, to Dolores, 'Watch this guy. He can be trouble.'

'Tell me about it,' said the kid.

'So what'll it be? Jack Daniels on the rocks, with a splash, and a vodka screwdriver – just a suggestion.'

'How did you know that's what I drink?' asked Dolores, incredulous, and the bartender smiled as he moved away, always busy.

'It's all over town,' he said, then began to sing the words as he went back to the bar.

'So,' said Joe Cleary, never a man to take long to get to the point, 'tell me about this guy you found dead in the freezer.'

'I've told you over and over. And over. Hey. I thought this was just you and me and a drink. Joe.' She paused the gas lighter on its way to her green cigarette.

Cleary smiled. 'Baby, you forgot to tell me you were fucking him.'

Well, she dropped the long cigarette and leaned down to catch it off the floor. Joe Cleary could not help observing her perfect, smallish breasts, as the black halter neck dress made space owing to the laws of gravity.

When Dolores straightened up, having given herself time to think, she swept her ash-blonde hair off her eyes and faced him, challenging.

'So what, officer? You think I killed him?'

'I think, Dolores, that you know who did.'

She looked completely shocked. 'I swear I don't.'

Cleary waited until a gaggle of people on a shoe convention moved further into the bar, from the street door. He flicked open his Zippo, which had the badge of US Navy Seal Team 6 on the side, and held the flame for her to get a light, his eyes searching hers.

'You maybe don't know you know them. But I think you probably have seen them, even heard them. Don't worry,' he leaned back, relaxed, 'this ain't about withholding.' He meant, withholding evidence, a serious misdemeanour.

The tall, good-looking kid – she was in fact stunning, he had decided some weeks ago – puffed on her cigarette in a way that suggested she was not really enjoying it, then she asked, 'How did you know he was a . . .'

'A John?'

She nodded, and seemed embarrassed.

Cleary shook his head and, as a Moroccan waiter, a minion of Norman's, served their drinks from a tray, he said, 'It was just a guess, kid. It's the only way us guys get from A to Zee.'

After a pause she said, quietly, 'You bastard.'

Joe nodded gravely. 'We both gotta survive, you and me. It ain't personal. And this won't go on the record, you got my word on that.' He raised his tumbler. 'You're beautiful, Dolores. Here's to you. Let's relax. You hungry? I know the *maître d'* here. Whadda you say?'

The girl picked up her glass, thoughtful. 'I did see him once with two other guys. Kind of foreign-looking,' she offered.

Four visits to the Bartello place, two to her apartment, three interviews downtown, in the Precinct. And all it took was whacking her pimp, defending her honour, bringing her to a classy joint and treating her like a goddam lady.

Bingo.

'In that case,' he announced, 'you could be in serious danger.'

Dolores took this in. 'I can take care of myself,' she decided, and Joe could not figure if that was bravado or sheer goddam stupidity.

8

Peek a Boo

'I'm looking at Cyprus,' said Alan Clair. He was sitting on a canvas chair at the stern of the *Criterion*, a powerful twin-engined forty-five-foot cruiser, named after a famous American thoroughbred who won the Kentucky Derby several times in the 1930s. The boat was the property of Joe Kippen, a Republican Senator, chairman of the Intelligence Oversight Committee and a long-time, trusted friend of Clair's.

Kippen hired the *Criterion* to the CIA Operations Director at a nominal rent, once or twice a year, whenever Alan Clair had a few days' leave and wanted to get away from Washington's intrigues and power struggles, and think in peace.

Sitting on a white life-raft cover was another old friend, David Jardine. The Englishman sipped rum and Coke from a chunky tumbler and turned his face to the setting sun, catching its gold-russet light, still strong in this part of the Florida coast.

They were moored alongside the marina at Sunday's wharf, in Key Biscayne, just a sweeping cantilever multi-lane bridge away from Miami's Bayshore and Coconut Grove.

'I'm looking at Cyprus and a couple of Vevak operatives butchered with a chainsaw, and you know what I see . . .?'

'What do you see?' asked Jardine, squinting at the prisms of colour the sunlight made through the dark liquid in his glass.

'I see a man without a nose. A woman likewise. Also their ears.'

'You have a disturbing memory for gruesome detail,' said Jardine, twisting the tumbler this way and that.

'And what do I begin to remember?'

Jardine shrugged. 'I'm not sure if I want to know.'

'I remember a guy found dead in a goddam freezer. In a mob restaurant in New York. Only this was no mob business . . .'

A grey pelican glided onto a mooring pole just feet away and settled his wings, folding them onto his body, and rested there. Soberly. Contemplating the glass-flat surface of the water and, it seemed to Jardine, making it clear he had no interest in their conversation.

'What a dignified bird,' he said. 'Do they live to a great age, like tortoises?'

'No, sir. This was a Vevak hit. On a Vevak operator. And you know what?'

'Or is it a myth? Maybe tortoises don't live all that long.'

'They do.' Clair scratched his ear, a sign he was becoming impatient. 'My wife's niece is an anthropologist on Ascension Island. They cut off his fucking nose . . .'

'The one in the freezer?'

'You know about it, come on. Harry Liebowitz sent the whole report to your office. For your eyes only, buddy. Your eyes only.'

In the silence, they could hear the laughter of young people across the harbour, where some lithe and animated teenage waitresses were flirting with three men who had tied up their expensive powerboat alongside the pier at the faded, gray-blue clapboard bar and restaurant that was Sunday's On The Beach.

The faint, deep chords of a live keyboard and bass guitar, tuning up, joined the muted sounds of laid-back hedonism.

David Jardine glanced at his watch. 'You want to eat over there? Have a few beers?'

'Harry figured the Bartello killing was a Vevak internal security team, pissed with one of their own. Now why would they be *that* pissed, DJ?'

Jardine nodded, touching the cold rim of his tumbler against his cheek. 'Maybe they found out.'

'Found out? Found out what?'

'Don't be tedious, Alan; they probably suspected he had been turned by somebody else.'

'Well, *we* didn't turn the guy. And he was good. FBI could

not get near his act. They still remain unconvinced he was a goddam spy, that's how good he was.'

Jardine sipped the rum. The live combo started to beat out a lazy Reggae number, 'No woman no cry . . .'

'Oh, he was very good, Al. He was really exceptional. And he was a friend. Brave man. I wish we could do something for his widow, but she thinks he's still alive. Plus she's in Tehran, working for the *majlis*, as a researcher. The moment we try to make contact, we've signed her death warrant. Don't you adore Jimi Hendrix?'

'Bob Marley. That's Bob Marley.' Clair lifted a tall glass of Wild Turkey bourbon on the rocks from a turquoise cold box and sniffed the liquor. 'So that was the double you were running in New York.'

Jardine inclined his head. 'We've been over all this. You knew from the start, Alan, I know you.' He smiled. 'And I'm quite glad I do. Sometimes.'

'What I'm getting at . . .' Clair climbed to his feet and sauntered over to the rail, eyeing up the waitresses on the far pier, 'is the mutilation signature is no coincidence.'

'No, I don't think it is,' agreed David Jardine.

'So.' The CIA man turned and looked his friend straight in the eye.

Jardine met his gaze. 'So, what?'

'So it seems, uh . . . what is it you guys say? "Not unlikely"? That the Cyprus victims were also interrogated and killed by their own Security people. By the same fucking sadist who did Muar Abbas, your guy in the freezer.'

David Jardine nodded his agreement. 'That is what my bright young people think too. That's the Catnap conclusion.'

Alan Clair moved along the rail, closer to Jardine.

'So . . .'

Jardine spread his hands, almost spilling his rum. 'Get to the fucking point, Alan.'

'So, ergo, these two dead Iranians, salami-ed deep-cover dead Iranian spooks . . . were they also on your SIS payroll? Were they too, "good friends" . . .?' He leaned down, closer to David Jardine. 'Do you have a whole nest of assets inside Tehran's secret world? David, this is too serious now, I can't let the Agency be cut out of something this serious. So tell me right now, in words of one syllable, were Mahmud and Benine Rashahi two of yours? Two *more* of yours . . .?'

Jardine gazed back, unblinking. After a long moment, he said, 'Absolutely not.'

This seemed to stop Clair in his tracks.

'And there's no possibility somebody, say, Marietta, is running sleepers without your knowledge.'

Jardine shook his head. 'I'd cut her balls off.'

After a pause, Alan Clair chuckled. 'You would need a damn sharp knife.'

They laughed. Then Clair asked if the Aldridge Ames thing, which by that time had resulted in Ames and his Colombian wife being arrested and jailed for selling CIA secrets to the new Russian Intelligence Service, was still influencing SIS when it came to sharing secrets with the Agency.

'Alan,' replied David Jardine, by this time in the main cabin where he was pulling on a clean shirt, 'you do know, old friend, I would never keep anything of any importance from you. We go too far back.' And he splashed some Trumper's Bay Rum astringent aftershave onto his face. 'Come on, let's take some shore leave and hit a few bars.'

Clair pulled a navy blue polo shirt over his head, looking thoughtful.

'If you're sure about Cyprus . . .' he said.

'Crystal clear, dear boy. So can we go?'

Clair finally relaxed. 'Sure thing.'

And as they climbed onto the dock, he said, 'Maybe it's turtles.'

'What about them?'

'Maybe it's turtles. Not tortoises.'

'Yep. Could be.'

'Who gives a shit . . .'

And the two good friends strolled towards the strains of Bob Marley. It was getting dark quite quickly now.

It was darker in Alaska. At the US Customs Post on the Canadian border, dividing the small Alaskan frontier town of Hyder from its neighbour, Stewart in British Columbia, Customs Officer Ed Donovan poured some hot coffee from an enamel pot and listened to the local weather news on the radio.

Local, in Hyder, encompassed an area of some 80,000 square miles, from Juno, in the north, to Prince Rupert, the nearest real airport in Canada, about 180 miles to the south.

Stewart had until 1979 been a booming mining town. Its copper mine had provided work for hundreds in the remote and mountainous region, not far from the junction between the Yukon and Klondyke rivers. The territorial border was no barrier to those American and Canadian men and women who lived in Hyder and Stewart and worked for the mine.

Then the mine had closed and, within a few years, the neatly laid out mining company streets and houses had fallen into disrepair.

These days, the main occupation for the few families left was trapping, hunting, salmon fishing and prospecting. The region was rich in wildlife. Deer, racoons, brown bears, black bears and grizzly bears thrived, along with packs of gray timber wolves and mountain cats. Bald eagles abounded and all kinds of wildfowl inhabited the dense forests that stretched for hundreds of desolate miles.

In the US Customs Post, Officer Donovan could hear the howling of the wolves, just a half mile or so away, in the steep mountain woods. In the middle of September, they were only advertising for mates. But when the deep snows came, they would come right down into the two small towns, foraging in garbage cans and on occasion luring domestic pets away from the safety of their warm cabins and the protection of their owners' hunting rifles.

There was one tribe of wolves which had perfected the art of sending their best-looking, sexiest young wolf bitches slinking through Stewart and Hyder, when they came on heat. The pungent scent and promise of unbridled passion was too much for many of the huge, red-blooded hounds, mostly Husky/German Shepherd crossbreeds whose owners worked them for hunting and protection, and they would follow the sexy she-wolves way out of town and up into the dark forest. Where they promptly became that evening's supper.

Ed Donovan smiled to himself as he thought about that. And he raised a hand to the two familiar six-wheel pick-ups cruising from Stewart across into Hyder where their occupants would down a few beers and play some pool in the First Chance & Last Chance Saloon, so called because, on the bar sign hanging outside the Hyder Inn, the side facing the nearby border announced 'First Chance Saloon', and on the reverse, facing into Alaska, was the legend 'Last Chance Saloon'.

'Ever been Hyderised?' asked a grizzled trapper in a thick plaid jacket and battered felt hat, decorated with the tails of small furry animals.

'What's that?' asked the Englishman who had hitched a ride from the King Edward Motel in Stewart, where he had come to photograph the bird life.

The trapper, John Mackenzie, grinned. 'Let's show him,' he said and the girl behind the bar put a bottle and four small tumblers on the counter. The brown, square bottle had an ominously lethal look to it, not alleviated by the name on the label, 'Yukon Jack'.

'One hundred and ten proof, son. Three of these and Dinah here'll give you a certificate, which states and confirms you have remained on yer feet. If you do . . .' He swept a couple of fingers through his moustaches and the other men laughed. 'And that document will say that you, so and so, have been well and truly Hyderised.' He poured four measures and handed one to the English guy. 'And what is your name again?'

'Andrew. Andrew Drummond,' replied James Gant, and he drained the liquor in one gulp, offering the empty glass for a refill.

Mackenzie and the other two men, a trapper and the owner of a Hyder workshop that made skidoos, a sort of motorcycle on skis, exchanged glances. 'Hey, kid,' growled the trapper, 'I like your style.'

By ten after ten that night, the First & Last Chance Saloon was noisy and smoky. Hyderised Certificates had been issued to Andrew Drummond and others besides. The road outside and the yard at the side of the inn were scattered with parked pick-ups and four-wheel-drive Jeeps and Dodges. They came and went back and forth to Stewart, on the other side of the border, once or twice every hour.

'Drummond' and his new-found trapper friends got pretty drunk. Then the Englishman joined in a series of pool games, where he lost a few dollars. Then the Backwood Mountain Boys arrived to a welcome of whooping and hollering and set up their electric guitars, electric fiddle and drums, so with all that excitement it was unremarkable that the four men who had arrived together soon became split up.

Next morning, nursing a trepanning hangover, eyes as bloodshot as a hungover vampire's, James Gant woke up on a pile of newly cured wolf and black-bear pelts in a lean-to at the back of the saloon.

He lurched to his feet and felt his way, delicately, to the yard, really just a dirt space with a couple of antique gas pumps, where he ran icy cold water from a spigot and splashed it over his aching head.

'Quite a night, mister . . .' said a friendly voice. 'Quite a night all right. You ready for breakfast? Eggs and French toast? Nice greasy racoon sausages?'

Gant's stomach revolved 360 degrees. He thought he was going to throw up. The speaker was about forty, fair haired, tanned complexion. Lean and fit. He was smiling.

'Why, just last night you were the life and soul of the party. Twice Hyderised is close to masochism. You want a ride?' He indicated a gargantuan truck, its rig the height of a modest house, all gleaming chrome pipes and scarlet and blue paint. Wheels taller than a man.

Gant winced and looked away from the bright colours. This was not part of the plan. His plan had been to stay in Stewart for a couple of days. Let the US Customs and the Canadian Mounties on the other side of the border get used to him wandering around, taking photographs of wildlife, then one day simply move on, having chosen one of the hundreds of places to cross the border without anyone noticing. In a society of drifters and bear hunters, nobody would think twice about his absence. And he had lodged a few hundred dollars with the owner of the King Edward Motel, so he would leave no debts, and no bad feeling. Which would turn fast into gossip in a desolate place like this.

That had been the plan. Gant's plan to enter the USA illegally. He had money, US dollars in five-hundred-dollar bills – forty thousand dollars' worth. All his savings. And he had four British passport blanks, and one Irish, along with forgers' inks and a collection of photos of himself with blond hair and dark hair, with moustache, without moustache, and likewise about glasses and the length and cut of his hair.

He also had computer discs and a small black diary with his proposed contact list and other vital details on every page, hidden among anodyne entries, in invisible ink.

And all of those things he still had on his person, in a body belt and two leg wallets, worn under his trousers, above the ankles, secured by Velcro straps.

He splashed more water over his face and straightened up, wincing as a team of tiny men with band saws went to work between his brains and his skull. 'Where you heading?' he asked the trucker.

The man paused, half-way up the side-ladder to his high cab, and answered over his shoulder, 'Ketchikan. For a load of timber.'

Gant nodded, which was a mistake. When the red mist cleared he said, sure, he would be glad of the ride.

So that is how James Sebastian Gant, alias Andrew Drummond, embarked on his first truly clandestine and totally illegal mission. A self-indentured smiter of terror, intent on the saving of around eighteen lives.

With the mother, father, and several ancestors of a hangover, the kind that has a dead badger swinging on your uvula, his plan, such as it had been, was abruptly altered on a snap judgement. For, he figured, since he had already entered the USA illegally and unnoticed, why make things more difficult?

And as the giant rig rumbled towards the snowline and the high forest mountain passes, Gant dozed and snored and from time to time sipped gratefully from a flask of piping hot black coffee as thick as a sort of caffeine soup. And he began to feel strangely relaxed.

For now he was committed. There was no going back.

Maybe it was the vestiges of Yukon Jack. Maybe it was too much coffee. But James Gant knew he was a man with a mission.

He smiled as he dozed, towering mountains and forests

drifting smoothly by, deep valleys with electric-blue glacier . . . hunks, toy building blocks of Behemoth children, littered in the gulleys. And he remembered the words of a number by Devo, a punk band of the seventies; 'I'm a man with a mission, I'm a boy with a gun, I got a picture in my pocket of the lucky one.'

Watch out, Zina Farouche, he thought as sleep overtook him. I'm coming after you . . .

Even if the Palestinian girl had been aware of James Gant's existence, it is unlikely she would have trembled in those Manolo Blahnik shoes of hers – a present from Hanna, who had bought them in London specially for her. (In fact, if Marietta Delice had been the totally omniscient spy of popular fiction, she would have known that Hanna al-Farah, Commander of the Assassins, was a size seven, while the feet of her lover were a more dainty five-and-a-half.)

But Zina Farouche had more to think about. In addition to working with the US Protective Task Force, arranging the minutiae of security for the Tunisian Delegation, and briefing her Tunisian colleagues and their diplomatic charges, she could not for a minute stop concentrating on her real reason for being in New York City.

And it was not particularly easy to make contact with the rest of the team. Ben Turabi was on the same floor of the Essex House hotel, with the Moroccan Foreign Minister. He was employed as a cook, a position arranged by Abu Nidal's Special Missions Committee, using a blackmailed asset in the Moroccan Foreign Ministry's Personnel Department.

But it was not wise for them to be seen to be on speaking terms, so Zina had arranged a complex programme of brush encounters in the elevators and the coffee lounge, where she could pass on instructions and details of more clandestine meetings, which she intended to keep to an absolute minimum.

Zafir Hammuda had been inserted into the Algerian Delegation, thanks to a favour owed to Hanna al-Farah by the Islamic Tide's Intelligence Director. Islamic Tide was engaged in a brutal terrorist campaign to destabilize the Algerian Government and establish a Fundamentalist state. Their agents and sympathisers had infiltrated every sector of the administration and it had been comparatively simple to furnish Hammuda with an Algerian passport, identity papers, driver's licence and a bank account. The Ministry of Foreign Affairs records had been altered to show that he had been employed there for four years, as driver and courier, with the necessary security clearances.

After consulting with her immediate superior, Hanna al-Farah, in Paris, in that former Gestapo house on the Avenue Foch, it had been agreed that, because of his lack of self control in raping and mutilating Denise Orué during the Biarritz assignment, Hammuda was to be given a severe reprimand and told next time he deviated from orders he would die very slowly indeed.

He was also appointed second-in-command of the hit team, for, if anything happened to Zina, Zafir Hammuda, crazy though he was, could be relied upon not to deviate from leading the mission to its bloody conclusion.

The system of clandestine contacts between Hammuda and Zina Farouche was arranged in a broad-spectrum calendar of locations, such as the drug store on the corner of 6th and 55th, the 7-Eleven on the corner of West 43rd and 6th, and so on. None of them knew when their cover jobs would permit attending such rendezvous, so there was a considerable number of show-up times each day. Often neither could make it. Sometimes only one. But the system succeeded in getting them together enough times to keep in touch.

There were actually six members of the Abu Nidal team.

There were the five who had been identified by Marietta Delice's Catnap network of terrorist watchers: Zina Farouche, Zafir Hammuda, Ben Turabi, Noor Jalud and Mustafa Sharik – the lesser-spotted Mustafa – on SIS files as an able planner who always got his killers away safely, after the event.

But the one terrorist Catnap had missed was perhaps the most dangerous, from the point of view of anyone attempting to get near the killing team. His name was Khaled Niknam, orphaned at six in Chatilla camp, Beirut, during a Christian Phalangist attack, which killed forty-six and left scores of maimed and bereaved.

He had killed his first Phalangist at the age of ten, and,

since then, Niknam had fought with Hamas in the Israeli-occupied West Bank, in the Lebanon and in Afghanistan with the Mujahadeen. He had also proved himself to be a brilliant deep-cover operator in Germany, Italy and England.

His forte was the total security of Special Missions teams and sleeper units, in hostile environments – what David Jardine's SIS termed 'Denied Areas'.

Khaled Niknam had a feline perception and an almost supernatural ability to smell out the interloper, the double dealer and the fake. Even the most professional and discreet attempts at surveillance had been winkled out and ruthlessly dealt with by him.

Niknam's secondment to her team had been specifically requested by Zina Farouche, and he had only been released from his other duties by Abu Nidal himself, after the Palestinian girl had persuaded her superior and lover, Hanna al-Farah, to intercede on her behalf.

So Khaled Niknam was now in New York City, working discreetly as the killing team's own security co-ordinator. It was a town he knew well, having helped to establish three sleeper units, worked as a courier during the setting up of the World Trade Centre bomb and as Abu Nidal's security liaison with a Vevak internal investigation team, which had unearthed a traitor among their own intelligence service operators. This was the guy who, after a horrific interrogation, was left dead and mutilated inside a food freezer in Barolo's Italian restaurant in Tribeca. To encourage the others.

And Khaled Niknam, a dangerous and profoundly experienced operator, was just twenty-one years old, blessed with an olive-skinned, smooth, almost cherubic countenance and big, full-of-fun, liquid brown eyes. Every middle-aged woman wanted to mother him, which was perhaps nature's way of compensating him for being an orphan.

He had learned fluent Spanish, working on joint ventures between the Abu Nidal Group and the Medellín, then the Cali cocaine Cartels. He had worked for a year in Colombia and could pass for a *paisa*, his features being very similar to those . Spanish/Jewish/Tolima Indian inhabitants of the Colombian province of Antioquía.

And that was how Khaled had come into the USA, for this

mission. The Cali Cartel *padrón*, Don Fabio Ochoa, had provided him with impeccable Colombian credentials and the Lebanese Arab even had a green card to work in New York as a Courier/Driver for Avianca, the Colombian airline.

Zina Farouche had planned well, for while the diplomatic cover she and three members of her assassination squad had acquired gave them valuable protection from the US authorities and their Federal counter-terrorist agencies – the FBI, the US Secret Service and NYPD's Intelligence Division – at the same time their movements were restricted, taking place, as they did, under the noses of those same agencies as well as the State Department's Diplomatic Security Service and the UN Week Protective Task Force, whose Special Agents and detectives like Joe Cleary had been assigned to guard each nation's visiting representatives, at every location they used or visited in New York City, right around the clock.

But Khaled Niknam, with his Avianca cover, was of no interest to anyone, provided he kept well clear of known Islamic extremists and their sympathisers, and kept his Colombian criminal contacts at arm's length. His work as a low-grade courier and driver permitted him to be in the same environment of hotels and restaurants as those team members with diplomatic cover. His profound understanding of what protective services' officers were looking for, in terms of potential threats, had allowed him, over the last several weeks, to establish his apparent innocence by merely working, quite indolently, at his cover job, and becoming a known and accepted face, at first noticed by astute Task Force advance operators, briefly checked out, then accepted as part of the landscape.

Zina had also inserted her team's master planner into New York without the inhibiting protection of diplomatic cover, so that he too could move around with complete freedom.

Mustafa Sharik, age twenty-nine, had been admitted as a postgrad student at New York University, scheduled to start his studies on 5 October, after the summer vacation. He had obtained a student's visa, using his impeccably forged Bosnian passport and other credentials, issued in Sarajevo by an official in that largely Muslim Government's consular department in return for a favour from the Abu Nidal group.

(The group had provided Bulgarian credentials for three agents of the Bosnian Intelligence Service, who were subsequently able to enter Serbia under cover as haulage company representatives, looking for a contract to smuggle oil into Bosnian Serb territory, in breach of the UN embargo.)

Mustafa had arrived in the USA four weeks earlier, through Boston airport. He had rented cars and travelled around the Eastern Seaboard, reaching New York unnoticed on 19 August, which was a Friday.

He had found an apartment with one room and a bathroom on the second floor of a brownstone building on Mercer Street, which was practically part of the campus. New York City being the polyglot place that it is, the lesser-spotted Mustafa, as Marietta Delice had labelled him, quickly became part of the teeming millions who inhabit Manhattan.

Thus Mustafa al-Sharik was able to go about his detailed preparations, to produce a watertight plan for the Beauregard massacre and the safe escape of the killers, in complete peace.

His only contact with the hit squad was in occasional meetings with Khaled Niknam. They met in the New York Public Library, at the Guggenheim Museum on the corner of Broadway and Prince – sometimes crossing the street to take a leisurely coffee or two at Dean & DeLucca's state-of-the-art delicatessen and espresso bar – and at the Strand Book Store on Broadway at 12th Street. To any casual or not-so-casual observer they seemed two fairly average Village types, of Latin or Semitic appearance. Mustafa checked out as a Bosnian student and his companion, whose papers were in the name of Andreas Murillo Guerrero, a Colombian driver with the national airline.

There were a million more unlikely acquaintances in New York City.

Noor Jalud, on the other hand, had no need of elaborate intrigue to get a place with the Kuwaiti Delegation, for she was a Kuwaiti national, born and bred. A Sunni Muslim, she had attended the Sorbonne where she had embraced radical politics and a succession of Palestinian lovers. One of these had been a recruiter for Abu Nidal and she had accompanied him back to Libya, where she had been interviewed by Abdel Aziz al-Khaliq, Controller of the faction's Membership Committee, and promptly denounced as a infiltrator and agent of the Saudi Intelligence Service.

Noor had been thrown into the merciless hands of Abdul-Salem Latif's interrogators at Station 16, in the Naji al-Ali terrorist camp, deep in the Libyan desert.

Like Zina Farouche, the Kuwaiti girl had survived her ordeal and had been admitted to a number of trial operations, to test her nerve, her loyalty, her discretion and her ruthlessness. She had progressed from daytime killings at point-blank range, in busy Beirut and Egyptian streets, to car bombs in Europe and an elaborate 'honey trap' to lure the loathed Yasser Arafat's Security Chief, commander of al-Fatah's Force 17, away from the safety of Fatah's offices in Tunisia to his long, slow death at the hands of a team of Iranian VEVAK interrogators in the al-Jarif camp near Khartoum, in the Sudan.

And, yes, his nose too had been cut off by one particular interrogator. And, yes, a chainsaw was used in the final hours of the man's ordeal. That had been four years earlier, when the girl Noor Jalud was merely twenty.

Her success as a *femme fatale* led Abu Nidal to direct his Special Missions controllers to mount an operation to return Noor to her native Kuwait, where her task was to infiltrate the Kuwaiti ruling family, and therefore its political leadership at the highest level.

Noor Jalud had done well. For the last fifteen months, she had been the lover of the favourite son of the Kuwaiti Foreign Minister, himself a member of the ruling family, who had a position with the Ministry of Foreign Affairs.

It had been Noor's suggestion that a trip to New York amid the exciting panoply of United Nations Week might be fun. And here they were, young Faisal as Minister Plenipotentiary – which entailed visiting the most expensive restaurants, obtaining the best seats at the theatre and the ballet for his father, and ordering a number of Chevrolet Corvettes and big Dodge six-wheels to be shipped back to oil city.

Noor Jalud had full diplomatic status as an official P/A to

the Foreign Minister himself. Since he was not scheduled to arrive until the weekend before UN Week, her duties were not exactly onerous.

So Zina Farouche had assigned the Kuwaiti girl to covert liaison with Khaled Niknam, alias Andreas Murillo Gueuero, and Noor Jalud was the team's only contact with him. She kept him up-to-date with the status of the other pseudo-diplomatic employees and he passed on his recommendations (orders, really) with regard to their continuing security and as much of the development of Mustafa al-Sharik's planning for the attack and their escape as he felt they needed to know.

Noor Jalud at no time was permitted to make contact with Mustafa. If they found themselves in the same place at the same time, they were to ignore each other.

The only person, apart from Khaled Niknam, with access to Mustafa was Zina Farouche herself. Because of the constantly changing demands on her time, meeting with Al Wiscynsky's DSS agents, NYPD, State Department and United Nations officials, and her own Tunisian security colleagues, she made arrangements for rendezvous at short notice, using a system of visual signals so simple as to be undetectable ... a green silk scarf protruding from her purse ... a pink chalk mark on a particular news-stand, on the sidewalk near the Hertz office in West 54th street. And so on.

Zina also had regular contact with Noor Jalud, who was her contact with Khaled Niknam.

For the benefit of anyone taking an interest, and she had to assume at all times that some form of security surveillance might be operating against her – the DSS had a very tight reputation for extreme thoroughness and such surveillance might, for all she knew, be routine – Zina had planned and gone through with a simple charade of being introduced to Noor Jalud at one of the State Department's welcoming functions, this one had been in the American suite of conference rooms and banqueting room in the UN Building, overlooking the East River.

The two women were past masters at appearing to get on well with each other, as soon as they first met, and it was no big deal for an intelligent young Tunisian to become friends with a pretty diplomatic secretary from the Kuwaiti delegation. What could be more natural?

So coffee in the mornings, or a quiet pasta in the evening at some mutually convenient restaurant, had soon become almost routine. It was so obvious that nobody noticed it.

Except, of course, Joe Cleary, for two babes, wearing neat, well-cut but unobtrusive European clothes, would at any time have won his admiring, casual interest. But he had met the Farouche girl that first cocktail welcome session on the eighth floor at the Hilton, she had been introduced to him by Big Al Wiscynsky, and something – he wasn't kidding himself, he had no illusions about his strange appeal to certain chicks – had sparked, briefly.

So when Zina and Noor Jalud met up in places like the piano bar in the Plaza Athenée, or in the Jockey Club lounge, he surely did notice.

And because Joe was a detective who had survived all those dangerous years in New York, first, and a no-account skirt-chaser, third (husband and doting father of Patrick Cheyenne came second), some sixth sense had caused him not to breeze up and say, 'Hi, remember me? I'm the guy looking after the Egyptians.'

Zina had noticed Joe Cleary too, a couple of times, and wondered why he, an obvious womaniser, had not acknowledged her presence. But it was part of her experience not to get paranoid, after all the man had an assignment that would take him over much of the same City territory as herself. When they passed each other on business, going in and coming out from briefings etcetera, they would smile briefly and nod. So if he did not feel like saying hello those couple of informal times, either the cop could not give a damn or he was a good professional.

She kind of thought it might be the second of these. Which confirmed her first instincts. If nice guy Joe was anywhere around on the day of the hit – the 27th, she had decided – he would be among the first to go.

Zina had already decided to include a snatched photo of him in her final briefing.

On this particular evening, she was working her cover job,

up front in the Tunisian Foreign Minister's armoured Cadillac, carrying a Beretta 9mm automatic pistol in her purse, cradled in her lap.

The driver was a trained bodyguard, a sergeant-major in the Tunisian Paratroop Brigade. In the back of the roomy limousine was Ambassador Belhassen Kefi and his wife Karin. Both were in their late forties.

Preceding the limo was a squat, ominous-looking Dodge patrol wagon, with black windows and the only sign of its lethal authority a discreet red and white strobe-light assembly, right across the roof of the cab, above the windshield.

Inside the Dodge were four Diplomatic Security Service Special Agents, two armed with .45mm Uzi sub-machine pistols, one with a short-barrelled Remington twelve-guage pump gun and the driver with a 9mm Mini-Uzi grease gun. They also carried issue Glock 19s with extended twenty-two-round magazines.

Travelling right behind the Cadillac was a black Plymouth sedan with no immediately visible law-enforcement or agency markings. Inside that were two more Special Agents backed up by two cops seconded from NYPD's Emergency Service Unit, which was New York's SWAT division. They too were heavily armed and able to use the hardware.

Behind them came a grey Ford sedan with four NYPD detectives, assigned from the 15th Precinct, known to Joe Public as Mid-Town North. These officers carried .45 Mac-10 Ingram machine-pistols and Glock pistols.

And all because the Foreign Minister had surprised everyone, from the US State Department to his own diplomats working in the USA, by arriving ten days early, so that he and his wife could enjoy a break in Manhattan and make informal contact with the US Administration and other foreign diplomats, for discussions on a wide-ranging menu of subjects.

An excuse, in other words, for a bit of a junket. And who could blame him? You get to be Foreign Minister in a North African autocracy, so go ahead, flaunt it. And here they were, escorted by a team of armed protectors.

Al Wiscynsky had taken it without a blink, shrugging and saying no problem. It would be a good chance to rehearse the protective team for its duties during the pandemonium of UN Week, in ten days' time.

All in all the tight, red-light-ignoring motorcade was a fearsome target to hit, considered Zina Farouche. Of course, if you knew where it was going to be, an RPG-7 hand-held rocket launcher would do the trick. And since the Ambassador always started out from the Essex House hotel, that would be the place to make the hit. Specially since Central Park and an easy escape were just across the street.

It occurred to the Palestinian girl, as the convoy cruised through New York towards the Metropolitan Opera House that night, that if some other killer team was in town, gunning for Ambassador Belhassen Kefi, she was duty bound to do her thing and protect his ass, even if it meant taking a bullet in the process.

Not just to maintain her cover, but because Tunisia had done nothing to offend her. Quite the opposite. They had given her shelter. It would be a debt of honour.

The beautiful girl smiled in the dark, as they sped across the intersection of 9th Avenue and 56th. How droll, if Zina Farouche were to die defending the life of a Sunni Muslim politician who had no interest in the cause of radical Islam.

She stroked the trigger guard of her Beretta and was caught off-balance by a sudden longing for the smooth and honey-sweet body of Hanna, for her cool breath. Her knowing touch.

Because it was dark, no one could see her blushing.

The journey to Juneau had taken all day. It was dark by the time the humungous rig roared into the harbour area and James Gant had been fast asleep for about six hours.

He rubbed the sleep from his eyes and looked around, blinking. The docks and piers were fairly crowded with tramp steamers, bigger cargo freighters and at least one cruise liner, with Russian Federation markings. Out in the bay were some fishing boats, heading off to sea and a long night's work, their red and green port and starboard lights and their white navigation lights blinking like wide-hipped, busy fireflies, hovering about the black surface of the ocean.

'You got someplace to stay?' asked the truck driver.

'Sure,' replied Gant automatically, remembering his training. There was no way he intended to prolong his acquaintanceship with this helpful stranger. He was glad he had been so hungover and bone-tired, for sleeping most of the journey had been an effective way to avoid being drawn into any meaningful conversation.

The trucker eyed him thoughtfully. 'You sure about that? I can put you together with a couple of cheap rooming houses.'

'I'm fine, really,' smiled Gant, 'I have a relation here.'

'Who's that?' The truck driver was busy securing his rig for the night; he was not really interested in the answer.

'Works for one of the shipping companies. Bookings side of things. Older than us, but I promised to look him up.'

The driver tugged down on a complicated system of ropes, keeping a tarpaulin over the cab. 'What the hell, maybe we could both take him out on the town. I mean, you sure know how to party . . .'

Shit, thought Gant. 'He's a lay preacher,' he invented, thinking fast. 'Maybe we could both join him at the gospel hall.'

His travelling companion stopped for a moment, frowning. Then he shook his head and said, 'Hell, man, what was I thinking of? This is Tuesday, right? I gotta phone my sister in Maine Tuesdays, she's just had her first papoose.'

James Gant smiled. As lies went, it was fair to middling, and most welcome. 'So, thanks for the ride. Can I pay for part of the gasoline?'

The Trucker, whose name was Jim Bridges, shook his head.

'All paid for, my friend. It was good to have company. You take it easy now and don't O.D. on the hallelujahs tonight, you hear?'

And that was that. The two men said so long and take it easy and they parted.

And James Gant was deep in American soil, with no whistles and no hue and cry. He shrugged and patted his money belt, then headed for the nearest waterfront hash house.

'Edith Treffewin isn't too well,' David Jardine remarked, pausing in the arched passage between the rest of the world and Magdalen College, to study the notice board outside the porters' lodge.

'The nice old lady who was a cabaret dancer?' asked Sally.

'That's the one. She paid her way through Somerville, on her tiny inheritance and a war widow's pension.'

'Dad, I'm perfectly happy with Bristol,' said Andrew, gazing around the mediaeval sandstone buildings and ecclesiastical architecture. It was a lazy, hot Saturday afternoon.

'They have wonderful fish in the pond at the other side of the quad.' Jardine moved on, gazing around, ambushed by memories of those days when the world had been his for the taking and he had realized he was falling in love with Sally's and Andrew's mother. Dorothy had been a year older, in her final term at Somerville. A considerable beauty in 1965, and reputedly unattainable.

'I'm not actually planning to do marine biology.'

'What are they called? Siamese carp. Something like that.'

'This is beautiful.' Sally turned round, gazing at the impressive quadrangle. It was a particularly splendid day, Jardine was always to remember. The sky that lazy pastel blue, and the autumn heat was stunning, mesmerising.

A faint hint of traffic sounds muttered from the town beyond. And tiny birds swooped around the spires and castellated roofs, chirruping idly, as if too warm from the sun to attempt too much.

'So is Cambridge,' said Andrew. More, thought Jardine, to stir things rather than as a reasoned contribution.

'Oh, I love Cambridge,' replied his sister, 'but this is very perfect.'

'Well, Bristol's fine.' Andrew was wearing jeans and a baggy shirt over a Jamaraquai T-shirt. David Jardine had no idea if Jamaraquai was a pop music group or a political cause. Andrew still seemed to imagine he was a Rastafarian or a child of the Bronx, from time to time.

'What's wrong with her?' enquired Sally Jardine.

Her father shrugged. 'Mild stroke, they suspect. Plus some problem with her pituitary gland.'

Sally nodded, she was in her fourth year of medicine, at Pembroke College, Cambridge. 'Beginning of the end, by the sounds of it.'

Jardine sighed. 'You think so?'

'Don't pay any attention to me, Dad, a little knowledge etcetera . . .' She slipped an arm through his. Sally had forgotten how fond her father was of so many of his colleagues, past and present, from 'the office'. It was a closed and remarkably civilized society, its practitioners urbane, cultivated and ruthless, quite clearly. But also fiercely loyal to their own, affectionate even, and surprisingly free-thinking. Quite unlike the reactionary image the notion of a secret service conjures up, she thought.

'Still, the old girl's a fair age. I'll pop in and see her on Monday.' Edith had been taken ill on the Thursday. And she was in intensive care at the King Edward VII Hospital for Officers, in London, near Harley Street.

They paused at the entrance to the Master's house, where Jardine had arranged for the present incumbent, John Allardyce, a former Ambassador to China and Fellow of All Souls – and an old and trusted colleague – to have tea with them and to take a look at Andrew. With the possibility of the boy finding a place in the college.

David Jardine gazed at his son. Andrew had really grown in the last couple of years and now he was at least as tall as his six-foot-three father. For all his cool, for all his rap-music argot, the boy had a lively intelligence and – if fathers can be objective – a really easy, pleasant personality.

And Jardine wanted the best for his son. And, for him, Oxford was the best. Although he would never let dear Sally know he thought that.

Maybe easing the young lad's academic path smacked of privilege, of nepotism. But it was a tough old world and kids needed a break.

Still. There was an expression in the boy's eyes which, standing there on the threshold of a fairly decisive tea party, made Jardine ask himself if he was doing this for Andrew, or for himself. If he was guilty of attempting to mould his son in his own image.

'You don't want to come to Oxford, do you?' he found himself asking, gently.

Was that a hint of fear in the boy's eyes? Surely to God not. Jardine smiled, 'It's all right. Really . . .'

And Andrew looked quite relieved.

'I don't think I do, Dad,' he said. 'As a matter of fact, I came and had a good look round, last term at school.'

In the silence, the chirruping of the idle birds, the faint hum of cars, the tinkle of a bicycle bell would stick in their memories.

'And you like the idea of Bristol.'

Andrew nodded. He seemed embarrassed, as if he was letting his father down. Sally had suddenly found the carp pond terribly interesting.

Jardine squeezed his son's arm. 'Then you should go there. Why don't you and Sally go and take a look around the town? I'll have a chat with John and we can meet up in the car park, in about a half hour.'

'I'll come up with you,' said Andrew. 'I don't mind explaining myself.'

They met each other's gaze. And smiled. Friends.

'Come on then,' announced Sally, joining them. 'I could kill for a cup of Earl Grey.'

The three of them had a pleasant half-hour with David Jardine's old chum, in the Master's sitting room, drinking not Earl Grey, as it happened, but PG Tips. Jardine was reminded of young James Gant's comment about monkeys on a television commercial for the brand. He wondered if the firm should try to get a message to James, about his dowager aunt.

The boy had been sent off on the office doctor's orders, to take a break, following his complaining of headaches and being diagnosed mildly hypertensive.

Where was it Gant had said he was going?

Climbing, Jardine seemed to recall. In the Dolomites.

John Allardyce had told them Bristol was a terrific place to study film, and he had brought the already much relieved Andrew out of himself, revealing a relaxed and cultivated young man, with not a hint of Ice T or Arrested Development about him.

They drove back to the Jardines' Wiltshire farmhouse in comfortable good humour, David Jardine having learnt that much more about the odyssey that is fatherhood, which he had begun to realize would never end.

Back home, Dorothy was waiting, just returned the previous day from a documentary shoot in Moscow, which those days seemed to be in the grip of gangsters and black-marketeers.

Ronnie Szabodo was coming down for the night. Jardine wanted to talk to him about the worrying coincidence of two of his most valuable assets, deep inside the Iranian Service, having been found mutilated and tortured – and, although thousands of miles apart, by the same sadistic interrogators.

'That bloody drag-artiste wants to build a tip,' remarked Dorothy as she chopped a bundle of carrots for the stew her husband was preparing. She was referring to a neighbouring landowner, who had a penchant for chiffon scarves and very young men from London's rougher environs.

'A tip? What sort of tip?' asked Jardine.

'Landfill. There's big money in it apparently.'

'Will we see it?'

'I don't know.' Dorothy Jardine dropped the sliced carrots into a saucepan by the handful. It was early evening and the radio was playing Purcell's *Dido and Aeneas*.

'A clove or two of garlic,' he pronounced, reaching for the terra-cotta garlic pot.

And as the aroma of lamb, and wine and olive oil and onions and herbs permeated the kitchen, he was transported back to that Friday evening, in the Post bar, in Oxford, when Dorothy had agreed to go to a horse race with him.

They had driven the 119 miles to Newmarket – it had not seemed so far in those days – and the tall and slender girl had been captivated by David Jardine's irredeemable and colourful father.

One of the 'Colonel's' horses had come in second and that had been cause enough for a celebratory dinner with his great pal Ryan Jarvis, another legendary Newmarket trainer.

Dorothy had never seen a racehorse, or even a horse race, close-up before, but the whole panoply of the turf had captivated her and, after that weekend, David Jardine and Dorothy Curwin had soon become an item.

And a couple of years after they had graduated, when Jardine was working in East Germany for Reuters, he had telephoned from Leipzig and asked her to marry him.

Now, twenty-something years later, having survived a long and nearly self-destroying fight with the bottle, Dorothy Jardine's career as a current affairs producer with the BBC was going strong. She had become David Jardine's stout, in every sense of the word, gravel-voiced companion and very best friend.

And, at the end of the day, it really was only Dorothy he truly loved. And even as he thought that thought, the irredeemable spymaster was visited by a guilty memory of the lithe and tanned Fiona Macleod, straddling him on a kitchen chair, gently rotating her immaculate pelvis as she pleasured him. You really are appalling, Jardine, he told himself. But we are all frail. Who could have resisted?

'How do you feel about rosemary?' he asked. 'Frankly, it does nothing for me.'

'David . . .' Dorothy smoothed her plump hands on the navy and white striped butcher's apron Andrew had given her for Christmas.

'Listen . . . Listen . . .' the opera had got to the part where King Aeneas is hoisting sail and departing, leaving a disconsolate Queen Dido – all the work of some wicked witches. And Jardine, who had a dreadful voice, short on tone and devoid of rhythm, as Edith Treffewin had put it all those years ago, joined in with gusto, singing, 'Come away all you sailors come away, let anchors be weighing and bold sails unfurling . . . Come away all you sailors come away . . .' and more in that vein.

'Those aren't the right words,' said Dorothy, fondly, knowing that was a lost cause.

And finally the chorus was over.

'I love Purcell,' announced Jardine. 'I really love him . . .'

'Well, you really would,' replied his wife, darkly. 'What time's Renfield coming down?'

Jardine glanced at her, slicing a clove of garlic into the big pot of lamb stew. 'Who told you he was called that?'

'Never you mind, I have my own secrets, what time?'

'Round about six, he said. Give or take half an hour.'

'Oh, he'll be bang on time. Ronnie knows when the free gin bottle opens.'

'Dorothy . . .' Jardine looked pained.

But Dorothy had returned to preparing more vegetables. Haricots verts this time. It seemed to Jardine, who was nothing if not perceptive, to be some kind of displacement activity.

'The plot's afoot . . .' droned Jardine, joining in with the witches. 'The game's forsook . . .'

'David.'

'Ha ha ha, ha ha ha, ha ha ha-ha-ha haaa . . .'

'You remember Angus Agnew?'

'Sure. Little shit who interviewed the Belgian Comique Ensemble in French and you had to put out an interview where nobody laughed at ten-forty one night with bloody subtitles.'

'That's him.'

'Pretentious little twerp. That was your verdict, I remember it very well,' he grinned. 'You were going to ritually disembowel him . . .'

Somehow, the way those moments happen, he knew precisely what she was going to say next. Somehow, he had known that warm, lazy afternoon, when idle finches had been chirruping happily around Magdalen's spires. And for all his 'little treats', and for all their living virtually separate lives, David Jardine's blood went cold, and his heart stood quite still.

'We have actually been seeing each other for some time,' she said, slowly slicing the green beans, 'and it's got to the stage we'll probably, we'd like . . .' she sighed, her cheeks wet with tears, 'to become closer. You know . . . what I'm saying, old sport, is, I think I'm going to leave you.'

Jardine gazed at her for a long time. At first, she couldn't look at him. Very gently, he removed the sharp little knife from her hand.

'Don't want to cut yourself,' he said, gently.

They were still standing there, in the stone-floored seventeenth-century kitchen, carrots and haricots boiling away, holding each other and crying quietly, when Andrew breezed in.

'Dracula's here,' he announced cheerily.

And Dorothy Jardine and David sniffed and held each other slightly apart. They started to smile.

'It's not Dracula, it's Renfield,' they both said at the same time.

Ronnie turned up at six on the stroke of the Jardines' long-case clock by Joseph Knibb, dated 1685. It had a peculiar chime, based on the locking-plate principle, whereby it would chime the number of hours, up to four – IV on the clock face – quite regularly, and, from four onwards, a deeper bell would come into play, mirroring the Roman numerals, so that four was 'ding-dong', five was 'dong', seven was 'dong-ding-ding' and nine would be 'ding-dong-dong'.

The clock, far more valuable than anything Jardine could have afforded, had been a present to the family from an illustrious and secret source, in recognition of a contribution David Jardine had made, in the unspoken affairs of his country.

'This is from the nation, Mister Jardine,' had said the august lady who arranged the gift. 'We have enjoyed it at Windsor and we have heard that clocks are your, um . . . thing.'

Jardine had been overwhelmed and so had Dorothy, who had been present at the informal luncheon with that regal personage, her indestructible mother and her eldest son, who was at that particular time newly married and free from the troubles that were to dog his and England's future.

'I suppose,' Dorothy had remarked later, 'you would've got a George Cross or something if you had been a soldier. Or a knighthood, but that would throw their bloody silly pecking order out of kilter.'

David Jardine had explained modestly (and not entirely accurately) that he had done nothing to earn a knighthood, a decoration for gallantry or even such a superb clock. But he had been absolutely thrilled, and every time he heard it chime its grave but profoundly silly sequence of dings and dongs, he sometimes smiled to himself and felt there must have been at least one time when he had done something right.

But as the clock struck six that September evening, Jardine had never felt further from smiling. Dorothy's sad announcement had just disintegrated the foundations of his very existence.

Of course he was away a hell of a lot. But then he always had been. And, yes, his affairs with a few women had been perhaps callous and selfish. But he had always been utterly discreet.

Oh, yes, David. So bloody discreet you ended up in a Bogotá graveyard defending yourself against an outraged and betrayed husband – a young man who had trusted you with his very life.

The echoes of that mad fusillade of gunfire were seldom very far away from what remained of David Jardine's conscience. But being the man he was, never once did he regret being faster with the bullets.

The plain fact was that, all his life, since falling for her all those years ago, there had never really been any woman for him but Dorothy. Sex – more lately the lack of it – had bugger all to do with the iron bond of devotion they had for each other. From Oxford, through babies, the demon drink, schools, careers and all, it had been a total love affair.

And now it was . . . gone? Certainly in real jeopardy.

'You all right, old man?' Ronnie Szabodo held a flaming taper from the log fire to his battered Petersen pipe, sucking steadily, as his eyes searched his boss's face.

They had gone into the study, an untidy room of bookcases, sporting paintings, Afghan rugs and ancient wood panels. And clocks, some of them in pieces, for Jardine liked to repair them.

The Hungarian had recruited Jardine, when the boss had been a young man working for Reuters in Leipzig. When Edith Treffewin had been Szabodo's controller, running the Gaslight circuit out of West Berlin.

There were no secrets between the two men. Well, almost none.

'I'm fine, Ronnie.' And Jardine rehearsed the history of their murdered agent Muar Abbas, codename Hindsight, found dead in that freezer in New York City, and of the Oversight team, Mahmud and Benine Rashahi, tortured and mutilated in too similar, too sick, a way for the two events to be coincidence. Particularly since, not only the methods of interrogation linked them, they also had in common that they were all deeply clandestine agents of SIS.

When he had finished, the room had acquired a pleasant aroma of Dunhill's Standard Mixture, Szabodo's favourite pipe tobacco (chosen because he had observed a former, titled, Foreign Secretary smoking that brand, and dear Ronnie was nothing if not a terrible snob).

Szabodo nodded, deep in thought. 'Are we thinking, Aldrich Ames here . . .?'

Jardine shook his head. 'Moonlight, Ronnie, is not something I have felt able to share with the Americans.'

'Moonlight' was the generic codename for SIS networks planted right at the heart of the Iranian Intelligence Services, their Government apparatus and the myriad client states, radical Islamic groups and terrorist organizations around the world, controlled by Tehran.

Even Ronnie Szabodo was not privy to the details and he often worried that, if the boss fell under a bus, or a big blonde, there would be no way of picking up the threads.

'Maybe Jamil Shahidi is a very good spy, David. Has that occurred to you?'

'Shahidi is a very good . . . organizer. He has a superbly devious mind. The Richelieu, if you like, of Motashemi's invisible empire. For special missions', Jardine meant acts of international terror, 'he is without equal. And their security procedures are . . . embarrassingly good.' David Jardine gazed into the heavy plain crystal tumbler of malt whisky he held cupped in his hands. He had not touched a drop. 'But counter-espionage, Ronnie? I don't think we have very much evidence they are so hot at that. Mmm?' His dark, intelligent eyes darted at Szabodo, like those of a snake.

Ronnie Szabodo raised his shoulders. 'We have no evidence. But then, if they were really so good. If they really were . . . unreproachable. We would not know, would we?'

Szabodo relaxed, pleased with that observation.

Jardine did not have the heart to tell the Magyar the word was irreproachable. He noticed Ronnie had worn his denture in honour of this rare visit to Dorothy and the Jardine stronghold.

'Problem is, old friend, I just feel in my bones that, um . . .'

'We have a rattlesnake.' Szabodo finished the sentence. 'A rat in the system.'

The log fire hissed and mewed gently in the silence. Ronnie puffed blue Dunhill's Standard into the darkening room. Jardine wondered if he should put a light on . . . If he should throw his drink into the fire and run out and find Dorothy and tell her he loved her and would die without her and he had been a bloody fool and –

'Are you sure you're all right?' The Hungarian seemed quietly worried.

'Never better. So, yes. I'm worried in case it's happening all over again.' The Director of Operations meant the horror story of Philby and Burgess and Maclean and Blake and the several lesser mortals who had been recruited by the KGB, a whole generation, or two, before.

The scandal had almost killed relations with the CIA and other US Intelligence organizations and it had taken thirty years to rebuild them. The embarrassment of SIS's American cousins at more recent US spy trials, like the Walkers, CIA renegade Ed Wilson, and more recently Aldrich Ames, had almost come as a relief, enabling both allies to chuckle ruefully and start with a clean sheet.

But something was wrong. Hindsight and Oversight had not been targeted by Vevak's sadistic amputator without somebody, somewhere, pointing the way.

'Maybe we should set a little trap,' said Szabodo, not unhappily. For he was a craftsman. He did not believe that anyone could elude his skill in the game of hide and seek, of peekaboo, that was counter-espionage.

And neither did David Jardine.

'Go for it, Ronnie,' he replied.

And both men knew that if there was a rat in the system, this time there would be no formal accusations, no damaging trial, no scandal.

Just a bereavement, in somebody's family . . .

9

Asset Strippers

'So whaddid he say? Exactly what.' Joe Cleary studied the business card. Harold K. Liebowitz, it announced, Room 441, Government Offices, Langley, Virginia. And the small, round gilt crest on the top left-hand corner was unambiguously that of the Central Intelligence Agency.

'Let me see . . .' Frank Grumman rested his chin on his left hand and stared out at the endless theatre that was Bleecker Street. They were sitting at one of the round, marble-topped tables in the Caffe Lucca, on the corner of Bleecker and Father Demo Square.

Those single-bladed roller skates seemed to be the big thing these days. And a two-hundred-pound deep-purple black butch queen in lavender satin hot-pants, a Madonna-type pointed gold lamé brassière and a pink feather boa gliding gracefully right down the centre of the street, backwards, naturally, his elegant arms moving as if conducting some silent melody, on roller blades, was just another, unsurprising feature of Village life.

'Um . . . yep, he said, "Mister Grumman my name is Harry Liebowitz and I work for the government." Then he handed me that.'

Cleary nodded, watching the guy's face. What made Joe Cleary such a terrific detective was that he always made absolutely sure he went right back to basics. What was the first thing that happened? Who said what? Where was so and so, were they standing or sitting or what?

And he never forgot a word anyone said to him. Sure, he might forget when Laurie asked him to bring home diapers or post a check to the gas company. But he never forgot a word, or a hesitation, or a look away, from any one of his hundreds of informers. Joe did not think of them as stoolies or snitches. The word he had coined for the army of low-lifes and grifters who fed him information in return for his . . . OK, for his protection, as far as it went . . . was 'whisperers'. And, without them, no cop would get past helping old ladies across the road.

So Joe Cleary looked approvingly at Frank Grumman and said, 'Good. Then what?'

Grumman was still watching the roller-blading queen, almost out of sight now, with something approaching wistfulness.

Ever since the unpleasantness at Martina's club, he had left his studs and leather duds at home in his wardrobe. The humiliation and abject fright of the first killing, then Joe Cleary's brutal gunfight with Henrietta, the six-foot-four Tina Turner diva with a twelve-gauge, had left him suffering, Frank had decided, from post-traumatic stress syndrome. And he no longer had the courage to strut his kinky motorcycle stuff.

Eventually he said, 'He said it was Government business and I was not to talk about it. With anybody. He said that was important. And he asked me "You got that?" and the way he said it you knew he meant business.'

'Well, I'm flattered, Frank. I'm really moved, man, that you feel you can talk to me. We won't leave you out on a branch on this one.' And as Cleary said that, he was visited by a vivid recollection of that monster tomcat, back arched, fur like an electrified porcupine and spitting like a . . . like a tomcat, with the sounds of 43rd Street traffic a couple of hundred feet of thin air below.

He touched his ear. You could still feel the slight indent, where the flailing claw had just missed making a Vincent van Gogh outa him.

'I can remember exactly that day. When he came into the morgue. You know how sometime you can have like . . . total recall?'

'Sure,' said Cleary, with his usual patience. He had gone to meet Grumman at this particular Village café in response to a phone call from the morgue attendant who 'had something to tell him, about that John Doe in the freezer case.'

But Frank wanted to talk and this was a good opportunity for the detective to go back over every detail the man could deliver. For he was pissed with the CIA for failing to respond to his faxes and letters on the subject, enquiring if the dead man was known to any US Intelligence agency. Cleary had not, at that time, revealed his awareness of Agent Liebowitz's visit to the Bellevue Hospital Morgue.

'I used the phone, to check him out,' went on Grumman, 'but I could not get a line. I asked him if it was, uh, fixed, you know.'

Cleary nodded.

'He said, "Whadda you think this is, Watergate?" Something like that.'

Joe Cleary grunted, amused.

'Then he asked about the John Doe.'

'What did he say?'

'Exactly?'

Cleary nodded.

'Um . . . "Frank, you have a body", no, "cadaver", he used the word "cadaver". "Frank, you have a cadaver, a John Doe brought in from an Italian place. Barolo. Am I right?"' Grumman shrugged, spread his hands. 'Something like that.'

They sipped some cappuccino.

'Oh, yeah, something happened,' went on Grumman, as if he had just remembered why he had phoned. Joe Cleary had begun to wonder if the man had just wanted somebody to talk to. He didn't mind that. Some of the best leads came out of such desultory conversations. He liked that word. It was in a Norman Mailer book he was reading. 'Something I forgot about. It was just before he left. Should I tell you now or, uh, keep it in sequence?'

Cleary was watching, out in the street, two young black guys in baggy pants, with big Reebok training shoes and loose jackets, ambling past the window, and across Father Demo Square. One had his hair long, in rats' tails, the other was a shave-head, with lines of close-cropped hair in some tribalistic design.

He recognized them as Narcotics detectives from the 30th Precinct, north of the Park. There was a regular switching of undercover cops on vice and dope details, from one police precinct to another. It confused the enemy.

'In sequence, Frank. I got all day . . .'

Thus encouraged, Cleary's gay whisperer went on, 'I asked if he had a tag number. He said something about missing fingers. I knew then he meant six-one-nine-nine.'

'Of course you did.' You could see the butt of a Glock 9mm sticking out from rats' tails' baggy black trouser pocket. The back pocket. Cleary signed to the waiter for two more coffees and rested a restraining hand on Frank Grumman's shoulder, as he started to get up.

'This is good, Frank. I'll be right back. Stay right there.' And Cleary moved easily across the café and out into Bleecker Street.

He walked quite quickly after the two young detectives until he was alongside, then passing them. Once he was a few yards in front, he stopped and looked around, glancing at his wristwatch, as if he was expecting to meet somebody.

As the two men reached him, he met their casual gaze and said, 'You guys wanna score?'

Big grins. Acres of white teeth. Amused, lazy brown eyes.

'Why sure, my man. What you got?' They could not believe their good fortune.

Cleary leaned closer. 'Sergeant Joe Cleary, Homicide. Fella, your gun is showing.'

Rats' tails' hand went instinctively to the butt of his piece. He shrugged his coat back over it.

'Thanks.'

Shave-head was not so trusting. 'You got ID, pal?'

'Go fuck yourself, I just did you a favour.'

Cleary looked so disgusted, both black men started to laugh. Somewhere an automobile backfired.

Shave-head punched him playfully on the arm. 'Hey, man, you can only be a Mick cop with a bad attitude like that.'

'Thanks. Take it easy,' grinned the Rasta man. And he held out a big, pink palm to the Irish detective.

Cleary patted his own palm against it and nodded, and the three of them parted. Joe Cleary got confused by the variety of ways these guys gave you some skin and he was reflecting on the easy cool of those two narcs, there was something at the same time likeable and most lethal about them, when a big commotion started back down the street, right outside the Caffe Lucca. One of the Italian waiters was waving his arms and calling for the cops.

Cleary hurried back, and through the window he could see a few people round the table he had been sitting at, with Frank. 'OK, OK, Police Officer, Police Officer . . .' Joe held his NYPD badge wallet open and in front of him, like an exorcist, and pushed his way past the gathering crowd of rubberneckers.

Frank Grumman was lying half across the chair that Cleary had been sitting on. The fresh coffee Joe had ordered was still steaming, on the floor and across the marble-topped table, where the cups had spilled.

The mortuary attendant's eyes were open. But there was nobody in. His shirt front was cherry-red and soaking. There was a small blue hole on his face, to the left of his nose. There was blood spattered on the marble and on the wall beside him, along with other stuff, maybe bone.

Cleary tugged his personal radio from his pocket. He gripped the older of the two waiters by the arm. 'Where's the shooter? Is he right here, is he still here?' And, even as he asked that, he slid his hand under his coat and across to the butt of his own gun.

'*Signor*, no.' This was the boy who collected dirty cups and plates. 'Big man. Tall. Very dark eyes. Long coat. Fastened at neck . . .'

'Yeah,' agreed the older waiter, 'fastened. Here.'

'Where'd he go?' Cleary was kneeling, feeling Frank Grumman's neck, feeling for a pulse from his carotid artery. But he had known from the dead eyes the man was a goner.

'He opened the door, *signore*, 'e did not-a look around.' The boy's words were tumbling over themselves. ''E knew just who to shoot, or maybe he was a crazy.' (This kid would make a cop, thought Cleary.) 'He just comes right in, stops, aims at this poor man and blam-blam-blam-blam-blam-blam. Shoots-a him dead an' spilling all the coffee.'

And he sure did spill the coffee. Joe Cleary looked at his witness, shock beginning to make the kid tremble. 'Six shots?'

'*Si.*' Then, unsure, 'I dunno. Maybe five. Seven.'

'So where did he go? What's your name?'

'Sal. Salvatore.'

'OK, Sal, you're a good man. Where did he go?'

Salvatore looked crestfallen. '*Signor* cop. All that noise. We screamed at each other and just . . . screamed. It was terrible frightening?'

Cleary nodded. This was not the movies and he had not the slightest intention of rushing out, gun in hand, looking for a fucking madman with a great big gun. A noisy one.

He lifted the radio and flicked it to speak. 'This is Eleven-Seventeen; I got a ten-fifty-six, location Caffe Lucca at 228 Bleecker, perp at large, armed and dangerous, location unknown, over.'

A woman's voice acknowledged the message and Cleary knew an armed response unit and a Crime Scene Supervisor were already on their way, for he had sent on the channel they shared with Control.

The two black Narcs appeared, pushing through the crowd. At first Cleary thought they were just coming to help, returning the favour, till he saw they had a big man, hands cuffed behind his back, the side of his face bleeding and blood on the shoulder of his long overcoat, buttoned up to the neck.

I don't believe it, thought Joe Cleary. We finally got a fuckin' break.

After James Gant had parted from the truck driver who brought him over the mountains from Hyder to Juneau, Alaska, he had found a hash house called Fat Nancy's and ordered a huge meal of hamburger, fries, fried onion rings and Caesar salad, followed by pecan pie with ice-cream, washed down with three Coca-Colas.

He had booked into the Meridian Hotel and Conference Center, a low, gray, anonymous pile which had just happened to be the nearest place to lay his head, and he had slept soundly from 10.10 p.m. until 7 the next morning.

Paying cash for the room had been tough, the woman on the hotel cashiers' desk was so conditioned to plastic that dollar bills seemed to confuse her. But a story about having left his valise on board the ship he had arrived in, along with his plastic, had been accepted, without a trace of good nature.

The flight from Juneau had been a breeze. At the airport, James Gant had paid cash for an American Airlines ticket, explaining that his rented car had been broken into and his credit cards and driver's licence stolen. But he had been carrying his per diem cash allowance from the mining company on his person.

This sob story was so boring that the clerk had said, 'Yeah, yeah, that's a drag,' and he issued a ticket in the name of Jay Koplowitz for the 09.25 flight to Seattle and that was that.

At Seattle, Gant took a cup of coffee, bought some American newspapers and purchased a United Airways one-way ticket to New York's La Guardia Airport. It was $242, including airport tax, and this time the good-looking girl booking-clerk took the money in fifties and twenties, and two one-dollar bills, without comment.

Flight UA 37 left Seattle at 14.40 and, at 16.07, allowing for the three-hour difference between Pacific and Eastern Standard time, the British Intelligence employee, whom his masters believed to be climbing in the Italian Dolomites, in southern Europe, walked out of the arrivals hall and got into a yellow cab.

'Where you goin'?' asked the driver, a lean man in late middle age. Wizened, leathery face.

'Corner of Mercer and Waverley, near Washington Square,' said Gant.

The taxi moved away and soon they had joined the solid traffic crawling relentlessly towards Manhattan.

'Bridge or tunnel?' asked the driver, whose name on his licence, displayed on the dashboard along with his mugshot, was Aristophanes Karavakas.

'Whatever you like,' said Gant.

They drove on in silence. Then the driver asked, 'You English?'

'Well, Scottish,' replied Gant, which was half true, for his mother had been Scottish.

And Aristophanes had proceeded to talk non-stop about English soccer until he stopped the cab on the corner of Waverley and Mercer, as requested.

James Gant paid him, wished him luck and strolled away,

feeling both elated and apprehensive. So far, as the falling man said while plummeting past the twenty-fourth floor, so good . . .

The room had bare wooden boards, with a moth-eaten carpet. There was a small bunk, with metal ends, very like the ones they had at Myg Trefwnny, the firm's training-farm in Wales, and a table, two chairs, a faded-brown easy chair with grease-lacquered arms, a solitary bulb hanging from a flex suspended from the tobacco-stained ceiling, a closet to hang clothes, a television, a big scuffed dresser for shirts and things, and a model of a Thunderbolt airplane, hanging from the ceiling on a couple of pieces of thread, which had been fixed there with drawing pins.

It was encrusted with dust, on the top. Four dead flies clung to the port wing, like fossilized stowaways.

There was a tiny kitchen off the room, and a small bathroom beyond that.

The two sash windows in the main room overlooked Greene Street, near its corner with West 4th. Heavy blue damask curtains, like funeral shrouds, hung from ceiling to floor. They smelled of dust and . . . sandalwood.

Gant smiled. Joss sticks. Sandalwood joss sticks, to disguise the smell of grass and smouldering cannabis resin.

After all, this was student country. The third-floor apartment was on the Campus of NY University. Gant had chosen it because the ages and races of New York's student population meant nobody stood out unless they wore a good suit and tie. Or rain overshoes. Since he intended to wear none of those, he felt comfortably anonymous.

The rent was $460 a month, payable in advance, with a $500 deposit. The agency was on Broadway, between a bookstore and a second-hand junk store. Nobody asked to see ID, other than the driver's licence Gant had stolen from that Good Samaritan who had given him the ride from Hyder to Juneau.

So he had booked in under the name of Tony Phillips. The name on the licence had originally been Phipps but that was kind of a weird name, one that people would remember, so Gant had signed in as Phillips and the Asian guy at the rental agency had taken his cash and given him the key to 116F Greene Street.

By this time it was 7.15 and James locked the door to his room, placed a chair against the handle and flopped down on the bunk. It was amazingly comfortable. Better than anything he had experienced in Bosnia or Kurdistan.

Thus far, his illegal entry into the USA had been more a sequence of opportunities and luck than the calculated, professional spy's method which he had planned.

Gant's decision to go all the way had, he knew, crystallized in the Buckingham pub just the previous Thursday evening, when he met Dosser Thackery, whom he had hardly seen since school. Get to travel? Dosser had asked and it had been like a sign from above. Too bloody right, James Gant had suddenly thought.

The arrogance of Jardine and his colleagues (Gant assumed the D/OPS could not possibly be acting alone) in even contemplating the sacrifice of about eighteen innocent people, in order to prove some political point, took his breath away.

Gant knew he had become obsessed with the Dante affair. He was sharp enough to understand that his childhood experience of the massacre at Rome airport was probably the driving force behind his resolve that, if nobody else was going to tackle Zina Farouche and her murder gang, then he certainly would. He was also aware that the particular trauma of Rome put him in a unique position, in the march of little histories, for Dante at last presented him with an opportunity to square his guilt, for having done nothing all those years ago.

His mind made up, James had applied himself, using Clerical 17's broad-spectrum access, to copying onto four 3.5″ discs every scrap of intelligence he thought might assist him in his solitary, self-indentured, clandestine mission.

He had purloined the classified records for details of the best, and most reliably discreet, forgers of documents, suppliers of equipment, from surveillance gear to weapons, and other, more sinister and deeply secret information. He had noted details of precisely where Zina Farouche and her gang, using their diplomatic cover, would most probably be, during the sixteen days remaining until the Curtises and the Selims were to gather at Beauregard, for their innocent break from the pressures of diplomacy.

Using the skills he had learned at the Farm, at Scarborough, at the Fort and with Marigold in Rome, he had acquired those passport blanks and drivers' licences, along with other false credentials, and he had withdrawn all but £1,500 of his entire savings. Gant had converted his money to US dollars, using a variety of exchange bureaux and airport banks, to avoid drawing attention to himself.

And right up to that point, reflected Gant, he had not really believed he would have the guts to go through with it. After all, the notion of a one-man vigilante taking on a professional and bloodily experienced terrorist gang, with its own vast resources was, bottom line, faintly ridiculous.

But suddenly his . . . game? experiment? indulgence? . . . to see just how far he could succeed in assembling all the intelligence, all the information and items he would require if he really were crazy enough to proceed – suddenly the game had taken him to the brink of reality.

Now, only his basic commensense stood between him and a step which James Gant completely understood would threaten at best his career and liberty, at worst his very life. What the hell, he decided, if no one else is going after this evil bitch Farouche, then I will. And he still believed, somewhere at the back of his mind, that he could still pull out, if he got cold feet.

Thus far, Gant had spent $2,814 in air fares, hotel bills, food, transportation, a valise and shaving kit he had purchased at Seattle, and some items of clothing, including Timberland boots, a leather zip-up jacket, a pair of cotton trousers, and some shirts, socks and underwear. He had phoned the King Edward Motel in Stuart, British Columbia, just across the border from Hyder, Alaska, and told them he had gone fishing for a couple of weeks, the weather being so great, and would they please keep his travelling bag and few belongings for him till he got back.

The manager had been very relaxed about that and it seemed such things happened not infrequently in the remote wilderness of the still north-west.

James Gant hauled his weary bones off the bunk and,

taking off his money-belt and ankle-wallets, emptied them onto the table and took stock of his assets.

There was $37,186 left in the money-belt. Just to be sure, he counted it twice. He checked the blank passports, the forgers' inks, the various ID photographs of himself, and the vital computer discs. Then he shifted the television to one side and prised open a floorboard, which had been beneath it.

Gant wrapped his paraphernalia up in oilcloth and gently placed it in the five-inch gap between the floorboards and dusty rubble on the battens over the ceiling of the apartment below. Then he pushed the television set back over the spot and began to relax. He pulled a can of root beer from the carton of food and stuff he had bought from the deli next door to the property agents and settled into the brown armchair, switching on CNN to catch up with events.

As the announcers droned on about some earth-tremor in California, Gant felt that mild surprise, it was quite a pleasant feeling, which he sometimes had experienced on being transported at a few hours' notice out of comfortable London to some remote corner of the world with his camera team, on assignments for the BBC.

Wow, he would think, here I am in the Philippines, or Kabul, or Mogadishu. Or Sarajevo. Little old me. Who'd have thought it?

But this time he was no longer a recorder of the world's more brutal events. This time, James Gant had the chance of being a player at the Devil's table.

He knew perfectly well he would be merely a tic on the hide of Islamic Tide's terror offensive. He was fully aware that scores, hundreds, of other innocents would undoubtedly die and be maimed in the name of the Fundamentalist Clergy's ruthless programme, aimed at stamping their will on the overwhelming majority of the world's gentle, pious and peace-loving Muslims, and punishing the Great (and all the Lesser) Satans.

This quixotic gesture was like just one grain of sand, in the desert of history, being moved a trifling distance by one little ant. But there was no way James could leave it lying there. Edith would understand.

So would Charlotte. The ancient Greeks had a thing that

certain men, caught up in momentous times, were simply not able to turn aside from their destiny. And, in a way, he felt, sitting in that threadbare Greenwich Village apartment, he had always known it would come to this . . .

'In a homicide or other serious case,' says the NYPD *Patrol Guide*, Serial No. 116–5, 'the ranking member of the Detective Bureau present will be in charge of the investigation.'

Well, Joe Cleary had not merely been the ranking Detective present – he had been the only one, he had been a Homicide cop, and he had been one of the last people to see the deceased alive. So UN Week Protective Task Force or not, the Frank Grumman murder was very much Cleary's case.

The perp had been held in the back of a police van, in the custody of the two arresting officers, whose undercover value, Joe Cleary grimly reflected, had been somewhat reduced by their prompt and courageous apprehending of the killer, who had tried to shoot his way out of trouble and had sustained a bullet wound to the shoulder and had apparently attacked Shave-Head's pistol butt with his face.

The Patrol Supervisor was an Irishman by the name of O'Hare, and the moment he had arrived on the crime scene, he had expressed surprise that the suspect had not been put on board the ambulance which was parked inside the police cordon expressly to convey the wounded killer to hospital.

Cleary had argued the man should be taken directly into Police custody, despite his gunshot wound. He pointed out that the bullet had merely grazed the suspect and he was just too dangerous to commit to hospital when he was perfectly fit, give or take the trauma of his violent arrest and a spot of bleeding from a 'minor flesh wound'.

O'Hare had said he was tempted to agree, because he did not at that moment have enough officers to guard the man in a hospital environment. But the rules were very specific and nobody wanted a serious complaint against the force.

'Where a suspect has been apprehended and is injured, he must receive prompt medical attention and hospital treatment if the doctor or ambulance attendant or paramedic attending the suspect so advises.' The *Patrol Guide* was not open to negotiation.

'Joe, I have to send him to Bellevue,' O'Hare had protested, 'you know I do; the guy's been shot, for Chrissake.'

And at that moment the duty pathologist had arrived, parking his dented Chevrolet – the words demolition Derby came to mind – half on the kerb and taking some orange and white plastic crime-scene tape with it.

This was Doctor Henry Grace, who saw more than a few suspicious cadavers in any one week. And he had a nose for the kind of forensic clues that Mickey Spillane would have given a whole typewriter for.

His hands shook slightly and his nose was redder than Rudolph's. But every working cop had a load of time for Henry E. Grace, which was why he still held a driver's licence.

'Henry,' said Cleary, taking him to one side, 'let me explain the problem.'

So Henry Grace had climbed into the van that had arrived for the suspect, and had examined the man; cleaned, sutured and dressed the flesh wound; had the long overcoat and the man's plaid shirt and bloodstained sweatshirt put into clear plastic evidence-bags and tagged; bathed the swollen and bruised face; taken the perp's, alleged perp's, blood pressure and pulse; shone a torch into his eyes and pronounced him fit to be taken into custody.

'Not often they let me loose on a live one,' he had muttered as he was helped out of the van, but luckily only Cleary and Pat O'Hare heard that.

The ambulance was dismissed and the perpetrator conveyed to the 6th Precinct.

Thus, round about when James Gant was sitting in that yellow taxi stuck in the evening rush hour, Sergeant of Detectives Joe Cleary leaned against the wall of the medical examination room on the second floor of the 6th Precinct House and studied his prisoner.

The man had a blanket round his shoulders. Blood from the bullet wound made a pink rose on the clean white gauze dressing. His face was bruised and there was a nasty swelling on the bridge of his nose. He was a big, spare, broad-shouldered man and on his right shoulder was a small tattoo of the 1930s Fleischer cartoon character Betty Boop.

Betty Boop is a sexy but innocent, happy, cheeky kid and her image radiates a sense of mischief and fun. Except, in this particular tattoo, she was holding a chainsaw.

'You want me to take the chains off?' asked Cleary. The man had been handcuffed to a steel table, which was bolted to the floor.

Silence.

'OK,' went on the detective, 'here's the deal. The arresting officers already read you your rights. I have a hunch you and Miranda are well acquainted,' (the Miranda Act was the one that stipulated a suspect must be informed of his legal rights immediately on his arrest), 'so, sure thing, you have the right to remain silent.' Joe Cleary watched the guy carefully. There was no hint of interest or emotion. This was a working cleaner who had gotten apprehended. Shit happens, was probably his inner feeling, if he had anything resembling personal awareness.

'And you have the right to an attorney. So who do we phone?'

More silence.

Cleary nodded, as if that was in some way a satisfactory response. And, in a way, it was. 'OK. If you do not have an attorney, we are bound to find one. You want me to arrange that?'

The man slowly turned his head and gazed at Cleary. It was a chilling gaze, and the eyes were intelligent. The man's hair was cut real short, and he wore a razor-short beard. Just a gnat's wing more than designer stubble.

But still he did not answer.

Joe Cleary inclined his head. He took a pack of Camel Filters from his jacket and shook out a couple, offering one to the prisoner. The eyes examining him flickered in a response that meant no.

'What's your name?'

A glint, this time, of . . . amusement.

'Fine. I see you got a tattoo there – Betty Boop, right? So, for ease of conversation, I'm gonna call you Betty, pal. OK?'

This had no effect.

'Right, Betty, the pistol you used to resist arrest is an Israeli piece. An IMI Desert Eagle. The magazine had one shell left in it. The four spares in your coat pockets each had nine rounds of forty-four magnum, so I am saying to myself, you probably fired eight times before you took that nine-millimetre copper-nose in the shoulder. The arresting officers say you fired three times at them. The man you killed took six forty-four magnum semi-jacket slugs in the head and chest.' Cleary pointed at his own breast-bone, 'Right here.'

'Betty' sat staring at the metal table in front of him.

Suddenly Joe Cleary propelled himself from the wall to shove his face inches from the prisoner's. He breathed calmly and examined the man's face, his eyes, his expression, for a long time.

'Are you gay, Betsy . . .?' he asked with chilling quietness. 'Are you a fuckin' pervert?' He let his face get even closer, still there was zero reaction. If anything, mild interest, in his technique. 'Is that what this is? A gay homicide? Was Frank Grumman your boyfriend? A little piece on the side?'

But Betty Boop was a cold customer. And neither Joe, nor Sam Vargos, his partner, who had come in to the precinct when he had heard what was going down, could get so much as a raised heartbeat outa the guy.

Round about 9 o'clock, when the medical room was stale from stubbed-out cigarette butts and half-eaten pizzas, Captain Capello, the officer running the 6th, finally told Cleary enough was enough and he assigned an attorney from the Public Pool to represent the unknown suspect.

The attorney was Jean Faccioponti, youngest sister of the DA who would be prosecuting 'Betty Boop' – the local New York City television news had already christened the slaying 'The Betty Boop Murder' – and she raged for a full half hour at Joe Cleary and Vargos for daring to interrogate her client without him having legal counsel.

And Bill Haldane, from the DA's Office, had been chewed off for allowing it.

So, from 9.23 through till 11.00, Joe and his partner went through the same questions all over again, this time with the lawyer present. And when Jean Faccioponti announced she was filing a complaint about a wounded man being interrogated without an attorney and deprived of medical attention,

Joe Cleary terminated the interview and told her he would be resuming at 3 a.m.

'This is not goddam Bolivia,' Faccioponti snarled, furious, 'this man is going to be examined by a doctor and it will be on his advice when my client can next be questioned.'

Cleary grinned. 'I got medical aid even while we were still at the crime scene, when Betty here was still wearing the goddam coat with four clips of forty-four in the pockets. Believe me, I brought him here on a doctor's authority.'

'A doctor?' Jean Faccioponti glanced at her client, who looked pale and ready to drop. 'Who? Doctor fuckin' Frankenstein?'

And Joe Cleary had smiled his friendliest smile at her and answered, 'Close.' And he left to spend a couple of hours at home with Laurie and hear all about Patrick Cheyenne's day.

Naturally he forgot the diapers.

'This', said Zina Farouche, 'is Beauregard.' She stood beside a carousel slide-projector, whose beam flashed onto the off-white wall of the basement room of the safe-house which she had chosen from among three, offered by Hanna al-Farah to the Team.

It was a four-storey town house on 71st Street, between Lexington and Third Avenue. It belonged to a Turkish fine-art dealer, specialising in Ottoman artefacts and sculpture. He was a member of the Near Orient Chamber of Commerce and a lecturer in Ottoman culture at Duke University.

He was also a sleeper, a 'submarine' in the Iranian Service's terminology, inserted five years earlier with the passport and other ID of one Çaglar Yüsel. Yüsel was a Turkish citizen whose proudest possession, an American Green Card, his permit to reside and work in the USA, had turned out to be his death warrant. Mr Yüsel had no living relatives, no acquaintances outside Los Angeles (where he had been residing until a recent move to New York City), and no business colleagues.

To be absolutely accurate, once Vevak had decided Çaglar Yüsel's identity and US Immigration Service permits were tailor-made for their needs, the man's only living relatives, his sister and brother-in-law, ceased to be a problem. They died in a car crash west of Istanbul within days of the man's disappearance while travelling in Syria, looking for artefacts to stock in his brand-new shop in Manhattan's East Side.

Thus the present incumbent, the current Çaglar Yüsel, was really Abdulkadir Talay, a Turk, certainly, and a Sunni Muslim, recruited by the Iranian Service while studying Islamic History at Shiraz University, trained as a deep-cover operative and now a wealthy and successful New York businessman who paid his taxes and made contributions to Republican Party funds.

He had lent his town house to Hanna al-Farah, while he went on a business trip to Europe.

The assassination squad had arrived at staggered intervals, on foot, after observing complicated 'dry-cleaning' procedures, to ensure they were not under surveillance.

Khaled Niknam had been the last to let himself in. He had observed the others from a nearby rooftop, where he had spent the last two days in faded blue overalls, painting a water tank and the safety rails with a dull brown, weather-resistant paint. If somebody had challenged him, he had an order form from his boss, a fly-by-night employer of casual labour, scribbled on a page torn out of a pocket notebook, which referred to a similar rooftop on East 41st Street, way downtown. But he had not anticipated anyone in anonymous Manhattan querying his tradesman's activity.

And nobody did.

From this vantage point, Niknam was able to scrutinize the safe-house and ascertain it had not attracted any interest from the several Security agencies busy doing their advances for UN Week, the local law, or indeed any of the foreign intelligence services who quietly worked in town.

He was also a solitary scout, observing the arrivals of the others, checking them for a tail and giving them points out of ten for their tradecraft. For Khaled Niknam was the Team's security officer. And if he became unhappy, any member of Zina's group could find themselves shipped out directly. Possibly in a box.

Or he could veto the operation, if he believed it was blown

or insecure. But thus far, he was satisfied the Team was operating well, and had attracted zero interest from anyone.

So here they were, sitting round a long table in the basement, watching Zina Farouche's detailed slide-show.

'And this', she said, clicking the remote switch, 'is the ground-floor layout. As you can see, the main room is really two already big rooms, made into one. As far as I can tell, there might only be one doorway, from the front hall. One way in . . .'

Mustafa Sharik grinned in the darkened room. 'And no way out . . .' he said.

'As far as you can tell, Eleanor?' Niknam, the youngest person in the room, was quiet, confident in himself, for his record as a sniper and booby-trap bomb maker had made him something of a legend among his fellow terrorists. It was he who had suggested they use nicknames when talking together, just in case of eavesdroppers, and it was he who had chosen the names of American Presidents and their wives. Thus, Zina Farouche was Eleanor, after Eleanor Roosevelt.

He continued, 'Perhaps we should make sure . . .'

The others looked at Zina. She gazed at the image on the wall for a long moment. Then she said, 'Abraham is of course correct. The reconnaissance by our support element' – she meant sleepers – 'has been very thorough, as far as it goes. On the day they gained access to the house, they started upstairs and worked down, disguised as electrical repair men. Unfortunately they had just entered this main room when Target Two returned with a woman friend and asked them to leave.' Zina pointed a remote wand at a large television set, beside the projected plan on the wall, and pressed a couple of switches.

The TV screen lit up and became bright blue.

The Palestinian girl pressed again and a videotape whirred into action. There on the screen was Beauregard, videotaped clandestinely, from a tiny camera hidden in a voltage meter, carried by one of the 'electricians'.

The six members of the killing team watched in silence as the interior of Beauregard was relentlessly exposed to them. The smiling South American maid who let them in, checked their ID cards and led them upstairs, hovered around, dusting and fixing things. Not letting them out of her sight, like a good maid.

'That girl', said Zafir Hammuda, 'can identify our people . . .'

'She's dead,' replied Zina Farouche. 'Nothing dramatic. As far as the Targets are concerned, she just didn't come back after a weekend with her boyfriend. Unreliable Colombians, they figured, according to the tapes.'

The others nodded, satisfied. Neither impressed at such ruthlessness, nor remotely shocked at the casual murder of an innocent stranger.

They continued to watch the mute exposure of hallways, rooms, bathrooms, stairways, kitchen and ground floor. The hidden camera had wandered into the vast double reception room and panned around, when it whipped back to the doorway, where Annabel Curtis and a smiling woman of about thirty-five, in jeans and expensive sweater, were just coming in.

Annabel, Target Two, was clearly asking the workmen to go and do whatever it was they were doing, elsewhere.

The camera took the watching group past the two women and out of the room, back into the hall.

Zina froze the image.

'I couldn't see any other door,' remarked Noor Jalud.

'There wasn't time,' said Ben Turabi.

'Wind it back,' said Hammuda.

So they played it over and over. And there was definitely one corner, obscured by a bookcase, which could have a doorway in it.

'So the question is,' commented Mustafa al-Sharik, who was the team's planner, 'do we risk putting someone back inside, at this stage, when the Targets' security people are beginning to do their advance?'

'It's up to you, Jack,' said Zina. 'If you think it's necessary, we'll do it.'

They sat in silence, while al-Sharik thought about it.

'What the hell,' he announced. 'A door is a door. We're not kids. It's no big deal . . .'

And Zina Farouche relaxed. Inserting a snooper now would be asking for trouble.

'Here are the children,' she said, clicking more slides onto the screen. 'Targets eight, nine and ten.'

And the smiling faces of two little boys aged five and nine, and a girl of about seven, appeared on the basement wall.

Sixty miles to the south of Tehran is the city of Ghom. The holy city of Ghom, where in the ninth century AD, Fatimeh, the sister of the Shi'ite Imam Reza, was buried and a shrine was constructed by Shah Abbas and subsequently embellished into the great and ornate religious complex it is today, by the Safavid Kings, keen to win favour with the clergy.

Ghom probably boasts the largest per capita number of mullahs and Shi'ite zealots in the whole of zealous and Shi'ite Iran. There are training colleges for aspiring clergymen and the holy city is a favourite weekend retreat for mullahs and ayatollahs from Tehran and many other places.

It is also an intellectual and political centre for the Hezbollahi, followers of the extreme Shi'ite Hezbollah – the Party of God.

As the Russian Gaz truck he was riding in rumbled through the main street, the Kheyabum-e Imam Khomeini, past wall-to-wall mullahs strolling, entering and leaving shops and restaurants, and clustered round the various entrances to the Astane, the Sanctuary, David Jardine mused that, all in all, this was not the very best place for the Director of Covert Operations of the Lesser Satan's Intelligence service to be.

And his presence there was indeed a secret. Not merely from the Iranians but also from Richard Sykes, Chief of SIS, 'C' to his minions, and from every single person inside the Firm, except for Ronnie Szabodo, who had arranged the trip and the very discreet back-up for his boss, should the fertilizer hit the revolving air-conditioner.

But needs must, as dear Edith Treffewin used to say, when the Devil drives. And his conversation with Ronnie that Saturday evening at the farmhouse, when they had resolved to identify the source of betrayal within SIS, had, perhaps inevitably, led directly to Jardine being in this truck, wearing Persian workman's clothes and carrying the credentials of a roofing fitter from Turkmenistan.

He had arrived in Turkmenistan by air from Moscow, travelling with the papers of one Alan Congreve, an English tour-company executive, looking for new places to run 'off the beaten track' holiday experiences.

In Turkmenistan he changed his papers to those of a Russian trader, a minor officer in the GRU, Russian Military Intelligence, and had gone to the house of a caviar producer, Agmet Belassian, who believed he himself had been recruited as an agent of the GRU, Russian Military Intelligence. This was a fairly routine procedure for intelligence services of most nationalities.

It was sometimes easier to acquire a source, or a helper, who earnestly believed he or she was working for whatever agency sat best with their inclinations or consciences.

Belassian ran a smuggling operation, shipping tons of caviar from Turkmenistan in the Russian Federation to Mazandaran Province in northern Iran. Iranian caviar was more expensive than Russian, and in recent years Iranian production had been greatly reduced.

So Agmet Belassian had done a deal with a mullah in the coastal Mazandaran town of Ramsar, tucked tightly between the mountains and the Caspian sea, to supply him with Russian Sevruga caviar, which the mullah arranged to be taken to his factory beside the Istba-e-Rasht river and canned in Iranian labelled tins. They split the tidy profit fifty-fifty.

Belassian had no problems accepting Jardine's US dollars in return for a passage on board one of the smuggler's fishing boats, to Ramsar, and for a driver to be arranged to take David Jardine to Tehran and a second driver, called Sayyed, to take him to Ghom, wait for him to go about his business, which Belassian was far too discreet to enquire about, and bring him back safely to Ramsar for a return trip across the Caspian Sea.

David Jardine spoke bad Farsi but fluent Russian, and, if the worst came to the worst, he would allow to be prised out of him that he was an ex-officer of the GRU hoping to arrange some black market deals in US dollars and contraband oil.

Such a combination neither offended the mullahs' faith,

nor threatened Iran's stability, and there was a fair chance an interrogator might succumb to the notion of a few thousand American dollars.

Still, thought David Jardine, we will not actually allow it to come to that.

As he gazed at the passing scene, the spymaster (flint-eyed, had been James Gant's impression) understood for the thousandth time something about himself. This was what he loved doing, more than anything else in life. He still felt that sense of wonder, of apprehension, the essential flow of adrenaline, at being deep in the heart of a hostile and potentially lethal environment.

Denied Areas, they were called. And it was the only game in town.

Surely this was irresponsible, for a most senior official of the British intelligence community? For an administrator.

Indubitably.

Jardine smiled. For some reason he found himself thinking about young James Gant, and the story of his convoluted efforts to make contact with Euan Stevenson in Rome. It was a story which had caused some gentle amusement among the few who had read about it.

But after the Rome posting, Euan had given the lad a good report. Gant's attachment to Marigold had been a new experiment, in slotting a probationer, an ingénu, straight into a black operational environment. The idea had been Kate Howard's, the Firm's Director of Security, at a general brainstorming session of senior executives.

In time of war, Kate had reasoned, the need for first-rate, freshly trained operators would rob SIS of the luxury of its standard procedure, treading carefully, taking as long as several years before committing its officers to a clandestine assignment, working without diplomatic cover.

And young Gant had done OK. Not a star player, but star players, prima donnas, could be more trouble than they were worth, reflected the senior British spook, blithely ignoring any comparison with his present situation. For if Jardine had a fault, it was possibly that he had always refused to accept there were certain vital operations, certain prize assets, that anyone else could run as well as he. It was an attitude that had caused many run-ins with the grey men in authority. And ruffled the feathers of his colleagues.

And was he right? Who could tell.

David Jardine continued to think about Edith's nephew, storming into the office and blowing a fuse about Dante and the Firm's handling of it.

David Jardine's handling of it.

Well, the boy had guts, he also had the high ground. Ethically and morally speaking.

Jardine devoutly wished his job allowed major decisions to be based on such principles. James Gant could not be allowed to know about Jardine's concern over a leaky CIA, or, as it now seemed, a traitor in his own outfit.

And he certainly could not be permitted even to guess at his boss's temptation to allow the Dante contract to go ahead, because it was such an enormous error of judgement by the Iranian extremists behind it. The horror might finally wake up the world's governments to precisely what they were faced with – a Tehran-directed programme of international terror to further the aims of Radical Islam. As the Gaz truck slowed to let a jeep full of Pasdaram Revolutionary Guards cut across its bows, David Jardine reflected, I'd like to see young James Gant, idealist and wet behind the ears, cope with a real grown-up clandestine job like this one.

A shockingly juvenile thought, for such an august . . . star? of the espionage firmament. Not, in truth, one he was proud of. And the moment he had thought it, the big man chastised himself for its hubris.

One day, boy, he said to himself, you're going to have to grow up. Then, like St Augustine, he added, but not just yet.

Up ahead, the jeepload of Pasdaram had stopped, at an angle across the next intersection. Jardine noticed the passers-by, mullahs and students and residents of the holy city, pause and stand as if listening.

He wound down his window and leaned close to the outside. A megaphone voice was speaking in Farsi, with that controlled urgency which is so typical of official panic in any language.

David Jardine's Farsi was, to coin Ronnie Szabodo's phrase,

'agricultural', but he could understand one or two words. Like '*khaktarnak*' used twice, which meant 'dangerous'. One word, '****', was repeated several times, but it was not a word he knew.

'What' he asked his driver, a stocky, small-time smuggler and black-marketeer, who said his name was Sayyed, 'does **** mean?'

He asked this in Russian.

'Lion,' replied Sayyed. Then he muttered, in Farsi, '*In khub nist . . . bash ey nist . . .*' Which basically meant, 'Oh, shit, this is bad.'

'What is it?'

Sayyed stepped on the fairly useless brakes and hauled on the handbrake at the same time as de-clutching down into first gear. He switched off the engine and watched as a lorry crammed with armed soldiers raced across the junction, from right to left.

Jardine waited. It did not seem, even though his heart had almost stopped beating, that his particular truck was the focus of anyone's attention.

Sayyed listened to the loudspeaker voice for several moments. Then he said, without looking at Jardine, 'There is a lion loose. It escaped from the zoo. It has killed its keeper and two other people. One of them a mullah. The streets are being sealed off.'

Jardine nodded. Everything had been going so well. And now, a bloody lion. Terrific.

He looked at his wristwatch. They had to be eight blocks further down the street in four minutes.

'So where is it?' he asked, meaning the escaped lion.

Sayyed raised his shoulders in a shrug.

'It could be anywhere,' he said.

James Gant woke at 6.10 in the morning. He had crashed out in the scruffy brown armchair and wakened at about 3 o'clock with *I Love Lucy* blaring out at him from the TV set. He had stumbled drowsily for a pee and flopped face down on the comfortable bunk, sleeping the sleep of the totally shattered for another three hours.

Now he yawned, stretched, and stood up. He put the kettle

on and went through to the tiny bathroom, shedding his clothing on the way.

By the time he had shaved and showered, and made some coffee, James Gant felt more than half-way human.

Since reporting sick, just six days before, and being examined by the office doctor at the Vauxhall Bridge headquarters – even though he told himself, reassured himself, that he could opt out at any stage – James had proceeded according to a very clear plan. He had sat up, that night after his confrontation with David Jardine, when the Director Ops had kicked his ass in no uncertain fashion, and written careful notes, based on his training at the hands of the best intelligence service in the world.

Aim: To stop the massacre of around 18 people, at the home of Ambassador Curtis in Essex County, Connecticut.

Situation: Six known members of Fatah: The Revolutionary Council (the Abu Nidal Group), under the command of Zina Farouche, have entered the USA under cover. The gang is codenamed Dante. They plan to carry out the massacre during the latter part of UN Week and make a safe getaway.

Mission: I will enter the USA under cover and, using my SIS training and natural resources, identify the Dante team and damage it sufficiently to cause them to abort their task.

Execution: Using information and equipment retrieved from SIS files I will acquire assets in New York City to furnish me with at least two sets of false identities. Also other assistance. I will pose as an operative of another nation's service.

Two of the Dante team will be neutralized. Their deaths will be arranged so that the Abu Nidal controllers understand their plan is compromised and, like any sane organization, they will cancel the mission.

If the deaths of two Dante operatives do not accomplish this, then I will go for three. Or four. They'll get the message.

Admin: I will use a combination of fluid-retention drugs and excessive exercise to produce symptoms of hypertension. I will report sick to the firm's MO, who will suggest I take some time off, due to stress.

I will say, how about me going climbing in the Dolomites,

> where the activity and fresh air will do me good. Since I am basically very healthy, he should go along with that.
>
> I will fly to Rome, then by shuttle to Paris and take an Air France flight under my own name to Canada. From there I will fly to Vancouver and take a connecting flight to Prince Rupert. Make my way from Prince Rupert to Stewart BC and enter the USA via Hyder, Alaska.

And so it went on. A detailed and comprehensive plan, well thought out and with copious notes, covering many eventualities and ending with his exfiltration back to Italy, where he would spend a few days in the mountains, before returning to London and anonymity.

Dear old Euan Stevenson would be proud of me, thought Gant. He has taught me well.

Of course, Euan Stevenson would have been no such thing.

Between one of the freshest of SIS freshmen taking it upon himself to venture into the darkest waters of politics and international terror, and one of the office's most seasoned and senior players going clandestine in Iran, it is difficult to guess which would have appalled him more.

At 9 that morning, Gant went to Komputer World, a cramped and seedy store on Broadway, and paid $1,225 cash for a Toshiba 3600CT Notebook Personal Computer and additonal 3.5″ floppy-disc drive.

He took it back to the Greene Street apartment and within ten minutes had it set up and running. He retrieved his floppy discs from their hiding place and spent the next half hour perusing highly classified SIS files on men and women who might provide him with the sort of less than legal facilities and services he was going to need. None of them were people, it seemed, one could take home to mother.

His work done, Gant protected those files now recorded within his slim computer (for those who knew where to look), replaced the discs, and stowed the Toshiba in the tiny kitchen, on a high shelf in the utility closet, which smelled of cleaning fluid.

Next, James took a taxi uptown and used a payphone at the Lincoln Centre to arrange a few things. At 10.14, he got out of a taxi in Fulton Street, in Brooklyn, and strolled a couple of blocks to Duffield Street, and just past the theatre, went into a brownstone apartment house and climbed the stairs to the third floor and rang the doorbell of Number 306.

The man who opened the door was so lean and fit-looking, wearing black chinos and a whiter-than-white sleeveless undershirt, with dark, bright eyes, above-average height, that James Gant thought he had come to the wrong place.

'Yep, what can I do for you?' bright-eyes demanded, checking him out, and the landing behind.

'I think I, um, I phoned.'

'Well, did you phoned or did you not phone, brother? You must know. Whadda you mean you *think* you phoned?'

Gant said, 'About ten to nine. I phoned and arranged to come over.' He paused, not usually so completely clusterfucked. 'Come on over, you said. Get here before ten-thirty . . .'

Bright-eyes nodded, amused. 'Sure, I recognize your British accent. Man, come in. I don't want the neighbours to see I got company.'

Gant stepped inside. The tall, fit man was on SIS files as a master counterfeiter, forger of any document you could name, for a price. His name was Jack Chisholm.

The sitting room had white walls and a kind of rope-carpet floor, in a natural gray-sacking shade. The furniture was good taste and expensive. Plain-wood bookshelves, but thick, plain iroko wood. Not cheap. State-of-the-art sound system, which was playing Ornette Coleman, softly.

James did not hear the door close but, when he glanced back, Chisholm was leaning against it, and he had a mean, unpromising look in his eye.

'When you *thought* you phoned,' his voice was one of those real low Mississippi Delta voices, a bass baritone, like Paul Robeson, 'what did you *think* you said that got me to agree to see you?'

'I said April sends her love, and hopes to see you in the spring. In the springtime.'

'Which?' The dark eyes were narrow now.

'Time. Springtime.'

Chisholm stroked his chin, considering. Then he asked, 'What do you want?'

'I heard you might be able to help me, um, fill in some forms.'

'You got a green card?'

'I don't even have a fucking visa.'

In the distance, a fire tender's throaty foghorn bellowed.

'When I say, did you got a green card, whadda you suppose to say?'

Gant smiled, the man was genuine. 'I say, no but I got a ticket to the Jets.'

Chisholm stared at him a moment or two longer. Then he relaxed. 'Wanna beer?'

Gant shook his head. 'I need some work on these . . .' He tugged a manila envelope from his jacket pocket and dropped it on the table.

Jack Chisholm slit open the envelope with a knife that had suddenly appeared in his hand, like a rabbit from a conjuror's sleeve. He shook out one Irish and two British passports, plus some full-face photographs of Gant.

He examined the passports and nodded, impressed.

'These are good enough to be real, man . . .'

They are real, thought Gant.

'Here are the details for each of the British ones.'

Chisholm was almost stroking the Irish one. 'And this one?'

'That's for you, along with your fee.'

'My fee is ten big ones, each.'

'Bullshit, your fee is five grand for the two, but I'll pay you six, plus the Irish blank – you can get five for that, no problem.'

The big man thought about this. 'You cheap Limey piece a shit,' he said. 'I tell you what, why don't you just take your crap outa here and I'll forget about rearranging your fuckin' teeth?' He crossed to the door and held it open, the blank Irish passport still in his hand. 'And I'll hold onto this, just for the inconvenience of . . . seeing you.'

Gant stared at the man. He shrugged. 'Is that your last word?'

Chisholm smiled. 'You should go while you have your pretty face, white boy.'

Gant sighed, he picked up the British passports from the

floor, where Chisholm had dropped them at his feet and, as he rose, James power-rammed his pointed knuckles hard and fast straight up towards where the ceiling would be – except Jack Chisholm's nuts, his family jewels, were in the way.

The big man's feet lifted off the ground, for a millisecond, his eyes popping and Gant, upright, stepped lightly to his right, almost gently took hold of Chisholm's left hand and wrist, in both of his own hands, and, with an Aikido twist known as the rattlesnake, flipped the forger in a full somersault, to crash on his back onto the kind of rope floor.

Before he could comprehend the completeness of the assault, Chisholm was rolled onto his belly and James Gant was sitting astride him, holding the other man's head right back, using his straight index finger along the base of the guy's nose, at his upper lip, and the very same knife that had slit open the envelope was touching, actually touching, big Jack's right eyeball.

Gant leaned really close to Chisholm's ear, and he whispered, very softly, intimately, 'How will you earn a living, wise-guy, if you have no fucking eyes? Mmmm?'

There was a long silence, then tears ran down Chisholm's face. 'Oh, Christ,' he gasped, 'you've really damaged my balls, man . . .'

'How, Jack?' Gant's voice was hard, and he wanted an answer. 'How? Without your eyes . . .' he caressed Chisholm's cheek with the knife.

'Whadda you want . . .?'

James Gant eased off, and, without any hostility, replied, 'I think it would really be better if we were to be friends, don't you?'

'Yes,' sobbed the forger.

'That's good. Now, when I let you go, you are going to want to kill me.'

Chisholm shook his head, distressed. 'No, man, no. No, I aksed for it, man . . .'

'Of course you will. Who wouldn't?' Gant eased the knife down to Chisholm's throat. 'So, just remember this. I know where your mother is,' Chisholm stiffened, 'and my people will skin her alive – that's not a metaphor, by the way, Jack. One-o-one-eight Park, that's Rockaway Park, right?'

This is about where your average spy, putting the arm on, like Gant was doing, prays to whatever God he owes his dues to, that the information on which he has predicated his particular, vile threat is not two years out of date and that said little old lady is not pushing up the daisies in Rockaway Cemetery.

But he could feel his opponent was beaten.

'I have my people very close to her, right now. Hell, Jack, all I want is a couple of lousy passports; come on, man . . . We don't *want* to hurt an old lady . . .'

That was it. The deed was done. Unarmed combat was one of the things he had done quite well at, down in the Fort. When Chisholm had got some ice on his swollen testicles, and Gant had helped him swallow some beta-blockers for his racing heart, the Englishman explained to him exactly what he required.

'OK,' said a subdued Jack Chisholm, 'Two days.'

'Tonight.'

'I need special ink, man.'

'Ah,' replied James Gant, 'I just happen to have some with me . . .'

The passports, he told Chisholm, were to be in the names of Peter Anthony Wilson, photographer, and Liam Russel Graham, free-lance journalist.

When he left the Duffield Street apartment, Gant went to a drugstore on Flatbush Avenue and used the payphone. He put in his quarter and dialled the number of Chisholm's sixty-eight-year-old mommy, on Rockaway Park.

But it was busy.

He smiled grimly and went about his other business.

Much earlier that day, the middle of the night really, while James Gant was sleeping, just before he woke up in that greasy brown armchair to the canned laughter of the *I Love Lucy* show, say about 2.54 a.m., Joe Cleary parked his '83 Pontiac beneath the 6th Precinct House and climbed the stairs into the front office. The desk sergeant was a wide man called Benwell, who had been at the 14th, Mid-Town South, before his recent promotion.

'How ya doin'?' greeted Cleary as he ambled past, still

groggy from two hours' sleep. Patrick Cheyenne had been teething and Laurie looked like she could do with some rest. He wondered how much a help would be, from maybe seven at night till twelve. Just to give her a break.

'Joe, you got company.'

'Yeah, Betty Boop's attorney, right?'

'Wrong. You, uh, you gotta go see Captain Capello.'

Alarm bells rang and the wiry little cop was suddenly wide awake. He stopped and pushed past two pimps in long leather coats and Rasta caps who were being led through to the cage by a posse of guys on Vice.

He leaned on the desk and stared at Benwell. 'What's up?'

Benwell raised his ample shoulders and glanced around, then he spoke softly, watching the door. 'Your collar is being taken to . . .' he peered at the big incident book he kept in front of him. Computers were OK but in the 6th they still kept a handwritten Register, like a captain's log, where every event in the day and night of the Precinct House was recorded, 'another jurisdiction.'

'You're kidding me.' Cleary was already furious.

Benwell shook his head. 'Soon as you come in, you go to Capello.' He pushed his uniform cap further back on his brow and turned a page, the conversation going nowhere else, as far as he was concerned.

Frank Capello glanced up as his office door banged open and Joe Cleary strode in, outraged.

'Joe,' he said.

'What the fuck is going on, moving my prisoner?'

Then Cleary became aware of two other men in the corner, sitting watching him.

Capello watched him take this in, then he said, 'Joe, these gentlemen are from', and here he lowered his voice and kind of mumbled, 'the, uh, from Washington.'

Joe stared at them, and slowly nodded. 'Yeah . . .' he breathed. 'Which one of you is called Liebowitz?'

And the one with gold-rimmed glasses looked Cleary straight in the eye, and said, 'I am. Harry K. Liebowitz. I'm with the Office of Investigations, CIA.' He took a business card from his top pocket.

Joe Cleary started to say forget it I got one already, the one you gave to Francis Paul Grumman, Deceased. But he stopped the words in that microspace between brain and tongue.

Something told him it would not be the smartest of moves . . .

10

Not Even Funny

When David Jardine lectured, as he did from time to time, at the Honey Farm, or up on the north-east coast, near Scarborough, or at the Fort, he was listened to with something approaching reverence. Not because he was the Director of Operations and a Very Senior Man, but because his reputation as an agent-runner, with more experience than almost anyone else of illegal missions in a hostile environment, was legendary.

'Mister Jardine', the Hungarian with two bullet scars in his left forearm used to say, 'is an agent-handler second to none. He has been there, children, he has been there more times than is decent or, indeed, prudent. And he has always come back, so far, so heed the man. And learn.'

Jardine sat by a small, bare table set against the open window of his small, spartan room, like a monk's cell, in the Mosāferkhūné Alī Shā, one of the hostels for the faithful, inside the Fātemeh shrine complex.

The room was on the third floor and he could see, across the lower rooftops of several ancient buildings, the golden cupola built by Fath AliShā, after whom his modest inn was named.

It was dark now, and the alleys and small squares, normally bustling with devout, but quietly impressed, even excited, mullahs and their families, were deserted.

The only sound to be heard was the distant, occasionally nearer, grumble of jeep engines and other military vehicles. Now and then a muffled, megaphone-distorted voice would issue fresh orders. Sometimes he could hear the patter of running feet, as some squad of nervous soldiery hurried across an open area of ground. Once, a shot had sounded – abrupt, sharp, then a brief echo. Doubtless a case of nerves.

Brilliant, thought Jardine. I arrive in Ghom for a deeply secret, professionally unnoticeable, face-to-face conversation with my most prized asset, a jewel in the crown of Islamic Jihad, and far from being lost in the crowd, in a city teeming with mullahs and pilgrims, the place has shut itself down, and locked itself in, because a bloody lion is on the prowl.

He was amazed at how the town had taken what was after all a fairly small drama. One lion, for God's sake. Probably mangy and old. And the holy city had retreated to lie under its collective covers. Was it because there was something grimly prophetic in such an event, in a totalitarian state run by religious zealots? Was it collective guilt? The potent symbolism of the lion shaking the populace out of a zealous daze?

And here I am, pondered the ace, even legendary, operator, the man who never put a foot wrong, sitting locked in a mullah's cell, gazing out at the deserted mediaeval shrine town. With a clock ticking and a big cat somewhere near, moving silently, in the shadows.

Is this your sense of humour, sir, he asked his God.

Are you *trying* to make me feel small, and alone, and . . . isolated? Vulnerable. Maybe just a little bit afraid, waiting for the rush of feet on the stairs and the harsh light, the bamboo on the soles of the feet. The pliers. Electric devices. The pain.

Well, he decided, with just the hint of a shudder. You have succeeded.

Hope it makes you feel good.

There was a bottle of local mineral water on the table, and a glass. Jardine took a plastic tub of plain yoghurt from the battered leather grip he had bought, ten thousand years before, on an operation in Colombia, which had eventually brought down Pablo Escobar, mega-rich boss of the Medellín Cartel.

He emptied the yoghurt into a jug and mixed it with some of the soda water, making a refreshing drink the northern Indians call lhassi.

Out there, beyond the open window, for the heat of the night was gruelling, in the angular gray and blue and brown shadows of buildings and minarets, nothing moved.

A distant whine of a jeep.

The muffled megaphone voices.

Jardine was tired now, but he had no intention of sleeping. He gazed out at the domes and rooftops of the shrine village and suddenly the Englishman felt at a very low ebb.

On the face of it, he had done better than he had dreamed of, all those years ago, when Ronnie and Nick Elliot had recruited him into the service. Just a couple of years back, he had felt sidelined, left to serve out his time on bloody committees. Then the Mossad, of all people, had presented him with an intelligence coup which had set him back on the inside track to a place above the salt. And now, as Director of Operations, he was the third most senior man in the organization, which was probably where he would stick, for he was perhaps no longer young enough to win the top job. After all, Richard was two years his junior.

Fresh blood had been the call. Let's give a new generation a chance. So, when Steven McCrae, Sir Steven, had accepted a job on the board of Barings Investment Bank, trading mainly with the Far East, the Chief had recommended to the anonymous Trustees of the Service, and they had agreed, that the three senior men most clearly in line for the position of C should be by-passed and the job offered to one of the best of the (comparatively) younger career intelligence officers in the firm.

The short list had been (and Jardine was not supposed to know this but, of course, he did) Marietta Delice, Richard Sykes and David Jardine himself. Richard had got the job and both Jardine and Marietta agreed it was a good choice.

So harmony reigned in Vauxhall, and David Jardine had been promoted to a job he was absolutely made for, with colleagues he liked and with whom he shared a mutual respect.

His children, Andrew and Sally, were well set in their academic choices, with good career prospects. He had provided for his family. They were comfortably enough off, with money in the bank and investments. And he had his health.

What more could he have asked for?

Dorothy.

That's what.

And, without her, there really was nothing worth having.

Christ, what a fool he had been. His arrogance in imagining that he could live forever in that indulgent limbo where slender, lissom young creatures, who very occasionally would smile on a randy, middle-aged spy, could be indulged in, while dear old, large old, 'I'd rather have a cup of tea these days' old Dorothy and he would just carry on forever. Once the most passionate pair of lovers, now 'very best chums', the most important people in each other's lives, blissfully content to approach the declining years together, plump chain-smoker's hand in calloused, blood-stained, tender paw – inseparable.

After all, had not Kate Howard, the only one of his 'little treats' David Jardine could have become really serious about, more than once said, 'But face it, David, in the real world, isn't Dorothy the only girl for you . . .?' And even in her bed, so warm and close, so close to falling for the incredible Kate, Jardine had not been able to deny the truth of it.

Yes, he had nodded, almost sadly, she is. The only girl for me. At the end of the day.

Jardine smiled grimly . . . what was that movement in the shadows down there? Beside a stall which sold religious mementoes of the Tomb of Fatemeh . . . at the end of the bloody day it had turned out that David Arbuthnot Jardine was not the only boy in the world for stout, boring old Dorothy.

And Angus Agnew. Of all people. That boring little cunt.

Boy oh boy. Jardine stared at the jug of lhassi and wished it was Isle of Jura, up to the bloody brim.

Tap-tap. Tap-tap-tap. Tap-tap-tap. A knocking at the bedroom door.

It was the arranged knock of Sayyed, the truck driver.

Jardine gently unlocked the door and held it open. Sayyed filtered in, like a pickpocket.

Jardine locked the door.

Sayyed's eyes were white as they checked out the room and the rooftops outside. When he spoke, it was – not even a whisper, just a breath, with words.

'It is impossible to move. It is not possible to get even to the next corner. Pasdarami and regular troops, and the police, are moving to shut off every street.'

'The lion,' breathed Jardine.

Sayyed nodded. 'Ashgar Shavary is Military Governor of Ghom. His wife and daughter were eaten by lions, during a visit to the Sudan. He has from that time both hated and been terrified of them.'

Jardine understood. 'So this one is not going to be allowed to get away.'

Sayyed spread his hands. He was a handsome man, with brown, intelligent eyes. Jardine wondered what had made him an agent of the KGB. 'It has already killed a nightwatchman, at a workshop which makes flails for the Penitent . . .'

The sense of having been transported back to the Middle Ages was almost thrilling. A million thoughts flashed through Jardine's mind, along the lines of, 'Have we been looking at the Islamic Fundamentalist threat from the wrong perspective?' Here in Ghom, one could almost touch a mediaeval ethos of stark simplicity, the heart of the fire of Jihad directed against the contemporary, more relaxed Islamic faithful.

Here in Ghom, the term 'Great Satan' was probably not a mere metaphor. From Ghom, the most powerful secular nation in the world probably *was* Satanic.

Suddenly David Jardine understood with shocking clarity precisely what Islamic Fundamentalists intended. They wanted to cleanse the world of unbelievers and install a sense of order according to the teachings of the Prophet and the Will of Allah The Merciful.

And if it took a tidal wave of violence and the slaughter of infidels, so be it. A small price to pay for spiritual fulfilment.

There was a stillness in the night, as he poured some of the lhassi from its jug into two glasses and offered one to Sayyed.

'Don't worry,' he said softly, in Arabic, which was the language they spoke, among others, 'tomorrow is another day.'

And as they sipped, a stair creaked, outside. Their eyes met, hearts suddenly pounding.

Jardine crossed to the window and glanced outside. Ten men in dark robes, holding AKS assault rifles, stood at intervals on the far side of the dusty street, watching him watching them.

These were special police from Tehran's 'Guidance Ministry', and they came under the direct command of Hojatolislam Farhad Nagazhian, Director of the Iranian Clergy's Intelligence and Security Bureau.

At that moment, the hammering on the door started, and, calm though he may have seemed to Sayyed, David Jardine's mild tenseness gave way to acute . . . apprehension.

Oh, God, he prayed, all those ways I meant to reform. Give me time to repent my sins.

But God was doubtless on other business for the door burst open, with a crash of splintering wood.

Jardine turned to face the three black-robed special policemen and their leader, a civilian in a dark suit, with the short, neat black beard and the collarless white shirt that was the custom among officials in Iran.

'Looking for the lion, gentlemen?' he asked, with a display of insouciance he far from felt.

And the white-shirted official smiled coldly and replied, 'You will wish it had been the lion who found you. In the name of Allah the Merciful, I am taking you into the custody of the Ministry of Guidance.'

Poor Sayyed, thought Jardine, who was known to take great care of his agents, his 'Joes'. They will torture him to the end of his stamina, the end of his courage, and he can tell them nothing. He wished he could have kept the man out of this.

The official turned to Sayyed, who was looking decidedly nervous. '*Motashakkeram*, Sayyed, *mojahed*,' he said.

Mojahed meant soldier of the Holy War, soldier of the *jihad*. And the first word was Farsi for thank you. This was one of life's little surprises which dear Alice Mayhew, David Jardine's first teacher in the art of espionage, had promised were to litter his future, usually in unpleasant circumstances.

Good old Alice. Right again . . .

He stared at Sayyed, who no longer pretended to be nervous.

'*Chizi nist* . . .' 'It's nothing', the truck driver replied, not taking his eyes off the man he believed to be a Russian intelligence officer.

'*Bolshoi spasiba*,' said Jardine. 'Thanks a bundle.'

Sayyed smiled. '*Nyechevo* . . . Don't mention it.'

Two of the policemen clamped manacles onto Jardine's hands and another held the door open.

'For what we are about to receive,' the big spymaster recited silently, 'may the Lord make us truly thankful . . .'

And he beamed his glare of flint into the bearded official's eyes and allowed himself to be hustled out of the room.

'I need time to get my things,' protested Dolores, raising her arms and letting a cotton-shift dress slide down over her head and nude body.

'There maybe ain't no time,' replied Joe Cleary, standing at the bedroom window and looking down on MacDougall Street, pretending to be completely unmoved by this provocative super-babe with her wilfully mischievous sexuality.

'So what's the big deal?' The tall restaurant manageress quickly shoved some things, underwear and make-up and stuff, into a big soft leather bag, along with her Filofax, a pocket-size Psion personal computer and wads of hundreds and fifties from her dressing-table drawer.

The kid, decided Cleary, has done this kind of thing before.

'The deal is maybe the people who killed the guy in the freezer are going to come looking for you.'

'After all this time? You're crazy, Joey.'

'Dolores, I don't like being called Joey.'

'Gee, I'll just go slash my wrists.' She checked her long, blonde hair in the mirror and met his eyes in the reflection.

'Who else knows you saw the dead man with some friends of his? C'mon c'mon . . .' He moved to the other window. There was that gay tart on the roller blades again. Maybe he was some kinda lead scout for the hit-men.

'Um . . . just you. And maybe some of the waiters at Barolo. We all talked about it – for God's sake, it's not every day you find a stiff in the ice box.'

'And had anyone else seen the victim accompanied?'

'No,' she replied, and almost demurely went on, 'I was with him in different circumstances.'

Then she understood.

'So I'm the only one who saw them . . .'

Joe shrugged. 'It's maybe nothing, Dolores. Maybe they don't know that. But just maybe word will eventually get to them that somebody can finger them. *Capisce*?'

Dolores nodded. She stepped into a pair of very nice navy blue Italian shoes, hefted up her soft leather bag and said, 'So let's go.'

Cleary took a final look at the street, six floors below, then he crossed to the hall and glanced back. 'Ain't you going to put on underwear?' he asked.

'You said to hurry,' she said, and lifted up her leather grip, giving him that look of hers.

For a microsecond Joe nearly weakened. He was only flesh and blood after all. But Patrick Cheyenne and fatherhood had changed his attitude to all that. Part of him hoped it might be a temporary thing.

'So let's go,' he agreed, and slipping the chain off the door, opened it carefully. The hallway was deserted.

The '83 Pontiac cruised into Mid-Town, the 14th Precinct's territory, past Grand Central Station and left into 42nd Street, right onto Madison, and paused at the lights.

Dolores had seemed subdued.

'Listen, it's just a precaution, kid,' offered Cleary, regretting having frightened her.

She shivered. 'Man, did you see what they did to Tony . . .?'

Tony was what the John Doe in the freezer had called himself, in the four times he had seen the girl from Barolo. Tony Maclean. Dolores had told Joe that, on the way back from the Jockey Club bar. Tony Maclean. He had paid his check the night he was murdered, in cash.

And Tony Maclean had introduced one of his business colleagues as Azil, she remembered. She could not recall the other guy's name, but he had been a tall guy. With glinting eyes, very alert.

'So where we going?'

'You'll see.' Joe Cleary swung right on 40th, slowing for a man taking advantage of the last flicker of the 'DON'T WALK' light. Automatically, subconsciously, Cleary registered him as male, Caucasian, six-one, medium build, athletic body movement, hair brown, steel-rimmed GI-issue glasses, tan chino-type trousers and a soft leather zip-up jacket. Maybe British, for the guy had looked right before stepping off the kerb, unless he did not know traffic on even numbers moved east.

Either way, a man from outa town.

That was the way Joe Cleary's cop's mind worked. He hardly thought about it. One thing, of course, he did not have was a name. Although, in years to come, he was never to forget it. For that passing stranger was to become part of his destiny, in the human comedy.

James Gant, unaware of the old Pontiac that had slowed to let him across the street, strolled on down Madison, casually alert and deep in thought. The night before, he had gone back to Jack Chisholm's Duffield Street apartment, in Brooklyn.

He had waited till twenty minutes after midnight. He had phoned the place from a payphone near the theatre.

'Yeah . . .?' Chisholm's voice had answered, almost immediately.

'It's me again,' James had said.

'Yeah. So?'

'You all set?'

Pause.

'Sure thing, come on up.'

'You come on down. Bring the stuff.'

Silence.

Then, 'Hey, friend, I don't feel too comfortable with that. You know what I'm sayin'?'

'Relax. You have taken copies of my mugshots and all the details on the merchandise. If I don't take good care of you, it would be . . . very silly of me.'

A slight pause, then a grim chuckle. 'Man, if you were not a Limey, I would swear this was a set up by the Federicks.'

'Be down at the drugstore across the street in exactly seven minutes, Jack. Then I'm out of your hair, provided you've done your usual perfect work.' And Gant had hung up.

Five minutes later, Jack Chisholm had padded cautiously down the emergency stairs at the back of his apartment block. They were badly lit and smelled of decay and piss. He had reached the third floor when a figure had stepped out from the shadows.

'Don't try to mug me, man, I bite,' had snarled Chisholm, producing a big Army Colt .45 from his back pocket.

'Relax, Jack. It's only me.' James had stepped into the dim light and lit a cigarette. He seemed unmoved by the artillery. 'You bring it?'

Chisholm had frowned. The temptation to blow the Limey away had been strong. But not on his own doorstep. And the wise-guy had obviously worked that out.

'It's all there . . .' He had put the pistol away and tugged a brown packet from under his tracksuit top.

Gant opened it and, using a jeweller's eyeglass and a slim, infra-red torch, had examined the passports, the driver's licences and the credit cards. He realized the big counterfeiter was watching, anxiously.

James had nodded, saying things like, 'Wow', and, 'Jesus', and, 'Wonderful'. Finally he put the torch away and blinked out the eyeglass. 'Jack,' he had announced, 'you are a fucking craftsman. An artist . . .'

And Jack Chisholm beamed, the tension of his labours evaporating.

'You see?' Gant had said, handing Chisholm a thick roll of $100 bills, plus the Irish passport blank, 'isn't this a lot better than shooting at each other?'

His eyes had met Chisholm's and here, perhaps for the first time in this the infancy of James Gant's secret odyssey, Edith Treffewin's hunch that he might do all right as an operator was proved right. For Jack Chisholm had held the Englishman's gaze and nodded, wiping the sweat from his hands on his tracksuit, then, slowly, he had smiled.

'I read you wrong, brother,' he had said. 'You're OK. You got respect, and you got balls.' And he had offered his hand.

Gant had gripped it and they both relaxed.

'How are they, by the way?'

'Ouch, man . . .' Chisholm had grimaced, then grinned. 'Not as bad as I guessed they would be.'

'Well, I didn't want to hurt you,' Gant had replied. And as Chisholm stood there, he had turned and moved off down the stairs, soon just his light footsteps the only reminder.

And Jack Chisholm had climbed back up to his apartment, thinking, that ain't the last we seen of *that* dude.

Dolores's eyes widened as Joe Cleary spun the wheel and the Pontiac's tyres squealed and kept on squealing while they descended the narrow, winding ramp to the basement car park of the World Trade Center.

'You're taking me to an apartment here?' Her eyes widened.

'Be cool. You'll be staying in my sister's place in Tribeca.'

'I don't like sharing, it never works.'

'She's outa town. Just for a week or so. I just want to keep you safe, kid. You're in the middle of something really bad; bad stuff is going down; I just want to keep you in one piece.' He drove slowly into a security fenced pen and stopped at a big triple-wire gate, on a serious tubular-steel frame. There were signs announcing this was Government Property and Keep Out and All Passes Must Be Shown and stuff like that.

A camera swivelled to include them both.

A uniformed guard in a dark-blue tunic, with a Smith & Wesson on his hip, stepped out from a hut set in the wire pen.

Cleary showed his NYPD Detective's ID wallet and a pink card with US State Department – Diplomatic Security Service, on it, with the State Department crest.

'OK, Sergeant.' The guard sauntered back and the steel-mesh gate slid aside.

'Where the hell is this?'

'I'm going to show you some photos, Dolores.'

'Joey, what is this? Where the fuck are we?'

'Don't swear, it don't sound nice, from somebody like you.'

She turned and looked at him, then her worried frown became a big grin. 'Hey, you can be a sweet guy . . .'

'Don't kiss me,' said Joe, holding a hand up as her lips moved towards his cheek. 'We should be businesslike, kid. I'm nothing but trouble, you get to know me.'

The stunning girl sat back, as he parked the car.

'Businesslike,' she repeated, like a little kid who had been given a telling-off.

'Yeah,' said the detective, and opened his door. 'Let's go.'

And the two of them walked through the parked Dodge four-wheels and grey DSS Oldsmobiles and beat-up, nondescript surveillance vehicles, to the elevators.

There, Joe Cleary pressed a combination of numbered buttons and the door slid open.

'Going up,' he said. 'Ladies' hose and stale coffee.'

'You know how to show a girl a good time, Joey,' complained Dolores, stepping in.

'Call me Joe, would you. While we're here . . . and don't speak except a coupla words that mean nothing, OK?'

'I was going to the movies tonight. With Martin.'

'Who's Martin?' asked Cleary as the doors slid shut.

'None of your business, Joseph.'

And the dank empty car park was silent once more.

Lights on the side of the elevator door showed it was going up pretty fast to the eighteenth floor.

Dawn in the Holy City of Ghom found David Jardine in a stinking cell inside the barracks of the Ministry of Guidance's Special Police Unit.

The night before, they had bundled him into the back of a canvas covered truck, put a thick, black hood over his head and driven him to a place which had rough concrete walls and dirt floors. It smelled of damp and cleaning fluid.

They had roughed him up, on the way along an echoing tiled corridor, and had pulled off the hood as they propelled him into the cramped cell, slamming the heavy wood door and locking it with three keys.

At first he had sat on the wooden bed along one wall, half-expecting to be taken out to some sinister interrogation room and given the full treatment he knew was meted out to prisoners at the Ghom barracks.

When no one had come, he had stretched out on the bench and contemplated his predicament. It had been bloody stupid coming here in the first place. He was pretty sure they believed he was a corrupt minor Russian intelligence man, but the whim of the Ministry of Guidance was unpredictable. What if he was dealt with by the wrong interrogator?

The very thought quickened his heartbeat.

What if they learned he was not really a Muslim? He had no illusions about his treatment then.

The only thing in the room, apart from the solid wood bed, was a metal pail with water in it. There was a spy hole in the heavy wood door, and someone was watching him. It was about then that David Jardine wondered if he had really made a terribly sensible decision in coming so deep into the lion's den. No pun intended, he thought, drily.

There was a small, brick-shaped window near the ceiling, about eight feet above. From outside came occasional sounds, incongruous but somehow familiar. Distant whine of jeep engines. Muffled megaphone voices, giving orders in Farsi.

Jardine wished most devoutly the escaped lion would come and chew on the sons of bitches who had worked him over; there had been no reason for the casual brutality, except that for them it had obviously become routine.

A key turned in the door and the SIS man prepared himself for more unpleasant surprises.

Two men came in, one late twenties, wiry; the other bull-necked, broad, aged about forty, wearing what Jardine recognized as French paratroopers' boots, called 'Rangers', black fatigues and gray T-shirts.

The young one held a complicated set of hand and ankle manacles, linked with steel chains. Jardine knew these too, they were manufactured by a British company in the Midlands, not far from Leeds. It was a company which had won a Queen's Award for Industry, for its thriving export trade in 'security' apparatus, including, it was rumoured, the occasional guillotine, which was considered one in the eye for their French rivals in the Third World market.

When they hauled him to his feet and fitted the chains, more than several muscles in Jardine's body ached from the roughing up they had given him the night before.

I am, actually, getting too damned old for this, he decided.

Without speaking, they led him out of the cell and along a long corridor, past other cells where he could hear groans and the disturbing sound of grown men weeping. When they reached a door, guarded by two black-robed Special Police, one policeman opened the door and Jardine was roughly shoved into a spacious room, where a straight-backed chair, empty, faced a long wooden bench.

There was a vaulting-horse, a wooden gymnastics box, wallbars along parts of the walls and piles of hessian mats on the polished wooden floor.

There were two high windows, and the faded, pale-blue sky of a hot late-summer Iranian day beyond.

Sitting on one pile of mats in this gymnasium was a spade-bearded man, with a long face, dark eyes and that certain arrogance which goes with the power of life and death. He wore a dark suit and a spotless, collarless white shirt, fastened to the neck.

The two jailers dumped Jardine on the high-backed chair and fixed his arms to the wood with well-worn leather straps.

This was not what I had in mind, Lord, the Englishman reflected, not without a prudent degree of reverence, when I asked for your help in getting close to this set-up.

There was a long moment when it was impossible to predict what was about to happen. David Jardine braced himself for the attack to begin. It had been eight years since he had last been in this position and he was not entirely sure he could endure it.

Jardine realized his mouth was as dry as a scarab beetle's shell. Perspiration ran down the hollow of his back. But the man in the suit merely inclined his head towards the door and the jailers ambled out, pulling the door shut.

Silence.

'*Vot izvoltye*,' said the man, softly, speaking in Russian. 'So here you are.'

Jardine controlled his breathing and kept his gaze fixed on the man. Some primitive instinct told him there were others in the room, somewhere behind him and out of his range of vision.

'*Znayete kto ya*?' the interrogator enquired. 'Do you know who I am?'

Jardine inclined his head. Oh, yes, he knew. This was Hojatolislam Javd Assadiyan, Deputy Director of the Iranian Clergy's Intelligence Bureau – Foreign Department – Commander of the Imam Special Missions Directorate and Deputy Chief Controller in the Ministry of Guidance.

There was very little that Javd Assadiyan did not know about Iranian secret operations, involving acts of terror in foreign countries. Assadiyan worked with Jamil Shahidi, who had sub-contracted their masters' wishes for a spectacular 'event' during UN Week in New York, to the Abu Nidal Group.

'*Shto sluchelos?*' asked Assadiyan, gently. 'What has happened?'

Jardine continued to watch him, warily.

Assadiyan glanced past him and seemed to meet the gaze of someone behind Jardine. 'I believe you are a former officer in the Glavnoye Razvedyvatelnoye Upravleniye,' said Assadiyan. He meant Russian Military Intelligence, the GRU. 'I know these things. There is no point in putting yourself through more of . . . this.'

'You couldn't be more mistaken,' replied Jardine in Russian.

Assadiyan smiled, it was a sad smile.

'Have you any idea of the extremes we go to, to protect the Islamic Republic?'

'I am a good Muslim,' replied David Jardine, and he felt a good Catholic's guilt as he said it. Not because he believed his own creed was the only one, the only way, but because he knew so many really good Muslims, thoroughly decent followers of Islam, who practised every day the kindness and tolerance taught by the Prophet Muhammad.

That was the real Islam and Jardine knew he could never match up to it. The truth was he was neither a good Muslim nor a good Christian. He was a man. Touched by Lucifer's kiss, like all mankind.

'I can even tell you what Division, what Detachment, you belonged to . . .'

Jardine remained silent.

'Fourth Division, Detachment 146. Special duties, *podpol-'naya rabota*,' he meant underground, undercover work, 'in Turkmenistan. Your assignment was to . . . arrange things, good services liaison, you call it, between your out-station in Krasnovodsk and deep-cover agents on the coast. Come on, Sergei, you know I am right.'

Jardine watched his interrogator. This man was good. He

permitted just sufficient of a flicker to pass between them, that anyone observing would deduce Assadiyan had succeeded in nailing his subject's hide to the wall.

After a long silence he said, 'You are mistaken.'

Assadiyan smiled. He rose and stretched his spare frame, elegantly, like a giraffe, working his neck this way and that. He shoved his hands in his pockets and walked, very slowly, as if to some inaudible tune, lightly, making what were like little, formal dance steps.

Then the Iranian paused, standing right beside David Jardine, looking down.

'If you confess, you can be of some small assistance,' he said. 'I mean, I know, Sergei, you came here using your old GRU contacts, merely to do some deals on the black market.' He chuckled. 'Illegal, of course. Immoral, without a doubt. But hardly a threat to the Revolution . . .'

He strolled right round the man on the chair, until he was standing on the other side.

'If you confess, Sergei, *and* if you agree to help the Islamic Republic, which as one of the faithful you should be proud to do, I guarantee you will be taken back across the border tonight. Sooner. For there is a mission you can perform for me. If you prefer that to days of beatings and a lifetime in prison.'

Jardine remained motionless. The ankle chains were chafing into his flesh.

'If, on the other hand, you do not . . .' Assadiyan stepped back and Jardine was aware of him nodding to whoever was standing behind, at the back of the gymnasium.

A sudden cough and splutter of something like a lawn-mower engine, or a small outboard motor, not quite firing.

Then with a deafening 'Brrarrr!' it ripped into life.

Its rasping whine filled the room. Jardine could smell the pungent gasoline/kerosene exhaust fumes.

Jesus Christ, a chainsaw . . . then, out of the corner of his good eye, he glimpsed the noisy machine. It was an electrical generator.

Oh, thank you, God, acknowledged David Jardine, they are only going for the old electrodes routine.

Slowly, like the sadist Assadiyan probably was, he kneeled

beside his prisoner. His dark, intelligent eyes inches from the Englishman's face, his bearded mouth even closer to Jardine's ear.

'*Shto eto*?' he murmured. 'What is it? We have to be quick.'

And he turned his head to lean an ear that smelled of cleanliness, of soap and Cologne, almost against Jardine's lips.

'We have a leak,' breathed Jardine, his voice inaudible in the din of the generator. The room was filling with acrid blue haze. 'London has a leak. Why did you not warn me? I can't believe you don't know . . . You yourself could be in danger.'

Assadiyan glanced at the two torturers standing about fifteen feet behind the chair and winked. They smiled. Director Assadiyan always got them to talk.

He turned back and murmured into Jardine's ear, 'I swear I did not know. But I will try to find out. This is a mad risk you have taken, bloody David bloody Jardine. But nothing else would have convinced me to take similar risks. You have my oath that I will . . .'

'I know that, Javd. We need your help before the entire enterprise starts to unravel.'

For several moments Javd Assadiyan alternately murmured into the prisoner's ear, sometimes seeming to threaten, sometimes giving instructions, and listened, his ear close to David Jardine's mouth.

Finally he smiled, patted Jardine like a good dog and climbed to his feet. He drew a finger across his throat and the portable generator stopped abruptly, leaving its noisy echo in the room.

To Assadiyan's men, such events were not unusual. They had seen him use minor criminals before, to go into neighbouring countries to gather information or perform simple tasks for the Revolution. Often they were subsequently disposed of. It was nothing to write home about. Which was why Assadiyan, recorded only as Agent 11061 on a Cosmic Top Secret file in an SIS safe, and Jardine had arranged their clandestine meeting like that.

'This prisoner will sign a confession,' Assadiyan announced. 'He is to be given first aid, cleaned up, provided with clean clothes and taken across the Turkmenistan border in this evening's operation *sharab*.'

Jardine was not certain whether *sharab* was Farsi for wine or moustache, the two words were close, but, either way, he would be safely back with Ronnie and his team, on the other, saner, side of the Iranian border by nightfall.

'Have you any questions?' Assadiyan asked 'Sergei'.

Jardine shook his head. 'I will make contact when I have something for you, *Mojahed*.'

'God is great . . .' pronounced Assadiyan.

'*Allah-ha Akbar*,' responded 'Sergei' and the two torturers behind him, automatically.

The guards watched as Assadiyan strolled out of the room. Then they approached and helped Jardine from the chair, surprisingly gently.

But he knew they would have tortured him to the edge of endurance with just as little emotion.

In the DSS office, on the twenty-fourth floor of the World Trade Center, the air-conditioning hummed and, from another room, the occasional muted chatter of a printer erupted as information and instructions arrived from Washington DC and State Department offices around the world.

Joe Cleary walked backwards into the office, exchanging a few words with Helen Sorensen, the FBI agent, and holding two plastic cups of hot coffee.

'. . . sure thing, Helen, I'm meeting with Rakesh first thing in the morning.'

He turned and laid one coffee cup beside Dolores, who was sitting at Joe's desk, flicking lazily through page after page of 8″ × 4″ black and white photographs of males aged between about twenty and fifty. She was bored as hell. Cardboard cartons of half-eaten pizza and pastrami on rye littered the desk top.

'Here. This'll waken you up,' said Cleary.

'Joe, I don't even remember what the guys looked like. I mean, one was . . . I dunno, real average.'

'What age?'

'Shit . . . thirty-five? Thirty-eight? Something like that.'

'And you ain't seen nobody . . .' Cleary indicated the four thick volumes of surveillance photographs or law-enforcement mugshots, two to a page. Hundreds of them.

'I need to get some sleep, I'm doing lunchtime tomorrow.'

'Yeah, we need to talk about that . . .'

'What do you mean?' She bridled, flipping another page over and glancing at him, ready to rebel.

'I spoke to Captain Gelardi in Police Plaza. He makes the decision on WP programmes.'

'What's WP?'

'Witness Protection.'

Dolores stared at him. 'What are you talking about?'

This was where Joe Cleary always felt like a medicine show man. How the hell was he going to be able to convince the patient this was good for her?

'The procedure is simple,' he said. 'The DA's office cites you as a potential witness in a major felony, in this case homicide' (he made it sound like jay-walking) 'and the City purse will provide a safe place for you with round-the-clock protection.'

'I would be like a goddam prisoner,' Dolores said. Her lip quivered. 'Joey, when you brought me here and said I should stay at your sister's place for a couple of days . . .' she shrugged and idly flipped over another page, 'I thought, well, no big deal . . . But I can't afford to lose my job. Jesus, Joe, I never enjoyed turning tricks but that's all I'd have left.'

'Bullshit!' announced the detective, suddenly, unexpectedly, angry at the dumb broad. 'You got such looks, so much poise . . . you could do anything, fashion model, uh, TV presenter, perfume counter at Bloomingdale's. Anything. You insult yourself turning tricks, Jesus Christ, God forgive me, where the fuck is your head at?' He paced up and down the room, spilling his coffee and burning his hand. 'Shit!'

In the silence that followed, the tall Sicilian girl sat, head bowed, thoughtful.

'You really think I could be a fashion model . . .?' she enquired, quietly.

Cleary leaned against the wall, shaking the coffee off his hand. 'Sure I do. You should work at finding the right connections.'

'Can't I just stay at your sister's place without all the big, uh, drama?'

Joe considered this. He nodded. 'If that's what you want. But you should stay away from Barolo for a while. You know, your own apartment and place of work. That's all they got on you.'

'And Johnny,' she contributed, lowering her eyes. Johnny Stomparelli had been her pimp.

'Yeah, well, leave that to me, babe.' And the cop's eyes had gone very cool when he said that.

Dolores considered that. Then she nodded. 'OK, Joe. I'll find a job someplace else.'

'Terrific.'

'You gotta come see me a lot.'

'Every day. Or Sam.' He meant Sam Vargos, his partner.

The kid nodded. 'How's your new baby?'

Cleary smiled. 'Patrick Cheyenne? He's a star.'

'This is him,' she remarked, softly, touching one of the photographs. 'This is one of them . . .'

'Which one?' His pulse quickening, Joe Cleary moved to look over her shoulder.

Dolores Caltagirone was touching the photograph of a tall man, coming out from between two parked automobiles to cross the street. It looked like West 54th, with the Hertz office kinda fuzzy behind him.

There was no mistaking that stubble, the long coat buttoned at the neck.

It was Betty Boop.

The sixteenth floor of the Essex House Hotel, uptown side, had a wonderful view over Central Park. Zina stood at the panoramic window, watching roller-skaters on the Wollman Rink and on the drive beside the Sheep Meadow, joggers, couples hand-in-hand, a pony-drawn *caliche* winding through West Drive past the Tavern On The Green towards the Boating Lake and Strawberry Fields.

She was pleased that she had identified every inch of the Park and had carried out a thorough recce, in the company of Zafir and Noor Jalud. They had made it a habit to go jogging in the early morning, around six – it had been Khaled Niknam who had suggested it was a perfect way for those members of the hit team with diplomatic cover to keep in touch, without being noticed, for the teeming city observed, almost to a man (or woman), each individual's right to personal space, and jogging around in brightly coloured sportswear, preferably fluorescent, was a pretty sure way to attract zero attention.

The Palestinian girl smiled as she recalled the three low-life muggers who had emerged from the bushes north of the Reservoir (the hotel information pack advised guests to 'enjoy the Park, during daylight hours, and on no account to venture north of the Reservoir') beside Harlem Meer, from which you could see the Martin Luther King Towers apartment blocks.

They had been on roller-skates, with navy and yellow baseball caps, worn sideways-on, extremely baggy pants and they each had a piece. Two snub-nosed .38 Saturday Nite Specials and a slightly jaded Star .38 Automatic.

'Money. Money. Money . . .' they had chanted, softly, as they skated effortlessly around the three Arabs. Zina had noticed they used roller-blades and had been impressed. It was a skill she had practised in the Bois de Boulogne in Paris but never had gotten the hang of it.

'Money. Money. Money. Money . . .'

Zafir, Noor and Zina had looked anxious and, fumbling inside their jogging tops, had at the same moment produced handy-size KF-AMP assault machine-pistols, the big .45 calibre, with twenty-round magazines and chosen one mugger each.

'Ready to rock and roll, brothers?' Zafir had asked, as the skaters had slewed to a halt.

'Take a fucking chance,' Zina Farouche had snarled, 'you might be faster than us.'

And just to swing the balance of the argument, Zafir Hammuda, the butcher of Biarritz, had suddenly raised his weapon head-high and pointed it inches from his personal target.

'Oh, please don't go,' he murmured, so softly it chilled the marrow, 'I want to kill you . . . Come on, stay and let me' and here he shouted so loud Zina and everybody else jumped, 'PUMP YOU FULL OF FUCKIN' LEAD!'

The one with the Star automatic immediately pissed himself, and he was not the roller-blader looking straight down the muzzle of Zafir's gun, the copper nose of the big .45 slug glinting at the end of the short barrel.

That guy, to be fair, had nodded, he nodded a couple of times, and lifted his hands up, not letting go of his little .38, but freeing his finger from the trigger and showing he had done so.

'OK, people. That's cool . . . We're outa here. Stay cool . . .'

He leaned backwards and moved away, without moving his feet, or any part of him. Zina had been envious of the ease of his control. The times she had tried them, the blades, she had almost broken an ankle.

The muggers had managed to skate away backwards, not taking their eyes off the seriously armed fluorescent joggers, and, as soon as they felt they had a chance, had spun round and rolled away to the furthest corner of the Universe. To be precise, Adam Clayton Powell Jr Boulevard.

Zina was still smiling when her Tunisian colleague opened the door and in walked Al Wiscynsky.

'Nice to see somebody happy,' he remarked, glancing around the room out of habit. He had been impressed the first time he had visited the Tunisians' makeshift security office to see how seriously they took the job.

Faxes, modems, wall maps, photographs of known Islamic extremists and right-wing Jewish Kalach activists known to be in New York, all testified to their professionalism.

'I'm sorry we couldn't give you more warning about the Ambassador coming in early,' said Zina.

Wiscynsky waved a dismissive hand. 'Forget it. We are so busy, one more doesn't get in the way. Is Ambassador Kefi comfortable? Anything we can do to help his stay in New York?'.

'He's fine, thank you.' Zina Farouche knew that behind such pleasantries was the US security man's other agenda, keeping tabs on what was happening, Belhassen Kefi's movements, who he was seeing in New York. 'The opera a couple of nights back went down really well.' She pulled her chair out and sat at her desk, lifting a file from a tray of several.

'I have to tell you,' said Wiscynsky confidentially, 'opera

drives me crazy. I can't understand the language and, if I could, I sure as hell could not figure out the plot.'

'A bit like United Nations Week,' smiled Zina.

He scratched his head and grinned. 'Just a tad.'

'So what can we do for you today, Al? Can I get you something, cup of tea?'

The man from State sat in the seat on the other side of her desk. 'What kind of weapons do you all carry?'

God, had he heard about Harlem Meer?

'I have a nine-millimetre Beretta, the big one. Plus we have KF-AMP Model Elevens. Good guns.' KFs were made in Stone Park, Illinois.

Wiscynsky tugged a pack of Marlboros from his jacket pocket, and gave that look which asked, is it OK to smoke?

'Go right ahead.'

Wiscynsky flicked his Zippo and lit up, then, exhaling, he said, 'You know, Zina, you really should not be carrying in the USA. That's our job.'

So that was what he had been leading up to, the incident in the Park had nothing to do with it. Illegal guns carried by foreign diplomatic security officers was a delicate problem, for the simple reason that some nations had an agreement with the US and NYPD authorities, others had an informal look-the-other-way arrangement and the rest either played by the rules or took a chance, the survival of their customers being paramount, and this was generally understood. Provided nobody behaved provocatively.

It was a subject Zina Farouche the Tunisian diplomat was prepared to argue.

'Some people carry,' she replied. 'The Israelis go armed here.'

'Not all the time. Plus they have to apply each time and there is a diplomatic protocol covering the arrangement.'

'Maybe we should have that too,' she said, glancing to Azouz Ben Larbi, the senior Economic and Press Counsellor, who had been in a corner, talking quietly with the other Security Attaché.

'Then you have to take it up with State.'

'Who exactly, Mister Wiscynsky? Who in State?'

Al Wiscynsky grinned slowly, she really was an attractive

young woman, and sassy with it. 'Me,' he admitted, then added, 'But we would only agree if DSS perceived there was a particular threat. And I don't think there is. At this point in time. I would love a cup of plain tea, without milk.'

'The Fundamentalists are getting more dangerous all the time,' contributed Ben Larbi.

Believe it. Thought Zina, grimly. And smiled pleasantly. 'I'm sure the Ambassador will make a formal request, if he is advised specifically.'

Wiscynsky appreciated the riposte. 'And who will advise him to do that?'

'I will, of course,' replied the young woman, and from the pile selected a gray-blue file, stamped 'secret' in Arabic. 'Here are his movements during United Nations Week.' She lifted the phone receiver. 'Sugar?'

'Two lumps.' Al Wiscynsky reached across and took the offered file. As he opened it and put on a pair of horn-rimmed reading glasses, he said, quietly, 'We know you carry when you're working, Zina. Just don't make it an issue, OK?'

Zina Farouche nodded. 'Sure. Thanks.'

'And for Chrissake don't shoot anybody. Now let's work out some routes here. And radio call signs . . .' The matter was over and Wiscynsky wanted to get on with his work.

'Two teas, Tahzi, no milk, one with two sugars. *Shukran*.'

'Your Ambassador is not planning any trips out of the city while he is here, is he?' enquired Wiscynsky, as he studied the itinerary.

'I don't think so. Why?'

'Oh, just one of my other ambassadors has decided to visit some old friends, right in the middle of all this.'

'How inconsiderate,' sympathized Zina.

'Yeah. Still, with all this stuff . . .' Al indicated the photos of about twenty known Arab terrorists and Jewish extremists on the wall beside them, 'he's probably safer out of town.'

'Unless they go looking for him,' commented Zina. 'I'm glad it's not my problem.'

Sixteen floors below, a tall, good-enough-looking young man, in a dark, lightweight suit, two-button jacket, button-down cotton shirt and unremarkable necktie, strolled into the busy lobby from the street and across to the reception desk, weaving through a group of Japanese businessmen who were being marshalled by an efficient Japanese lady in a striped Armani business suit and built like a wrestler.

'Hi, how can I help you?' enquired the neatly dressed clerk behind the counter.

'I have a reservation for a few nights. Name of Wilson.'

'Wilson ... Let me see ...' The clerk's fingers flicked across his computer keyboard. He glanced up, without moving his head. 'Would that be J.T.? Mister James Wilson from Idaho?'

'Tony. Anthony Wilson. London. England.'

Silence as the clerk summoned up more data. Behind them, who just ambled in but Khaled Niknam. Without a care in the world. Casually dressed in jeans and a slightly faded sweatshirt with Georgetown University on the back, he moved past them to a magazine, candy and cigarette kiosk just off the main lobby. He bought a copy of *The New Yorker* and came out, checking his wristwatch and choosing a place on the comfortable brown leather seats around the walls. Just another tourist, waiting for somebody.

'There you are, Mister Wilson.' The clerk scanned Gant's signing-in card one last time, then handed him a plastic, one-time room key and his Amex credit card. It was a company card, it had a worn look to it and it was in the name of Signet Photo-optics of Leatherhead, Surrey. P.A. Wilson was the name of the cardholder. The clerk's routine enquiry had shown the card was good for very serious credit. 'Room 1824. Elevators are to the left, just over there.'

'Thanks.' Gant lifted his soft leather grip and headed for the elevator, walking past the Palestinian activist, unaware of the small drama of the moment. For, although this was the first time he had shared space with a member of the Dante Group, it meant nothing to either of them.

James Gant took an elevator to the eighteenth floor. He found his room, along a corridor to the left of the lobby, and, as he slid the key-card into its slot, waiting for the tiny green pin-point of light to announce the door was unlocked, he felt a tinge of excitement and apprehension.

He was actually doing this thing.

All the way through, up till then, the young Englishman had known he could always jump off his one-man mission before it gathered speed.

But now he was moving out of shallow waters towards the deep end. He knew Zina Farouche was two floors below him, with the Tunisian delegation. He had criminally obtained two counterfeit British passports, complete with open-ended US visas, franked to show he had entered the USA via Miami International Airport on 29 August and New York's JFK on 2 September, respectively.

And he had used that counterfeit credit card – from a source he had discreetly approached, using a series of phone calls and passwords updated just three weeks before by SIS's New York outstation. It had turned out to be a character with the worst wig Gant had ever seen, whose front was a surveillance and counter-surveillance store off Hudson Street. 'We don't use stolen cards, son, we simply keep an update on folks who are spending a few weeks in hospital, or in jail, and have good credit ratings. And we do that in seven countries world-wide. It's kids and candy time with the electronic superhighway.'

Whichever way you looked at it, Gant was just that much further from being able to run home out of trouble.

He locked his door and flopped down on the bed, flicking on the television and browsing among the channels, his mind filled with events of the last four days.

That had been something. A big moment in his life. Truth to tell, he had never been a rough kid, at school or with the film units. Gant had played rugby football and had been a member of the school judo team. And he had rowed and won his rowing blue at Oxford, so he was no couch potato. But the decision, coldly made, to lay hands on another human being, going all the way, if that's what it took, and doing it with speed and surprise, had never been one he had been required to make.

Until yesterday.

The success of his attack on the rock-solid and aggressive passport forger Jack Chisholm had amazed him almost as much as his sudden decision to do it. He had been so stoked up on adrenaline he had thought his heart would thump its way clean through his breast bone. Mouth dry as a Mormon's wine cellar. It had been hard to force the words out, such was the near-clinical state of shock he had been in.

But he had managed not to let it show. God knew how.

And James had a feeling the next time would not be so unfamiliar.

On the CNN channel was news footage of a sniper and mortar attack on Sarajevo. How far away it all seemed now. And yet, remembering that too-thin girl, and her letters for some Bosnian in Tufnell Park, London, probably dead by now, or cowering in the city as the bullying and murderous Serbian artillery picked off the most helpless and innocent targets they could find, Gant felt grimly satisfied that he was here in New York City, taking a little bit of rough justice to another bunch of murderous and cowardly bastards.

I'll give them Swords of God, he promised himself, and fell into a profound and dreamless slumber.

11

Dead Men's Shoes

Ronnie had been waiting at the house of Agmet Belassian, on the shore of the Caspian Sea not far from the old fortified port, Stary Karakum, in Turkmenistan. He had been visibly relieved when the blue Tatra pick-up truck had approached through the sand dunes, headlights bumping and flickering in the moonlit night and his boss had got out and, thanking the driver, had strolled, shoulders slightly hunched, in that way of his, with his hands thrust deep in his trouser pockets.

Jardine had paused, at the front door, and gazed at the Hungarian.

'So you managed to get a black eye,' said Szabodo, by way of greeting.

'Pour us a large vodka, old boy. There's a good chap.'

And Jardine had laid a hand on his old friend's shoulder, for a long moment, before stepping inside.

Well, of course Ronnie Szabodo had brought a bottle of Talisker malt whisky along, and by six in the morning – David Jardine had arrived back from his fishing-boat journey from Ramsar, on Iran's northern coast, at ten minutes after three – there were about four inches left in the bottle. And both men had been stone cold sober, for they had been discussing matters of life and death.

Now they were 120 feet above the M3 Motorway, as the Aeroflot Ilyushin IV passenger jet, Flight SU 241 from Moscow, delicately wobbled its great descending mass into position for imminent contact with the concrete of Heathrow airport's No. 4 Runway.

Szabodo gently shook his travelling companion but Jardine was sleeping soundly. The Hungarian placed an open palm on the boss's chest and allowed it to sink with the exhalation of air, then stayed firmly in place when the lungs tried to take in more oxygen. It is a technique guaranteed to waken all but the very dead.

Jardine's eyes opened, slightly startled.

'Just landing,' said Ronnie Szabodo.

They sat in silence as the aircraft's ten huge tyres inched relentlessly closer to the runway and, with the merest bump, they were back in England. David Jardine always liked this moment – arriving home, after an operation. It was something he did not particularly think about, or look forward to, when working in the field – such sentiments were potentially negative – but every time, just like now, when he was gazing at the dull old square buildings of Terminal 2 rumble past, he was pleasantly surprised to have made it, one more time.

For a second he wondered if Dorothy would be there to meet him. She had a way of winkling out, from the normally discreet Heather, estimated times of arrival for Jardine's return flights. Then he remembered. Dorothy was no longer an item.

She had been talking about renting a small flat in Holland Park, and moving her London things out from the Tite Street maisonette. She confided that The Creep, which was one of David Jardine's milder terms for him, in his private thoughts, wanted to set up house together, but Dorothy being nobody's fool felt she needed some private space for a while. Just to see how things worked out.

An office Scorpio was waiting, with a driver called Trevor, and Heather was on the pavement outside Terminal 2. She smiled brightly as Jardine and Ronnie emerged, carrying their light luggage.

'Morning, David. Hi, Ronnie.' She waited while Trevor opened the trunk and put the men's bags inside. As Trevor moved to the rear passenger door and held it open, she nodded to Szabodo to go in first and said to her boss, 'Richard wants to see you. As soon as we get to town.'

'Whoopee,' Jardine replied, and moved to the front door, to sit beside the driver.

'How'd you get the black eye?'

'Banged into a wardrobe. You know, strange hotels in the dark . . .'

'I most certainly do not.' His PA smiled. 'And, if I did, you would be the last to know.'

On the route into London, Jardine asked Trevor about his mum and her arthritis, and learned she had now been waiting eight months for a hip replacement. When the car pulled up in the underground car park beneath the green palace, Richard Sykes's own PA, the formidable Mrs Budgen, was waiting by the armoured-glass security pen, attended by two uniformed janitors.

Ronnie took Jardine's ancient leather Colombian travelling bag and joined Heather, loping on into the elevator lobby.

Mrs Budgen had smiled to David Jardine and said, 'Welcome back' in that hushed tone she used when inferring she was well aware of what the returning operator had recently been through.

In Jardine's case, he devoutly hoped she believed he had been in Moscow attending a conference on monitoring nuclear warheads in the more restless Islamic states in the Federation.

Once in the direct elevator to the Chief's suite of offices, Enid Budgen murmured, 'Bit of a flap on.'

'Really . . .' David Jardine managed to look concerned. 'What's up?'

'Someone's being paraded on Iranian television. Confession time. And he says he spied for Britain. Well, actually, for you.'

Do you ever have one of those weeks, Jardine reflected.

'Ah, well, let's see how I can talk my way out of this,' he murmured and Mrs Budgen blushed as he smiled, the way he did.

'It is not really all that funny,' said Richard Sykes. He was wearing the town tie of his school, which Jardine had noted was generally worn on days the Chief lunched with the Foreign Secretary. Patrick, on the other hand, having gone to Eton, never indulged in such spreading of tail feathers. He didn't need to compete, was the unspoken message in the arcane code of English snobbery.

'I'm seeing Patrick at twelve.' Aha, thought Jardine, I

should've been a spy. 'And his PUS has already been on the telephone. Twice.'

Twice was serious.

'It was a smile of pain, Richard. This has been a dreadful end to a truly dreadful week. First Dorothy declares she is moving out . . .'

'Oh, God that's terrible.' Richard actually looked concerned. That was the thing with Richard. You never could tell if he meant it. The man was a master confidence trickster. Not a bad qualification for the job, come to think of it.

'Thanks. Then I risk life and limb to make contact with one of our prize assets.'

'Bit risky, in your position; you must learn to delegate these things.'

'I know, I know, you're right, of course.'

'Where was this? I should know but –' Sykes indicated the desk behind him, piles of Top Secret files leaning precariously, like miniature Towers of cardboard Pisa.

'Ghom,' replied Jardine.

The Chief's eyes darkened. 'Ghom where?'

'It's, um, in Iran. Eighty clicks south of Tehran.'

'Oh, Jesus Christ . . .'

'I chose Ghom because it is teeming with strangers – all mullahs but mostly strangers – and guess what? A bloody lion chose that day to escape. You will not, I fear, be overly elated when I tell you who I made contact with.'

He gazed pointedly over the Chief's shoulder.

Richard Sykes turned slowly to gaze at the three large, flat video screens set into the wall – a new toy designed by his predecessor for this new, hi-tec building. On the left-hand screen was a photo of Hojatolislam Javd Assadiyan, VEVAK Colonel and right-hand man of Ayatollah Sheik Jamil Shahidi, Director of the Iranian Clergy's Intelligence Bureau – Foreign Department.

On the right-hand screen was a mute sequence from the Iran News Service's noon television news programme. A man with a bruised face, head bowed, was speaking to somebody behind the camera. This too was Assadiyan. And, although no lip reader, David Jardine was sure (wrongly, it turned out) he could at least twice make out the word 'Jardine'.

'According to his confession,' said Sykes, 'he was contacted by one of your agents, two days ago.'

'Did he name the contact?'

'He does. He alleges it is someone called Baxter.'

'Baxter.'

'And this Baxter was an illegal working from over the border, in Turkimanstan.'

'Turkmenistan . . .'

'Trust me, David. This is not a good time to come all over pedantic.'

Jardine remained silent.

'So, damage limitation. Patrick wants to know, how do we play this?'

David Jardine looked pained. Javd Assadiyan was one of the cruellest men he had ever known. He was also one of the bravest. His use of the name Baxter was a message to Jardine that he would hold out for twenty-four hours, nobody could expect more, when faced with the mullahs' torturers in Tehran's Elim prison.

'Say nothing, of course.'

Sykes seemed annoyed, angry even. 'Nothing? Get off the glue. The Foreign Secretary wants to be briefed. And I was thinking –'

Jardine held up a hand, what Richard meant was, maybe his D/Ops could go and take the flak. 'Don't. I have twenty-four hours to save as much as I can of a network. I'll be in the dungeon and please consider a Do Not Disturb sign is pinned to the door.' He glanced at his watch, pointedly.

'I can't just say nothing,' Sykes complained, not without sympathy. 'The halcyon days of this office being able to do what it pleased, without oversight, are almost over. We are a government department, I am repeatedly told by those who supply our secret fund, and we are answerable, David.' And as he contemplated the daily rows with bloody politicians, his sympathy turned, out of frustration, to annoyance. 'What the hell do you think this is, anyway, Five Go to bloody Smuggler's Top?'

David Jardine ambled over to the window and looked across the terrace below, and over the weird, pagoda-like beams of iroko wood, laid over sand-coloured stone supports, like a giant lost pergola, landed, perhaps by some whirlwind, on the north face of the great green palace. Beyond were the swirling waters of the Thames, surging around the buttresses of Vauxhall Bridge.

A column of massive barges, noses joined to tails like floating elephants, emerged from under the bridge, moving sedately downstream.

'I really must do what I can to salvage Moonlight Four,' he remarked, gently.

Richard Sykes stared at his old friend and sparring partner. David had a way of getting the right, as opposed to correct, perspective on things. 'My dear chap, of course we must. Javd Assadiyan and his people deserve at least that. Do what it takes. Take my agreement as read. Use my personal authority.'

Jardine smiled. 'As if I wouldn't.'

'But David . . .'

'Mm-hmm?'

'I'm presuming here, that you are Baxter.'

Jardine nodded.

Sykes went on 'Have you asked yourself – look, I'm sorry, it's your Joe on the rack – have you asked yourself if this . . . excursion of yours, which seems typically rash if you don't mind my saying so, might have fucked things up?'

David Jardine turned, his big frame dark against the window, even with its slightly green-tinted glass.

'I have asked myself little else,' he replied, and the Chief crossed to the door, and held it open for him.

'I shall tell Patrick nothing.'

'It's probably best.'

And as he passed to leave the room, Sykes laid a hand on his shoulder. 'But you and I shall take wine with him at White's tonight. And, there, you bloody well tell him the lot.'

Jardine met his steely gaze. 'Off the record.'

The Chief of MI 6 smiled. 'Of course.'

So, in a quiet corner of one of London's more senior gentlemen's clubs, redolent of noble birth and slightly scruffy gentility, Foreign Secretary Patrick Orde, SIS Chief Richard Sykes and his Director of Operations, David Arbuthnot Jardine, CMG, MC, sat around an ancient card table and Jardine related to Orde the following story.

At the time of his painful television appearance on Iran News, Vevak Colonel Javd Assadiyan had been working for SIS for seven nightmare years. At first on the staff of Sheikh Hussein al-Mussawi, co-ordinating Vevak domination of Hezbollah, then as Deputy Director Intelligence and Special Missions, under Jamil Shahidi, he had been a jewel in the crown of SIS Operations, recruited and run, in the beginning, by a forty-four-year-old Controller in Mid-East Ops called Richard Brereton Sykes, who had handed him on to David Jardine, about two years earlier.

Assadiyan had once had a sister, a student at Persepolis, working for a degree in ancient Farsi. She had, rashly, rejected the advances of the head of her faculty, a minor mullah, and at the same time sided with a brave group of students who were protesting (mildly, for Iran is a dangerous climate in which to voice dissent) at the expulsion of three Christian students from their course, an implementation of government policy.

The protest group had been arrested at ten past three one Sunday morning and taken to the local prison for interrogation.

Susha, Javd Assadiyan's youngest and favourite sister, had been released into the custody of her faculty head, the mullah who desired her. He took her in shackles to his villa and, after getting her drunk on whisky, had raped her repeatedly.

After ten days of this, Susha had stabbed him in the eye with the key to her chains, which she had asked him to remove because she was, she had said, aroused by his manhood. She had stabbed him so hard the key penetrated the brain and the man had died after emergency surgery.

The nineteen-year-old girl had been taken to Elim special prison in Tehran, from which had emanated rumours too appalling to relate, and had, finally, been reported 'executed for offences against the State'.

And Javd Assadiyan's father had been charged the equivalent of 80 US cents for the cost of the bullet which killed her, a standard procedure when criminals were executed in Iran.

'With a regime like that,' Richard Sykes remarked to Orde, 'we hardly need to exert ourselves to find recruits.'

Jardine went on to tell the Foreign Secretary, strictly for his ears only, that Assadiyan had been the leader of a network of dissident Iranians inside their intelligence and military apparatus, codenamed Moonlight 4. It was so secret that only the Chief and he himself had full access to the identities of its agents. And it was out of Moonlight 4 that secret intelligence about the radical Islamic Fundamentalist clergy's Special Missions Directorate had come.

In the months to come, the examiners of carcasses of wrecked operations, at Ryemarsh, believed, on balance, Patrick Orde's recollection that no mention of Dante, or New York, or Connecticut, had been made that evening at White's.

David Jardine would say, in mitigation, that while Javd Assadiyan had been one source of intelligence concerning Dante, he had felt constrained to protect another, and more valuable, agent, right at the heart of the affair.

The one thing he was never to admit to a living soul was that, of course, it had been the Foreign Secretary himself who had asked, all those months earlier, whether Jardine was aware of anything which might 'jolt Washington' into understanding the seriousness of the threat from Tehran.

Jardine did, however, in the presence of Richard Sykes, tell Orde about the torture and death of Major Muar Abbas, found mutilated in the freezer of an Italian restaurant in New York, and about Mahmud and Benine Rashahi, discovered tortured and mutilated on board their yacht *Pyramus* in Limassol harbour.

'The modus was too similar to be a coincidence,' said Sykes.

'And they were both . . . ours,' the Foreign Secretary, a politician to his bootstraps, found it difficult to utter that last word.

'They were our fully paid-up agents, reliable and effective,' agreed Jardine. He explained that it was probably a fault of his, but there were certain agents, certain operations, he believed that he and only he should have final control of, and to Richard Sykes's surprise, and perhaps to his chagrin, David Jardine's former comrade in arms nodded, understandingly.

Thus encouraged, Jardine disclosed that, suspecting a leak in the system, a rat in the works, he had made a secret visit to Ghom and tasked Javd Assadiyan with finding out if VEVAK or any of its sister organisations was running an SIS mole.

'That was three days ago,' concluded Jardine, 'and the rest, as they say, is history.'

'Poor guy,' sympathised Orde. 'I expect he'll tell them everything.'

David Jardine nodded gravely. 'Of course he will. But he has sent me a signal, in the form of his televised confession, that he is holding out until I can try to save something of the network.'

Orde considered this. Then he gently moved Jardine's tumbler of Perrier mineral water away from him and enquired, softly, 'So shouldn't you be somewhere else?'

The tall spy climbed to his feet and nodded. 'Thanks, Paddy. Richard and I will keep you fully informed.'

'Good lord,' replied the Foreign Secretary. He turned his gaze upwards. 'Can that really be a pig I see . . .?' And his arm moved as if following a slow flying object.

David Jardine and his colleagues got something like nine hours' sleep between them over the next forty-eight hours, warning the Javd network and arranging for the lucky ones to flee over Iran's borders into certain neighbouring countries.

Round about two in the morning of the second night, Jardine and Ronnie Szabodo found themselves not far from the car-repair and paint shop that was London Facilities Section, in the Atlantic Café in Brixton, a district in south-east London with a Caribbean predominance.

The Atlantic was owned and run by a former Yardie enforcer, name of Willie John Campbell, who had become a Christian while doing a ten stretch in the Scrubs. He was now a Baptist lay preacher and, at six-four and twenty-two pounds, the man was accorded a measure of respect. He kept a clean joint and did what he could to make folk of all shades and beliefs feel at ease in his place.

Sitting in a corner, at one of the cramped Formica tables, sipping coffee and Appleton's Gold rum, toying with a mess of spicy alligator gumbo (two spoons), David Jardine asked how the Hungarian was getting on, had been getting on, before the shit hit the fan, with the beginnings of his enquiry into the identity of an Iranian-run rat in the firm.

Szabodo raised his broad shoulders and squinted over his spoonful. 'As you know, David, access to Moonlight is extremely limited.'

'That should make life simpler.' Jardine dropped a lump of sugar into his coffee.

'*You* know everything, everyone. The grand design. I know the framework, plus the nuts and bolts. Marietta has pieces of the jigsaw. Also, she has her own operations, world-wide. Sometimes we duplicate each other. Kate Howard knows the identity of our own black operators and contract people. And most of our illegals working that territory. Plus the boss. Plus certain of our . . . underlings.'

'We try to say "colleagues" these days.'

'Please yourself. Officers in certain stations and outstations. Tehran. That's of course where I start, you can understand, my dear chap. But we try not to burden Tehran Station with anything outside Moonlight One. Moonlight Two is handled from Cyprus. Parts of One and Four. New York and the USA are cleared for elements of Two and Three.'

'Spare us the bloody overview, Ronnie, what's your point?'

'Only you, boss, have the big picture.'

Jardine smiled. He was very, very tired. His body ached from the going-over Javd's religious police had given him. They must, he reflected, look an unprepossessing pair, the Magyar with his front tooth missing and himself with his broken nose, the scar on his face livid from fatigue. And his black eye. Hardly the unremarkable spies the Firm tried to cultivate.

'By that reasoning, I'm the prime suspect . . .' He lifted a spoonful of alligator meat and eyed it warily.

'My point is,' Szabodo ignored that contribution, 'whoever it is, they can't tell the opposition anything too absolutely damaging.'

Jardine touched the thin scar, Szabodo wondered if it felt numb, like the two bullet wounds in his left forearm, and the boss went on, 'That's not really a good enough reason to avoid shutting down the other Moonlight circuits.'

The squat Magyar's eyes narrowed. Not for the first time, David Jardine thanked God the man was on our side.

'Their product, David, is coming in quick and fast.' Jardine supposed he meant thick and fast. 'Whatever you decide to do about Dante, you will need every blinking last item, to help you make your decision the right one . . .'

David Jardine had not ever heard the word blinking used except maybe twice in black and white British movies from the 1940s. But Ronnie had a point, the question was, was it worth deliberately risking the lives of nineteen brave, blackmailed or bribed Iranians in sensitive positions of secret access, just to keep tabs on Zina Farouche and her assassination team.

He decided it was.

'OK.' His eyes met the Hungarian's, briefly, and he took the plunge and popped the alligator meat into his mouth.

It tasted surprisingly good. Slightly sweet and not, giving the lie to Ronnie's opinion, in the least like chicken.

Jardine's thoughts, as he chewed, remained on that murderous gang, doing diplomatic things in Manhattan.

'Ronnie,' he said, suddenly feeling the burden of his responsibility too great, 'you know I have a problem with this Dante business.'

Szabodo watched him carefully, wiping the gumbo gravy from his chin. 'I know,' he replied, and after a long silence added, 'and it's your problem, sport.'

His eyes remained empty of condemnation, or encouragement.

You are on your own, was the message. And Jardine sent out a silent prayer. 'Be a chum, Lord. This burden is too great for one man to bear.'

And in his heart he sensed quite clearly the celestial reply, 'But that was your choice, my dear boy . . .'

Joe Cleary had no such problems *vis-à-vis* Jehovah, the Grand Design, his ethical motivation or the merest smidgen of metaphysics. As he swung his '83 Pontiac coupé into the visitors' car park on the north spur of the CIA Headquarters Complex, he was in even spirits but his mouth had that determined set Laurie called 'Oh, shit, the man means business'.

In the reception facility at F Entrance, he showed his silver NYPD Detective's badge in its leather ID wallet, the metal burnished with years of use, and his DSS ID with his photo in its clear plastic sealer.

'Sergeant Cleary, NYPD Homicide,' he declared, with that same warm glow of pride he had experienced the first day of his promotion, eight years before. 'To see Mister Semprino.'

'Open the case, please,' said one of the two agents on security detail. Then he was told to report to the reception desk.

'To see . . .?' enquired the CIA staffer at the desk. She was about thirty-five, in a sober but stylish suit by one of the European names. Not Armani, Dolores had said that Armani was yesterday.

'Semprino. Mister Anthony.'

'Mister Anthony . . .?' She opened her much-thumbed staff directory book.

'Anthony Semprino.'

'Uh-huh.' The woman closed the book and consulted an appointments diary. 'Stand on the tape, please.'

Joe frowned, then looked around the tiled floor and found a strip of gray masking tape, about six inches by one. They had these at the DSS Office in Manhattan. He stepped up to the tape and gazed, expressionless, at the lens of a small video camera.

'Thanks.' The woman behind the desk smiled and waited patiently until a squat brushed-metal box slowly emitted a pale-green, pass-sized card, with Cleary's photo in the top left corner, and a large 'V' superimposed. She slipped the pass into a piece of laminated plastic, with a clip on the top.

'Please wear this at all times. Mr Semprino is sending somebody down for you.'

'Thanks.' Cleary clipped the pass to his top pocket and, sticking his hands in his pockets, ambled around the spacious lobby. Above the revolving-door cylinders was a big CIA crest. A fountain tinkled over-enthusiastically in one corner and Cleary realised he urgently needed to take a leak.

While he waited, men and women, some of them mere

girls, came and went. It was a very different atmosphere to the noisy and untidy bustle of the lobby at 1 Police Plaza, the NYPD equivalent of this place. Most people seemed to know each other, but it was more like a goddam library than a law-enforcement agency.

But, of course, these people were not into law-enforcement. They were spooks. And that was precisely why he was here. It had been surprisingly easy to get taken seriously, once he knew the dance steps, and it had been big Al Wiscynsky who had shown him how. 'Al,' Cleary had said one night, on a DSS advance, checking out the hotel where the Egyptian Ambassador would be staying, 'how the heck do you get the CIA to reply to goddam faxes; how do I get them to understand I will not go away . . .?'

And Wiscynsky had asked what was the problem and Joe Cleary had told him the bare bones of his investigation, without giving anything away.

'Simple,' Al had replied; 'phone this number in Langley, it's their Office of Security Investigations. Tell them you are investigating a crime that has interstate connotations and involves the Agency. Say that, because of the Federal aspect, you are inclined to go directly to the FBI, but because a Langley man is in your sights you wondered if they would like to be consulted.'

'Will that do the trick?' Cleary had asked, and Al Wiscynsky had just grinned.

'Joe. Hi. Tony Semprino. Glad to meet you. Thanks for coming on down . . .' The CIA man was a tanned and dark-haired guy in his early forties. Say about forty-two.

'Tony. It's a pleasure.'

They shook hands, each using enough pressure to show they had a sincere grip, without getting into an Indian arm-wrestling contest.

'You want something?' Semprino had a good-sized office, with a desk of light oak, a coffee pot on a hot plate, numerous framed photos of Semprino with guys on various courses, one of Semprino in a baseball-team group photograph, and one of a youthful Semprino in untidy fatigues with a bandanna round his head, in the company of three other soldiers in the same kind of stuff. They were grinning and carrying a couple of M-16s, a Remington pump-action twelve-gauge and a Chinese Type 56-1 assault rifle.

Also in the picture were two smiling Montagnard tribesmen, who had been more than willing to fight alongside US Special Forces teams in Vietnam.

'Was that with this outfit?' asked Joe Cleary, leaning forward to examine the photo.

'No way, man, that was where men were men and the Agency was on the other end of the goddam phone . . .'

Cleary glanced quickly at the guy and was rewarded by a genuine grin. He nodded and straightened up. 'Where'd you train? Bragg?'

'Sure, and Loc Than. I was nineteen. My folks wanted me to plead education to stay Stateside.' He meant, avoid the Draft. 'But I was young and stupid. Now I'm not so young. Coffee?'

'Great. As she comes.' He was going to mention his own war but why break the habit of a lifetime?

'And you were with UDT, Marcowitz's team. How was that?'

Of course, this spook was nobody's fool. Cleary shrugged. 'Yeah, I was nineteen, too. Musta been crazy.'

'Straight up, right?' Semprino passed him a mug of black coffee.

'Thanks.'

'Silver star, purple heart. And the big one. You must've been *totally* insane.' The CIA man flopped down on one of two easy chairs and a couch, with a coffee-table in between.

By this time Joe needed to take a leak like real badly, but things were moving in the right direction. 'We were both lucky to get back,' he said quietly and sat on the couch, holding the coffee mug.

'Amen.' Tony Semprino nodded. 'So what's the beef, Joe? Why you bullying the poor old CIA?'

The detective told him about the cadaver, the John Doe, in Barolo's freezer store, and about the CIA man Harry K. Liebowitz first visiting Frank Grumman's Bellevue Morgue then turning up to spirit away Frank's killer, known only to NYPD Homicide as Unidentified Suspect 19935 and to Joe

Cleary as Betty Boop. He told Semprino about his many faxes and phone calls to the CIA's Legal Department, and about the lack of co-operation.

When Joe had finished, Tony Semprino nodded. 'You never touched your coffee. Will I get you fresh?'

'It's fine, I like it just warm. You get kinda used to it, you know what I mean?'

'Sure do. Joe, do you have copies of any of those faxes? Dates of phone calls?'

'Every single one.' Cleary opened the black leather briefcase, a present from Laurie four birthdays ago, and spun it on the coffee table to face Semprino.

Tony Semprino picked up the file inside, labelled 'Boop/Betty', and started to read.

'If you want to use the John,' he said, without looking up, 'it's out the door and third door on the left.'

Cleary grinned. 'You shoulda been a detective,' he said and stood up.

'Well, I am, sort of,' the CIA man replied.

When a much relieved Joe Cleary returned, Semprino had put the file back in the briefcase and was looking thoughtful. Cleary automatically glanced around, looking for a photocopier, smelling for the trace of heated paper.

Semprino smiled. 'Can I take copies of these, Joe?'

Cleary nodded. 'Sure.' He sat down and reached for the coffee cup.

'Are you sure you don't want a fresh cup?'

'Positive.' Joe Cleary tried to look as if he was enjoying the lukewarm sludge.

'This Betty Boop. Harry Liebowitz has never heard of him.'

'You're kidding me. The guy was in the Precinct House; he spoke to my boss, Capello.'

Semprino gazed at Cleary as if the detective was a bright but innocent child. 'He's coming over.'

'Liebowitz?'

'Sure. He'll be here presently. Do you have a photo of Betty?'

'Here ...' Cleary took a brown envelope from the back panel of his briefcase and handed it over.

Semprino removed two NYPD Homicide Dept 8″ × 10″ black and white mugshots of the arrested killer.

'Maybe I know who this is,' he said, which confused the cop because either you knew who the guy was or you did not. What Semprino probably meant was like when Guido Lucchese used to say, 'Maybe I can help you', when he meant, 'But I gotta ask the Capo'.

'So who?' asked Cleary.

'Joe, this is classified stuff but I promise not to snow you, and I guarantee right now that the Agency will co-operate with your investigation. Believe me, the last thing we need right now is the Bureau crawling all over us. The Aldrich Ames thing has been a nightmare.'

Cleary and the rest of America knew all about the Ames scandal. And Joe Cleary had read that the FBI had been called in to investigate the affair. He could understand Tony Semprino's chagrin, for nobody loved the Feds.

'I hope this won't come to that,' he replied, deadpan.

'Sounds like a threat, Sergeant.' Semprino put the photos back into their envelope and glanced at Cleary.

'Better believe it.'

At which moment the door opened and a lean, quiet-looking man in a light brown suit, button-down shirt and red and blue bow tie came in. He had a crew cut and was probably about thirty-eight. Cleary wondered if this was Tony Semprino's boss.

'This is Sergeant Joe Cleary, NYPD Homicide.' Semprino indicated Joe.

'Joe,' said the stranger, 'we seem to have a problem and I'm grateful to you for bringing it to our attention.'

Cleary had gotten to his feet and the man offered his hand. 'I'm Harry Liebowitz,' he announced.

'This is him in the lobby.' Khaled Niknam pushed a small photograph across the table. Zina Farouche gazed at it, one of five such items spread in front of her. They were in the fenced-in patio of an Italian café called Amici Miei, on the corner of West Houston and West Broadway.

Mustafa Sharik sat at another table, watching the street. And Zafir Hammuda was just inside the café, sitting near the door, reading a book and keeping an eye open for any hint of surveillance.

The photographs, all snatched by Niknam or Sharik, were at awkward angles, fuzzy and indistinct. But the subject in each of them was the same. It was a young man, sometimes wearing steel-rimmed glasses, sometimes not. Wearing a jacket and necktie in two, a sober suit in one, casual jeans and a leather jacket in another, and like that.

'He calls himself different things,' murmured Niknam, looking even younger than his twenty-one years, Zina thought. 'In your hotel it was Wilson. Here,' he touched another photo, 'it was Graham . . .'

The Palestinian girl contemplated. There was something familiar about the man's face. She could not remember where from, or if she was imagining it.

'Maybe he's a private detective. Collecting evidence for . . . I don't know. A divorce?'

'He doesn't behave like that.'

'A thief . . .?'

Niknam frowned, then nodded. 'Could be. He could be a thief.'

'There are a thousand cops and spooks doing advances for next week, maybe that's it. It would explain him turning up in the same places as you.'

Khaled Niknam gazed at Zina. 'As *us* . . .' he replied and immediately regretted the smart reply, for when Zina gave out that look, braver men than he quaked in their shoes.

'Make sure the whole team has copies of these,' she said.

'I have them ready.' Niknam patted his pouch pocket.

Zina Farouche considered. If somebody was taking an interest in the team, nothing could be more serious. It either meant one or more of them had attracted suspicion, or worse, that the enemy had received warning of their presence in New York. Maybe even their intentions. And, if that was the case, she would either have to abort the mission or move it forward. But, as far as she knew, the earliest date for the Curtises and the Selims to be together in Connecticut was the Wednesday of the following week. Eight days away.

The idea of aborting the assignment filled her with dread. She knew what fate awaited leaders of failed missions.

Khaled Niknam sensed her reservations.

'Listen,' he said, 'why don't Mustafa and me put a few questions to him?'

'No, you listen to me.' Zina Farouche had just about had enough of this kid dictating all kinds of stuff, just because he had been designated Security Member of the team. 'We have no evidence he is interested in us. I mean, have you or Mustafa even seen him looking at us? Or checking out where we work, or where we eat? Anything like that?'

Khaled Niknam shook his head, but he was a survivor from the bloody streets of Beirut and the Palestinian West Bank. 'This beggar used to turn up all over Gaza, in the days before the traitor Arafat turned it into an Israeli colony . . .'

Zina glanced around, alarmed. 'Keep quiet about such things,' she hissed. 'You should know better.'

'I was fourteen at the time.' Niknam pressed on, annoyed at having felt intimidated by his leader. 'You know, Zina, I told the Tamimis, the two vounger ones, they were running things at the time,' the Tamimi brothers had controlled Hamas, the Palestinian West Bank resistance, 'and they said just the same as you. "A beggar is a beggar, the guy sleeps among piles of garbage, go and do something useful, like spray *Intifada* slogans on walls. Throw rocks at Kike jeeps."' He plopped two cubes of sugar into his coffee. 'But I had a feeling, I just had a feeling about that beggar, so I followed him, without him ever knowing it. And one day, he got into the back of a Shin Beth van and was driven away, like a long lost friend.' He shook his head. 'By the time I got to the safe-house of Tariq al-Tamimi, Tariq and his bodyguard had both been shot four times in the head and the house had been blown up to cover the corpses.'

He stirred his coffee, with a rock-steady hand. 'He should have listened to me . . .'

In the name of God, this kid is dangerous, thought Zina Farouche. She had certainly chosen her team well.

'That was another place and another time,' she replied gently. 'I will put others onto this man. Your job is to look after our team. Nothing else. We will all keep an eye open for him. But you will not follow him, or even look twice at him. If you find yourself in the same elevator, ignore him. Control your curiosity, for if he does happen to be a pro, he will sense it, OK? He will smell it.'

Khaled considered this. He met her gaze. 'You will put a support cell onto him?'

'At once.'

The youth nodded. 'So be it. *Insha'Allah* . . .'

James Gant had been in New York for five days. He had used the Essex House Hotel, not as a second address, and certainly not as any kind of a safe-house. Quite the opposite. With the level of DSS and Secret Service – not to mention FBI and local police – advance coverage, prior to the next week's United Nations General Assembly, Gant had deliberately used the hotel so that his comings and goings would attract no attention. By breakfasting in the restaurant, buying magazines and maps in the lobby and just travelling in the elevators, sometimes sharing them with security people on their way to and from the floors where diplomats were staying, Gant's presence had become a mere part of the scenery. Or so he hoped.

He had also used what Euan Stevenson had described as the Mark 1 eyeball to confirm that Noor Jalud was with the Kuwaiti delegation at the Pierre Hotel, and Zafir Hammuda was at the Regency with the Algerian Foreign Minister, where his cover was as a courier and driver with the visiting diplomats.

The whereabouts of Mustafa Sharik had not been communicated to SIS by the time Gant had left London. Or, if it had, he had not been able to retrieve the information from Clerical 17's computer base.

Carrying out a reconnaissance of Beauregard was high on his agenda, but he knew from his training – VIP Protection and Liaison with other Agencies – that security around the Connecticut house would be discreet but tight, and the Diplomatic Security Service had some very observant special agents, among the best in the business. So it would have to be something low-key.

Early on the Tuesday before the UN Assembly, James Gant rented an unremarkable Cherokee Jeep from a downtown Budget office and made the three-hour drive to Essex, where he parked in the main street by the marina and treated himself to a T-bone steak and French fries in the Griswold Inn, where a bunch of people were celebrating something. He was not sure exactly what.

Then Gant drove to the cable ferry at East Lyme and crossed the broad, sluggish river to the far side and, after missing the turn off a couple of times, found the track leading to Beauregard and another, smaller house, located further along the river bank.

The thrill of operating in the field hits one in odd ways. And it was when he recognised that the tall, good-looking, fair-haired woman, elegant even in faded jeans, tennis shoes and a pink sweatshirt, who reined in her chestnut hunter and smiled as he waved a thank you, was Annabel Curtis, that James Gant finally understood he was actually doing this thing. There she was, not a photo from a computer printout, or even a video from some snatched surveillance job, but a warm, living, breathing, Mark I human being. Wife, mother, neighbour . . . target.

There was not much more Gant could accomplish without drawing attention to himself, so he turned the Jeep around and motored on back to New York City.

Never imagine you will not benefit from even the most cursory recce, the Hungarian had dinned into them on Intake 44. You will always be ten times more prepared than when you first arrived in the environment.

The next day, at about 10.50 a.m., James Gant stood in the Windsor Pharmacy, on Sixth Avenue, examining a display of vitamin pills and, while appearing convincingly uninterested, the way they had taught him and the others on Intake 44, and the way he had practised in Rome, with Op Marigold, as a probationer intelligence operator, Gant had observed a slightly plump, Mid-Eastern-looking young man standing at the counter at the back of the drugstore. The guy was trying to get the pharmacist behind the counter there to sell him some Zovirax cold-sore ointment without a prescription.

The pharmacist was having none of it, but the mild altercation gave the young Englishman time to make a positive ID on Ben Turabi. And the Zovirax thing was a bonus, because an SIS file on Turabi recorded that the terrorist suffered from herpes simplex two, a minor, sometimes sexually transmitted, disease which recurred at intervals over a period of years. Zovirax was a standard treatment, and stress was known to bring on attacks.

Presumably even a member of Abu Nidal's murder gang could suffer from stress, in the run-up to a bloody massacre. In any event, Gant was satisfied he had a positive make on another Dante player, and that made three. Which made him feel he was maybe doing quite good in his unauthorised and quite illegal mission.

He stayed there, browsing, as the Palestinian finally gave up and left, after paying at the cash desk for some Breath Savers and a comb. Then, just as Gant made his way to the same desk, with a packet of vitamin C capsules and some shaving gel, in walked a slender, tanned and undeniably attractive young woman, wearing a navy blue suit, long jacket and short skirt – maybe Jean Muir for it was similar to Charlotte's navy Jean Muir and the skirt had so aroused James that they had made love in the underground car park beneath the Canteen restaurant at Chelsea Harbour Marina, up against a pillar, *before* going up in the elevator to eat, but that was another story. Anyway, in strolls this elegant, good-looking . . . babe, and it was all Gant could do to ignore her and pay for his stuff for it was as if bright neon signs were pointing at the girl, shrieking, 'Zina Farouche! Zina Farouche!' There was no doubting the identity of the woman whose image, in a dozen snatched surveillance photographs, had occupied his every waking, and not a few sleeping, moments.

By the time he had gathered his change and sauntered outside, walking away purposefully, just in case she was being protected by a back-up team of some kind, sweat was running down the small of his back and his heart was thumping with an unwelcome influx of adrenaline. OK, to be pedantic, he thought, noradrenaline for the body's entire physiology had been dinned into him during Maintenance In The Field, which had been Week Eleven of the Fort's Continuation Course, for those who had survived the elimination process of Basic Induction.

Gant had been right, about some kind of security support for the Farouche girl, and, to be fair to the embryonic secret agent, his professional surveillance skills were not at all bad, and they had been, if not honed, at least smoothed, during his operational experience in Italy.

He was, in fact, probably good enough to avoid the attention of busy, overworked DSS and other US protection officers, who predicated their work on intelligence warnings and assessments, and relied to a great extent on overt, saturation coverage of their clients.

That he had not escaped the notice of Khaled Niknam was because Niknam had only one task and that was sniffing out professionally trained spooks like Gant. If a question mark remained over whether or not James was working them over, it was probably because his very inexperience had not yet evaporated to leave that inescapable stamp which one clandestine operator instinctively recognises in another.

He had also used his five days to acquire equipment. One of the deeply classified computer files he had pirated from the office contained details of three competent and reliable contract killers on the east coast, two of them in New York City.

One in particular had interested Gant, and for about forty-eight hours he had debated whether or not to go through the prescribed motions, to arrange a contract on one of his targets. But the fight with Jack Chisholm and the disturbing loopiness of the credit-card provider in the Spy-Counter-Spy store had unsettled him. Already there were two men in town who could identify him as a lawbreaker. Did he really need to risk a nausea over the complex minuet required to touch base with a pro mechanic?

James Gant did not think so.

Which meant he was going to have to take a deep breath and do the thing himself. So, still telling himself he could get off this rollercoaster while it was slowly gathering momentum, Gant had consulted his electronic gazetteer to the cornucopia of near-legal and downright illegal merchandise available in Manhattan and surrounding districts, if you knew where to look.

It was amazing, they agreed later, that Ronnie Szabodo had not gotten wind of his sorties into that world, using conduits and passwords normally employed only by a very limited number of menacing and worryingly capable operators who moved sharklike through those waters, way, way beyond the merely deniable and expendable categories of clandestine employment.

But James Gant had quietly succeeded in acquiring a number of items he would need in his self-appointed task, namely the murder – there was no gentler word for it – of at least two members of the Dante team of assassins.

He had no particular target yet but, on balance, it seemed that Noor Jalud and Ben Turabi were more accessible. Since Zina Farouche was the boss, it would be pointless to kill her, Gant felt, for it would be she who would have to give the order abandoning the planned massacre.

And Zafir Hammuda, let's face it, he thought, is such a dangerous looking bastard, there is no point in making life too difficult.

The dark blue Sikorsky S-70C maintained a steady 175 knots, about 200 miles per hour, flying at a height of just 2,000 feet, leaving Keyport, New Jersey, a few miles behind, to the south-east. Ahead, Joe Cleary could just make out the haze and glittering skyscrapers of his home town, Manhattan.

It was kinda strange to be sitting beside Harry Liebowitz, who wasn't Harry Liebowitz, but who was the real Harry Liebowitz. Joe felt less than comfortable with this world of spies and half-truths.

And yet, they had been more than straight. On the face of it, they had been quite forthcoming. 'The situation is this,' Liebowitz and Tony Semprino had briefed him. 'We at the Agency are aware of some guy who has represented himself as Harold K. Liebowitz, some asshole. First at Bellevue Hospital, when he arrived at the morgue and took a look at the cadaver who was found dead in the freezer at Barolo. The cadaver you have been going apeshit trying to ID. The reason we did not respond to your faxes and phone calls is that we knew from the description and photos you sent to us that this was a serious player in the espionage circuit. And the case, as far as CIA was concerned, at that moment became classified Top Secret. Like that.

'So nobody had any need to visit Bellevue and draw attention to our interest.

'And, second, this same ersatz Harry K. Liebowitz arrives at your Precinct House, presenting immaculate forged Agency ID, goes through all the kosher legal jargon, complete with a counterfeit Federal Warrant, and spirits the killer of Frank Grumman away, into the night. Betty Boop.

'Both of these cases were your cases, Joe,' the real Harry Liebowitz had said, 'so in the matter of the brutal slaying of poor Frank Grumman, sitting where you had been sitting until just a few minutes before, what conclusion can you draw, you being a detective and all . . .?'

You dunce, Joe Cleary had accused himself, you dumb waste of space. He had nodded and without a blush had replied. 'Sure. It's too obvious. I was the fuckin' target.'

Harry had excused himself, leaving Joe to chew the fat with Semprino for about twenty minutes. Then he had returned, with a classified file stamped Top Secret.

'Read this in the helicopter,' he had said, holding the door open. 'And you are not to divulge what you read to a soul. You dig?'

'Where we going?'

'New York. Right now.'

'But my car is here, man.'

'It'll be driven up. Don't worry about the car, we have to be there in an hour. Joe, I think you can help us . . .'

Cleary had thought hard. If these guys were offering him a chance to ID his John Doe *and* go after Betty Boop, it was an offer he would not refuse. But be careful, Joseph, he told himself, these fucking spooks don't know how *not* to shaft you. Sideways.

'OK.' He had nodded. 'You'll need the keys.' And Harry Liebowitz and Semprino had given him a pitying look.

So here he was in the Sikorsky, the civilian version, with leather seats and fold-down desks, with special lighting, and a cute secretary who served coffee. Very different from 'Nam.

The file had been codenamed Jade and even with the Seal Underwater Demolition Teams in the war, when Marcowitz's team had been privy to some hot-shit secrets, Joe Cleary had never been near such deep spook dynamite.

The gist was that the British had set up a number of networks inside the Iranian Intelligence, Security, Military and Fundamentalist Clergy, who were running all kinds of secret terror campaigns, targeting other Islamic nations, plus the Western Alliance and, of most interest to the CIA, the United States of America.

But the Brits were not sharing their most secret stuff, codenamed Moonlight, and that was divided into at least four self-contained, watertight parts.

So the Agency, under direct control of the D-Ops, Alan Clair, had mounted a penetration operation against the British. And they had been successful in recruiting two of the SIS assets, one Major Muar Abbas, working under cover in New York City, and a couple of VEVAK agents, turned in 1987 by some guy called Richard Sykes, and subsequently run by a David Jardine.

The couple had operated as a husband and wife team, until they had been found tortured and murdered on board a sailboat moored off Limassol harbour, on the island of Cyprus, which Cleary learned was in the Mediterranean Sea, with Europe around its north coasts and the Lebanon and North Africa to the east and south.

And Muar Abbas, double or triple agent, for Iran, Britain and the CIA, was of course the JD in the freezer.

Well, good for us, thought Joe Cleary. We steal two of the Brits' assets and pretty damn soon they are butchermeat.

Is this what I pay my taxes for?

No fucking wonder they want the help of a New York cop.

Cleary did not know why he was not surprised to see Al Wiscynsky, the Diplomatic Security Service co-ordinator, waiting on the roof of the US Mission to the United Nations building, between First and Second, at 44th Street, as the Sikorsky descended amid a bluster and roar of rotor blades to land delicately on the helipad there.

Harry Liebowitz led the way, dropping down from the chopper and ducking his head as they scuttled forwards, out of the swishing circle of lethal blades, the downdraught too close for comfort.

Wiscynsky nodded to Liebowitz and shepherded them to a plain gray doorway, which was guarded by two men in suits. Inside was a small entrance hall, covered by closed-circuit

TV cameras and three steel doors, each with an electronic security box. Al Wiscynsky slipped a plastic card into one and a heavy lock clunked as the door gave way to his push.

They went down a flight of steep stairs to a landing, with two elevator doors. The DSS man pressed the down button and a green light went on above the left-hand elevator. The door sighed open and the three men went in.

In the cabin, nobody spoke, but Cleary noticed both men were at ease in each other's company. They stopped at the eleventh floor and a female voice enquired, 'Yes, gentlemen?'

'Nightingale, three,' responded Wiscynsky.

'Nightingale three persons thank you have a pleasant evening.' And the door slid open. On the other side was an open-plan office, with eight desks, only two of which were occupied by a couple of staffers working at computer terminals.

Al Wiscynsky and Harry Liebowitz led the way through the office to a smaller room in the far corner. It was quite spacious, and functional. A large, flat illuminated screen on one wall had a detailed plan of Manhattan Mid-Town and Lower but Cleary felt it could just as easily show Boris Yeltsin's back yard at the touch of a switch. He could hear the muted hum of a humidifier, otherwise the room was soundproofed.

'So, coffee?' asked Wiscynsky.

'I got coffee coming outa my eyeballs, Al,' replied the detective.

'Right.' Liebowitz shrugged off his jacket and draped it over the back of a chair, loosening his necktie. 'Joe, you know Al.'

'Sure. DSS, right?' But Joe Cleary was no longer sure of exactly how this game of secret suits was being played.

'Al and I would be grateful for your help.'

Would you now? Would you? Where the fuck were you when I was trying to get a handle on my John Doe, huh? That was what Cleary felt like replying, but he just said, 'Sure.' For the detective was nothing if not a realist.

'You see,' said Wiscynsky, 'I have a feeling in my bones, Joe. I think something is going down here, something very heavy, for next week.'

'You got a whisper . . .' Joe Cleary did not think Big Al paid much attention to hunches. He was a busy guy. Overworked.

The way Wiscynsky and Liebowitz exchanged discreet glances said it all.

'OK. How can I help?'

Harry Liebowitz flicked a switch and, sure enough, the illuminated wall map became a screen split into five rectangles, each with a different surveillance photograph of Betty Boop.

'Just by doing your job, Joe. Just do your job.'

Wiscynsky smiled. 'With a bit of help from your friends . . .'

Boy oh boy, thought Cleary. With friends like you two I would be better off back on that fourteenth-floor fire-escape with Arthur the fuckin' tomcat.

Iran's Prime Minister read the transcript of the interrogation of Sheik Javd Assadiyan with growing anger.

It was not the minutiae of the intelligence boss's acts of betrayal which angered him, not Javd's work for the Iranian regime's enemies – misguided, treasonous nationals who wished to overthrow the Fundamentalist legacy of the Ayatollah Khomeini, aided in this instance by the British Intelligence Service – but the revelation that yet again, extreme elements of the clergy, who ran virtually their own police and security services, had been usurping the role of his Government's most sensitive Special Missions Directorate.

Special Missions included the funding and training of terrorist groups, in Iran and in the neighbouring Sudan.

Terror, the Russian revolutionary Lenin once said, is merely the extension of diplomacy by clandestine force. And in a world which had become a tinderbox of nuclear and chemical warheads, the occasional, spectacular act of terror could be profitably employed to punctuate the political process, without engaging in all-out war.

Now, the Premier was no wimp, and he had not shrunk, nor would he, from authorising such acts when he considered, after consultation, that the result would be a plus rather than a minus.

But control was everything in the business of international clandestine violence, and the interrogation transcript in his hands reported that Javd Assadiyan had been involved in a secret plan by the Ayatollahs and Mullahs of the extreme and powerful Islamic Tide movement to arrange a major act of terror during the week of the United Nations General Assembly. Just days away.

And worse, by Assadiyan's treason, the British SIS had knowledge that, although farmed out to the Palestinian renegade Abu Nidal, in order to keep the atrocity at arm's length, a senior Iranian intelligence official, Brigadier Sheik Jamil Shahidi, had ordered the thing.

Anger was perhaps not the best word to describe the Prime Minister's feelings.

Had he not, for the last three years, fought through more regular diplomatic channels to open all those doors firmly shut against his country? Doors to international trade, to profitable treaties, to cultural and economic links with the major powers. Doors which had slammed shut against the very excesses his nation's blinkered Fundamentalist, Gestapo-like mullahs espoused with such fervour.

Allah in his all-seeing wisdom must know just how hard he had struggled to contain the damage being caused to Iran by its inflexible clergy's zeal for cruelty. God, Allah, was surely to be loved, rather than feared, or obeyed out of oppression.

As a religious man, and a patriot, the Prime Minister was determined to make his country a respected member of the international community. And to this end, he had spent years consolidating his own power base, with his own loyal followers in all areas of the machinery of administration, including the Revolutionary Guard, Vevak, Savama, the military and, indeed, inside the clergy.

So anger was too mild a word to describe his feelings upon learning that the massacre planned in Connecticut had been authorised and set in train without his being consulted. He had been . . . outraged.

But, upon reflection, he divined a way to turn the potential catastrophe to his advantage. For direct confrontation with the Mullahs of Islamic Tide would not necessarily go his way.

He had come to power and held it by understanding precisely that.

Hashemi Rafsanjani picked up the telephone on his teak desk, inlaid with mother-of-pearl, and dialled the home telephone number of his most trusted confidant, General Yussef Faroukrouz, Director of Security in SAVAMA, the foreign intelligence service. Faroukrouz was his cousin, and an implacable enemy of Sheik Jamil Shahidi.

'Yussef,' he murmured, 'come and take some tea with me. We have a matter of some delicacy to arrange.'

12

Little Red Rooster

'I am picking Marietta's Catnap apart with a fine cock's comb,' Ronnie Szabodo said. They were leaving a 1930s apartment block, self-contained with shopping mall, restaurant, bar and swimming pool, just along the Embankment from Vauxhall Cross and the London Station office in Pimlico. The firm kept a number of apartments there as safe-houses and debriefing and planning environments for those they preferred to keep away from the green palace. The vast complex, anonymous and impervious to the rest of the neighbourhood, was called Dolphin Square.

Jardine and his Renfield had been there to speak with a couple of agents, a Peruvian diplomat and a Moscow newspaper owner, nothing to do with the Moonlight affair but life had to go on for there were over a hundred networks around the world to keep an eye on, encourage, prod and instruct.

'And what do you find?' enquired the big spymaster.

'Zilch.'

They turned into the Thames embankment, across from a ghastly monstrosity of a club or something called The Elephant, and Szabodo followed his boss's direction, which was away from the office and towards Chelsea Bridge.

'Thank God for that.' David Jardine did not know what he would do if the rat turned out to be in Marietta's outfit.

Or, unthinkable, Marietta . . .

'But I have not finished yet.'

They walked briskly, the Hungarian having to stretch his stocky legs to keep up.

'Also,' he continued, 'I am looking very hard at Cyprus Station.'

Jardine had a momentary vision of Fiona's glistening thighs. Her tanned, flat belly. 'Cyprus has to be a serious possibility,' he replied, unabashed.

'I have reports from my watchers. Phone taps. Goings and comings . . .'

Jardine's head reeled. '*You* have watchers and intercepts on Cyprus Station . . .?'

Ronnie shrugged. 'David, this is not Five Go Smuggling Happily.' He was alluding, Jardine assumed, to the children's book by Enid Blyton called *Five Go to Smuggler's Top*. 'My job description is to use all means necessary, to ensure our foreign operations are clean and free from compromise.'

'Are you sure, Ronnie?' Jardine had never heard that one before. The firm had an excellent Security Section, run by his former (briefly) lover, the delectable Kate Howard. She would hardly be thrilled to learn that dear old Renfield here had taken on some of her responsibilities, and was probably breaking the laws of a dozen countries in the process.

'Of course,' replied Szabodo unfazed, 'it is a mission I was tasked with by a previous Chief.' He spread his calloused East European bouncer's hands. 'It has never been rescinded.'

'That's because nobody knew about it, old sport. Who the hell gave you that, um, mission?'

Szabodo smiled beatifically. 'Sir Maurice,' he said, without a trace of embarrassment.

Maurice Oldfield, a former 'C', had been dead for about fourteen years. It was typical of the squat Magyar to go for the big lie. Dead men can't contradict you. Also, Maurice was just about the only chief who might just have made such an irregular arrangement.

'Nothing in writing, of course,' said Jardine, with a jaundiced glance at this sorcerer's apprentice of his.

Ronnie Szabodo sucked through the gap in his teeth and shook his head. 'Not the way Maurice worked, dear boy . . .'

And David Jardine just shook his head.

'I don't share the tapes with anyone,' went on Szabodo. 'Occasionally, if things warrant it, I let Kate know by a sort of roundabout system of mine.'

'You lie to her.'

'This is not a nice business, David, maybe you should have been, um, a penicillin racketeer, or a banker.'

'Fuck off.' Jardine grinned, it was hard to be annoyed with Ronnie.

'So that's Cyprus. Then there's Washington . . .'

'Please don't tell me you are bugging the Embassy.'

Ronnie Szabodo shook his head. 'No, but I have their homes under surveillance. I flew in some help from Miami.' West 8 was running a big operation against the Colombian Cartels in Miami. Some things never changed, thought Jardine.

'And Clerical 17. You know, David, far too much sensitive stuff goes through that desk. The people in Clerical 17 must know, in fact in all the Clericals, they must know almost as much as you and your Senior Controllers.'

They could see the traffic lights at the Lupus Street junction. A tourist bus had knocked an electric-blue motorcycle and its rider to the ground, cutting the corner. It must have just happened, for people were stopping and moving to help.

'So who do you think? At this stage?'

For a long few moments, Jardine wondered if the Hungarian had not heard him. Then Szabodo replied, 'It's early days. This could take years. And, if we are not careful, it will become a witch-finding.'

David Jardine contemplated this. Ronnie was, as so often, dead right. Witch-hunts, chasing after imagined, or even real, moles, had a history of destroying services. That was why he had not shared his suspicions with Kate, or Richard, or anyone apart from Renfield.

'Don't let that happen, old man,' he murmured, and, raising a hand, hailed a taxi.

As the vehicle pulled up, its diesel engine ticking, he opened the door and ushered Szabodo in.

'Where to, guv?' enquired the driver.

'Wherever this gentleman wants to go,' said Jardine and met Ronnie's eye. 'I'm seeing Dorothy; you take care of yourself and, really, Ronnie, using Maurice's name for your sins. You ought to be ashamed.'

'*Jamais*,' grinned Szabodo and pulled the door shut.

*

Dorothy liked eating at Bibendum. Jardine enjoyed the airy, light room, with its tall and wide, stained-glass Art Deco Michelin Man and Pneu Michelin windows. On a sunny day, it was like being on a cruise liner in the 1930s. The clientele, on the other hand, was just a touch too media-luvvy for his taste. But the food was good and the waiters and staff friendly without being familiar.

'I always spend too much when I come here,' announced Dorothy, helping herself to a freshly baked bread roll, offered by a child waitress in a shortish black pleated skirt, black shirt and long white apron. Her pretty face was – cut it out, David, Jardine said to himself, you are supposed to be here to try and rescue your marriage.

'Expensive wine . . .?' he enquired politely.

'In the shop, downstairs.'

'Ah.'

Dorothy smiled. 'The Conran shop. They have wonderful things, from bath oil to Indian cotton fabrics. And none of them cheap.'

Jardine sipped some Perrier mineral water. He had too much on his mind to go back to work less than 100 per cent sober.

'David, you will have some wine, won't you?'

'Of course,' he replied. 'Some of that Californian Chardonnay would be nice. Frog's Breath, or whatever it's called.'

Dorothy laughed. 'I know the one. How's work?'

Isn't it strange, mused David Jardine. Twenty-three years of marriage, two children and a lifetime's companionship with all its laughter and all the tears. And suddenly we're struggling to make smalltalk.

'Oh, you know. Usual boring stuff.'

'Is that how you banged your face?'

Jardine touched the almost-healed bruising on his cheek and around his eye. He smiled.

'Getting too old', said his wife, 'for all that rough stuff.'

'I know.' He cut into the poached-egg and haddock starter. 'I do know, kid. I am really tempted to promote somebody. Richard thinks I should have a Deputy Director, and take a more sedate role.' And he glanced up into her eyes. 'Spend more time at home. What do you think?'

Dorothy Jardine gazed back, levelly, her left hand tapping a piece of bread on its plate, deep in thought. 'I think you would be very lonely,' she replied, then added, 'unless of course you marry again.'

In the silence, a cold wind seemed to rustle through Bibendum.

And that was that.

The really quite startlingly attractive young waitress, moving past, gave him a quick and, at any other time, welcome little smile, a little stolen smile. But the man whose marriage had just died did not feel like smiling back.

'There is really no doubt about it,' Zina Farouche said to Hanna al-Farah. She had taken two hours using taxis, the Subway, walking through department stores and generally dry-cleaning her journey before arriving at the luxury apartment on 66th, overlooking the 7th Regiment Armory. 'He is turning up in too many places my team uses, for it to be just coincidence.'

She took a small envelope from her leather Enni purse and shook out the surveillance photos of James Gant onto a thick glass coffee table, on an African iroko-wood base.

Hanna al-Farah spread them out and studied them carefully.

'But he makes contact with no one,' Zina went on. 'Reports to nobody. Uses no telephones. Not even a payphone. No letters posted. No dead drops.'

Hanna nodded. 'Brush contacts . . .?'

'My support cell is very experienced. So, not as far as they could tell.'

The older woman tugged a Winston cigarette from a gold Cartier case and lit it as she gazed at the photographs. 'It could yet be coincidence.'

Zina wanted to ask for a cigarette, but even after all they had done together, all the intimate, mutual pleasure they had given to, and taken from, each other, this was still the legendary Hanna al-Farah, Commander of the Assassins, and the menace of that awful pit, at the Naji al-Ali camp in the Libyan desert, still lingered over every interchange.

'Would you like one?' Hanna asked, offering Zina the gold case as if she could read the girl's thoughts.

'Thank you. *Shukran*.'

Al-Farah ran a hand through her shortish, elegantly cut blonde hair. 'What's your gut feeling?' she asked, in Arabic.

'Zafir wants to interrogate him,' Zina said, by way of explaining how her entire team felt. It was bad for their confidence, even the suggestion that somebody was onto them.

'He is definitely English?' Hanna pushed the photographs around, as if playing patience.

'He uses two names, two sets of ID. Both English. One of the support cell was born in Birmingham, England. She says he sounded British when talking to a waiter in the Pot Bellied Stove.'

'What's that?'

'It's a diner in the Village.' Zina lit her cigarette and sat down on a big tan leather couch, under a teak wall shelf arranged with priceless Etruscan artefacts.

Hanna al-Farah looked thoughtful; she moved slowly to a winged armchair covered in an oatmeal, cotton-calico fabric and sat down, crossing her slender, tanned legs. 'Could he be a journalist?'

Zina shrugged. 'He just does not communicate with anyone. He observes, quote, professionally trained counter-surveillance techniques, and he has been seen making purchases at electronic and survival stores.'

Hanna thought about this. 'Maybe he's going to make a hit on somebody we don't even know. This diplomatic circus is all over town.'

'You know,' said the Palestinian girl, 'that is about the only thing that makes sense.'

Hanna allowed a long trickle of blue smoke to leave her mouth, as she looked at the Palestinian girl appraisingly. An ormolu clock on the mantelpiece ticked gently.

'If you interrogate him,' she said and Zina noted she had not said if *we* interrogate him, 'and he is part of a team, a security or counter-terror team, it is all over.' And from her gaze, Zina Farouche knew she meant, for you, it will be all over for you.

'But if you arrange for him to die in say some kind of accident, or a mugging – this is Mugger City – then you would be able to spot any . . . replacement.'

In the silence, Zina Farouche shook her head in wonder. 'My sister, you are incredible.'

Hanna al-Farah smiled, and flicked the ash into the fireplace. 'Experience, child.'

Zina looked at her wristwatch. 'I will have it done at once.'

'Don't you have details to arrange? Brief your back-up cell? Who will do the thing?'

Zina Farouche was already at the phone – she was too professional to use a portable, they were too easily intercepted – and she looked quite pleased with herself as she replied, 'A mugging was one option we have prepared for.' And she dialled the number of the Kuwaiti Delegation, Noor Jalud's extension.

Noor was waiting by the telephone, as she had been instructed to do, and she would be there all day.

'Noor, hi, it's me,' said Zina. 'Another three for drinks at six. *Ciao, cara.*' And, replacing the handset, she turned to Hanna al-Farah like a schoolgirl who had done well. 'He will be dead pretty soon.'

'Good.' Al-Farah stubbed out her cigarette and her gaze softened. 'You must be exhausted, child.'

Zina, to her disquiet, felt her heart beat faster. 'Not really. I find this work quite . . . stimulating.'

'Do you . . .?' Hanna al-Farah unwound, supple as a cobra, and rose from the easy-chair, her voice with that hoarseness Zina knew so well. 'So do I.' She reached out for Zina and once again the Abu Nidal fighter descended into that confusion of self-disgust and slick, sweet pleasure which by now frightened her, for she was beginning to look forward to those moments, and she had never intended to do so.

In one of those coincidences of fate, James Gant, at that same moment, sat in his room near Washington Square, gazing at a snatched SIS photo of Zina Farouche. The girl was coming off a tennis court at the private club in the Bois de Boulogne, rubbing sweat from her neck with a flannel.

She looked young and glowing with health, and, no getting away from it, attractive. As he studied the photograph, Gant frowned. In the recesses of his memory, something stirred. Hadn't he seen her somewhere? Before all this began. But the moment slipped past and James let it go.

What in the name of God, he asked himself for the hundredth time, has made this woman into such a monster? Among the computer files he had filched from the office, was a detailed report from the French DST on the massacre at Biarritz. It read like a horror story. Stephen King could not have bettered it.

And there was a note, in Marietta Delice's neat hand, for SIS eyes only, identifying the killers as the Dante group, who were codenamed by Abu Nidal's Special Missions Committee, 'Sword of God'. Led by Zina Farouche.

Also spread over the table were snatched photographs of Ben Turabi, Noor Jalud, Zafir Hammuda and Mustafa Sharik. Gant had decided, after identifying his targets and noting their accessibility, their vulnerability, and possible escape routes in each environment, that he would first kill Ben Turabi, then Zafir Hammuda. He had abandoned his first choice, Noor Jalud, on the grounds that she was closely related to the Kuwaiti ruling family and, as PA to the Foreign Minister, her murder would attract too much flak.

He was also not too keen on the idea of killing a woman.

He had not been able to locate Mustafa Sharik, and the only intelligence he could glean from the files was that he would be using the cover of a student at NYU, with false papers.

And, of course, James Gant had no idea of the very existence of Khaled Niknam, for the simple reason that neither did those whose files he had purloined.

He reached out for a lined pad of A4 note-paper and studied his plans for the next day's work. James was methodical and painstaking, with all the considerable attention to detail one would expect from a former BBC news and current affairs editor.

Two hours later, just before he reached for the ice-cold can of root beer he had promised himself, he wrote in large, red letters, 'Remember the enemy does not have the same script!' This was something the Hungarian Szabodo had dinned into them at the Fort and on exercises. And his operational experience with Euan Stevenson had proved the point on several occasions.

However, you did have to start with a plan, provided you knew it would almost certainly require flexibility and improvization on the day.

Turabi, a cook with the Moroccan Delegation on Floor 16 of Essex House, was to be first. Gant had watched him leave at around ten every morning, to visit drugstores and those garish 'everything must go/prices slashed' antique and jade stores around Central Park South and Sixth Avenue. And the method he had planned was simplicity itself.

After the root beer, Gant stripped to his undershorts and spent the next forty minutes in a vigorous workout, culminating in a hundred sit-ups and sixty squat-jumps, invented in Marine Corps hell, called burpees.

With sweat pouring down his body he stood under a cold shower and waited for his respiration to return to normal. And, as he did so, James Gant smiled with cold satisfaction.

By Christ, he had sorted Jack Chisholm out, no problem at all. It was reassuring that all the unarmed combat and knife fighting those SAS non-coms taught at the Fort really worked.

'Remember,' just call me Steve had said, 'there is not the slightest consideration of not winning. You have to *know* you have beaten the opposition before you start. You work fast, hard, and without mercy. Surprise and power. Awesome fucking power, so hard, so fucking awesome you wonder after where the hell it came from. And where does it come from?' Steve would tap his head and then his abdomen. 'Here, and here. Your spirit, and your fighting spirit.'

At which instant he would emit a blood-curdling shriek so loud, so powerful, that the assembled seven students would feel buffeted, as if in a wind, '. . . the *ki-ai*.' He would then say, in a mild voice, 'Your spirit-shout. Now try it.'

And they would practise, and practise and practise, until after days, weeks, of that, the intake of men and young women were lean and whip-fit, and dangerous, lethal weapons.

And poor old Jack Chisholm had picked the wrong sucker.

Still smiling, quite pleased with himself, Gant stepped out

of the shower and towelled himself dry. Until then, he had been a bundle of nerves. Am I doing the right thing? Have I taken leave of my senses? Is this just a sad attempt to avenge the nightmares after Rome?

But now, his mind was clear, and free from doubt. I am the avenging angel for your *future* crimes, he promised Dante. I am the guardian of those families at Beauregard, whom you will never get to harm. For I am here to stop you. And by God, I shall . . .

The night nurse slipped quietly into the room and smiled politely to Jardine, as she checked the progress sheet on a clipboard at the end of Edith's bed. Then she looked at the life-support monitor screen and sat on the edge of the bed, to take the old lady's pulse.

Edith was aware of none of this. Her head was back on the pillows, almost too far back, and her shallow, gurgling breathing was a struggle to listen to.

'Shall I leave,' whispered Jardine.

The nurse shook her head. 'I think she knows you are here. It's comforting.'

David Jardine nodded. When the nurse had done, she straightened Edith's bedclothes with surprising tenderness and fixed the old woman's wispy hair, in its thin curls.

'Cup of tea?' she asked Jardine. And, from long practice, pretended not to notice the tears on his face when he glanced up.

'That would be splendid,' he said, and she thought what a gentle, polite man he was.

There he was again. Gliding, sweeping, now moving backwards, but never colliding, spinning gently, arrogantly . . . menacingly? The tall, two-hundred-pound butch queen, handsome, maybe Somali, features, in pink Lurex tights, electric-green hotpants and aluminium brassière, a Sunset Boulevard-type toque covering his dyed blond Afro.

And his roller-blade boots were gold and scarlet.

Maybe this guy was some kind of exterminating angel. Joe had never seen him till that day of the Frank Grumman hit. Since then he had never been far from the detective's path.

'Who is that faggot on the skates?' he asked the other two.

'Where?' enquired Sam Vargos, who had been sharing a foot-and-a-half-long Frankfurter with their companion, Dolores Caltagirone, and muttering wisecrack asides to her the way Sam did, and making her laugh a lot.

'You musta seen him Sam, come on . . .'

Vargos gazed around, and saw the head and shoulders of the roller-blader, disappearing among the traffic and the people on the sidewalk.

'I ain't seen him around.'

'Maybe I'm going crazy. Dolores, who the hell is he?'

'Who, Joey?'

'Aw, forget it.'

They were strolling on West 10th Street, near 6th Avenue, and the peace of the sultry September night was somehow undisturbed by the myriad muted sounds of jazz and rock music from the open windows of apartments and the many small bars and cafés in the neighbourhood. The aroma of roasting virgin coffee beans, from the Schapira Coffee Company, a little shop where they make their own brand right on the premises, lingered in Joe Cleary's nostrils.

He realized this was a wild goose chase, taking the Sicilian kid back through the places she had been with the murdered triple agent Muar Abbas, where she had met the killer Betty Boop not once, but twice, in the company of another man whose photo she had not been able to find.

Betty Boop had been introduced to her as Azil, Dolores had finally remembered. And Harry Liebowitz had told Cleary, under conditions of national secrecy, that the man was a known mechanic, a 'cleaner', in the pay of the Iranian Intelligence Service, which apparently was called Savama.

He reputedly lived among Iranian exiles, enemies of Khamenie's regime, and had a green card to work as a taxi driver and elevator repair man. His papers were in the name of Mahmoud Dashti. Since obtaining a visa and green card, Dashti – Betty Boop – had disappeared into the teeming masses of New York City.

Still, Joe Cleary had been asked by the real Liebowitz to help. And both Al Wiscynsky and the CIA man had told him they believed the 8th Street/10th Street/Greenwich Avenue area, and surrounding environs, might not be a bad place to start looking. Also, the Sicilian kid might remember other stuff, by walking the same streets she did with the dead man.

Dolores shivered, although the night was warm. Maybe the vibes were getting to her. After all, it was Dolores who had found the stiff in the freezer.

'What's the matter, kid?' asked Cleary, glad to interrupt his partner's phallic interchange with the long Frankfurter, although, of course, he was not jealous, him being a newly born father and all.

'Nothing,' said Dolores.

'Come on, something just got to you. I seen you shiver, did you see that, Sam?'

Sam nodded, sure, he'd seen her shiver.

'Well,' said Dolores, tentatively, and glanced sideways at Joe. 'Maybe I shouldn't.'

'Listen, you can say anything, you're a Federal witness, kid. Nothing ain't gonna incriminate you.'

Still uncertain, Dolores shrugged and said. 'Hell, Joe, I was just thinking about these drapes in your sister's apartment. It's like the place was decorated by Helen Keller . . .'

Sam spluttered on the mustard-filled frankfurter bun.

'You musta seen that queen on the roller skates.'

'It's blades, Joey. I'm sorry, but you asked, after all . . .'

Then she stopped and clutched Sam Vargos's arm, swaying slightly.

'Jesus, you look pale,' muttered Vargos, steadying her.

'What is it now?' asked Joe Cleary, 'the fuckin' wallpaper?'

Dolores shook her head. 'Keep walking, keep moving,' she said, and they did.

Cleary was impressed by how fast the slender kid, one-time call girl, regained her composure. After they had moved on a few yards, say about thirty feet, she paused to fix her hair in the reflection of a café window. Joe and Vargos leaned casually against it, facing the street, each man mentally checking he could reach his piece, Joe's in a holster under his belt on the left front, Sam Vargos's stuck in his jeans, in the small of his back.

Joe Cleary felt his pulse quicken as adrenaline kicked into

the bloodstream. Fuckin' roller blader. Harbinger of doom, sure enough, he could feel danger in the air.

Cool, happy people strolled past, oblivious to the situation.

'OK Dolores, what is it?' he asked.

'That dead-end street, the courtyard.' She meant Patchin Place, a quiet, tree-lined cul-de-sac, shut off from 10th Street by an iron gate, almost opposite Jefferson Market library.

'Yeah.' Cleary looked across at it, while his partner continued to watch all around them.

'He was the other man, with Tony and Azil, the one you call Betty Boop.'

'Who was?'

'He just opened the gate with a key and went in. Then he turned and looked around, like he was checking for something, like he was checking for a tail.'

'You sure it was him?'

She nodded. 'He came to the Met with us.'

Vargos asked, 'Tony watched the Mets?'

'Metropolitan Museum of Modern Art,' replied Dolores.

'Well, pardon me . . .'

Cleary hunched his shoulders and said, 'So he went in, did he lock the gate behind him?'

'I guess he was opening the gate to allow a car in. You can walk in either side of the gates. It's to keep it private from cars, that's why they have iron gates across the street. It's not a gate actually blocking the place off.'

'Enough of gates already,' said the cop.

'The sidewalk either side is open. You can walk in.' Dolores pressed on. 'So he must have been waiting for a car.'

'So where is it? I didn't see a car . . .' Sam peered at the gates, blocking off Patchin Place from West 10th Street.

'So maybe he was expecting a car, and it didn't turn up.'

'You think maybe he is living in one of the houses there . . . Can you remember a name?' This from Sam, whom Joe Cleary had briefed with as much as Vargos needed to know to partner him on this job. Also he had needed to explain why they had been assigned to such a task in the middle of a hectic fortnight.

She shook her head. 'Shit, I've tried. Tony MacLean, Azil . . . and, I dunno.'

'A regular name or another Arab name?' Good question from Sam, thought Cleary. Although he had already been round and round that one with Dolores.

'It was a name like a, like a horse; it reminded me of a horse.'

'Like Francis?'

'That was a mule. I mean my papa used to be a bookie, we all knew so many horses, all the winners, all the placers. All the fixed mares. By the time I was sixteen there was not a horse racing in the USA I did not know by name and trainer.'

'So who won the Kentucky Derby in 1989?' Vargos was a cynic.

'Rapido Express,' announced the Sicilian girl without hesitation.

'Was that his name? Rapido? Ring any bells?' Joe Cleary chuckled and they started to stroll back the way they had come.

'Just say we're your clients,' Joe went on. 'We're going to make a four with another working girl. If he comes out and recognizes you.'

'You ain't; no offence, Joey, but you ain't got the class for the tricks I used to do. Now and again.'

'No kidding,' replied the detective, drily.

'So tell him we're your pimps,' volunteered Vargos.

She gave him a withering look. 'With threads like these? Gimme a break.'

Sam glanced at Joe with a plaintive 'Do we have to take this?' expression.

'Wrong drapes, wrong threads; we sure are not style victims, Sam I am.' Joe Cleary had taken to calling Vargos that since fatherhood and bedtime picture books had invaded his life.

They were outside the Jefferson Market library, and able to gaze into Patchin Place, which lots of folk did because it was an oasis of near-charm in this part of the Village.

'Well, he has not come out,' said Sam.

'And there is no exit from the other end,' remarked Cleary, for he had twice cornered perps in Patchin Place's dead-end north side.

For a few moments they examined each doorway, each

house, in the Place, secure and conservative behind its iron-railed, arched gates.

And just then, a blue-panel truck, with 'QUICK BACK LAUNDRY' on the side, in yellow letters, slowed down and signalled that it was turning into the cul-de-sac. The guy beside the driver got out – he was wearing blue coveralls with the same laundry legend on the back – and pushed the gates open.

The truck rolled in, through the gates, and the driver's buddy pulled the iron gates shut.

'So how did he know the gates would be unlocked . . .?' breathed Dolores.

'I said it before, you would make a detective, kid,' smiled Cleary, not taking his eyes off the van. It stopped outside a house near the far end. Number 7. The driver got out. His buddy was walking back from closing the gate, to join him. The driver pressed the bell at Number 7 and the door opened. His companion opened the side of the truck and climbed inside.

At which moment a lean, broad-shouldered man in white shirt, no collar and dark trousers emerged from the house and with the driver went to the sidewalk to help unload the van.

Dolores watched intently. Joe Cleary noticed she was trembling, like a sniffer dog, when it detects explosives, or dope.

'Like a racehorse . . .' he murmured.

'That is he . . .' She was back in the time when the dead guy in the freezer was still paying for her body and showing her the good life, and introducing her to his friends . . . his killers, Cleary was sure. If Betty fuckin' Boop was one of them.

'Joe,' she whispered.

'Yeah?' Cleary replied.

'That's his name. Joe.'

'There was a racehorse called Joe?' Vargos seemed sceptical.

'Jo Majik,' she said, as if sad anyone could be so ignorant. 'Don't you remember Magic Joe? He was breaking bookies all over the east coast. Bust his heart on the Maryland Handicap Cup. Vets figured somebody had fed him on speed.'

'Gee,' Joe rolled his eyes, 'they don't dope horses do they?'

'Sure they –' and Dolores stopped. She dug her elbow into his ribs. 'Joe Majik. Check it out.'

But Cleary and Vargos had suddenly become all professional. The three men in the leafy, sleepy cul-de-sac were unloading boxes and carrying them into the house.

'OK, we're outa here.' Cleary turned and led them on along the street, walking steadily, his left hand resting on the butt of his 9mm Glock 19. If anyone had been looking for watchers, Cleary and his two pals had fitted the bill. 'Don't use your radio or look back,' he ordered, leading them right, into Sixth Avenue, and not stopping till they reached the Coach House restaurant on Waverley.

'Don't you want to raid the place? Call on some back-up?' asked Dolores and the glance Sam Vargos gave her seemed to agree. But Joe Cleary had fulfilled his unlikely assignment. On this, their second trawl of the neighbourhood suggested by Harry Liebowitz just two nights before, they seemed to have achieved a result.

And the CIA man's instructions had been very clear. If you find them, tell us. Do nothing else. Even if it's Dashti – Betty Boop – forget your cop's instinct to take him there and then. This is too important.

So Joe Cleary took them past the Coach House and radioed for one of the four unmarked back-up cars that neither Sam nor the girl knew existed. Within forty seconds, a dark green Cherokee Jeep pulled up at the kerb, just beside them. There were three young men in it, casually dressed in jeans and sweat shirts, with a variety of casual jackets.

The back door opened and Joe said to Vargos, 'Sam take the kid and get in the jeep.'

'Who are they?' Vargos was going nowhere that easily.

'Agency. It's cool. Stay with Dolores, they'll want to ask her about Majik Joe. I'll catch you later.'

And Sam ushered the Sicilian girl into the Cherokee, which moved away, effortlessly, and was soon out of sight.

The Irish detective used his radio again and watched with professional approval as a yellow cab stopped to let Harry Liebowitz out. Liebowitz walked back along Waverley to Popolino's Pasta place, on the corner with Mercer, and went inside.

A few minutes later, at a quiet table for two, Joe Cleary joined him.

'I'm impressed,' said Liebowitz.

'You ever heard of a racehorse called Magic Joe?' enquired Cleary, testily.

'Sure. Blew its heart out in the eighty-seven Maryland Handicap. Doped to the eyeballs. Shame. Good horse.'

Joe Cleary was beginning to hate the CIA. But he had an ace up his sleeve, for he had made Joe Majik. This was the very same guy who had presented himself at the 6th Precinct House, calling himself H. Liebowitz. And doubtless also the phoney who had visited Frank Grumman's morgue, to check out John Doe Number 6199, who now had more names and aliases than most of the living.

Just round the corner from Popolino's, in his Greene Street rented room with kitchen and shower room, James Gant was preparing to make his first hit. As he dressed, starting with an ankle-holster fastened to his leg with Velcro tape, and two razor-sharp flat-hilted fighting knives with four-inch blades taped with plaster to his rib cage, under each armpit, hilts down, Gant was reminded of the Robert de Niro movie *Taxi Driver*. He devoutly hoped he was not in the least like the sick twist the actor played in that scenario.

As a matter of fact, James Gant seemed to recall reading that de Niro had an office further downtown, on Greenwich Street, at the Tribeca Film Center, and he wished his clandestine, Quixotic trip to the USA had allowed him to touch base there, for he was still a cameraman and editor at heart.

Checking his rig in the mirror, as he fastened a body belt, with separate holsters for a screw-in Ceiner silencer and 9mm Sig-Sauer P-226 fifteen-round automatic pistol he had chosen over the current, vogue, spook's personal weapon, the Glock, James continued to feel more than vaguely ridiculous. He remembered the crazed taxi driver of the eponymous movie facing up to his image in a long mirror, lip curled and mouthing 'You looking at *me* . . .?' in some psychotic charade which turned, that was what the movie was about, into bloody reality.

Then he remembered why he was doing this and all his

doubts were gone. Removing his gear, Gant cleaned his weapons for probably the eighth time and slept until dawn.

In the hour after midnight, the green pyramid that was SIS Headquarters was more or less deserted, apart from those teams running operations in other time zones, communications staff and the janitors.

David Jardine sat in his leather swivel chair and turned away from his desk to gaze out of his window at the lights and rooftops of Pimlico, across the river. He was gently winding the Thomas Mudge carriage clock, aware of the peaty aroma from a large crystal tumbler of Knockandoe malt whisky on the desk behind him.

The craggy, untidy man, who managed to look roughly assembled even in the beautifully cut Huntsman suits he usually wore to work, felt, somehow, empty. Dorothy had given him the clock as a wedding-anniversary present, at a time when she really could not afford it, knowing his appreciation of antique timepieces.

'When you love somebody,' she had said, in answer to his quietly pleased protests, 'you just take the plunge. Keep it in your office and think of me.'

And that's just what he was doing. Thinking of her. Self-pity, Jardine, he told himself, is a pretty sad indulgence. If ever a man asked to lose his life's companion it was you, mate. And he marvelled at his naivety, his purblind arrogance, in imagining that she would not be aware of his predilection for slender, upper-class, ever-so-slightly decadent young women. Or, more insulting when you come to think of it, that she would somehow understand his needs and turn a blind eye.

Why?

Because you are so truly wonderful in every other way?

Get a life. As Andrew and Sally would say.

Delicately, he extracted the key and gently closed the back of the clock.

'Working late?' a familiar voice asked. And when he slowly swung the chair round, there was Kate Howard.

He took a second crystal tumbler from a drawer in his desk and placed it beside the whisky bottle.

'Help yourself.'

Kate was carrying a file holder. Although it was a warm night out there, the office air-conditioning was running cool and she wore that shapeless grey cardigan over a cream shirt and pleated skirt. Aquascutum, decided Jardine, who flattered himself he knew about such things.

'What's up?' she enquired, putting the file on his desk and picking up the bottle. Their brief fling, about three years before, might so easily have made for a difficult working relationship after he had found the then Chief's cufflinks in her bathroom cabinet.

Surprisingly, although neither had ever mentioned the entire episode again, Kate had been amusedly warm and . . . relaxed in her professional relationship with David Jardine, to the extent of supporting him when others at the top table had been gunning for him. In fact, they had remained good chums, and only Ronnie, Jardine felt, had guessed that something more intimate had occurred between them. But then, Ronnie would.

Kate was now Director of Security and she was, at the age of thirty-three, one of the best the office had ever had. Jardine knew that the boss of the Security Service, MI 5, in its fortress of a building across the river and just a half mile away, had tried to poach her. But Kate Howard was both loyal and ambitious, and Jardine knew she harboured an ambition to become the first woman Chief of SIS which she, quite rightly, considered to be the more prestigious position.

He did not doubt Kate might just make it. Although she had never heard a shot fired in anger, unlike the courageous – Jardine reluctantly conceded – boss of the Other Service.

He waited until she had poured a generous measure into her glass, then raised his own drink and, gazing over the rim, met her eyes.

'*L'chaim*.'

'Break a leg.' She sipped the malt. 'Mmmm. So I say again, what's wrong?' Kate looked around and pulled a seat to the side of the desk. She sat down and pushed a wisp of hair off her brow.

Jardine smiled. The one thing the firm had over any other outfit he knew of was a remarkable camaraderie, a closeness between its practitioners of this, the second oldest profession. Quietly élitist, once inside the charmed circle there was only mutual warmth, support and . . . understanding.

'Edith Treffewin. Ring a bell?' he asked.

Kate frowned. 'Dowager Viscountess. Put James Gant up for the firm. Um . . . ran our Berlin Operation, sixty-eight to seventy-five. Retired seventeen years ago. Foreign Office and Cabinet Office committees till ninety-one. Your first boss. How did I score?'

'She died at nine o'clock tonight.' And to Jardine's surprise, his lip suddenly trembled and grief clutched at his throat. He blinked and rammed the tumbler to his mouth, sipping to hide his silliness.

Kate Howard laid her drink on the desk and came round to him. Standing behind him she leaned over and kissed him gently on the forehead.

'You are really quite fine,' she said, softly. 'But I promise to keep it a secret.'

Jardine touched her hand and chuckled, ruefully. What happened next, they were to agree later, had probably always been inevitable.

For he turned and their eyes met, and they kissed properly.

At which moment Marietta Delice appeared silently in the open doorway, from the outer office, manned by young Heather during the working day.

Marietta knew about Dorothy and David separating. Actually, everyone in the office above the rank of Controller knew about Dorothy. And neither David Jardine nor Kate Howard, Director of Security, would ever know that Marietta had been there.

The older woman had no idea what had gone before that moment but she was familiar with the way things sometimes panned out in the firm's close family and, as she tiptoed out, across the outer office to the corridor, she flicked on the red 'In Conference' light and closed the door behind her, remembering quite fondly all those years ago, when it might have been herself to whom the big ox would have turned, in his loneliness.

It was several minutes before the couple in the Director of Operations's office finally disengaged.

'Are you sure about this,' he asked, aroused and very clearly too, for by then she was on his lap.

Kate leaned back and gazed at him. 'Not in the slightest,' she replied, with a serious expression.

David Jardine stared at this beautiful, intelligent, understanding, desirable woman. 'Listen, I'm a complete bastard, take my advice and run screaming from the room.'

'Excellent advice. And tempting.'

Jardine gently started to undo the buttons on her linen shirt.

'Dorothy and I are getting divorced,' he said, pushing the shirt open.

'I know.' She firmly lifted his hand from her immaculate breast, slipped the bra cup back over it and buttoned her shirt. 'This is rather embarrassing; I didn't intend anything like this, David.'

Bless her, thought Jardine, she really is embarrassed.

'I liked it . . .' he said, simply, helping to fasten the top button.

She met his gaze, their hearts still pounding, fighting – not lust, they could each handle that – what was alarming them was more dangerous.

'I don't know. Maybe when you're free. If that really happens.'

In the silence, the carriage clock ticked noncomittally.

David Jardine's shoulders sagged, he cut out the randy, live-life-for-the-moment façade and said, simply, 'Believe me, Katherine, it is over. I am, for what it's worth, free. To tell you the truth, it's been a bit of a blow.' He let her examine his face, trying to be as open and honest as any spook could ever be. 'And if you don't come home and sleep with me, I think I will burst into tears.'

After a long moment, she shook her head and laughed quietly, then kissed him gently and replied, 'You are such a shit.'

'What did you come over here for, anyway?' Jardine glanced at the file on his desk.

'Somebody's activating a few deep-black facilities in New York. Using all the right passwords and work codes. I expect one of your operators there has been too busy to file his day reports.'

Jardine frowned. 'What sort of facilities?'

'Um, forged papers, credit cards, firearms and things like that.'

The spymaster shook his head and they got to their feet. As he crossed to the door, shrugging on his jacket and straightening his tie, he said, 'Bring that with you and read it to me in the car.'

As they left the office Jardine, presuming it was Kate who had switched on the red 'In Conference' light, switched it off, with a degree of insouciance he had not felt for ages.

He felt that old lightness in his step, accompanied by a feeling he was perhaps back on form, and could handle anything. Making all the right decisions, just like the old days.

It could not have come a minute too soon.

It took the CIA remarkably little time to put Number 7 Patchin Place and its occupants under observation. This was partly because the build-up to UN Week had caused the Agency to assign an extra 114 field officers to the City and because they were able to liaise with the Diplomatic Security Service to borrow certain State Department personnel based in Manhattan, so within minutes of Dolores having made a positive ID, backed up by the suspicious activity of the blue-panel truck, Urban Surveillance Routine 36 had begun, with twenty-eight agents assigned in two shifts, plus two NYPD Homicide Detectives, Joe Cleary and Sam Vargos.

Routine 36 (R-36 in Agency parlance) was about deep-cover work, both static and mobile. Performed well, it was state-of-the-art, for the targets were generally highly aware, professional espionage hoods, armed and extremely dangerous.

The nearest undercover operators had moved into position even while Cleary was hurrying along Waverley to join Harry Liebowitz in Popolino's, and within fifteen minutes the address and surrounding environment were under discreet scrutiny.

Now, the circumstances in which the Agency is permitted to carry out such work on domestic US territory are limited to the point of non-existence, but there are ways round most regulations, provided you don't get caught.

In this case, using a strictly informal and legally questionable facility, the CIA team used a cover story, with credentials to match, for the benefit of any unwanted curiosity from local law-enforcement or Federal officers.

The spooks were provided with DSS credentials and reported to a control room in the DSS Office in the World Trade Center, manned jointly by Al Wiscynsky's deputy and an Agency Assistant Director called Bill Nelson.

Once Cleary had briefed Liebowitz on the situation, more watchers and long-range eavesdroppers were drafted in, and, before an hour had elapsed, an application had been faxed to Langley for dedicated access to an orbiting NASA satellite, codenamed Minerva, to intercept any radio messages and phone calls to and from the Patchin Street house.

'Might be nothing,' said Liebowitz to Cleary, 'but if these are the guys who put your John Doe in that freezer, they sure as hell are not in town for the ball game.'

Back at the US Delegation building, across First Avenue from the UN Plaza, Dolores and Sam Vargos were shown a number of black and white photographs, clandestinely obtained, of several men of European appearance.

'Sure. That's him. That's Joe Majik,' the girl said, tapping one photo. Tony Semprino scratched his ear and glanced to Vargos. 'What do you think, Sam?'

Vargos stared at the picture, long and hard. Eventually he nodded. 'Yeah. That could be him . . .'

'Then somebody's in deep shit,' announced Semprino. 'That is Morteza.'

'Who's he?' Dolores was beginning to acclimatize to all this high-powered spookery. And Semprino was kind of cute.

Tony Semprino considered his reply. 'Was that the guy you met with, um, with Tony MacLean? Are you . . . certain?'

Dolores nodded. 'I never forget a face.'

'Or a horse,' added Vargos, helpfully.

'OK,' went on Semprino, 'he is very bad news. Miss Caltagirone, do you know about the Federal Witness Protection Programme?'

She shook her head vehemently. 'I sure do and I ain't joining.'

Tony Semprino shrugged. He turned away and took a cup of water from the dispenser. 'And have you also heard of a Federal warrant to put prime witnesses into Protective Custody?'

Silence. Sam watched the Sicilian girl, and felt a pang of sympathy, for she suddenly realized she was in way over her head.

'Mister, can't I just stay at Joey's sister's . . .?'

'I thought you hated the wallpaper,' said Vargos.

'The drapes, it's the drapes, but I don't want to go to jail, man.'

'Right now,' said Semprino, 'I need to keep you alive and out of harm's way. So if you co-operate, we can take you someplace real comfortable, like . . . Montana.'

'You ain't entitled to inflict cruel and unusual punishment, I know my goddam rights.'

Sam laughed.

'Whatever,' replied Tony Semprino. 'Just agree to help and we will treat you well, Ma'am. And with courtesy. OK, maybe Montana is kind of quiet. How about Chicago?'

'Better,' agreed Dolores reluctantly, by now in a huff.

'Plus we can probably arrange some expenses, OK?'

'Maybe I never saw the guy in my life, how about that?'

'Don't fuck with me, lady.'

And Dolores Caltagirone did what any reasonable girl would do in her position. She burst into tears.

Now, the reason Semprino was coming on so strong was because the suspect identified by Dolores and Sam was one Major Morteza Azmoudeh, of the Security Enforcement Division of the Iranian Foreign Intelligence Service, Savama. He was the commander of a roving unit, with a world-wide remit, tasked with seeking out infiltrators, traitors, unreliable assets and, in general, any agents or sub-agents, or contracted operators who had become an embarrassment to the security of the Tehran-based Savama.

The Enforcement Division was part of Savama's Directorate of Security, and Morteza Azmoudeh's immediate boss, who trusted him implicitly, for Morteza was married to his sister, was General Yussef Faroukrouz, Director of Security.

All this was on file at Langley. And, in truth, from the

moment Joe Cleary's first fax had found its way onto Tony Semprino's desk, the CIA man had strongly suspected that Morteza Azmoudeh was somehow involved.

For Morteza did like to interrogate by torture. And he did like to leave his trademark. Which involved mutilation by scalpel and, if there was time, by chainsaw.

But Betty Boop, who had been with Morteza and the doomed Muar Abbas – 'Tony MacLean' – was more of a straightforward button man, an executioner, and very good he was too.

Quite a team.

Semprino left the sobbing kid and went through to his operations room where he spoke to Bill Nelson. For, if Morteza was in town, somebody was scheduled for a great deal of unhappiness, of the terminal kind.

This, said James Gant to himself, emerging from a bookshop near Grand Central Station, could just be a dummy run. I mean, time is on my side. If the scene does not feel right, I might decide to abort and go for the second target.

Bullshit, Gant, came the reply. You have maybe five days, could be four if the Connecticut family gathering has been moved forward. If you mean business, Ben Turabi's ass will be grass in about fifty minutes time.

If you are chickening out, run back to London and your nice safe job in intelligence – Rear Echelon.

James Gant smiled thinly. His emotions after the violence with Jack Chisholm had been interesting. Not only had he managed to defeat the well-built counterfeiter one-on-one – he had really enjoyed it.

So, as far as he was concerned, he had not come all this way to fool around. Ben Turabi, old boy, he affirmed silently, your ass is sheep food.

As Gant went through his routine counter-surveillance techniques, changing direction, taking taxis in random directions, riding on the subway and entering and leaving department stores by different doors, he understood that the unusual course he had chosen might end in his own death.

That was something he was prepared to accept. He would not have chosen hazardous assignments, as a BBC cameraman, if he had been unduly bothered by the prospect. James's philosophy had always been, when the good Lord wants you, he will tap you on the shoulder, and no amount of dodging and weaving will avoid the moment. And if one particular day is not that fatal day, you will survive. Till your number is up.

He also believed in taking every sensible precaution to minimize risks and stay one step ahead of the grim reaper.

But Ben Turabi was a seasoned killer, an alert and ruthless survivor. Gant was nothing if not a realist, and he was well aware that the wrong move, at the wrong instant, could easily leave him as one more statistic, one more unknown cadaver, on the streets of New York. Or at the bottom of some elevator shaft.

The subway train slowed down as it pulled into Queensboro Plaza and Gant got to his feet and waited to get out, along with a couple of Chinese kids and a tall, shabby guy carrying what seemed to be his laundry in about five plastic bags.

Walking along the platform, he found himself thinking about Charlotte. Would she be able to manage without him? He did not doubt it, although his death would be another blow in her young life.

He made his way across a series of underground walkways to Queen's Plaza, where he would catch a BMT train back over East River to 57th Street, prior to his final approach, on foot, towards the Hertz office on West 54th, where Ben Turabi would, if he stuck to his morning schedule, be strolling past between 11.15 and 11.35 a.m., on his way back to the Moroccan Delegation's accommodation on the sixteenth floor.

As he descended some stairs to the next platform, Gant became aware of a strange phenomenon. The hairs on the back of his neck began, quite literally, to rise.

Almost at once, he noticed three men, Afro-Americans, in their mid twenties, overtaking him, not all that quickly, and not speaking. They wore the baggy pants and huge Reeboks of the posse culture, with dark shirts, worn outside the jeans, loose vests and baseball caps on back-to-front. And yet . . . something was wrong. Maybe they were just a few years too old for the gear they were wearing.

The blade was dull and James almost did not see it, but his body's self-preservation mechanism was already in overdrive, the hair-rising and adrenaline surge not a second too soon, and he swayed to his right as the hoodlum lunged, colliding with the one overtaking him, who wrapped an arm round Gant's neck and hauled him backwards, presenting the Englishman's front to the knife man. Knife *men*, for the third mugger had a switchblade suddenly open in his hand.

Gant heaved his weight against the one holding him and launched his feet in twin, ramrod-hard, simultaneous kicks into the chests of his attackers. As the two men checked, winded, he rolled to his right and bent his legs, so that he and the guy with the arm round his throat both tumbled down the remaining steps onto the platform. It was a move known, they had taught at the Fort, as *sutemi-waza* – a sacrifice move, using your inert body to take the assailant where you want him to go.

As they struggled on the platform, James ignored the stranglehold, tensing his neck muscles, and, reaching down with his free left hand, ripped the compact Smith & Wesson ASP 9mm seven-round automatic from his ankle-holster and shot his attacker once in the lower left thigh and, as the man howled and immediately let go of Gant's neck, the SIS man rolled laterally, several times along the platform, prone with arms above his head, like he had done so many hundreds of times in practice, holding the pistol two-handed and firing controlled, rapid, aimed shots into the two knife men, who had leaped over their wounded accomplice and were coming in for the kill.

The one on the left, with green vest and blue cap, just stopped, as if he had walked into a wall. The mugger on the right spun satisfyingly – there was no denying it – and toppled over onto his back, gore spurting in a bloody fountain from his throat.

The would-be strangler, his left jeans leg saturated in darkest red, struggled to get some kind of equaliser out from under his jacket.

Gant shot him in the head – his last bullet, because the slide of the pistol stayed back, behind the butt.

The remaining attacker had still been standing, looking . . .

surprised, legs akimbo. Then, very slowly, he dropped to his knees, pointed at Gant as if about to say something, and fell forward, abruptly, and lay there, face down.

Surprisingly calm, James Gant climbed to his feet, and looked around, in time to see the last of the few people who had been on the platform disappearing up the stairs at the far end. This was New Jack City. Nobody wanted to know. Nobody wanted to be a witness.

Then, from behind a pillar, with a sign advertising Mabel's Yoghurt Drink – Raspberry, Banana & Chocolite – stepped a slender, olive-skinned young man, wearing a leather Avirex zip-up, white T-shirt and faded jeans. And shades. He held a Glock .45 pistol, with a longer-than-average magazine-clip protruding from the butt – you notice detail like that, the instructors had told Gant, and they had been right – and, as he raised the weapon, he said, 'Not bad. But you should have counted your bullets . . .'

His finger was tightening on the trigger as James Gant rolled right, drawing the Sig-Sauer P-226, a big, serious piece of artillery, from his waist harness and both men fired at the same time. But Gant was fighting for his life, for the very first time, whereas Khaled Niknam had got used to being the killer.

It was probably that near-complacency which killed Niknam, for James Gant emptied ten slugs so fast into the Palestinian's upper torso that witnesses later attested they had heard a sub-machine gun, while a mere three plugs of lead cracked past his own head.

Even Gant's hairy-arsed SAS close-combat instructors would have given him a grudging 'not exactly piss-poor', for this first blooding by fire, his speeding brain registered, in the timeless animal flush of victory.

At this moment, the platform now deserted (the entire encounter had lasted just eighteen seconds), the rushing, roaring sound of an approaching train grew louder and Gant managed to distance himself some twenty yards from the four corpses as it swished out from the tunnel and alongside the platform.

Doors sighed open and about twenty people came out. Some hesitated when they saw the bodies and the blood. A woman screamed. Consternation reigned. One or two passengers glanced around, wary, then hurried towards the far stairway.

Others withdrew back inside the safety of the carriages and James Gant was among them, for everyone was using different doors and, in the confusion, nobody was counting.

Somebody yelled to get the hell out of there and the doors hissed shut and the train began to move out of the underground station, back into the next tunnel.

Gant, soaked in perspiration, heart pounding hard against his chest, sat down in a seat, his weapons safely back in concealment.

Jesus, he thought, the big-time assassin nearly mugged. That'll larn you. And even in his state of some shock, he told himself it was good for the mission that he had acquitted himself so well. So lethally.

But what a coincidence. I mean, they were hardly out to get me, in particular, he told himself.

Or were they?

Next question. Do we proceed with Plan A? The killing of Ben Turabi, or do we abort and go home to lick our wounds?

Bullshit, decided James Gant. Nobody said it would be a picnic, let's strike while the iron is hot . . .

13

Dead Drop in Midtown

Seven in the morning in the Tite Street maisonette. David Jardine awoke to the sound of a helicopter clattering over the rooftops on its way to Chelsea Barracks, where the parade ground doubled as a landing pad. He wondered if anyone he knew was in it.

Then he became aware of a warm, smooth, naked Katherine Howard, MA, snuggled up with her back to him, fast asleep, her fair hair spread on the pillow.

Well, he thought to himself, there's a turn-up for the book. And he wondered if he had taken the delectable Kate back due to total inability to control his sex drive – no, that was not actually fair, self-control was not a problem – or as a gesture of defiance at the disastrous state of his so-very-private real personal life. Or had he just felt low, and been hurting, and needing a warm and affectionate, moist womb to give him comfort?

That's quite enough self-analysis, he decided and, turning, touched his new companion, tenderly, on the shoulder, and planted a delicate kiss on the nape of her neck.

'Mmmm . . .' She pressed herself against him.

And, after this, David Jardine contemplated, an early start at the office . . . find out precisely who is drawing counterfeit stuff in New York and forgetting their paperwork. Update on Dante. And young James Gant. Contact him in the Dolomites and tell him his poor aunt Edith is dead. He supposed somebody had the boy's contact number.

'Jesus, David, that is so naughty . . .'

But first things first, the irredeemable spymaster decided.

'How about . . . this?'
'Yes, please . . .'

They think they are so goddam smart, reflected Joe Cleary, but most cops on the detective squad can do this.

Morteza was on the move, and he was being shadowed all the way by the Agency's R-36 surveillance team. Cleary and Sam Vargos were with the detail, as much so that they could smooth things out with any local police difficulty as for their streetwise understanding of Manhattan.

The blue van had left, soon after its arrival, taking both QUICK BACK LAUNDRY men with it. Morteza had worked in the back room of his Patchin Place house till late. Then he had risen at ten before seven and worked out, mainly sit-ups and push-ups, showered and prayed facing Mecca, before breakfasting on yoghurt and honey, with coffee, according to a subsequent search of his garbage.

Now, at 10.37, he had just walked up and down and through that glittering Taj Mahal of dedicated shoppers after everything from jade to high-class perfumery to giant antique, almost life-size ivory veneered camels that was Trump Tower, in Mid-Town South, before getting into a taxi and leaving it on Broadway, not far from Columbus Circle.

Joe Cleary and Al Wiscynsky got out from the beige Ford sedan just a block away and in a few seconds were strolling about forty feet behind the Iranian security man. They both wore cordless hearing-aid earpiece receivers and throat microphones fixed by clear Band-Aid to the sides of their necks.

A running series of meaningless words and phrases meandered through the airwaves as the R-36 team passed across or in front of the man being tailed, none for more than a few brief moments, so that the most professional surveillance spotter (and that sure was Morteza) would notice nothing alarming.

Hand it to them, conceded Cleary, even he was not aware of the process, except from the radio commentary. Students, sightseers, meter maids, businessmen, beggars, the team employed all those disguises and more.

A voice in his ear said what appeared to be an order for two pizzas but it meant that Morteza had linked up with another male.

Joe Cleary and Wiscynsky quickened their pace in time to see the Iranian enforcer gazing into a cheap jewellery shop, and talking to a tall man standing beside him. A tall guy with his overcoat buttoned to the neck, like Fester in the Adams Family movies. Stubble of beard and short haircut.

Betty fuckin' Boop.

'Betty Boop . . .' muttered Cleary.

'Sure. Stay back.'

'Man, we can charge them.'

'This is not a law-enforcement matter, Joe. Stay cool.'

So, with reluctance, the Homicide cop allowed himself to be guided to a yellow taxi where he and Wiscynsky made a dumb charade out of asking how much to Rockaway Beach or some such environ, using the side mirror to observe the two subjects.

Then Morteza held something for Betty Boop to look at.

'What's he showing him. What is it?' asked Wiscynsky, peering into the mirror, frustrated.

'It's a fuckin' photograph, that's what it is,' replied Cleary, looking around, instinctively, for a tall, black fairy in gold lamé on roller-blades and most religiously hoping it was not his face the two Iranians were studying.

Only two blocks away, on that September morning, James Gant passed his Minnesota driver's licence to the plump, wisecracking Puerto Rican woman at the Hertz counter in West 54th. She punched in the details to their computer and slid it back across the counter.

'Will you be doing more than one hundred miles?' she asked.

'Just to the Hamptons and back,' replied Gant.

'OK, you should take the low-mileage rate.' The clerk entered that, then took the credit card in the name of Wilson and ran it through her machine. She slid the carbon-backed slip round for Gant to sign. 'Sign here.' She handed him a ball-point pen.

Gant scribbled a signature and passed the slip back.

'You need a map?' she asked.

'No thanks.'

'Mmm-hmm. Here you go, Mister Wilson. Have a nice day.'

'You too.' Gant took the folder of documents and the keys. Resisting the urge to look at his watch, he left by the side door and strolled down the curving ramp, echoing to the squeal of distant car tyres, and, in the first level of the underground garage, soon located the smoke-blue Oldsmobile coupé he had rented.

He unlocked the car and opened the trunk, where he dumped the jacket he had been wearing on the subway platform, during the recent excitement. On the train, he had taken it off and had been carrying it folded inside out.

On the way to the Hertz rental office, James had purchased two items from a store on Sixth Avenue – a cheap brown raincoat and a plain navy sweat shirt. Now he took the sweat shirt from its plastic bag and, glancing around to check he was unobserved, pulled it on, over his head. He opened the driver's door and got in. It was 11.08.

Gant eased the empty ammo clip from his short Smith & Wesson in its ankle-holster and slid in a fresh one. Seven more rounds. The beauty of the 9mm ASP was it had been machined smooth, with no projections, for easy quick-draw in urgent, unpleasant situations. ASP stood for Armament Systems & Procedures, the name of the firm that adapted the pistol for clandestine operators, but at the Special Combat School near Scarborough, the Poet had said the letters should really mean As Soon as Possible, and now James Gant knew the piece was worth the $870 he had paid for it at a no-questions-asked gunshop in Queens. For it had saved his life.

Holding the bigger Sig-Sauer automatic under the brown raincoat on his lap, Gant deftly screwed the Ceiner sound suppressor into the muzzle, all the time checking he was unobserved.

A full clip into the butt and he was ready. One silenced round and he was out of it, that was the plan, but events of the day so far had proved nothing was certain. To tell the truth, he still felt pretty shaky after the struggle on that subway platform, the noise of gunfire still lurking in his ears.

Gant carefully rolled the weapon up in the raincoat, so that he could carry the coat on his left forearm and reach the trigger, inside the garment, with his right hand, which at least was not shaking, for he checked.

It was 11.12. Time to party.

He got out, locked the car, and strolled across to the side stairwell. 'Please check you have handed your keys and documents to reception' enjoined a sign, black letters on yellow.

Outside on East 54th, it was hot and bright. Gant strolled casually towards Sixth Avenue – The Avenue of the Americas.

Three minutes later, on the lookout – on the hunt – for Ben Turabi, he was more than somewhat surprised to see the one member of the Dante group he had written off as untraceable, in the limited time at his disposal – Mustafa Sharik. The straggling fringe of black beard, the dark skin, prominent front teeth and dropped shoulder were unmistakable.

Sharik was the wild card in the Dante pack.

But here he was, crossing 54th Street, 6th Avenue intersection, heading for Central Park South.

Well, well. Expect the unexpected – every single one of Gant's instructors and operational bosses had dinned it into him. OK, so I did not expect this, he admitted. I was looking for Ben Turabi and up pops a different member of the gang. But, as the Poet said, remember the other guys do not have the same script.

Gant's plan had been to take out Turabi and be back in his rented Oldsmobile with an innocent expression, making his way sedately from the underground garage, while the crime scene was being taped off. Or maybe even sooner.

But this could be a once-and-for-all chance to kill Mustafa Sharik. Did it really matter which of the low-lifes he wasted, just so long as it got the massacre aborted?

And James Gant, as he shortened the distance between himself and the terrorist, had only seconds to decide what to do.

Morteza and Betty Boop had strolled on, leaving the jewellery-shop window, Morteza creating a gap of about twenty feet between himself and the Iranian hit man, who walked behind.

They were under observation by a constantly changing

permutation of twelve men and women from the CIA's R-36 surveillance team. Joe Cleary and Wiscynsky kept well back, for the last thing they needed was for Betty Boop to get spooked by seeing the Irish detective.

Ben Turabi had been in the Harley Davidson café, buying a purple and navy motorcycle jacket which had set him back $320. He was pleased with his purchase and when he got home to Beirut he intended to show it off as much as possible. He was also thinking about buying a yellow New York taxi and shipping it back to Morocco with the returning delegation, which had done some serious shopping in the Big Apple, as he liked to call it.

He paused at the 55th Street intersection, the crossing light said WALK but it had begun to flash and a cavalcade of black-windowed Secret Service Dodge four-wheels and Pontiac sedans, all with blue lights strobing and sirens whooping, approached right down the middle of the street and across, heading east towards 5th Avenue.

When the five vehicles had swept by, the Palestinian saw Mustafa on the other side of the street, walking with that loping gait of his towards Central Park South and looking . . . agitated. Turabi changed direction to take advantage of the crossing-lights and hurried across, keeping his eye on Mustafa Sharik, wondering what the problem was.

There! Gant glimpsed Ben Turabi hovering on the intersection, as the VIP convoy sped past. He saw the terrorist notice Mustafa Sharik and, after pausing, starting to cross the six-lane Avenue of the Americas.

Sharik was ahead of Turabi, and Gant had no wish to expose his back by hitting on the man in front. But Ben Turabi appeared to be unprotected. Gant automatically checked out the environment. Nobody seemed to be taking any interest, so . . . decision time.

OK, he decided, it's Plan A. Turabi gets the lucky bullet.

James Gant quickened his pace and vectored in on Ben Turabi, as the Arab reached the pavement.

Seven paces behind.

Gant was gaining. He cradled the rolled-up brown raincoat

and slipped his right hand underneath, to grip the butt of his pistol and he let his trigger-finger lie along the trigger guard.

Four paces.

Gant's concentration was focused. Two shots, he decided, we haven't come all this way to leave it in doubt. He would fire and keep on walking, looking neither right nor left. The City Center Theater, on the 56th Street corner, was just yards ahead, he would turn left there and walk round the couple of blocks to the Hertz Garage and his rented car.

Two paces.

Ben Turabi was shorter than Gant and his thick, black hair was neatly cut. The man was chubbier than in the snatched photos and the first couple of times Gant had seen him, early in his reconnaissance of the Essex and its surrounding streets, he had not quite recognized him.

Maybe it was the cooking that had affected his calorie intake.

One pace.

Gant's finger curled to rest gently on the trigger. A big man in a topcoat suddenly barged into Turabi; James had no idea where he came from but it was a hefty shove and Gant swiftly got his finger off the trigger and side-stepped out of the way, just like the four or five passers-by, who simultaneously made space and ignored the collision.

Shit, thought Gant, I'll move ahead and wait for him.

But a woman started screaming and he glanced round to see Ben Turabi slowly corkscrewing to his knees, his neck a crimson second mouth, horribly wider than any real mouth and gurgling blood spewing down his white T-shirt front.

The stricken man's arms flailed and the Harley-Davidson carrier bag he was clutching tumbled to the pavement.

Jesus, so much blood it was in a rapidly spreading pool around his knees as Turabi's arm movements became weaker, even as the horrified crowd collected to watch, and, after a very long thirty seconds, the life had gone from his staring, desperate, pleading eyes and the corpse of Ben Turabi, international terrorist, crumpled into his own gore.

'Holy shit,' breathed Cleary, drawing his piece. He had broken into a run but Wiscynsky caught up with him and restrained him.

'What the fuck? Get outa my goddam way!'

'Joe, cool it! Just cool it. This is a Federal matter.'

Wiscynsky turned his head, holding his earpiece and listened, nodding a couple of times and saying 'Copy that' and 'Sure thing'. And like that. And all the time he kept a tight grip on the outraged Cleary's sleeve.

Then he put his face close to the cop's and said, 'We still have him in the box, Joe. Morteza fingered him and Betty Boop did the business. We still have them both in sight and we aim to keep a loose surveillance pattern.'

Cleary shook his head, as they approached the crowd of rubberneckers and the dead body of some guy, male, middle twenties, sallow complexion, his head half severed from a sweeping cut with a sharp, a very, very sharp, instrument. And all the time Wiscynsky was listening and he said, 'We still have them. They've split up but we have them both. Did you see that man? Boy oh boy, was that a pro hit or what?'

Joe Cleary glanced at Wiscynsky and shook his head. 'Man, you're some sick twist; whose side are you on?'

'The side of keeping one hundred seventy-two foreign diplomats alive for the next eleven days, bud. That's what. We lift Dashti, Betty Boop as you call him, and he won't talk. We lift Morteza and ten-to-one he'll pull some diplomatic immune protocol shit. And we never know what this is all about, what exactly is going down here. And, believe me, my friend, Washington is demanding to know.'

As Joe Cleary considered all that, a 14th Precinct Patrol car screeched to a stop and the two cops inside got out, hefting their belts laden with night sticks, revolvers, radio batteries and stuff, the way Cleary could remember doing himself, before he made detective.

A tall guy with steel-rimmed glasses, like GI issue, carrying a cheap brown raincoat, on the edge of the group of shocked New Yorkers, turned and strolled away, past gathering rubberneckers.

He sure is a very cool fellow, thought Cleary to himself, not many people just stroll away when a bloody piece of street drama has just occurred.

‘Do you ace spooks have this on video, perchance?’ he enquired, still watching the cool fellow head for West 56th and disappear round the corner.

Some 3,414 miles to the east, on the fifth floor of the great green monstrosity, it was 4.32 in the afternoon.

‘Did he say which, um, which *bit* of the Dolomites he was going to? I mean, did anyone take the trouble to actually ask?’ David Jardine pushed his thick hair off his forehead and waited for an answer.

‘I do not’, replied Heather patiently, ‘have anything to do with Clerical Seventeen. It’s not my fault if they don’t observe operational procedures, and why should they? Actually. They hardly need to be instantly contactable if the fertilizer hits the air conditioning.’

‘James Gant was Edith’s favourite nephew and he was fond of her too. He’s not a bad young man, so be a sport, Heather . . .’ His P.A. frowned, for she hated what she called ‘southern British patronizing’. ‘And do your level best to find him. He’s somewhere in the Dolomites, apparently. Climbing. Use our Dolomite out-station.’

‘We don’t have a Dolomite out-station.’

‘Well, I don’t know. Use the nearest one. Milan. Venice. Use your loaf.’

‘You don’t know where the Dolomites are.’ It suddenly dawned on his Scottish P.A.

‘Don’t be damned silly, of course I do.’

‘If I bring a map in here, a world atlas, I bet you can’t put your finger on them. Without cheating.’

‘Come on, come on. We don’t have time for this.’

‘I’m just amazed, that’s all. Here we are, Director of Operations in MI 6 and you don’t know . . . precisely . . . which major Italian city is closest to the Dolomites.’

Silence.

‘Heather, I’m not actually in the mood. Just find James Gant and tell him his auntie’s funeral is on Wednesday.’

His secretary shrugged and went to the door to her outer office, then paused and enquired, ‘Why not use Ronnie? He probably has illegals disguised as . . . mountain goats.’

Jardine finally grinned. ‘It’s not *that* important,’ he said.

It was not a statement Heather would let him forget.

Zina Farouche kept calm. Her heart was racing but she forced herself to think and act coolly. The cryptic message, from an internal hotel phone – which by-passed wire-taps – had been simple. 'Those flowers have started to die. Would you like to cancel the order?'

As code-speak went, it was pretty transparent. We have fatalities, it said, do we abort and save our skins?

Shit, shit, shit, shit. This is not thinking clearly, Zina berated herself. With steady hands, she lifted her purse and her radio handset. She smiled to her Tunisian colleague. 'I need some fresh air, Muhammad, call if you need me.'

'*Aiwa*,' he replied, not looking up from the liaison schedule the DSS had sent over. Thirty-six pages of it.

Zina took the elevator to the twenty-fourth floor and walked along the corridor, deserted except for a Latin American housekeeper using a noisy vacuum cleaner. She stopped at Room 2416 and knocked. A very frightened Mustafa Sharik opened the door.

Inside, they went over to the window, which Sharik had opened wide. Traffic noise from the streets below drifted up. A helicopter droned past, a couple of hundred feet above them. Sharik had also turned the TV set on quite loud, so they could probably talk without fear of eavesdroppers.

Zina Farouche leaned out and gazed down at the rooftops and windows of other buildings. Room 2416 was at the back of the hotel.

Sharik joined her, clearly shaken. So the subway mugging went bad, Zina thought. OK, it could be worse. She thanked God she had insisted on using three black Islamic Americans from the support cell, who could in no way be linked to her own hit-team.

'Khaled is dead,' announced Sharik.

And this was where Zina Farouche's painstaking mission began to fall apart. Her belly turned to cobwebs as she heard how the English target had taken on his attackers and killed all three in a matter of a few seconds.

'You should have seen him. Like Bruce Willis in *Die Hard*, the first one.'

'What the hell are you talking about?' demanded Zina. She had been chained in a pit in the Libyan desert while that movie was doing the rounds.

'Then Niknam steps out from behind a pillar.'

'You're joking.' Zina knew what was coming and anger at the dumb youth won over dawning panic.

'He said something, I was on the stairs, getting out of it like everyone else, Zina. I could not make out the words. Then Henry' – they had codenamed Gant, Henry – 'suddenly has a big Sig in his hands and they are trading bullets.'

This can't be happening, she told herself, the leering faces of her desert tormentors suddenly looming in her mind.

Mustafa Sharik told her how 'Henry' had killed Khaled Niknam and he, Mustafa, had escaped up the stairway and out into Queens, along with a couple of dozen other terrified subway travellers.

Zina Farouche took deep breaths; think calmly, be a leader, you have survived worse, she told herself. Khaled is dead because he disobeyed his orders, he cannot be linked to the rest of us. After a few moments she laid a hand on Sharik's arm.

'Find out how many are gathered at Beauregard today. We can hit them tonight. It was always a flexible plan . . .'

Mustafa Sharik looked away. He bit the back of his thumb, something he did when upset.

'It gets worse. Ben too is dead,' he finally said. 'Throat cut.' He glanced at his watch. 'Nine minutes ago, just outside here, in Sixth Avenue. And you know who was there, when I looked back?'

'The Englishman . . .' she breathed.

'Oh, he was there. But so was someone else.'

From the open window, Zina could see office workers, like tiny, safe ants, in the many rectangles of windows on buildings nearby.

'Who?'

'Morteza Azmoudeh.'

The geometric shapes of buildings and rooftops rippled, as if in a haze. Zina Farouche clutched at the window sill. Betrayed. She had been betrayed. And Tehran had sent its people after her.

Did Abu Nidal know? Had this always been the plan? Or was Tehran out to embarrass Fatah – The Revolutionary Council.

Either way, Morteza's goons made Zina Farouche's assassination squad look like amateurs. She glanced back into the room, at the door, fearful. For, once Morteza had been activated, he did not stop until he had done his awful work.

'Do you believe in God, Mustafa?' she asked, quietly.

'Of course. God is great and there is no God but He.'

She nodded, and smiled, sadly. 'That is good. Because, *mojahed*, I think we will very soon be with Him.'

And at that moment, the desperately angry and apprehensive girl received a lesson, a reminder about who she was, and why she had embraced the life she had.

'I am a soldier of God,' said Mustafa Sharik, calmly and simply. 'I believe in His plan. I would not have killed so many times if I did not know that was His will. Whatever is to happen, it is the will of Allah the Merciful. You are my sister and my brother.' He stepped into the room, switched off the noise of some obscene quiz show and with dignity and simplicity, knelt and prostrated himself towards Mecca, bowing his head several times on the rug and murmuring words from the Koran.

Then Mustafa Sharik climbed to his feet, calm and controlled. 'We must warn the others,' he said.

The little seamen's chapel in Narrow Street, in London's Limehouse, where in the early part of the century Chinese stowaways from the ships that unloaded in the Isle of Dogs waterfront had teemed and set up a whole community, with tailors and laundries, and little restaurants, was an oasis of quiet.

David Jardine knelt in a narrow pew, near the table of burning candles, and, head bowed, communed with his Maker.

Somewhere, the murmured voices of penitent and confessor made the profound silence more human.

Dear Lord, prayed Jardine – too chastened for flippantries – I am such a sinner that I could not blame you for not answering this call. But I need you.

My beloved wife, whom I have betrayed in the flesh but never, ever, with my heart, has left me. Serves me right, but this is really my first and most important supplication . . . please put us both together again.

Quite frankly, life is not much fun without her. Even the illicit fun is not much fun because it's no longer illicit. Yes, I do know I chose my path but really I am asking for a tiny miracle, sir. Please send her back.

(What a wimp, he thought to himself. But God knew he meant it.)

Next, about Kate. Now, listen, Lord, she's a beautiful young woman and you know I am flattered by her . . . affection. But she really could get very hurt being involved with this servant of yours, so I suppose, what I'm saying, praying, is, give me the strength to deny her charms, and her warmth. She deserves better.

(A wimp *and* a hypocrite, he reflected, you're doing well today, Jardine.)

Now, dear Lord, you know all about Dante and the Connecticut business. I have made a cold, logical case, convincing myself and Richard of the benefits – namely the net saving of many human lives, in the long term – of sitting back (masterly inactivity, we call it), and allowing the planned Beauregard act of terror to go ahead.

That has been my advice to my betters, and they are ready to accept it, and yet . . . I have searched my heart, and I do not think, actually, old sport, that I can live with it. So, unless you can give me some quite dramatic sign . . . I'm going to have to warn the Yanks.

There. When he had knelt down to pray, David Jardine had not known he was about to admit that, despite all the human tragedy he had seen in his years with the service, all the ruthless and sometimes bloody decisions he had midwifed, the deliberate murder of around eighteen men, women and infants at Beauregard was not something he could, at the eleventh hour, permit.

With that understanding, a great peace came over him. And, as he gazed up at the wooden carving of Jesus on the Cross, a broad beam of light fell across it.

A shadow moved, on the statue. Jardine turned and saw that the light came from the doors to Narrow Street.

One was ajar, and a stocky man, with a gap where his false tooth was absent, was moving quietly towards him. He carried a brown envelope and genuflected, crossing himself like the good Hungarian Catholic he was, as he reached the pews where his boss was kneeling.

Ronnie Szabodo sat on the pew and bowed his head, gazing around to ensure they were alone.

'You have to see this,' he said, head still bowed, rested on one gnarled fist. He passed the envelope to Jardine. 'It comes from Albatross.'

Albatross was the codename for David Jardine's most prized asset, deep inside the Abu Nidal terror network. Even Ronnie did not know the identity of the source.

'And where was this?' enquired Jardine, easing himself onto the pew.

'New York. Sigmund Three answered a routine chalk mark. Dead drop in Mid-Town. It took a few days because Roly didn't think it was urgent . . .'

Sigmund was the firm's New York outstation. Roly Benedict was the local boss. It was Roly, a good operator, who had been servicing Muar Abbas, prior to the man turning up in that freezer.

Jardine slowly gazed around. The confessional was still occupied, he could hear muted voices. He gently tugged out the contents of the envelope. And there was a one-page note from his secret asset, and four grainy, poorly focused surveillance photographs of James Gant.

Jardine scratched his nose and, glancing way past the wooden figure to the arched eaves of the centuries-old vaulted ceiling, he murmured something Ronnie could not catch, except for the last word, which was 'Amen'.

'What?' asked Szabodo.

'I said, so he's not in the Dolomites.'

'He's in New York. Playing silly buggers.'

'Oh, wonderful.' David Jardine climbed to his feet and, as he started towards the door, he looked back at the candles. 'As signs go, you could have picked something mildly less . . . catastrophic,' he said, quietly, for he suddenly understood that his famous antennae, his legendary bloody sixth sense, had totally missed the warning signs when James Gant had stormed into his office declaring the firm could not just sit on its hands and allow the Dante atrocity to happen.

'Not with you, old boy.'

'Outside,' replied Jardine and walked on, deep in thought.

In Narrow Street, one of Ronnie's perks from the Brixton car-repair and stereo shop was parked, down the street from the church. It was a dark green 1978 Porsche 911.

'Ronnie,' Jardine tapped the brown envelope, as they moved towards the Porsche, 'I want every single officer who has ever been in contact with this young man to be interviewed in the course of the next ten hours. Get hold of Kate, activate her Security Section, work together with her. And, Ronnie . . .'

Szabodo nodded, 'Sure, maximum hush.'

The last thing either David Jardine or Renfield Szabodo wanted was for it to become common knowledge that the one career officer they personally had recruited, in recent years, appeared to have lost his senses . . . at the very best analysis.

James Gant sat in a cheap movie house, near Gramercy Park, one of about ten people in the almost empty place. He was in the back row, near the left aisle, where he could watch the doors, and everyone else in the darkened auditorium.

At least here he had a breathing space. Time to work out what the hell was happening. What mistakes he had made, for such mayhem, such deadly confusion to have wrecked his plans.

On the screen was a poor-quality print of *Blade Runner – The Director's Cut*. And the sombre, surreal, doomed drama, interspersed with violence and menace, reflected Gant's mood.

It was not lost on him that he had first seen the movie just one day before that fateful evening-meeting with 'Fred Estergomy' and his fake niece. His very last day in Wonderland, as it had turned out.

The bloody murder of Ben Turabi had left him deeply shocked, in a way that the fight with those four muggers had not. Then, he had been motivated to survive, and using his training and his weapons had come naturally to him. But, at the end of the day, he had crossed the Rubicon. He had taken lives. He was no longer the man behind the lens.

Every millisecond of the killing – the tall man shunting into Turabi, the instinctive movement of passers-by away from the so-brief incident, the crimson gash, pouring blood, the terrified eyes of the man, dying even as he staggered on the sidewalk, hands spread in confusion – played and replayed through his mind.

Could coincidence be such that two completely random acts of casual brutality had touched him within the space of an hour?

I don't think so, he decided. And he shrugged off the memory of Ben Turabi's death to concentrate on the Queen's subway attack.

Three black muggers. One . . . let's face it, Middle-Eastern type. Prepared to kill him. That had been no mugging. The knife was coming straight at his chest when he had thrown himself and the guy holding him down the stairs.

And the fourth assailant – the one who had stepped out from behind the platform pillar – he had quite simply tried to shoot Gant.

So who would want to murder him?

James's mind raced.

Maybe the Firm had cottoned on to him. Would SIS sanction the murder of one of their officers, because he had gone over the side, targeting on his own initiative a terrorist gang?

Gant just did not know. Nothing in his eight months' experience of the outfit suggested such extreme sanctions, in fact he had been mildly disappointed at how reluctant his service was, in the real world, to get involved in anything remotely aggressive.

We like a quiet life, laddie, Euan Stevenson had said, time and again; our work is watching, listening, filing reports, guessing the future. James Bond would not have lasted ten seconds in the real world of intelligence.

So who else would be aware of him? Who else would have benefited from his death?

Gant flushed at the realization he might have come to the notice of Zina Farouche and her Dante group. What a turkey that would make him. Of course they must have back-up cells, unseen watchers on the sidelines, protecting their security, he had been aware of that. Taken every precaution he had learned.

It had just not occurred to him they might be better at it than he was.

'*Do you truly understand*', enquired a sinister character on the big screen, '*what it is you have done . . .?*'

Oh, yes, thought Gant, it's just hitting me.

'*Have you any concept of the meaning of real fear? Of terror?*' the voice went on.

Gant almost nodded, sitting there in the darkness.

Now the game was no longer a game. No longer a ridiculous indulgence. Will I kill them? Will I not? What an absurdity. Had he really been so dumb as to imagine those professional international political killers, with tens of millions of dollars funding them, could have been vulnerable to a new kid on the block?

He was perspiring. Oh, yes, James Gant finally knew the meaning of real fear all right. He truly did.

Who was that slipping in the door near the screen?

A bag person. Looking for someplace to rest.

Or was it?

Heart thumping, the would-be avenger, the Walter Mitty scourge of terrorism, cowered in his cinema seat.

It was not lost on Gant that he had run to the dark womb of a movie theatre, the land of make-believe, when the shit hit the fan.

An hour later, he was still there, watching the sad, almost Wagnerian drama unfold on the screen.

What was he to do?

Make a run for home? Slip back into Clerical 17 and hope that no one would ever find out what a dangerous idiot he had been?

Jesus, just think of the horror story if it came out that a serving SIS officer had been running around New York City during the UN Assembly, armed to the teeth, committed to murder on American soil.

Then, slowly, Gant began to smile. His racing pulse subsided. All it took was a gunfight and a near beheading to bring you back to reality, he thought to himself.

Well, you had better sort this out. Start thinking, boy. How do we salvage something from this . . . catastrophe?

And gradually, as the flickering fantasy on the screen unfolded, he worked out a sort of plan.

And even at Ryemarsh, in the months to come, it was grudgingly agreed, the boy had finally begun to think like a man . . .

'I'm afraid the place is a bit of a mess.' Charlotte Gant arched her neck to glance up at David Jardine who, at six feet three inches, towered above her. After examining him, in friendly fashion, she smiled and led the way into the sitting room.

'I never get time to tidy up,' sympathized Jardine. 'This is a model of good housekeeping compared to my place.' He noted the framed photo of a young RAF pilot in flying rig, standing grinning beneath a Harrier jet fighter. There was an ironing board with a man's blue striped shirt from Hawes & Curtis in Jermyn Street, half-ironed, and a pile of other things for the same treatment. A can of Coke was on the mantelpiece and the television set was on, mute, with a programme about round-the-world yacht racing.

It was something David Jardine had wanted to watch, that evening, instead of trailing round James Gant's nearest and dearest, trying to get the measure of the young man and to figure out just what the hell he might be playing at, in New York City, sleuthing around one of the most dangerous, and experienced, terrorist gangs in existence.

The Harrier fighter was camouflaged in desert colours and, as Jardine peered at it, he said, 'Was this Desert Storm?'

Charlotte nodded and moved a neat pile of laundered and ironed shirts and things, clearing a place for her visitor to sit down. He had telephoned just twenty minutes before and said he worked with James, in the Foreign Office, and he had to do this boring, routine enquiry, for Personnel.

Like many well brought up young ladies, who moved in Tudor Hall and City banking circles, Charlotte knew all about the Positive Vetting system, whereby certain people in the military, or in government employ had to be investigated and found to be fit to handle Top Secret information. So the visit by someone from James's office was no surprise.

'Would you like something? Cup of tea? A beer?'

'I would love a beer, if you've got one to spare . . .' Jardine smiled and sat down on the rust coloured, heavy linen covered sofa. Tulley's, he thought to himself. Tulley's three-seater. Every young persons' flat within a three mile radius of the Fulham Road seemed to get its solid, long-lasting heavy furniture from Tulley's.

'It's Rolling Rock,' came Charlotte's voice from the kitchen, 'or one of those cans of draught that give you a real head.'

'Rolling Rock will be fine,' replied Jardine to the open doorway.

The sitting room was comfortable and only superficially untidy. It was furnished in relaxed, easy going good taste.

'Who's the pilot?' he enquired when Charlotte came back in, carrying the bottle and a tall glass which she had probably forgotten to hand back to some pub or other.

'Hugo.' She lifted the can of Coke from the mantelpiece and curled up on the other couch, lowering her head slightly and watching him from under a fringe of hair, which she flicked away, like a neat little suntanned pony.

'And is it Hugo who has such good taste in shirts?' Jardine inclined his gaze to the neat pile of ironing, and tilted some beer into his purloined glass.

'Do you know, I could kill him. He spent two hundred and sixty pounds on five shirts. The week before we went on holiday . . .'

'Go anywhere nice?'

'Corsica. Propriano.'

Ah, Propriano. Twenty-two years before, a young David Jardine had strangled a man in Propriano, on the verandah of a rented villa, looking down over the sheltered bay. A Moscow hood by the name of Grishov, in the good old days when everyone knew who the enemy was, and who your friends were.

'Wonderful sunsets, as I recall . . .' he said, politely.

'Absolute heaven.' And she told Jardine about Hugo and losing his eye and leaving the Royal Air Force, and just recently qualifying as a barrister. The way she told him showed a quiet trust that any colleague of her brother's must be OK, and it also was very clear that she loved this Hugo, which made him a very lucky chap, for Charlotte Gant was a quietly desirable young woman. Not so much a classic beauty, more . . . unattainable tomboy, with just a suggestion of controlled abandon, for the chosen few.

'I'm terribly sorry about Edith,' said Jardine. 'She was a real friend to me, when I was about your age.'

'That's where I've seen you before.' Charlotte pointed her Coke can at him.

'Where?'

'Coming out of King Edward's hospital. About a week ago. A week last Monday.'

She's right, he realized. 'Yes, I was there then.'

Silence.

'I don't think she suffered,' Jardine suggested, as, on the television screen, a sleek ocean yacht rose and fell, battered by huge seas off Cape Horn.

'James was closer to Edith, in a way, than I was. I think, not to be unkind, I think she became more . . . animated, in the company of men.'

Spot on, agreed Jardine. 'She thought you and your brother got on well; that pleased her. After your mother died.'

Just for a millisecond, a whisper of . . . guilt? – the merest shadow – touched her pretty face before the sun came back.

'We're like, um . . . sister and brother.' She smiled and her pale, gray-blue eyes flashed as they met his.

'Has James told you what he does, with the Foreign Office?'

'Dull as shit, he says. Oh, sorry, that can't be a great help.'

Jardine laughed. 'Actually, it is a great help. But what does he do there? Has he explained?'

'Boring PR, he says. Very close, old James. He never tells anyone anything.' Except that he loves me, she comforted herself, masking her secret with a frank gaze, and feeling that longing in her loins.

'Whereabouts has he gone, actually,' enquired Jardine, 'for this climbing holiday?'

Charlotte shrugged. 'Italy someplace. I wanted him to take me, but he said he needed some space.'

She doesn't know a thing, decided Jardine. 'Is he ever, does he ever do anything . . . rash? Take enormous risks that would otherwise be totally out of character?'

Only the one, mused Charlotte.

'He's quite brave,' she replied. 'He's been to Bosnia. Colombia. All that macho stuff . . . but how do you mean, rash?'

'Say . . . a fight starts in a bar, two guys gang up on one, or big guy, small man. You know the sort of thing. Would he jump over a table and wade in?'

Charlotte grinned. 'I think we must drink in totally different social circles, Mister Jardine.' She screwed up her face and thought for a moment. 'I suppose the answer is . . . yes. And no.'

Jardine waited, interested to note – not because he was a sad case of arrested development, but because there was very little he did not notice, when he was at work – that the girl's nipples had become prominent, under her white shirt. Was it the talk of violence? Or was there a cool draught, perhaps, from the open window? Or did she find him attractive?

None of these reasons seemed appropriate and he continued to study the label on his bottle of beer.

'Yes,' went on Charlotte, 'if there was no alternative. And no, because he really would not want to . . . wade in, if he could possibly avoid it. But if no one else looked like doing a blind thing about it . . .? Then he wouldn't flinch.' She smiled quietly, and added, 'He's really very physical. And Jimmy has never been one to stand by and let shit happen. Beneath the surface, there is something quite . . . dangerous, about my brother.'

Which was precisely what David Jardine had not wanted to hear.

Hanna was changing safe-houses twice a day. Some of the people she was staying with were Abu Nidal sympathisers, others acquaintances she had made over the years in Paris, London and New York, who would have been horrified to learn that they were harbouring an international terrorist.

She kept away from the organization's deep-cover support cells, unless she needed to communicate some instruction, for she was using her time in the city to check on the several other assignments the network of sleepers had been tasked with, and to fine-tune their general efficiency.

Zina Farouche had a phone-pager number to ring in case of emergency. It was this number she had used, with the bed and a heavy dresser pushed against the door of Room 2416, to raise her commander. After forty-five long minutes, a reply had reached her own pager. Deciphered, it specified the location where Hanna al-Farah would be in three hours' time.

Once Zina had left the claustrophobic hotel room – where Mustafa, unbelievably, had suggested sex, since their time on this earth was probably limited – she had taken an elevator directly to the second floor and used a house phone to call her colleagues with the Tunisian security team, to say she would be out all day, busy in discussions with the American police and State Department officials.

Next, she had descended to the lobby and walked straight out, getting into a cab which had just deposited two large-backsided folk, festooned with camcorders and plastic bags of tourist T-shirts, from out of town.

She had forced herself to go through a painstaking 'dry-cleaning' journey before reaching Hanna's current safe haven, a ninth floor apartment on Riverside Drive, not far from the Baptist Church, overlooking the Hudson River.

Hanna had the door open as the Palestinian girl reached it, half-way along a silent, plush carpeted corridor with Art Deco lighting.

She did not speak until they were both inside. It was a big apartment, with spacious rooms and it had been decorated, although not, Zina felt, recently, in slightly over-rich good taste. She herself preferred plain whites, dark, rich woods and rugs and furniture which reflected her Middle-Eastern background.

This place was more European. Good antique furniture, much of it bigger than the average apartment might accommodate, but perhaps the sort of thing a movie-set designer would provide, or a realty developer would put into a show-apartment, for photography in *New York Living*, or *Vogue* magazine.

Hanna al-Farah treble-locked the heavy door and led Zina through the open-plan entrance hall to the sitting room with its wide picture window and a breathtaking panorama of the Hudson, the treetops of the park immediately below and on the far bank, the waterfront at Cliffside and Edgewater.

'Are you all right?' asked Hanna, concerned.

'I'm fine. Khaled is dead. Also Mustafa.'

Hanna al-Farah leaned against a rosewood table, gleaming with the patina of age and care. She waited, with not the merest trace of alarm or surprise.

Zina Farouche went on to relate the details of both men's deaths, along with the Englishman's shooting of the three 'muggers'.

Hanna listened, not interrupting, until the younger woman had finished. 'And this Englishman was also present when Mustafa was killed . . .?' she asked.

Zina nodded. There were paintings by Chagall and Joan Miró on the green and ochre-patterned walls. Somebody had ruined this flat. The rugs were no doubt priceless, but they were of extravagant Chinese silk, such as vulgarly wealthy Saudi businessmen cluttered their marble floors with.

The work of North Africa's Berber hill people cost a hundredth of the price and exuded serenity and memories of home. That was what Zina Farouche would have put into an apartment like this.

'Did he do the work?' Hanna meant, had Gant slashed Ben Turabi's throat.

'Mustafa says no. But,' Zina had kept the worst news to the last, 'you know a Tehran enforcer called Morteza Azmoudeh?'

'I have always tried to avoid him. He enjoys doing things with a chainsaw.'

'He was there, watching. Too far away, Mustafa says, to have done the killing.'

'He prefers to have someone else do that sort of thing. Who else, what else, did Mustafa notice?'

'The Englishman was getting out of the way, even while everyone was in shock. And he was carrying a raincoat, which could have hidden a weapon . . . are these Chagall's or reproductions?'

Hanna glanced at the paintings dismissively. 'Whatever the Englishman's role is in this, the principal threat is from Morteza; he is a Savama man first and last. If he had anything to do with killing Ben Turabi, there is no room for doubt that was on Tehran's orders.'

'And Khaled . . .?'

'Khaled was different, child. The Englishman killed defending his own life. He could have had no idea, at the moment he was attacked, who was behind it.' Hanna paused. 'Khaled Niknam made an error of judgement. He should have faded from the scene and reported what was, after all, a minor embarrassment which could not have been traced to you.' She looked away. 'They are probably fakes; this place belongs to a bit of a charlatan.'

You, Zina noticed, not *us*.

Hanna al-Farah frowned, taking a long Marlboro filter from a silver box on the table, 'Could the Englishman be Iranian? Maybe he speaks with an accent because he went to school there. It's quite common.'

Zina shook her head. 'He is British. Maybe Irish. Maybe even Israeli. And I have seen some *paisas* from Antioquía in Colombia with the same complexion and features. But Iranian . . .? I don't think so.'

The truth was, although the Abu Nidal Group had made its peace with the Iranians and co-operated in joint training and undertook deniable missions, like the Connecticut job, Fatah were Palestinian Arabs and there was little love lost between them and the mullahs of Tehran, who had a singularly monocular vision of an Islamic Fundamentalist world dominated by them. What Zina Farouche was saying was that she could tell an Iranian spook a mile away and 'Henry' was not one of them.

'Do you sleep here?' enquired the young woman, gazing around. 'It really is not as . . . perfect as your usual places.'

'It belongs to a friend, whom I trust. Zina, you understand I will have to seek guidance . . .'

Zina sighed. Guidance entailed breaking the golden rule not to communicate with Abu Nidal's Special Missions Directorate. It would almost inevitably lead to the mission being called off, and her own execution.

Her blood chilled as it suddenly occurred to her that they might suspect her, Zina Farouche, of betraying them to the mullahs.

'Are you OK?' Hanna asked, concerned. 'Let me get you something.'

She helped Zina to a couch and sat her down. Then opened

a Chinese lacquer dresser to reveal a mirrored drinks cabinet. Hanna poured two glasses of cold milk from the cold compartment and, as she returned to sit with her protégée, asked, 'Have you warned the others?'

Zina said she had. The particular order she had given had confined Zafir Hammuda and Noor Jalud to their own diplomatic missions, Algerian and Kuwaiti respectively, where they would be safer.

Hanna al-Farah sat deep in thought, for several minutes.

Zina flicked through a September copy of *Vogue* on the chunky glass coffee table, feeling nervous and confused. Ever since her rehabilitation, at the tender hands of Hanna, her placement in the Tunisian Embassy in Paris and her efficient recruiting of the assassination team, she had grown in confidence and had been in total control.

The Biarritz rehearsal had gone so well. Hanna had even told her Abu Nidal himself had expressed approval. And now, everything was collapsing around her ears.

The mistake was, she knew, but was wise enough never to have expressed it, that the absolute terror of being returned to the interrogators of Station 16, in the Libyan desert, motivated team leaders like her to press on with a task which any sensible operator would have abandoned at the first sign of discovery.

Finally, Hanna al-Farah asked, 'Reduced to four, do you still have the capability of proceeding?'

Relief flooded Zina's heart. 'I believe we could accomplish the operation with two, provided one is Zafir, for he is like ten men when the blood is up.'

Hanna nodded. She smiled and laid a comforting hand on the beautiful girl's arm. 'Then go about your cover work as normal. These are dangerous times but we thrive on that. Just think of New York as Beirut and focus on the mission, Abu Nidal himself has big plans for your future, Zina. I shall activate a support cell here in New York to provide cover for you and . . . discourage Morteza Azmoudeh and his goons. It will be difficult, but you must strike at Beauregard at the first opportunity. The Egyptian and his family arrive there tomorrow around noon. Do this thing and you will be a hero in the eyes of Abu Nidal and of the Sisters of Islam.'

Zina Farouche sipped her milk, like an obedient child, and examined Hanna's face, reading her expression. It was clear the older woman cared for her. Zina was quietly thrilled to hear al-Farah mention the most secret of Islamic womanhood's movements: the Sisters of Islam existed, deeply underground, to support each other in a largely male-dominated society.

Hanna touched Zina's smooth, olive-complexioned cheek. 'And if the worst happens . . . if we lose each other, you will be a martyr of God and of Islamic womanhood. Poems will be written, and songs sung in the souk, for centuries to come. Portraits of Zina Farouche will be carried in religious processions and will hang in Jerusalem, when we have won it back.'

The young woman trembled slightly. She knew that martyrdom was preferable to failure. She shuddered inside at the prospect of a return to that foul desert torture camp. And Zina Farouche smiled slightly, bravely, and met Hanna's gaze. 'Thank you for giving me the option,' she said.

Hanna al-Farah clasped the young woman's hand. 'Try not to contact me until it is all over, child.' She kissed Zina softly on the forehead. 'I will see you in Khartoum.'

And Zina Farouche, being the survivor she was, even in that apartment which seemed so . . . foreign to the Hanna she knew, moved her face so that their mouths were close, and moved her hand gently along the inside of her commander's silky thigh. 'Remember me like this . . .' she whispered.

14

Dropping Betty

Three-ten in the morning. The hunt was on to locate and interview every single person in the secret world who had come into contact with James Sebastian Gant. Two senior officers of SIS sat in an almost vintage Porsche, colour slate green, in the shadow between two lampposts. The tall, space-age column that was the Post Office Tower reached into a wind-blown sky, where scruffy, rain-filled clouds bustled under a pale, highwayman's moon.

'So how do you feel about him . . . Gant?' asked Ronnie Szabodo as he offered his slim, round hip-flask to the office's Director of Security, first unscrewing the cap with courtly delicacy.

'I'm confused. He seems everyone's idea of a really able, quiet, reserved, observant, pleasant guy,' replied Kate Howard, accepting the vessel, burnished with use from countless surveillance operations, investigations and other, less legal, occasions. She held it suspiciously, sniffing at the neck. They were both close to exhaustion, having started fourteen hours earlier to interview, as Jardine had ordered, 'every single person in the Firm who has had even the remotest contact with Gant.'

'That's what they said about Kim Philby,' the Hungarian remarked as he fitted a Krook-Lok bar to the steering wheel of the green Porsche.

'Are you suggesting Gant is two-timing us? What is this?'

'Hungarian Eau de Vie,' Szabodo announced blandly and tugging a slender tape recorder from his tweed sports coat checked that it was in working order. 'No. I have a horrible feeling he has jumped on his Don Quixote horse and gone off to smite Dante all on his ownsome.'

'Moonshine, more likely.' She sniffed at the neck of the silver container.

Szabodo smiled, revealing the gap in his front teeth, and, replacing the tape recorder, produced a thin black leather notebook. 'It might be.' He turned a few pages and peered in the gloom. 'Three-o-eight. Leviathan. It says here.'

Kate shrugged and took a swig.

'God almighty,' she croaked.

'Keeps the cold out. Ronceval.'

'What?' Kate's eyes were nipping with fatigue.

'The horse. It was called Ronceval.' He took the flask back and poured some of the liquor down his throat. Then he screwed the top back on and asked, 'All set . . .?'

'Poor woman, it's ten past three in the morning. I mean, Ronnie, it's a fairly routine enquiry.'

'But urgent. Plus she should be at home; don't you just hate calling when they are out?' The Hungarian leaned across and unlocked the passenger door for her, then shouldered his own open and heaved himself out.

The apartment was on the third floor of a serviced block. It had been child's play for Ronnie to bypass the front-door security system. The carpeted common parts suggested a quietly well-run property for middling professional people. There had been a lingering smell of last night's curry, when they had come out of the elevator.

Outside Apartment 308, they rang the doorbell four times, each one longer than the time before, at thirty-second intervals.

'Maybe she's not in,' Kate suggested.

Ronnie shook his head. 'No, somebody's there. Can't you hear?'

And Kate, who wanted nothing more than to be a field operative, out there doing spying things, shook her head, and listened more intently. She was still doing that when the door was opened a few inches, held on a chain.

The plump, pink face of Angeline Moresby-Thomas appeared in the crack.

'Yes . . .?'

'Sorry to bother you so late,' whispered Kate Howard. 'Are

you Angeline?'

'Who are you?'

'We're from the Office. Can we come in?'

'What office?'

'The one that pays your wages.' Ronnie Szabodo beamed a disarming smile. 'We just need the answers to one or two questions.'

'ID,' the pink face demanded, at the same time alarmed and groggy with sleep.

Kate produced her blue card, the Service's identification document. It had her photo on one corner, and certain diagonal stripes which were the Firm's mark. It was in laminated plastic, inside a small leather wallet.

Angeline undid the chain lock and opened the door.

The sitting room was quite small, with a rectangular window overlooking a communal garden square, and a glimpse of the Post Office Tower, beyond the rooftops.

'Is this Marylebone?' enquired Kate, gazing out at the limited skyline, 'or Bloomsbury.'

'Bloomsbury,' replied Angeline, re-tying her ankle-length Chinese silk robe. She glanced at her gold Rolex and blinked, as if unable to believe what it told her.

'Angeline, I'm really sorry to burst in on you so late,' went on Kate, 'and without calling. Can we sit down . . .?'

Angeline looked sharply at her, then at Ronnie. She motioned with one hand, as if distracted. 'Why not? Now that you're here. Can I, um, offer you something . . .?'

Szabodo chose a corner of a Scandinavian three-seater sofa in white wood and green, rib-patterned calico-type cloth.

Kate could not help noticing a few small grey stains on the unoccupied centre cushion. And at the same time she felt tacky for noticing, and disapproving that the plump woman had not bothered to clean it up.

She perched herself on a high-backed leather chair, beside a modern teak writing-bureau which came, she recognised, from the Conran shop in Sloane Avenue. It had been labelled £3,200 two summers ago. Kate remembered that, because she had liked it, but had not been able to afford it.

'So,' said Ronnie, whose cool professionalism in their eleven previous calls, starting at one in the afternoon, had been quite instructive, even to Kate, with all her experience, 'can you guess why we're here?'

Angeline's pink face reddened. 'Absolutely not. I haven't the slightest idea.'

'It concerns Clerical Seventeen, Miss Moresby-Thomas,' said Kate. 'Does that help?'

The woman shook her head. It occurred to Kate that a man might be responsible for those stains. Yeugh.

And almost immediately she wondered if he might be in the flat, lying in bed, in a room along the dark corridor, behind Angeline. Listening, anxious. Perhaps a stranger, someone from Wonderland who should not be privy to this . . . interview.

'Are you alone?' she enquired, smiling to convey, Listen, we're all human, it's OK.

'What do you mean?' Angeline's face went from scarlet to death-bed white in an instant.

'If you are not, please tell us,' said Szabodo, not in the slightest bit pleasantly. 'This is a matter of Security, Miss Thomas. Katherine here is our Director . . .'

For a long time, perhaps a full minute, Angeline sat silently. You could see her heartbeat thumping too rapidly against her chest, between the now somehow sad globes, which had seen some fun in their time.

Kate was about to say something but she caught the sudden urgency in Ronnie's warning glance, and kept her mouth firmly shut.

Finally Angeline said, very softly, 'Have you been following him . . .?'

Szabodo almost lifted a hand in warning but Kate was now in tune with the moment. Here was something awesome, a revelation, lurking, ready to . . . astonish them. So instead of saying, following who? Kate asked, softly, 'What do you think?'

And abruptly tears, unstoppable, rolled one after the other, down Angeline Moresby-Thomas's cheeks.

'I knew you would find out, one day,' she whispered. 'I knew it would end like this . . .'

Szabodo frowned, and when he spoke, his voice was barely audible. 'Is he armed . . .?' was all he said, and Kate Howard's blood stopped in her veins.

But Angeline blinked, angered, through her tears and replied. 'Of course he's not armed. Abdullah is a diplomat.' And she turned and looked towards the bedroom in its dark little corridor.

The stocky Hungarian, lighter on his feet than Kate would ever have imagined, was already off the couch and standing by the wall beside the open doorway. He had a .45 Glock automatic in his right hand, drawn from his left front as his left arm swept his jacket aside. Angeline started to climb to her feet but Kate moved across and, pushing her shoulder down, indicated the woman should keep quiet.

In just three seconds, Ronnie Szabodo had darted swiftly into the short corridor and, kicking open the left- hand door, had emerged, roughly shoving a lean, tanned man of Middle-Eastern appearance, who was wearing only boxer shorts with a Teddy Bear pattern and a pair of black nylon socks.

Szabodo had the man's right arm jammed hard up behind his back, using an aikido wrist and thumb lock, and the Glock's muzzle was pressed against the base of the prisoner's skull. He was muttering something, clearly insulting, in fluent and rapid Arabic

'I am a diplomat.' the man gasped, furious and afraid. 'You are in big trouble . . .'

Szabodo stopped and flipped his grip in such a way that the diplomat stumbled onto the floor and half knelt, half sat there, while the SIS man kept his gun aimed at him.

'Oh! Oh!' protested Angeline. 'There is no need for this!'

'Shut up.' Kate roughly hauled the plump, shaking woman to her feet and, pulling her hands behind her back, bound them with plastic handcuffing flex, tossed to her by the Hungarian. She never ceased to be amazed at the cornucopia of objects secreted in the pockets of that shapeless coat.

'Leave the lady alone, you will most certainly be the subject of an official complaint,' snarled the man called Abdullah, which, to Kate's mind, displayed a certain optimism of spirit, considering his predicament.

'I have awfully bad news for you, old sport,' said Szabodo, in his best Oxford voice, fractured by those Magyar consonants.

'You are Abdullah Gurafi Fadul. Second-in-charge of the Sudanese Intelligence Service in Europe, with special responsibility for political intelligence and counter-espionage. Your chances of being granted diplomatic immunity are rather slimmish. We are not the police, you do appreciate, my dear sir. We are the nasty people who take diplomats to some very damp and smelly cellars and beat the shit out of them. We are the people you meet, before you become just another missing person, in this lawless metropolis of ours . . .'

He stood over Abdullah's head and let the gun touch the man's ear, at the same time cocking the hammer with his thumb.

Angeline began to weep, her shoulders heaving under the silk robe.

'I demand to phone the Minister Plenipotentiary at the Embassy of the Sudan,' said the diplomat, markedly less aggressive. 'You are the Hungarian, Szabodo. And I heard you introduce your colleague. My own people will have observed you entering this building. If I do not walk out, unhampered, they will report precisely who, in the British Intelligence Service, is responsible. So put the gun away and let us face up to reality.'

Ronnie thought about this. He and Kate exchanged glances. Neither of them had really bothered to check out the area, before coming up to Apartment 308. So there easily might have been a back-up 'sentinel' team, watching Abdullah's back.

Kate was in a state of some shock. At first she had presumed Angeline had broken down and confessed to some tiresome affair with a minor Arab diplomat. Since her own field was Security of SIS business and personnel, and not counter-espionage like Ronnie's, she had never heard of Abdullah Fadul and she actually was wondering if perhaps Szabodo had got it wrong, when Angeline sniffed loudly, wiped her pink nose on a Chinese silk sleeve and, regaining a little composure, enquired meekly, 'What am I looking at? Fifteen to twenty years?' And added, 'Would it help if I made a statement?'

Paydirt!

Kate took a snow-white hanky from her bag and dabbed,

none too gently, the streaming tears from the face of Angeline Moresby-Thomas, the mole, the rat in the barrel, the rotten apple. 'I'm sure your co-operation will influence a judge and jury.'

Angeline considered this.

Once, Abdullah Fadul, who was watching her like a dog watching a half-empty plate, seemed about to say something, and from his expression it was not going to be words of encouragement. But Ronnie Szabodo knelt beside him and, holding Fadul's thick, black hair in one hand, caressed the skin between his eyes with the muzzle of the Glock.

Finally, Angeline declared, with prim simplicity, 'I wish to make a full statement, explaining how I became an agent of the Sudan Government's Directorate for Special Intelligence. I have been a fool. But I really am in love with this man, whose identity you clearly know.'

Szabodo spoke quietly into Fadul's ear and, all histrionics and bluster gone, the man nodded and turned to lie on his back, hands stretched above his head, knuckles touching the carpet, legs spread-eagled. Ronnie draped a cloth from a small table, over Fadul's face, to obstruct his vision, then he crossed to the telephone and, lifting the receiver, dialled a number.

'I'll need a street sweep, two laundry vans, a Special Branch DI and two females with the party,' he murmured, quietly, and replaced the receiver.

'Nothing to do now but wait,' he announced, sitting down on the green couch. And he smiled his cold, alligator's smile at Angeline. 'You will find it such relief, to get rid of your awful burden, my dear . . .'

And his sincerity was such, even Kate almost believed him.

On the eleventh floor of the US Mission to the United Nations building, on Second Avenue, across from the UN Plaza (built upon the former site of the old S & S Slaughter Houses), Al Wiscynsky, the real Harry Liebowitz, Tony Semprino and Joe Cleary sat in conference.

On the table in front of them were crime-scene photographs of the murdered Ben Turabi. In black and white, they seemed bleak and final, which was of course exactly right.

There were also typed-up reports by Wiscynsky and Cleary, along with snatched photographs of Morteza and Mahmoud Dashti, whom even the Agency officers were now calling Betty Boop, taken during the current surveillance operation.

The large, flat computerised screen on the wall of the room – Ops Room 4, Cleary had learned – with its detailed plan of Manhattan, had acquired all kinds of constantly updating information, including the time, the number and identity of agents working the R-36 surveillance routine, plus two bright pink dots positioning precisely the location of the two subjects, Morteza and Betty Boop.

After the killing they had moved, on foot, by taxi and subway, to different parts of the city, traversing the bridges and tunnels linking Manhattan Island to Queens and The Bronx. Classic 'dry cleaning' procedure, and carried out so well that the CIA teams had very nearly lost them a half dozen times.

Right now, the pink dots, and the blue and purple dots of the two R-36 teams, were not moving. Morteza had returned to the Patchin Street safe-house, which Harry Liebowitz had vetoed bugging from the inside, relying on the satellite Minerva electronic eavesdropping facility, which monitored telephone, radio and fax traffic to and from the place, in addition to picking up conversations from any room which had a telephone handset, a plugged-in radio or a TV set.

Minerva was only possible to detect with sophisticated equipment, and Minerva was programmed to switch off, the millisecond such a device was employed.

Thus far, Morteza had phoned or faxed nobody, but two men and a woman had visited the apartment. They had not spoken, inside, which suggested they communicated with the Tehran intelligence man by writing things down, or retreated to the bathroom, which was the one room out of range of Minerva's big ears.

This was a very professional operation Morteza was running and Harry Liebowitz had no wish to dissipate the watchers at his disposal by hiving off smaller teams to tail any of the three visitors.

Betty Boop had gone to ground in a cheap rooming house across the East River, in Queens. He had no phone, but there was a payphone in the lobby, where an unshaven man in his sixties doubled as concierge and receptionist.

This payphone was intercepted by a DSS team from a black windowed Toyota 4 × 4 parked in a nearby street.

'So. Joe. How do you see all this, from a cop's perspective?' asked Semprino.

Joe Cleary leaned his chair back, so that the two front legs were off the floor. He took a Winston cigarette from its pack and tapped it on the table, gazing at the photographs, the maps, the Crime Scene reports and the illuminated wall screen.

'How did the Moroccans react?' he said, 'When you told them the bad news. Did they seem surprised? Angry? Afraid . . .?'

'OK,' Al Wiscynsky answered, 'on his body, in a wallet in his back trouser pocket, was ID making him a cook with the Moroccan delegation to the UN General Assembly. I went, with your partner, Detective Vargos, to their office in the Essex Hotel and asked if they had a Monsieur Turabi, working as a cook. A . . .' he consulted his notes, 'Monsieur Abdel-Fateh, a Second Secretary with the Moroccan Ministry of Foreign Affairs, confirmed this. I told him a man with those credentials had been involved in an incident, a street-mugging perhaps, and would he please identify the cadaver.'

'Which he did at . . .' Cleary checked his own notes, 'ten after one, this afternoon. Police Pathology Morgue. Who was with him?'

'Detective Vargos.'

'And Sam reported the diplomat, this Second Secretary, was no more and no less shaken by the formality than anyone else being shown an employee with his gullet split wide open . . .' Joe nodded, then glanced back at the wall screen, as if trying to see beyond it, into the rooms where Betty Boop and Morteza were at that second.

'Just like that,' said Wiscynsky.

The Irish detective frowned. 'Well, from Homicide's point of view, we have a pro-killing, in broad daylight; we have a multiple ID of the perp for he did it while under serious CIA surveillance; and . . .' he spread his arms, cigarette still unlit, 'we are sitting on our fannies doing squat about it.'

Liebowitz and Semprino exchanged looks. 'Listen, Joe,' Tony Semprino leaned forward, 'gimme a break. This is being run from Washington. It is not fucking Watergate, we do intend to protect our foreign guests from these two killers, but, if we pull them in right now, how do we know there is not a fall-back position, where more targets are hit and we would be really in the fuckin' dark. Huh? Is that what you are beefing about?'

Joe Cleary smiled, he had seen it all before. These guys were just like the mayor's office. Vested interests beat natural justice any day. The Agency were more interested in finding out what Morteza was up to than saving lives.

'You asked how I saw it from a cop's perspective. The law-enforcement point of view. I told you. If you mean, what do I personally figure is going down here? That's different. We suspect Morteza tortured and killed one Iranian spook earlier this year and left him in a freezer in a restaurant in Tribeca. My homicide, incidentally. We believe he tortured and killed two Iranian secret agents on a yacht in the Mediterranean Sea, half-way across the world, a couple of months later. Not, I am happy to say, my problem.'

Joe flicked his Seal Zippo and lit the Winston, exhaling a cloud of blue smoke in the direction of a NO SMOKING sign, then gazed at each intelligence man in turn. 'And this was not unconnected with you and the British not sharing, and us trying to be real smart and steal their agents. And look what happened. Another triumph for Uncle Sam.'

Harry Liebowitz looked pained. Tony Semprino merely put on his we're-all-on-the-same-team act and said, 'Let's get to right now, Joe. In your police officer's opinion, where's the link between the earlier killings and today?' He pushed a photo of the murdered Ben Turabi across the table, towards Cleary. 'Where does this victim fit in?'

'This,' said Joe Cleary, 'is what they banged into my head at detective training school I should never do.'

'Which is what?' enquired Liebowitz, warily.

'Jump to conclusions. For myself, I don't think this guy was a spy – at least, not one known to you people. Just look at yourselves. You no longer understand Morteza's mission. Whereas before, it was open and shut. But this deceased cook? I don't think he was of any interest to the CIA at all. Prior to his somewhat dramatic demise.'

Harry Liebowitz shrugged, passing a hand in front of his face to get rid of a loitering stratum of cigarette haze. 'We had no interest in Ben Turabi. He's a stranger to us. Joe, you're right. His murder is a mystery.'

Cleary let his seat bump back to earth. 'Why don't we accept, just for argument, there is no connection?' he suggested. 'And assume Morteza is not here for anything to do with the earlier homicides, here or in Cyprus. This is one busy guy. It's hard work being a Tehran enforcer.' He waved the dwindling Winston at the CIA men. 'Morteza baby is here on a whole new mission. Fresh deck, gentlemen. Forget the past. And what is his task? We have no idea, it's a whole new ballgame . . . and right now, you don't have a ticket.'

At Beauregard, Annabel and Mike Curtis stood smiling on the porch of the sprawling, two-storey, Georgian-pillared colonial house, as two squat, dark-blue, darkened windowed Dodge 4 × 4s preceded a black Chrysler limo up the dirt track from the ferry road to the house. Another Dodge four-wheel-drive followed and, behind that, a smoke-blue DSS sedan with four more agents inside.

The Chrysler stopped at the four steps to the porch and Special Agents from DSS and the CIA's Protective Services Division, including three women, stepped out and surrounded the limo, facing outwards, with hands on their guns, listening to the continuous commentary in their deaf-aid radio earpieces.

Egyptian Ambassador Ramses Selim, his wife, and their daughter Leila, carrying their grandson, eight-month-old Nassir, in her arms, climbed out from the Chrysler and Mike and Annabel Curtis embraced them and strolled up the steps and into the house.

Inside the big double drawing room, with its feeling of space and New England good taste, a kind of mixture of Grandma Moses and American *Vogue*, Mike Curtis led everyone to a group of comfortable sofas, arranged in a square in a lone part of the room, like covered wagons from the Yukon trail. 'Well, Ramses, have you been promoted or something I haven't heard about?'

Selim grinned. He said, 'You mean the security. I suppose it is because of the troubles we are having back home.'

'We had troubles last year too,' his wife said, smiling at Annabel and pointing to her new, shorter hair style with signs of approval, 'but we only had three car-loads, not five.'

'Ah . . . troubled times,' commiserated Curtis. 'Now, would you like something? A drink? Cup of tea? Before you freshen up?'

Ramses Selim plumped down on one of the couches and chuckled. 'Freshen up? Is that a hint?'

'Of course not,' replied Annabel Curtis. 'Mike's a diplomat.'

And everybody laughed.

'Mine's the usual,' said Selim, by which he meant a large Scotch.

'I would love a cup of tea, Annabel . . .' said the Egyptian's elegant but diminutive wife, clearly happy to be back among old friends.

'Of course. Mikey, will you do the drinks, darling?' And then Annabel smiled to her Colombian maid. 'And tea for us, Consuela, thank you.'

Leila, cradling the sleeping baby, said, 'Annabel, do you mind? I would like to splash some water on my face and change Nassir.'

'Hell, let the nurse change Nassir, Leila,' commented Mike Curtis, busy at the pale-ochre drinks cabinet, set into one wall. 'You just sit down and I'll throw some water over you . . .' He gestured with a full jug and Leila grinned.

'I won't be long,' she said, and headed for the far corner, beyond the crammed bookshelves.

'Oh, we got rid of that doorway, Leila. To extend Mike's library. Try the door we came in . . .' And Annabel indicated the door to the front hall.

As the young woman left, with the baby, Ramses Selim relaxed and held out a grateful hand for the chunky tumbler of Scotch, clinking with ice. 'Ah, my friends,' he murmured, 'how safe it feels to be back in Connecticut. I always feel, when we are here, at total peace with the world . . .'

As her husband clinked glasses with the Egyptian, Annabel Curtis smiled and said, 'Well, if you are not safe here in Connecticut, where on earth could you be?'

And Ramses Selim raised his tumbler to her, in a silent toast.

New York City, that same evening, had many frightened people walking its streets, sitting in bars, huddled in rooms, and like that. It was that kind of city.

But no two of its teeming millions could have been more coldly apprehensive than James Gant and his adversary, Zina Farouche. Both twenty-seven years old, each was engaged in an enterprise which, dangerous at the best of times, had become a walk with imminent death, and they both knew they would be lucky if it came fast.

Zina had left that strangely unsuitable apartment her leader, Hanna al-Farah, was using, and had made her way downtown to Gramercy Park, where she had the keys to a small place rented by Khaled, for just such an eventuality. It was on the sixth floor at the back of a block on East 18th Street, between Park and Irving.

Only she and the dead Khaled Niknam knew of the existence of the place, and the rent of $600 a week had been paid in cash for the next seven weeks, along with a $2,000 deposit, to a Russian currency dealer who lived in one of those neat, well-kept Jewish communities near Forest Hills on the west side of Queens.

As she turned the keys in the four heavy, double locks, Zina listened for any hint of another presence. In her big drawstring purse was the same compact machine-pistol she had used to frighten off those three roller-blading muggers in Central Park, and, as the last tumblers of the last lock clicked open, she slipped her right hand into the purse and took a grip of the piece, flicking the safety to 'auto'.

Inside, the main room had that dusty, fusty gloom of all unlived in places. And there was always a silence about such so-called 'safe-houses', like the silence of a town after midnight, blanketed with snow. Or Beirut during the troubles, when the bombardments occasionally had stopped.

The bedroom was silent, sullen even, and the tiny kitchen had mildew on the walls and rust around the drainage hole.

Walking back, delicately, into the quiet sitting room, machine-pistol in her hands now, ready for use, the Palestinian girl wondered if the familiar noise of shattered glass, always micro-seconds before the sickening cataclysm of a bomb, was only instants away, although, with Morteza running things, such measures might be considered far too humane.

But Zina got to the door unscathed. She treble-locked it and, taking a slim telephone from her bag, knelt on the floor and found a vacant plug, beneath a cheap coffee table.

Now that the worst had happened, now that her mission was close to falling around her ears, the attack of panic had gone. Hanna al-Farah's message had been clear. If you succeed, even against the threat from Tehran and its executioner, Morteza, Abu Nidal himself will welcome you to the inner circle of the Revolutionary Council, and defend you from anything, and anyone.

And if you fail, at least you will die a martyr.

The hidden clause was about what would certainly happen to Zina if she gave up now.

The girl shivered. And as she dialled the first of three telephone numbers, she could not shake off flashes of – recollections of – those final moments of pleasure. Of intense physical emotions and smooth flesh and slick . . . lust.

As the ringing tone sounded, Zina reflected it had never been like that before. And she knew, instinctively, that for all the other woman's experience and tender guidance, and capacity for sensual excitement, that had been the first time that Hanna al-Farah, Commander of the Assassins, had so totally abandoned herself, to such exquisite fulfilment. Crying out as she gave way to loss of dignity and self-control.

And when they had finally subsided, lying slippery in each other's arms, Zina had leaned over, gently, to kiss her mistress.

And, eyes hooded with spent lust, but cold as a rattlesnake's, Hanna had gazed back and said just the one word, '*Saida*' . . . 'Goodbye.'

'This is the Kuwaiti Delegation to the United Nations,' announced a familiar voice on the other end of the line.

'Ah, Noor,' said Zina Farouche, as calm and in command as ever, 'here is what I want you to do . . .'

When James Gant left the Movie theatre (like his quarry he had quelled the rising panic by sheer force of will) he had, maybe for the first time since that self-important, self-indulgent, decision taken in the comfortable safety of the firm's Clerical 17 office in Whitehall, a coherent and sensible plan to stop the Connecticut massacre. He would locate the leader of the murder team, Zina Farouche, and convince her she was walking right into a trap, using a combination of fact and fiction, just as they had taught him at the Honey Farm, and just as he had learned from Euan Stevenson in Rome. If he succeeded, the Palestinian girl would call off her mission.

And if he failed? Gant would kill her. He had no option.

As he walked, Gant reflected on the day's events, for the hundredth time. Recalling every detail. Trying to make some sense out of the mayhem. The killing of Ben Turabi was a problem. For all Gant was aware, maybe Farouche herself had ordered it, for some transgression against the Dante team's brutal code. Or perhaps the cook/terrorist had actually been mugged – God knew, the streets of New York had enough crack-dosed crazies to slash a man's throat and just stroll away.

Either way, it would have set the assassination team on edge, and he would have to try to extract maximum leverage from that.

His deliberations in the cinema had led James Gant to the correct conclusion: that the distressing events on the subway platform at Queensboro had been ordered by Zina Farouche, because Gant had come to their attention, as he had carried out his surveillance of their group. OK, so he had failed in his first endeavour, by being discovered, but his effective, trained fighter's reaction would go a long way to convincing her of his professional credentials.

Something like that. It was not much of a plan. But he now had a clear understanding of the frightening minefield, with violent surprises all along the way, that his ill-conceived one-man war against Dante had become.

And the diplomatic horror story, if it was discovered that a serving SIS officer was engaged in an unauthorized shooting war in the second city of a major ally, left him almost blushing with guilt at his thoughtless, self-indentured mission.

To continue down this route could only end in his own death, or a major international scandal. Or both.

The almost paralysing terror of the last few hours had affected him more deeply than anything which had gone before in his eventful young life. More than the random and cowardly cruelty of Serbian shells and snipers in Sarajevo, or the tribal wars of Central Africa, or the dumb evil of the Provisional IRA's murder campaign against ordinary men, women and children in Ulster and England.

James had filmed the grisly results of bombs planted in public places by the brave boys of the 'rah', and his anger had always insulated him from fear, even in South Armagh and the Creggan housing estate, where life was cheaper than in the slums of Rio.

His news team directors and hardened reporters like Kate Adie and Sandy Gall had nicknamed him 'The Man With No Fear', and Gant had always been quietly proud of the sobriquet.

But this was different. The men on that subway platform had come for him, to kill *him*, James Gant, and the guy who had stepped out, after the first three went down – he had also quite simply been intent on murder.

Gant shrugged. The attack of anxiety was passing, and, as he walked back towards his cheap room, he was relieved to feel his fear drop away, like water after a squall.

Fuck them.

He started planning how he could get close to Zina Farouche, with all the Abu Nidal panoply of support teams and clandestine watchers.

In London, the Sudanese diplomat Abdullah Fadul was taken in a green, box-backed van, known as a Luton van, for that was where it was made, through the almost deserted night streets on a journey which lasted twenty-seven minutes, through Grosvenor Square, passing a sleeping American Embassy, down Park Lane, past Sloane Square and over Chelsea Bridge, to arrive eventually in a derelict and untidy yard, behind a Brixton street, where a car paintshop and stereo workshop had their rough and ready premises.

The van was backed into a loading bay and his four escorts, wearing blue boiler suits and neutral expressions, tapped the prisoner, now attired in white overalls, his head inside a thick, black hood, his hands handcuffed in front of him, and guided him carefully out from the van and onto a wooden elevator hoist.

The hoist seemed big and echoing, to Fadul, and it descended very slowly for twenty seconds, before coming to a stop.

He was led along a dank, musty corridor, hard, maybe concrete, under foot, until a heavy metal door was opened and he was led inside.

Calloused hands helped him to stand against a wall, the handcuffs were removed and his arms raised, spread at an angle, to be secured to tight, uncomfortable leather clamps.

Other straps were fastened to his ankles, after his legs were spread apart.

The comfortable, black velvet hood was whipped off and Fadul groaned and twisted his head, screwing up his eyes against the whitest of white light.

'Well now, Abdul,' said an urbane voice, behind the light, 'the quicker you unburden yourself, the less chance there will be of permanent blindness. And nobody wants that, do we . . .?'

An icy spasm fluttered over Abdullah Fadul's entire body surface.

It had never, anywhere, in all his efficient, well-funded intelligence service's files ever been suggested that the effete and decadent English behaved like . . . like he did.

'I demand to be returned to my Embassy,' he said, and was annoyed by the tremor in his voice.

'Well, I don't think we ever can, Abdullah. Do you? Not after all we're going to do to you . . .'

Then he heard, beyond the white, all-enveloping glare, the hum of an electric generator.

'Come on, son,' said the voice of the Hungarian who had found him in that awful infidel woman's apartment, and it was a sympathetic, friendly voice, 'we know about the property you own on the shore of Lake Lucerne. We know about the Kruger-rands in Colombia. Apart from being permanently blind, you will be a wanted man. Khartoum does not like its revolutionaries to cheat on it. That money is supposed to be running whole . . . networks of agents.'

Fadul fought to control racing, all-enveloping fear. He could feel his retinae shrivelling. He could imagine the reaction of his masters in the Revolutionary Intelligence Committee in Khartoum, to his years of fraud and embezzlement.

In the silence, the generator hummed and buzzed.

'I have nineteen minutes to get your full co-operation,' this came from the other voice, the one in command, 'so forget trying to hold out, for you, of all people, must know that you will shortly be gibbering to deliver. Ask yourself, Abdullah, do you really need to put yourself through all that. I'm in a hurry so you have to decide right now.'

And Fadul heard another voice say quietly, 'If it's all the same to you, Boss, I don't want to be here when they . . .' He could not make out the last words but his heart was racing towards a point where loss of consciousness was likely.

On the other side of the battery of lamps, normally used to illuminate the paint-shop bays, a couple of floors above, David Jardine leaned against a work-bench cluttered with bits of car radios and electronic gadgetry and studied their attempt at recreating the kind of scenario which someone as used to torture and sadistic brutality as a middle-ranking spook from the Sudan's Counter-Espionage Directorate would accept as routine.

The Harley-Davidson calendar of scantily clad, but somehow innocent young women on the wall beside the work bench, the half-full bottle of Johnny Walker and the radio-controlled model Jeep Ronnie had been fixing for a neighbour's eight-year-old son, rather gave the lie to the deception, Jardine supposed, but not having great experience of such places (the most recent being a gymnasium in Ghom) he could not really be sure.

But the man strapped to the brightly lit, white-washed wall seemed to accept completely that he was in some SIS 'hard' interrogation facility.

And, sure enough, just after Ronnie had mentioned that

perhaps he should put a rubber sheet under the prisoner (for reasons David Jardine hesitated to contemplate, he sometimes worried about the darker recesses of Renfield's mind), the diplomat blurted out, 'I recruited her in nineteen-eighty-nine.'

Jardine could scarcely believe they had broken him in just those few moments, and it rather appalled him that the man clearly believed the firm was capable of whatever it was he imagined was going to happen.

Such was the power of suggestion.

'Her code name is Yaum Al-ahad,' went on Abdullah Fadul; 'it means "Sunday" in Arabic.'

In the silence, the generator hummed and buzzed.

And soon there was no stopping the man – names, code-names, all the years of classified intelligence concerning whatever Angeline had learned about SIS operations inside Iran and its satellite, the Sudan. Fadul had an incredible memory, like any good spy, and it all came tumbling out, amid tearful pleas not to do whatever it was he thought they had been going to do to him.

As Jardine left the underground chamber, he heard Ronnie ask, conversationally, 'Please give me details of those networks being rounded up, as a result of Colonel Javd Assadiyan's interrogation . . .'

Outside, in the corridor two levels beneath the paint shops, the Director of Operations leaned against the wall, feeling physically sick. Those two little shits, Angeline Thomas and Abdullah Fadul, were directly responsible for the rounding up, the unspeakable ordeals and deaths of the members of his Moonlight circuits: some of the bravest and most able agents he had ever run.

He knew the law insisted on the Sudanese diplomat in this underground 'facility' of UK OPS being returned to his embassy, unless the bastard wanted to apply for political asylum. But the Foreign Office would not agree to that for they would not relish the nausea of angering the Sudanese radicals and their Tehran puppet-masters.

So, really, it would probably be best to milk Fadul for all he had, then drug him and drop him off at the tradesman's entrance to the Sudanese Embassy, with a doctored tape of his de-briefing in his pocket. Experience of such things did not lead Jardine to expect any formal protest.

Then, glancing at his watch, he decided to catch the 11 a.m. Concorde to New York, where a hunt was already under way, directed from Manhattan Outstation, for James Sebastian Gant.

It was just after midnight. James Gant had taken two hours to case the immediate area around his Greene Street apartment block and, so far as he could tell, although his faith in his training had been dented by the ease with which he had been noticed by the Dante Group *and* ambushed in the Queensboro subway station, there was nobody taking an interest in the place.

Before that, he had gone to a left-luggage locker in Grand Central Station, where he had removed a small grip. He had gone to the men's rest room and locked himself in a cubicle, where he had set up a mirror and cut his longish hair into a thick, shorter style. Then, with a plastic bowl and clean water from the WC, he had applied a Just For Men blond hair dye (good for six weeks), and had included his eyebrows and body hair, rinsing it out after six minutes, to alter his appearance.

A pair of contact lenses replaced his steel-rimmed glasses and a modest, slightly drooping moustache, dyed the same colour, completed the transformation.

Into the grip had gone his leather jacket, which he had become maybe too fond of, and in its place he settled for a cotton polo shirt of neutral colour and a mossy green linen jacket, with faded blue jeans and worn Reeboks.

By ten that night, he was back in his room. He cleaned his two handguns, then prised open the floorboard over his cache and spent the next twenty minutes changing the photos on his counterfeit passports and other ID.

After stripping and cleaning a Mini-Uzi machine-pistol, and loading four magazines, each with twenty-five rounds, he replaced his materials and nailed down the piece of floorboard, replacing a rug and lifting the television set back into place.

Around 11.20, he had still not worked out the best way to make contact with Zina Farouche without,

a. Getting blown away either by her or her back-up.
b. Finding himself held by one of the most dangerous terrorist gangs in existence.
c. Or b. followed by a., with the kind of thing he really did not want to think about in between.

The temptation to walk out, lock the door, drive to Seattle and fly home had never been stronger. He doubted if the Firm would ever suspect what he had been up to, and, even if they did, so what? The worst they could do would be to fire him.

He had left the radio and television switched off, so that he could hear any movement on the stairs outside his door, but it had been one hell of a day and young Gant dozed off soon after these inconclusive deliberations.

It was the creaking of that one stair, three from the landing, that woke him. It had always creaked and Gant had been able to make it worse (or better for his purposes) in order to be warned of anyone outside.

Now, at 12.09, he was wide awake. He reached swiftly, silently, for the Mini-Uzi and moved, lightly, to the wall on the lock-side of the door.

Heart pounding, but not too quickly, for experience was hardening the man into a survivor – or maybe honing the survivor he had always been – James listened. Sensed. Even using his nostrils.

The sounds of traffic, a distant radio at some open window, an ambulance siren, all seemed quite remote, as if he were on a window ledge, high above the affairs of mortals.

The sound, when it came, was from the floor, at the foot of the door. And, as James Gant's gaze travelled down, a slip of paper, from one of those telephone memo pads, appeared, being shoved under the crack.

It had the crest of the Essex House Hotel on the top. And a neat hand had penned, 'This is Zina. Flag of truce. I need to parley.'

Having treble-locked the door, James could not do what his instinct told him and haul it open, to confront the person outside at gunpoint.

Shit.

What would Euan Stevenson do? What – and he realised he had been asking himself this ever since things had turned sour – would David Jardine do?

And he probably did the right thing.

'Are you alone?' he asked, gripping the Uzi, aimed at the door, using the wall for what cover it might afford.

'Yes,' said a surprisingly quiet, well-mannered even, woman's voice.

'What do you want . . .?'

'Don't be absurd. Open the bloody door.'

Gant thought about this, then, still sheltering against the wall, he tugged the keys from his pocket and unlocked the three locks. Every sound in the neighbourhood seemed amplified, but still remote, as he turned the main lock and slid the catch which held it open.

Then he moved to the corner of the room, gun held two-handed, trained at the door and all the time checking out the window, just in case.

'OK, it's open . . .'

And the door slowly swung open and the slender, olive-skinned young woman who had occupied his every moment, for weeks on end, stepped inside. She carried a drawstring bag and wore the simple brief skirt and jacket he had seen her wear for meetings over coffee with Noor Jalud, at the Hotel Pierre on Fifth Avenue.

She gazed around the room and her eyes settled on Gant, who felt more than somewhat foolish, behind the Uzi, which moved steadily between his visitor and the open door.

'Blond does not suit you so much,' she said and, glancing around, sat down on the high-backed wooden chair beside the table that doubled as his desk and added, ignoring the artillery, 'And the moustache is very silly. Who exactly are you?'

Gant was suddenly aware of how stiff and painful almost every muscle in his body was, after the fight in the subway, more than twelve hours before. He decided to leave the door open. At least he could see who was outside.

'Put your bag down and kick it away from you.'

Zina shrugged and did as she was told. The weight of the bag, as she shoved it across the floor, spoke for itself.

James moved to the window and looked down at Greene

Street, below. It seemed quiet enough. Then he turned to look at the girl. Always be ready for surprises. How right the instructors at Scarborough had been.

'What do you mean? Parley?' he asked.

'Does a girl get a drink?' she replied.

'Well, um, what do you want? I've got Michelob. Or Doctor Pepper . . .'

'Doctor Pepper would be fine.' She crossed her legs and smiled. 'Would you like me to hold that for you?'

Listen, boy, a small voice reminded him, this is a murderer. Killed her first people at fourteen. Hand-grenade, thrown into a seafront café at Junieh, in the Lebanon. You are not Noël fucking Coward or Ian Fleming, so hold on to the gun and tread with very great care.

Still, for the first time in days, James Gant realised he was enjoying himself. This was living. And the truth, when it came, arrived with a lightness of touch completely out of step with the gravity of his situation. For it occurred to the young man that he might have done all this, not because of some long-nursed angst over the Rome airport slaughter, but because he needed an adventure. That he had done it for fun. That it was a total break from the complexities of being in love with his sister and the boredom of Clerical 17.

How very irresponsible. He remembered Euan Stevenson saying, 'Fun? Fun? Never, ever let them hear you say that, laddie. They don't like the notion of any bugger enjoying themselves in Accounts Section . . .'

'What are you smiling at?' enquired the Palestinian girl.

'Oh, myself, I suppose. Here . . .' And he threw her a can of cherry soda which she only just caught. 'Why are you here?'

Zina Farouche glanced at the yawning door, as she opened the can. Gant realised she was . . . not frightened, but on edge.

'There was a murder, in Sixth Avenue. A cook with the Moroccan Delegation staying at my hotel. You were seen there. Are you with Morteza?'

The look of mystification on James Gant's face spoke for itself.

'Who is Morteza?'

Zina drank from the can. She was thirsty. Then she wiped her mouth on the back of her elegant, tanned wrist and said, 'Pray you never find out. He does . . . enforcement, dirty work, for Savama. He is a major in their service.' And she examined Gant's face and asked, 'The man who killed the cook. You saw him?'

Gant nodded. 'Sure. He was about . . . maybe taller than me. Small head for such a large frame. Coat buttoned to the neck. Bit of stubble . . .' James touched his own jaw, to illustrate, 'wool hat. He was a pro-killer; at first I thought they had just bumped into each other.'

Zina Farouche was nodding, thoughtful.

'You know him?' enquired Gant.

'I think so. Why, have you been following me? Spying on me . . .?'

Gant sat on the arm of the old brown chair. He was now working on instinct, and, deep down, he felt this was what he had been created for, what he had always been destined for. It gave him a kind of buzz, this dawning of his vocation.

Time to up the ante, he decided, and said, 'You are saying that the Iranian Intelligence Service had Ben Turabi murdered on the streets of New York?'

And this brought the response he had hoped for.

'How do you know his name?'

'Zina, I know all about you. I know about the murdered man, Turabi, the so-called cook.' Her eyes were on him, like a mongoose with a cobra, locked, unwavering. 'I know about Noor Jalud, and Zafir Hammuda. And Biarritz. I know all about you and, Zina, I am not alone . . .'

The tension in the room was suddenly electric. He knew Farouche was calculating whether she could reach her heavy bag, on the floor near her feet. But James Gant ploughed on. 'I had given up trying to locate Mustafa Sharik, but there he was, just a few yards ahead of Turabi. Did he get in touch? Report the hit? Of course he did. What else can I tell you. Maybe it's your turn . . .'

Zina Farouche was working, like a computer, through a hundred permutations, setting to one side, discarding, those that did not fit. Trying to get a fix on this Englishman.

'Are you SIS?' she asked.

'I am the man who can . . . maybe, just perhaps, get you out of the mess you are in.'

'What mess . . .?'

'Come on, Zina. Why else are you here? If you were not in real trouble. You would have hit me with another bunch of hoods like the ones at the subway station, not knocked on the door and asked to parley. Why did you want me dead, anyway?'

'It would have looked like a mugging,' said the girl, without animosity. 'If you had been replaced, I would have had to take other steps. If not?' she shrugged, 'we would have been mistaken.'

'Neat thinking.' Gant listened but could hear no footfalls, no hint of anyone on the stairs. 'Those other steps, would they have included calling off Operation Swords of Allah?'

Shit. Thought Zina Farouche, her mind racing. This is worse than I had ever feared. The Englishman was either SIS or maybe with the CIA. No, the CIA would never have permitted things to develop this far. Or, her heart froze, he *is* with Morteza. She recalled the rumours about English men and women, converts to Islam, being used by the Iranian Service.

'At least tell me your name,' she said, moving the can from hand to hand, weighing it up as a potential weapon.

'It's Alec,' said Gant. 'And have you called it off? Have you called off Connecticut?'

She shook her head, then looked him directly in the eye and said, 'If you tell me precisely who you are, and can prove it, maybe we can do business.'

Allah the Merciful, she thought, if Hanna could hear me, she would personally drag me to the edge of that pit. But things had happened since leaving Hanna's place that afternoon which made survival the only imperative. At whatever cost . . .

It had been earlier, after phoning her orders from the Gramercy Park apartment. Zina had arranged a rendezvous in Mickey Mantle's bar and restaurant, on 59th Street, facing Central Park South.

One by one, the others, the survivors of her team of killers, had turned up.

If James Gant had put on his television, the local news would have told him all about it, for what had happened there was dominating the news. On every channel.

In the absence of Khaled Niknam, now lying on a slab somewhere, yet another John Doe in a busy city morgue system, Zina Farouche had kept watch on the rendezvous from the corner of East Drive and Central Park South, looking for any sign of Morteza or his associates – in particular, Sergeant-Major Parviz Rahmani, who was known to the US authorities as Mahmoud Dashti, or, more usually these days, thanks to Joe Cleary, as Betty Boop.

She had watched as Noor Jalud went into the restaurant. Four minutes later, bang on time, Zafir Hammuda, and three minutes after that, also on schedule, Mustafa Sharik, who had been reluctant to leave the safety of room 2016, in the Essex House Hotel.

Using her Minolta camera's zoom lens, trying to look like any tourist, Zina had carefully checked out the environment, then, relatively satisfied that her team had not been shadowed, and that the place was not under surveillance, the Dante leader had crossed the street, at the Ritz Plaza, and, after one final check, had gone into Mickey Mantle's, where a good-looking manageress had smiled and asked how many?

'I think my friends are already here,' Zina had said and had gone through to the back of the restaurant, past the oval bar and a half dozen television sets showing tapes of baseball games past and present. She had descended a couple of steps into the rear area, and there were the others, sitting round a table for four, in the corner, where they could cover the floor.

A waiter had taken their drinks order, two cappuccinos, an iced tea and a Coke, before Zina Farouche was able to give her instructions.

She told them that the operation had been brought forward. She had been in touch with the leadership and they were to carry out the job the next morning, preferably hitting the place just before lunch.

'Are we not totally compromised?' Noor had asked. 'At least till we know who killed Ben Turabi . . .?'

'NYPD have arrested the perpetrator,' Zina had lied. 'He is a vagrant with a history of mental disorder.'

The others had relaxed, relieved. Zafir Hammuda commented that he agreed it was sensible to bring the massacre forward and Sharik, the team's planner, had then given, orally, details of the location and back-up location where the weapons and other equipment were to be collected, in caches pre-positioned by a quartermaster cell of Abu Nidal's clandestine New York network.

The atmosphere had been positive, and Zina had conveyed her final orders for the attack. They had rehearsed it, weeks ago, over and over again, at a mock-up replica of Beauregard built near the Adarama terrorist training camp, on the banks of the Nahr 'Atbara river, in Eastern Sudan.

'Primary clients are the bodyguards and the heads of family; after that, the youngest, after that . . .'

'Everyone . . .' had concluded Zafir Hammuda, with a sly grin.

'OK. We get out fast on the rubber boat, just like rehearsals. If anyone gets separated –' Zina had glimpsed the delivery man, a tall, shambling figure, walking backwards from the kitchen at the side of the dining room, pulling a wheelbarrow. He was wearing a green canvas jacket with RYDER TRUCK RENTAL on a patch on the back, and she had felt the fine hair on the back of her neck rise, horizontally, but it was all too late, and Zafir Hammuda had pushed her to one side, saving her life as the delivery man had turned, firing his compact but lethal Ingram MAC-10 .45 on full auto and hitting the wall exactly behind where she had been sitting; switching left, shredding the pretty head of Noor Jalud and spraying blood and brains across the iced tea and half-finished cappuccinos and Coke; and a tad more left and whacking Mustafa in the gut as he rose, twisting, his big Colt automatic drawn and firing and firing again and again, even as the slugs had thumped him backwards, and still firing even as the right side of his head lifted away. And it was Mustafa's cold, angry courage that saved the lives of Zina Farouche, who had scrambled fast towards the steps up to the main dining area where everybody was scrambling for cover and screaming and crying, and of Zafir Hammuda, who had stood, legs spread,

KF-11-AMP machine pistol held two-handed and unleashing its thirty-six .45-calibre copper jacketed bullets in half-second bursts of six, ignoring the gunfire directed at him and felling the seemingly indestructible Betty Boop as methodically as a woodsman drops a tree.

For a long five seconds both men stood immovable as rocks, trading lead, but the Iranian killer had been hit bad by Zafir's first burst, which had destroyed most of his right shoulder and, even as Zina Farouche had reached the street entrance, stumbling over terrified customers who had hit the floor, she had turned to watch, fascinated, as one of Tehran's most efficient enforcers staggered backwards, dropped his gun and clutched at his head, somehow pathetic in his last moments of life, blood flowing between his fingers, and that final, longer burst from Zafir, the one that did it, destroying the seemingly indestructible as the huge man crumpled onto his side.

Zina had not hesitated. She was unscathed, apart from a graze on her left knee and leg and she had walked away from the restaurant pushing through the gathering crowd of by-standers and had stepped into a yellow taxi outside the Ritz Hotel with the instruction to drive to Gramercy Park and use Park Avenue. She needed to be alone and, back in the 'safe-house' apartment off Irving Place, she had locked the door, piled furniture against it and had collapsed on the stale, dank bed and sobbed her heart out.

She had wept for everything from her dead baby, Sami, and her father, murdered in the massacre at Chatilla, to her nightmarish time in the pit, to shame at her behaviour with Hanna, to regret at the abrupt death of Noor Jalud and, finally, pity for Mustafa Sharik, who had been so terrified out of his mind ever since that morning, he had just wanted to stay in Room 2016 and stare at Bugs Bunny cartoons on television.

Pity was a very rare, in fact unknown, emotion, for Zina Farouche. For pity did not get you very far in Beirut or in Abu Nidal's organisation. But here, for perhaps the first time in her life, Zina Farouche had felt compassion for poor Mustafa, who had turned up at the rendezvous, bright eyed with fear. Knowing he was due to die.

But mostly, Zina Farouche had wept tears of rage, for somebody had betrayed her. Whether it was Abu Nidal himself, or his enemies in Tehran, somebody had wrecked her chance of becoming a heroine in the eyes of her masters.

And as the sobbing had ebbed, she had found herself reflecting on those last moments with Hanna al-Farah.

Those final moments.

For there had been something chillingly inevitable in the finality of Hanna's parting words.

'*Saida*,' she had said, in Arabic. 'Goodbye.'

As she had lain there, in that dismal apartment, her face wet with tears, breast heaving with distress, with fear, Zina Farouche had remembered the very first word her mistress, her boss, the Commander of the Assassins, had said to her, in that clean, comfortable bedroom at Abu Nidal's orange farm not far from Tripoli Airport, in Libya.

'*Marhabbah* . . .' she had whispered. 'Welcome.'

So there it was.

Hello and goodbye.

Stark in its simplicity. When you came to think about it. When you came to think about it over and over again.

You will either return as a hero, or be remembered as a martyr, Hanna had whispered, as the two women had dressed, muted, almost unable to look at each other, after their final tryst.

Well, I am no martyr, Zina had resolved. You got me confused with somebody else. I took up arms to recover Palestine, to avenge Sami and my papa. But martyrdom?

You have to be kidding. Zina Farouche is first and foremost a survivor.

And that was when she remembered the first time she had seen the young man Khaled Niknam had photographed, worried in case he had been spying on them.

It had been in Rome. In Serafimo restaurant. The day she had rendezvoused with Zafir Hammuda.

The young man had come in, glanced at her table, and gone on, with an older man, to a table in the far corner.

The second most favourable table, for an operator to choose.

Shit.

The guy had been on their case since then. Plus he had killed Khaled and his team of muggers. This man was a pro. And a pro had an organisation behind him.

So, lying there, as the sun went down on Manhattan, Zina Farouche had worked out a whole new plan for survival. For somebody had ruined her hopes of escape from the shadow of the pit.

And somebody, the young woman had vowed, as she regained her composure, was going to pay . . .

15

Beauregard

Number 4 Ops Room was going crazy. Ever since Morteza had given them the slip, from right under their noses, Joe Cleary had figured something outrageous was going to happen.

It had occurred to him that it was a mistake, earlier that day, not to put a tail on the three people who had visited the house at 7 Patchin Street. But the Irish detective had no inclination to interfere with the Agency operation.

Say nothing, you get blamed for nothing, was not his usual way, but he had a notion that nobody was telling him the whole story and he had no wish to carry the can for any major fuck-ups.

So when Betty Boop had turned up in Mickey Mantle's, turning the place into his own private Alamo, when those neat pink dots were assuring everybody he and his controller were sitting quietly in their respective hidey holes, Cleary had not been surprised when the Agency assault team had hit the Patchin Street place and found, not Morteza, but the tallish woman who had been logged as entering the premises at 2.17 p.m. and leaving with one male suspect at 3.09 p.m.

Morteza must have changed clothes with her, Tony Semprino had ventured.

Naw. You're kidding me. Joe Cleary had thought.

And the room in Queens. Was Betty Boop there, to justify that pink dot on the high-tec screen?

Well, how could he be when he was lying shot to pieces on the floor of a fast-food place on Central Park South?

Right now it was five in the morning and all kinds of CIA

whiz-kids were busting their brains trying to put the pieces together again.

Cleary had been down to the morgue with the real Harry Liebowitz, to ID the two Arabs killed in the shoot out. Harry had asked him and Sam Vargos to bring in the Kuwaiti Security chief to identify Noor Jalud, which was only possible by taking prints off the cadaver.

On the body of Mustafa Sharik had been a Bosnian passport and driver's licence, along with a faded, much-folded letter from New York University, informing him he had been admitted as a post-grad and was to report to the campus admin office on 5 October.

Neither Cleary nor Liebowitz were impressed with this; not many people in New York City wandered around with such neat confirmation of their status, so a mugshot of the dead Mustafa Sharik, plus prints of his ten fingers and his palms, were circulated to the Federal Fingerprint Computer via the CIA's New York Field Office and the NYPD Intelligence Division. Also to Interpol in Europe.

Joe had gone home about nine to shower and shave, and change his clothes. He had phoned Laurie and coo-cooed to Patrick Cheyenne down the line, and now he pushed open the door to the smoke-filled Ops Room 4, where more hotshots had been flown in from Washington and many phones were being used, old-fashioned computer files were being searched, agents were huddled in consultation and little attention was being paid to the magic screen on the wall.

'Anyone call for a pizza?' shouted Joe and grinned and held up his hands as they all turned with anxious looks, expecting to be gunned down. 'Just kidding . . .'

Tony Semprino put an arm round Cleary and led him into the inner office, where the controllers of this operation, which had acquired the codename Jade Fragment, had set up shop.

'OK, Joe, tell me how you see this.' He pushed a fax copy across the big table, with four seats around it, and helped himself to coffee from a vacuum flask, adding three sugar lumps.

Joe Cleary scratched his ear and sat down. It was Liebowitz's chair but the spook was not around. He studied the fax. It was from Interpol.

JALUD, NOOR: DOB 23/7/70. NAT KUWAIT – b. KUWAIT CITY. ED RIYADH, SAUDI ARABIA + SORBONNE PARIS. MISTRESS S. OF KUWAIT FOREIGN MINISTER. ALLEGED BY INFORMANT 1986 [SEE DST 21/9/86 AL/A/23510891/JN] TO BE CLOSE TO STUDENT DAOUD, ABDUL-SALEM [DST VAR. CT/P/462937/DA] SUSPECTED MEMBER FATAH-THE REVOLUTIONARY COUNCIL [ABU NIDAL]. NO FURTHER.

The palm and fingerprints of Mustafa Sharik were not on file at either the Federal Fingerprint Register or with Interpol. And the Bosnian office at the UN had faxed to confirm the dead man held a passport issued in Sarajevo.

'One common denominator,' said Cleary. 'They are both Islamic.'

'Stray dogs . . .?' wondered Semprino.

'Say what?'

'The Iranians send hit squads after people who have offended them. Received wisdom is, so long as they only target each other, maybe it's better to let sleeping stray dogs lie.'

'Not in my fuckin' town they don't.'

Semprino smiled. 'Al Wiscynsky is screaming, two Arab diplomats, minor players, murdered in the same day by your friend Betty Boop. A Tehran enforcer. Who's next? And who were the two at the same table who escaped? And why were the two victims and the guy who blew away Dashti, Betty Boop, armed like Arnie Schwarzenegger?'

'I got a picture of the guy who traded lead with Betty,' said Cleary, quietly.

'You have?'

Joe Cleary pulled an envelope from his inside pocket and placed it on the table. 'It's from the surveillance cameras at Mickey Mantle's.'

'Why didn't you bring this in immediately?' asked Harry Liebowitz, who had just walked in.

'I could not believe you guys would not have got one for yourselves.' Joe could not help it, these so-called pros would not last two days in Homicide.

They studied the poor-quality, black and gray and white photo, from a high angle, of Zafir Hammuda, his pistol held two-handed and spitting flame.

'I'm sorry, Sergeant Cleary.' Liebowitz pushed a hand

through his hair and flopped down on a chair beside Joe. 'We should, too . . .' He pulled the photo to him and studied it, hard. 'I know this face,' he murmured, eventually. 'Tony, wire this to Langley and have it ID-d. I can't remember the name, but the connection is Abu Nidal, I'm pretty sure.'

Cleary glanced back at the report on Noor Jalud. 'Alleged to be close to Daoud, Abdul-Salem, suspected member . . . Abu Nidal.'

'Would there be any occasion, any . . . situation, where the guys in Tehran would order a hit on some Abu Nidals in New York City?'

And Semprino stared at Harry Liebowitz. 'During the week of the UN Assembly . . .'

After the briefest of pauses, the CIA man lifted a phone and said into it, 'Get me Al Wiscynsky, wherever he is. Right now.'

Daylight had long since spread through the room, and James Gant woke up abruptly, heart pounding. No idea where he was or what country he was in. Then it all came back. He had been sitting in the old brown armchair, Mini-Uzi machine-pistol in his lap, at about three in the morning, watching the Palestinian girl step out of her Chanel suit, with its short skirt and longish jacket. It was not an unpleasant sight. Zina had folded her suit neatly over one of the kitchen chairs. She had borrowed a bath towel and had stepped into the shower for four or five long minutes, during which time Gant had reflected on the previous hours of conversation.

He had told her a legend not entirely without foundation; that he was an officer of SIS, based in London. That Zina's terror group was known to SIS and there was an operation under way to ambush the Dante murder team, as soon as they had collected their weapons, just prior to the attack on Beauregard.

He had told her that he, James Gant, was merely a backroom analyst, and that, and here he contrived to seem embarrassed, he had fallen for Zina, from surveillance photos and tape recordings of her voice, that he understood how she had arrived at the position she was in, and that he had travelled to New York, on his own initiative, in the hope that he could cause her to abort the mission and thus not die in a hail of lead.

He had felt it was not a brilliant story, but his halting sincerity, the very outrageousness of such a tale, and her own agitation and anxiety seemed to have combined to lead the Farouche girl to believe it.

At the same time, he could hear the groans of Euan Stevenson and the instructors at the Honey Farm. Dear God, laddie, he could just hear Euan say, is that the best you can come up with . . .?

Then he must have fallen asleep. And now it was daylight. Tense, gun held ready, he gazed slowly around the room.

Her suit was still folded over the kitchen chair. Her expensive shoes on the floor beside it. And there on the bed, covered by just a sheet, for it had been a hot September night, lay Zina Farouche, master terrorist, killer of her first innocents at the age of fourteen, butcher of Biarritz, sleeping like a child, her pretty face innocent and at peace.

It was coming back to him. She had listened, the professional in her appalled at the amateurism and stupidity of his tale, and she had shaken her head in disbelief more than once.

Then she had asked him just four questions. Who was SIS Head of Station in Beirut?

Gant had said he could not discuss that.

Who was Director of Operations in London?

Again he had refused to answer.

How much did he earn, as an analyst in the Intelligence Directorate?

About £23,000, with no London living allowance, he had felt it safe to disclose.

And what was the telephone number of SIS at Vauxhall Bridge?

It was, since the Government's new, open policy, in the phone book, so he told her.

And Zina Farouche had nodded. 'You're authentic,' she had decided. Probably thinking, no other agency on earth would have sent a turkey like you.

And she had made her proposition. If SIS could guarantee her immediate safety, and if they could spirit her out of the USA and back to Europe, providing her with a new identity, a British passport, a lump sum and an income, she would tell them all she knew about the Abu Nidal organisation, its ongoing plans, its secret networks in Europe and the USA, agents, methods, everything.

Gant had said he might be able arrange such things, provided she could assure him the Beauregard massacre had definitely been called off.

And Zina had smiled ruefully and said, thanks to Morteza and his goons, there was no Dante team left to complete the mission.

Then she had taken the shower, and James, the ace operator, had fallen fast asleep.

He sat there, contemplating the fear, the drama and the . . . exhilaration of the previous twenty-four hours.

Privately, things were turning out better than he could have hoped, sitting lonely and afraid in that movie theatre yesterday, watching *Blade Runner* without seeing or hearing it.

Zina Farouche walking in, as they called it. This was brilliant. He would contact New York Outstation and arrange for the Palestinian to be taken into protective custody, prior to being spirited out of the country.

This would, of course, not best please David Jardine, Director of Operations, who was apparently prepared to allow the terrorist outrage to happen, for his own reasons – for the greater 'net saving' of human lives. Meaning theoretical human lives, at some time in the hypothetical future.

Well, tough luck, Jardine, thought James Gant. Too bad. And bringing in a prize like Zina Farouche might just get me off with a mild reprimand, for this little adventure.

At which moment, Zina opened her eyes and turned her head to gaze back at Gant. She smiled.

'Did you really get yourself into this mess just for me . . .?' she asked, softly.

James Gant smiled. Oh, boy, he thought. What a player. And what a temptation. There was a degree of symbiosis about getting into bed with the Dante leader, before delivering her to the Firm. In fact, the stuff that legends were made of.

He could imagine David Jardine doing just that. It would be in keeping.

'We should make tracks,' he said. 'This Morteza chap must still be looking for you.'

She shrugged, and pushing the sheet back, stretched luxuriously, completely naked.

Jesus, what a body, thought the young man, and he stood up, glancing around. 'I'll make some coffee and then contact my people,' he declared, matter-of-fact.

She rolled onto one side and looked him up and down.

'You have an erection,' she murmured, ever the survivor.

'Sure,' James replied. 'It's at the thought of keeping my job. Do you take sugar?'

As the slim, delta-winged Concorde banked over Long Island Sound, David Jardine was still turning over in his mind the astonishing events of the previous night. As so often with hindsight, Angeline Moresby-Thomas fitted all the parameters. She was good at her job, but considered herself undervalued, having been passed over twice for promotion. She was over-sexed but underendowed with looks or physical attractiveness. So she had been flattered by the attentions of a foreign diplomat, who had treated her like a lady, listened to her opinions, shared her love of Woody Allen movies and the music of André Previn and who had proved a talented lover with, apparently, considerable stamina.

It had been a few short steps from there to supplying him with an internal directory of the firm's London personnel and its establishment; after all, the office was in the phone book these days. And she had been quietly pleased to have been recruited into a foreign intelligence service, who had 'promoted' her twice in three years, so that poor Angeline actually believed she held the rank of Lieutenant-Colonel in the Sudanese Intelligence Directorate, with the 'Lion of Khartoum' medal, 1st Class, for services to security.

Jardine shook his head, it was grotesque, when you thought of the awful suffering of those betrayed agents in Tehran's Elim prison, that a few bonks and a piece of tin could so easily seduce an SIS employee with Cosmic security clearance.

And at the back of his mind, he was well aware, he had been almost ready to believe Fiona Macleod might be the mole. Based, he ruefully admitted, on not much more than a feeling of guilt at having allowed himself to be so delightfully seduced by her, during his last stop-over in Cyprus, to investigate the murder of his two agents on board the yacht *Pyramus*, in Limassol bay.

But now, he shook off all that, like an old suit, and turned his attention to the reason for his journey to New York. To stop the Dante group, without allowing his American friends ever to know how close he had come to allowing the Beauregard massacre to happen. And in the normal run of things clandestine, that would not have been too difficult. But the office's American Liaison Desk had passed him reports of the murder of Ben Turabi and the gunfight in Mickey Mantle's, where Mustafa Sharik and Noor Jalud had died, just as fast as they had come in.

That left just the Dante team leader and the psychopath Zafir Hammuda, hardly enough for the planned massacre, but it was more than possible Farouche could reinforce from Abu Nidal's US network of illegals. How Jardine would give anything for information about that. His prize asset, Albatross, was in Manhattan, and he hoped to learn more details when they met, in about fifty minutes' time.

As the undercarriage groaned down, until it locked open with a solid clunk, and the supersonic aircraft slowed to a whisper on its landing approach, Jardine concentrated on his rogue officer James Gant. The firm's loose cannon. And he wondered what hand the young man had had, in yesterday's mayhem, and, as he did, he knew that a political and diplomatic catastrophe on a grand scale was looming close.

He understood, after reading a digest of all the interviews with Gant's colleagues and superiors, just what he was dealing with. And why the lad had gone off the rails.

In fact, if he had known – if, more accurately, he had realised the implications – that James had been present at the 1985 Rome Airport massacre and how deeply it had scarred him, Jardine guessed he would probably not have entertained the idea of recruiting Gant in the first place, and he felt annoyed with the late Edith Treffewin for failing to mention it.

But the milk was spilled.

And truth to tell, there had been occasions when Jardine had been a young field operator, when he too had ignored the wishes of his controllers and gone off, quite illegally, to prod small events in the tide of history, in the direction he had felt would benefit the affairs of his service, or of the nation.

The fundamental difference was, the young David Jardine had never been found out.

What exactly was James Gant up to? That was the question. Well, there was little Jardine could do about it. Roly Benedict's New York watchers and streetfighters were out in force, searching for the boy. And, but for yesterday's excitement, they would doubtless have collared him by now, lurking around the Dante players.

But the two survivors, Zina Farouche and Zafir Hammuda, would have gone to ground, regrouping or, pray God, be fleeing the country, all plans for Beauregard abandoned.

'Joe, you wanted to know if we had video coverage of the Ben Turabi hit . . .' a young CIA staffer called Wendy Torres leaned in the open door to the Planning Room. The table was untidy with files and reports and maps and photographs of the fast-food crime scene. Dead cigarettes were piled in saucers (no ashtrays for this was a 'No Smoking Facility') and floated in stale coffee cups.

'Did I? Yeah. Sure thing.'

Wendy came in, carrying a mountain of requested files, and dropped a tape cassette on the table. 'You want anything? Teddy's sending out for sandwiches and stuff.'

'No. Yeah. Pastrami on rye and two Pepsis.'

'Six dollars twenty.'

Cleary sat back and pushed his aching shoulders against the chair. He took some notes from the pocket of his jacket, hanging over the back of the seat, and handed her two fins.

'Mustard?'

'The works.'

Four minutes later, Joe Cleary was sitting in a corner of the main ops room, playing and winding back, and replaying, a few feet of the seconds just after Ben Turabi got his throat sliced open. The operator had missed the attack, it would have been too much to hope for that he had captured it on tape, but he had been enough of a pro to concentrate on the bystanders, and not the dying man.

And there he was. The guy with the raincoat folded over his arm. Walking calmly away. Too calmly.

In fact, if the Irish cop had not seen with his own eyes Betty Boop do the business, this would have been suspect *numero uno*.

Forward, stop, play, rewind, play, and like that, for seven minutes. The digital facility allowed Cleary to freeze and zoom in on the man. Steel-rimmed glasses. Tall.

Where the hell had he seen that guy before? Then Joe Cleary, being the excellent cop that he was, remembered. It had been with Dolores, making a right into 44th Street, on their way to the DSS Office at the World Trade Center.

This schmook had been crossing the street, on a flashing DON'T WALK light, and looking the wrong way. English, Joe had registered, the way cops do. Or at least from outa town.

He took a print of the guy's close-up, from the screen. Plus a wider angle.

And just at that moment, Semprino banged down a telephone, at the far end of the room and yelled, 'They just picked up Morteza! He's in a burgundy Pontiac, on Amsterdam at Ninety-Four, heading south!'

A ragged cheer went up and agents climbed to their feet, shoulder holsters over their shirts, grabbed coats and casual jackets and headed for the elevators.

Cleary clicked on his Police radio handset and spoke into it.

Three minutes later, Sam Vargos was at the back of the US Government building, with their tan unmarked car.

'What's up?' he asked as Joe Cleary came out at the double, gripping a pastrami sandwich and a can of Pepsi.

'They got the Iranian. I drive, you break into the spook net. This time we make a fucking arrest, Sam. Fuck Washington, this is New York City and there's been enough killing over this bullshit . . .'

But even Sergeant Joe Cleary could not be right all the time.

*

Going through Immigration at JFK, with his diplomatic passport, David Jardine spotted Alan Clair, along with two senior CIA men from Political Analysis, waiting in the short space between the Immigration Line and Customs.

There were maybe twenty people between them but, being taller than average, Jardine was hard to miss and he was aware of the Agency's operations boss noticing him, first out of the corner of his eye, then turning his head to give Jardine the full eyeball.

The Englishman glanced around, affected to see Clair for the first time and raised his beat-up old Colombian grip, in salute.

For a long moment, the man who had introduced him to the clandestine game in Vietnam, on the eve of the Tet offensive, and who had shared a parallel career in what had until very recently been a sister service, stared back. Then, almost sadly, he slowly raised a hand to his brow, in an ironic parody of a military salute.

Jardine nodded. He grinned that lopsided grin of his and held his friend's gaze. Then he strode on, for there had been no mistaking the finality of Clair's message.

Is that all there is? As the late great Peggy Lee used to sing. After all those years . . .?

Well it sure looked like *sayonara* to me, considered Jardine, his stomach going cold with guilt at the dread thought that the CIA man might have found out about Dante, and James Gant and the total and deliberate failure of SIS to provide the merest whisper of a warning.

No, that can't be so, he reasoned. Or the shit would have hit the fan and I would have been recalled via the Concorde radio net.

Even so, David Jardine felt pretty jittery as he emerged from the Customs line into JFK's Arrivals Hall, where an unremarkable man in his mid-thirties, wearing a lightweight gray tweed jacket and a quiet necktie, fairish brown hair, smiled a muted greeting and, turning, strolled out to the taxi rank.

Roly Benedict was yet another of the firm's men who had been educated at Sherborne, a solid High Church boys' boarding school, gently iconoclastic, buried in a mediaeval town in Dorset, in the West of England. It turned out good-natured, able, courteous men, who seemed to hold a very private affection for the old place.

Roly, after a lifetime of espionage in the Middle East, South America and South Africa, had been given New York Outstation to run, because he was very good at working a high-profile SIS liaison office, glad-handing every intelligence officer in the UN and the US Intel community, while at the same time running a lethal and deeply buried and quite shockingly illegal (not to mention the bad manners of it) espionage network without arousing the slightest suspicion.

Ronnie Szabodo loved him.

Roly opened the door of a yellow cab. Jardine got in and moved across to the far side and Benedict climbed in after his boss.

'So, David,' he murmured, as the taxi moved away, some taxi captain on the cab line yelling at the driver he should wait for something or other, 'how does it feel. The fucking power of it all? D-Ops, how does it feel . . .?'

'It feels great,' replied Jardine, awash with relief that the half-expected crisis had not materialised. Not yet, but who knew what Gant was up to at that very moment? He went on, more urbane than he felt, 'But you would be surprised how PC they're trying to make it. The Cabinet Office wants a finger in the Secret Allocation.' Of funds, he meant.

'Resist, dear boy. Resist the whole damned lot of them. We have a business to run and they don't know how fucking lucky they are to have us.'

David Jardine smiled. He had forgotten how much he liked Roly.

'Maybe,' he replied. 'But we have to be very careful, nay, devious. These days.'

'*Plus ça change . . .*' said Roly, and settled down, content as ever, to enjoy the ride.

'Where, actually, old sport, are we going?' Jardine enquired.

Roly frowned, 'Didn't you want an RV with Albatross . . .?'

'Of course.'

'Well that's where we're going.'

*

The yellow taxi, one of Roly's better ideas, driven by Ian Ramsay, an ex-SAS warrant officer who had been contracted to the Firm as a thinking man's minder, crossed the East River on the Triborough Bridge and made its way west on 125th Street, until they made a left into Riverside Drive and pulled up at the kerb, on the corner of West 122nd Street, just down from Grant's Tomb.

A green Cherokee was parked further down, opposite an exclusive-looking apartment block. Inside, two of Ramsay's colleagues were keeping an eye on the entrance to the block which, carved stonework above the doors announced, was called Jerome Van Dam House.

Inside, accompanied by Ramsay, David Jardine and Roly Benedict took an elevator to the ninth floor and strolled along the plush carpeted corridor, lit by Art-Deco wall and ceiling lamps, to Apartment 903.

Roly glanced to Ramsay, who spoke briefly into a small radio handset.

And they waited.

'Taking their time . . .' commented Roly.

And waited.

'Hell's teeth. I'll use the key.' Roly took a keyring from his pocket.

'Just a minute, boss.' Ramsay took the keys and dropped them in his pocket. He took a short device, like a pen cap, with a suction pad, and stuck it to the heavy, polished wooded door.

Then he took a small brace-shaped tool from his leather coat and, inserting it into the other end, swiftly drilled a hole through the wood.

Removing the tool, Ramsay next took a short length of dark cable from another pocket and, inserting into the hole, connected it to a cigarette carton-sized video receiver and switched the thing on.

The three men watched as the screen revealed an open-plan entrance hall with rooms leading off. As Ramsay manipulated the cable, other parts of the immediate foreground became visible.

'Maybe they've gone out . . .' suggested Jardine.

'If they have, I'll skin them alive,' grunted Roly, who,

having had enough of this, took the keys back from Ramsay and opened the door.

It turned out not to have been a felicitous remark.

As soon as they moved across the entrance hall, the smell of fresh blood was overpowering. And lying, half on that couch where she and Zina Farouche had caressed their last farewells, was what was left of Hanna al-Farah, Commander of the Assassins.

'Jesus Christ . . .' breathed Roly, and the brave Squadron Sergeant-Major Ramsay gagged and turned away to heave his guts out on the silk Chinese carpet.

'What the fuck are you playing at, Roly? I thought this was supposed to be a safe-house.' Jardine, working on instinct, went through to the bedrooms and, sure enough, the bodies of two SIS officers, a nice young woman called Jo Granger and Colin Bain, the New York Outstations Security Officer, lay at awkward angles on the floor. Somebody had made them kneel and had killed them with single shots to the back of the head.

'She hadn't wanted anyone inside the place,' said Roly, and even in his anger, David Jardine could not help feeling sorry for him. This was a major fuck-up.

'Until last night, after all the excitement in town, I over-valued her.' He was grim-faced and so white, Jardine wondered if Roly Benedict was going to faint. 'So I sent Colin and Jo round . . . to babysit.'

Poor bastards, thought the big spymaster. No match for Morteza and his pals.

'You should have sent me,' said Ramsay, wiping his mouth on his sleeve. Then, forcing himself to examine the mutilated corpse, he commented, 'Taking off broad strips like that . . . we're talking about a very sharp hunting knife.' He held out his hands. 'About this long.'

But Jardine was not listening. He knelt and gazed into what was left of the face of Hanna al-Farah.

'Poor Albatross . . .' he said. 'She never really got a chance to spread her wings. Roly, how soon can you erase all this?'

'Initial laundry, within the hour. Carpets, wallpaper, furniture and curtains? Say by nightfall.'

'Do it,' ordered Jardine. 'And for Christ's sake find that bloody fool Gant. Before it's too late.'

After making a pot of fresh coffee, and a pile of toasted raisin and pecan bread, James Gant had offered Zina some cornflakes but she had raided the fridge and helped herself to yoghurt and honey.

The television news channel was broadcasting an update on the Mickey Mantle gun battle and an astute reporter was linking that to the murder earlier the same day of a cook with the Moroccan Delegation to the UN Assembly, name of Turabi.

Is this some kind of inter-Arab or Islamic feud, we're seeing here on the streets of New York, he was asking Lieutenant Ray O'Donnell, of NYPD's Public Affairs Bureau, and the detective was saying at this stage nobody was sure if there was any connection. Coincidences happen, was O'Donnell's message.

'Miraculously,' went on the reporter, 'no innocent bystanders were hurt in the brutal exchange of gunfire. Two men and a woman died, including the perpetrator, whose identity has not yet been established. Police want to interview a young woman and male aged about thirty, who fled the restaurant, immediately after the attack. The man is armed and may be wounded.'

As she put the bowl down on his table, watching the television screen, Gant took a clean shirt from a dresser drawer and handed it to her. 'Zina, put this on, I'm only flesh and blood.'

She smiled and shrugged into the garment, fastening one or two buttons. Then Zina Farouche sat down and wolfed the breakfast as if she had not eaten for days.

James went over and over his two hours of questioning, the night before, then he said, 'Zafir Hammuda. Where would he have gone? Back to the Algerian Delegation? Or the Embassy?'

She shook her head, 'He will have gone to ground. One of the first things we did, each of us, when we arrived here, was to make our own private arrangements to run for cover.' She ran a finger round the empty bowl and licked it. 'That way, none of us can betray the others, under the worst interrogation.'

'So what will he do? Do you think he was wounded?'

Zina Farouche shrugged. 'I got out of there. Who knows . . .?'

Gant kept at it. From Farouche's detailed biography of Hammuda, the night before, including his rape and mutilation of the Basque ETA-Negro woman in Biarritz, the man was a psychotic terrorist and in James's estimation, was the one member of the decimated Dante team who might just decide to head for Connecticut and do his worst.

'You said he knows the location of the weapons caches . . .' he asked.

Zina nodded, munching into her third slice of toast, spread thick with butter and strawberry jam, not taking her eyes off him. Gant reminded himself how very dangerous this stunningly attractive young woman was, and ignored the strong animal instincts she was arousing in him.

'Well, if he can move at all,' persisted Gant, 'I have a horrible feeling Zafir Hammuda will try his damnedest to carry out your mission on his own . . .'

Zina munched, contemplating this. Then she grinned and nodded. 'Yep,' she said. 'So do I.'

'Fuck you, Zina, if one single person at Beauregard is as much as . . . scratched, the deal is off and you're on your own. No new identity. No big cash payment. Zero. Plus I will probably blow your fucking head off. *Capisce*?'

This amused her even more.

'*You* . . . blow *my* head off?' She scratched her left tit, under the half-open shirt. 'I don't think so.'

No, actually, neither did James.

'Why don't I phone him?'

Gant's mind reeled, 'What?'

'Why don't I phone him? If he was not hit in the gunfight, he's on the phone; how do you think we planned to get in touch with each other, if we had to split up?'

She had lifted her drawstring bag before he could stop her and the heavy KF-AMP machine-pistol was in her hand. She looked at it, the way other women would check their wallet, and laid it on the table, beside the toast. Then she lifted out a slim portable phone.

'Smallest in existence. State of the art. Satellite access. You like?'

Mouth suddenly dry, Gant nodded.

'I'll give it to you, Alec, after this is over.'

'Um, thanks.'

'No problem.' And rapidly she keyed in a set of numbers, then listened, drumming the fingers of her free hand on the table. Then . . . 'Jackson? *Al'humdolelah. Ke falik, mohajen . . .?*'

. . . '*Ne baba!*'

. . . '*E khatarnak . . . Kei?*'

. . . '*Dast-e chap.*'

She listened, then checked her Rolex wristwatch. '*Sa'at-e do b'ad az zohr. Bletti! Kaf kardam.*'

. . . '*Bash e.* It's cool. See you.' And she flipped the phone shut and put it on the table.

Gant stared at her. 'Two o'clock where? And what's dangerous?'

'You speak Farsi?' She was less than impressed. 'Two o'clock means noon and the where is where we rendezvous. And *khaternak*?' She meant dangerous. 'Well, hitting Beauregard with two people is probably quite dangerous.'

She wiped her hands together, a different woman. It was as if contact with another member of her team had given her a shot of adrenaline. Gant hoped most fervently, specially with the gun at her right hand, that the girl had not suddenly changed her mind.

'You know what *kaf kardam* means?' she asked.

'It means you're pissed, had enough, annoyed.'

She nodded, 'He says if I don't make the rendezvous by ten after noon, he's going ahead by himself.'

'What's in the weapons cache?'

She examined her fingernails. 'M-16's, Heckler and Koch grease guns, Colt forty-five handguns, machetes, hand-grenades, including phosphorous . . . and eight sixty-six millimetre four-shot M two-o-two A-twos.'

'What's that?'

'Portable four-shot rocket launcher. Loaded with high explosive and napalm.'

Silence.

Gant had understood at once. 'So he doesn't need to breach the perimeter . . .'

'Six hundred yards would do it.'

James had made the journey from Manhattan to Beauregard three times. As part of his general reconnaissance and preparation. The journey had taken between two hours forty and three hours twenty-four. It was five minutes to eight.

'Get dressed,' he said, and, switching off the television set, shoved it away from the floorboard over his own stash of artillery.

'You're going to take on Zafir?' asked Zina, alarmed. 'Listen, Alec, the man has killed over sixty people. Yesterday he traded bullets with a top Tehran hit man and walked away. Forget it. Get me to safe custody and call the US Security Service. Here . . .' she rummaged in her bag, 'call Al Wiscynsky, he's in charge. Let them ambush Zafir and protect Beauregard; they're very good at it, believe me.'

As he chose his weapons and loaded the body-harness rig, Gant was tempted by this sensible suggestion. But he felt instinctively that unless he could solve this last piece of the Dante madness by himself, there was no way back into the Firm's good graces.

After all, David Jardine was Director of Operations. He was the man who had brought Gant into the firm, and he had his own reasons, in perhaps a grander design, for keeping his knowledge of Dante from the Americans.

So, partly from natural loyalty to his superior, partly from a belated sense of self-preservation, James had no intention of blowing the whistle on his own boss by blurting the whole mess out to the US authorities.

Perhaps he was wrong. They still examine his motives, discuss his rationale, the porers over entrails. But, having made up his mind, James Gant was determined to go for it, balls to the wall.

He watched as Zina stepped into her clothes. She went into the bathroom, and he stood at the door, feeling the surges of adrenaline as he psyched himself up for a fast drive and whatever lay at the end of it.

Zina Farouche brushed her teeth and mumbled through the foam, 'You do the same; you'll feel like shit later, if you don't.'

Ah, those little personal hygiene hints for your pre-terrorist atrocity grooming, reflected Gant. How touching.

The tan Ford was on East 23rd Street, Joe Cleary at the wheel and Sam tuned in to the CIA short wave band, as Morteza's burgundy Pontiac travelled sedately, never running a light, pausing to let pedestrians across, on its journey from Amsterdam Avenue, heading downtown from wherever it was he had been. Which was of course the Van Dam apartment block on Riverside Drive.

'Subject entering Union Square from Broadway . . .' crackled a voice on the CIA net.

Cleary made a left into Sixth Avenue, flicking on his blue and red strobe lights as he drove against six lanes of traffic that was scrambling to get out of his way.

'You like doing that,' accused Vargos, instinctively flinching as a bus lurched across their bows.

'I wanna get ahead of him,' replied Joe, happy at his work. He spun the wheel, turned left off the Avenue into 22nd Street and, stepping on the gas, overtook a gaggle of cars and taxis and almost killed a messenger bike as he slewed right into Fifth Avenue and carved his way through the traffic, lights flashing but siren off.

'Turning off Broadway into . . . Wannamaker Place.'

'He's going somewhere,' contributed Vargos.

'Of course he's going some fuckin' where. Jeez. you think he went for a drive?' Cleary slowed and, switching off his lights, turned left into West 9th Street, which became Wannamaker Place, a couple of blocks further east.

'I see him . . .' breathed Vargos.

'Copy that,' said Joe Cleary.

'. . . turning left into . . .'

'Greene,' said Cleary. 'He's looking for something.'

'An address?' suggested Sam.

'No the *Graf Spee*,' grunted his partner and made a left into University Place, which was just beside Greene Street, sharing the block.

'What sort of car do you have . . .?' asked Zina Farouche, descending from his room down the shabby staircase.

'The fastest one I can find,' he grinned, as they passed an old woman in curlers, standing at an open doorway.

She gaped after them, shaking her head in disapproval and muttering, 'Damn junkies . . .'

The tan Ford paused on Waverley, at the Greene Street intersection.

'He's stopped.' Vargos and Cleary watched as Morteza parked the Pontiac. The airwaves were busy with CIA static.

'Observe and report.' Cleary recognised Semprino's voice. 'Repeat. Be ready to move, but the aim of this is observe and report . . .'

'Yeah, kiss my ass,' muttered Joe Cleary. He drove over the intersection and parked at the kerb, on Waverley Place.

Cleary and Sam Vargos climbed out, taking their time, loosening their neckties and instinctively touching where they kept their pieces. They could only be two guys from Homicide.

Gant paused at the door and, half-opening it, checked out the street. Maybe if he had looked right first, instead of left, but that was not the way the door opened. Whatever, it gave Morteza the fraction of a second to side-step into a doorway.

Gant stood there, listening, his cheap brown raincoat over his left arm. He frowned.

'What is it . . .?' asked Zina.

He sniffed. 'I'm not sure. Something . . .'

After a long pause, he shrugged. 'Stagefright, I suppose.' And he stepped out onto the street, asking, only several hours too late, 'How did you know where to find me?'

'Khaled followed you. But he's dead.'

They walked along the street, looking at the parked cars, looking for a fast one to hotwire.

'Tell anyone else?' he meant of course, Zafir Hammuda.

'No. Oh, just Hanna. But she won't tell anyone.'

Too right.

'How about that one . . .' he indicated a burgundy coloured Pontiac coupé, half-way along the block.

Joe Cleary and Vargos were walking past the Pontiac, taking it easy. Joe could feel the eyes of a dozen CIA agents on him; he could almost hear the dialogue along the lines of what the fuck is *he* doing here? Get him off the street. And stuff like that.

'Do you see him?' he asked, quietly.

'No.' Vargos was walking on eggs, his cop's antennae stretched.

'Feet,' breathed Cleary.

'Where?'

'Doorway. Thirty feet right.'

'Seen.'

At which moment a purple Mustang with flames painted on the side pulled up with a squeal of rubber right beside them and the driver climbed out, real athletic like, and bounced around the hood coming straight at Joe Cleary.

It was Johnny Stomparelli.

'You fuck!' he was yelling. 'You fuckin' fuck!'

'This fellow has a way with words, Sam.'

Johnny the Stomp was puce with anger as he reached them, his right fist having found a Colt Silver Eagle automatic since jumping round the hood of his automobile.

'You bust my fuckin' ear-drums you fuckin' motherfuckin' fuck!!' And he stuck his heater right under Joe Cleary's chin, trembling with the rush of long anticipated revenge.

'Like this?' enquired Homicide Sergeant Joseph Cleary and clapped his flat hands hard together, with the Stomp's head in the middle.

As they strolled on, leaving the hoodlum keening on his knees, hands nursing his busted ears, Colt kicked into the gutter, Sam Vargos remarked, 'Rock'nroll nights will never be the same again, for one dumb pimp.'

James Gant and Zina Farouche had stopped, watching this minor drama only fifty feet away.

'The Mustang would be better,' he murmured.

'The Mustang will be good . . .' she agreed but Gant was already reacting to the male shape stepping out from a doorway just a few yards away, holding an HK-MP5 9mm submachine pistol at head height, arms extended, and, even as the muzzle flashed, James was shouldering Zina to the left and rolling to his right, firing the Sig pistol he had been carrying under the raincoat.

It was the culmination of his training, his hard-won experience on the streets of New York and his survival instincts honed from staying alive in places like Beirut and Sarajevo's Snipers' Alley.

The gunfire was deafening and, even in the heat of it, Gant could not figure out why that was so, for the gunman's weapon had a big fat silencer. It was only as the Iranian enforcer crumpled to the ground, that behind him Gant saw that the two men who had been involved in the minor drama seconds before were both also shooting at the man Joe Cleary recognised as Morteza.

As the Iranian rolled over, breathing in awful gurgling rasps, his arms twitching, his shirt, jacket and pants all soaked in crimson gore, Gant moved over to Zina. She was sitting half against the wall, and had not even had a chance to get her gun out of the drawstring bag.

'Where did he get you?' asked Gant.

She grimaced. The right shoulder of her Chanel jacket was rapidly saturating with blood. Gant gently lifted it away from the bullet wound and pulled the shoulder strap of her crimson-wet body down over the girl's upper arm. Then he tugged his shirt off, over his head and wiped away the blood, examining her shoulder and arm.

She shivered, but kept silent, as he undid the leather belt round his jeans and wrapped it around her upper right arm, before folding the shirt into a tight wad and pressing it hard into the opened flesh.

'Can you move your fingers?' he asked.

She flexed her fingers.

'The hand and wrist?'

She obliged.

'Bend the elbow . . .'

Zina bent her elbow.

Gant relaxed. 'OK . . . let's just see if you are hit anywhere else . . .'

She rested, like an injured animal, trusting this big, patently reliable man, who had moved so much faster than she – and Zina Farouche was reckoned to have better reactions than most.

'You're going to live,' Gant smiled. 'One slug tore your upper arm muscle. Nothing to get excited about . . .'

The wounded girl examined his face, then managed a pale grin and said, 'I take it back.'

'What?' asked Gant.

'You're quite good.'

At which point the two men who had shot the would-be assassin arrived, speaking into personal radios, still holding their Glock pistols.

'Fast moving, buddy,' complimented Joe Cleary, and indicated with a nod of his head, James Gant's Sig-Sauer 9mm pistol, which Gant had laid on the concrete as he tended to Zina.

Sam Vargos scooped it up. The slide was jammed open.

'So how's the patient?' enquired Cleary, holstering his piece.

'Just a scratch,' replied Zina Farouche, calmer than she felt, and, using Gant for support, allowed him to haul her to her feet.

'Grazed the flesh,' added Gant. 'Bleeding's superficial – looks worse than it is.' The shock of what had just happened was beginning to hit him, but already he was working out how to get to Beauregard in time to stop Zafir Hammuda.

The shorter of the two men, they seemed to be cops, had taken a folded piece of paper from his inside pocket, and was opening it out.

While Vargos checked out Morteza, gasping in agony, his life's blood ebbing around the sidewalk, Joe Cleary studied the computer printout of the video picture of Gant, strolling away from the murder of Ben Turabi. He checked it with the blond guy in front of him.

'What did you dye your hair for? It doesn't suit you,' he said.

'I told him already . . .' said Zina Farouche.

'Who are you?' demanded Cleary.

'This lady is an employee of the British Foreign Service, as am I,' replied James Gant. And he produced the passport he had been keeping for just such an occasion. It was his own. 'Please arrange for the British Mission to the UN to be informed. Her immediate boss is a Mister Benedict. I am taking her there right now, and of course will be happy to make a witness statement later.'

'Mister, tell it to the desk sergeant.' Cleary glanced at the dying Morteza. 'I'm detaining you as a material witness . . .'

'We have urgent business, officer.'

Cleary glanced to Sam Vargos, who had produced a battle-field dressing from one inside pocket and a metal whiskey flask from another. The Irish cop chuckled, shaking his head. 'What a goddam town,' he said, and turned to Gant. 'You have a licence for a concealed weapon?'

Gant shrugged eloquently and concentrated on helping Vargos pour whiskey over Zina's flesh wound.

'This looks worse than it is; you was dead lucky,' counselled Sam Vargos to the young woman.

In the distance a rising whine commenced of approaching sirens of all manner of police and ambulance vehicles.

A blue Toyota 4 × 4 hurtled in from West 4th Street, two of its wheels lifting off the ground, and skidded to a stop beside them.

The front passenger-door opened and Tony Semprino, clearly furious, beckoned to Cleary, who sauntered over.

'What the hell do you imagine you were playing at? Can't you obey orders, Sergeant Cleary?'

'Listen, pal, I take my orders from New York City Police Department and, you know what? They don't sit still for multiple homicide so that you assholes from Langley can play spookey-spookey. These two people would have been dead right now and what would you be doing? Tailing the fuckin' perp and watching pink lights on a goddam wall . . .!!'

It was probably a long time since anyone had yelled at the Assistant to the Deputy Director/Intelligence of the CIA like that. Semprino opened his mouth. Shut it. Went very pale with anger and said, 'I can not have a classified argument with outsiders present. Suffice it to say, Sergeant, your career with the police is History. Next time I see you, will be on a school-crossing detail . . .'

And he slammed the door and the vehicle moved away, a red light flashing on its dashboard.

Joe Cleary shook his head and turned back to Gant and Zina Farouche.

'Problems?' enquired Gant, sympathetically.

'Fuckin' spooks,' commented Joe Cleary, and he looked at Gant. 'I suppose you're one too . . .?'

Gant said, 'Not in so many words. Thanks for saving my life.'

Cleary met his honest gaze and, finally, he grinned. 'You know, all your bullets went wide?'

James Gant nodded, ruefully. 'I had an idea . . .'

'In a surprise gunfight like that . . .' advised the wiry little cop, 'are you right handed?'

'Yes.'

'In a quick-draw situation, nine times outa ten you're gonna shoot high and to your left. See here . . .' he prodded at the dying Morteza's right shoulder, 'your first slug tore through the shoulder pad of his coat.'

'Ah.'

'After that, they all went high.'

Gant thanked Joe Cleary for this impromptu lesson.

'So, in future. Shoot low and right. In such a situation . . .'

'You can bet on it.'

The howling sirens seemed to be all around them, but not yet in the street.

'So, who you with, some Limey outfit?'

James smiled, and to his surprise, found himself saying, 'Yep. And I'm in deep shit.'

'You too.' Cleary smiled and took a pack of Winstons from his pocket. 'Smoke?'

Gant, who did not smoke, accepted one. It was a small courtesy that was to make all the difference.

'Well, pal, I have to take you guys in. Get statements. This is months of goddam paperwork.' He flicked his Seal Zippo and held it for Gant.

Police Squad cars and ESU Vans and unmarked carloads of detectives were suddenly cluttering the street, their flashing, strobing lights lending a surreal, carnival atmosphere.

'My name is Joe Cleary. Homicide. What's yours?' Joe dragged on his Winston.

'James Gant.' And Gant made a decision, for right now his stupid, personal mission was on the brink of turning to ashes, diplomatic catastrophe, probable criminal charges, dismissal from the Service . . . total disaster.

'Nice lighter,' he said, turning it over in his hand. 'Were you a SEAL?'

'Sure thing. Vietnam, South and North, Jimmy. I was there.'

'And SEALs are Special Forces, am I right?' This will never work, James, he said to himself, but what do you have to lose?

'That's right. Just like your SAS, but with flippers.'

James Gant nodded. This guy has something on his mind, recognised the detective.

Gant took a wary Joe Cleary by the elbow, and gathered Zina Farouche with his other arm, taking them aside from the police paramedics, who were trying, fruitlessly to do something for the gravely wounded Morteza, who was now lying motionless.

'Joe, this is a very serious question, OK?'

Cleary nodded. 'OK.'

James took a deep breath and glanced at Zina, then he said, 'Suppose a crazy person had obtained a portable rocket launcher, you know the kind that fires high explosive with napalm combined?'

'Yeah, the M-Two-O-Two springs to mind.'

'That's the one,' contributed Zina, who seemed to have guessed what Gant was up to.

'Now, as a Special Forces soldier . . .'

'I was a Special Forces *sailor*, buddy, but I'm listening.'

'As a Special Forces man, say you know this crazy is determined to kill as many innocent people – men, women and kids – with his napalm rockets as he can. A fanatic. And you knew exactly where to find him . . .'

'Precisely where to find him,' added Zina Farouche.

'Would you,' asked Gant, 'mobilise all the firepower of the CIA, the DSS, the US Secret Service, the local sheriff and the National Guard? With helicopters and flashing lights and stuff? Or would you send a . . . three-man patrol to take him out?'

Joe Cleary spread his hands. 'Fella, there's no question. If you know where he is, you send the three-man patrol, now we gotta get down to the Precinct.'

As he turned, James Gant held onto his arm, and spoke

closer to Cleary's ear. 'He's in Connecticut. He has four of those things and if this young woman here does not RV with him by ten after noon, he is going to hit two families at a big house on the Essex River.'

Joe Cleary's blood went cold. You know when destiny touches you on the shoulder, he thought to himself; this is surely it. And he was not surprised at the answer to his question, where exactly?

'It's a place called Beauregard . . .'

Of course it was. Joe Cleary studied the young guy hard, examining his face. The man had been through a thing or two, he could see that. And the chick? She was a piece of work all right. Made Dolores Caltagirone look like a kid outa high school.

'You are sure of this, James?' he asked. 'Just one guy, not ten?'

'He is the last of a team sent from the Middle East, on the orders of Tehran,' said Zina. 'This man here' she glanced at Morteza's body 'has killed the rest.'

Joe Cleary considered this. It made a kind of sense. He had felt it coming since the first day he set foot inside Beauregard. If ever there was a victim it was Annabel Curtis. It had been shouting at him.

'I am probably crazy,' he said, 'but if we are going to reach Connecticut in time to do something, we gotta move right now.' He sighed. What a day. Then, as he motioned for Sam Vargos to join them, he warned, 'If you are fuckin' with me I will blow your balls off.'

Vargos walked up and said, 'Johnny Stomparelli is filing a complaint. Assault and battery.'

'Wow, see me shaking,' said Cleary. 'Sam, get us to the World Trade Center. We need a top for this lady, a shirt for this man and a fast chopper. Let's move it.'

Zafir Hammuda was everything that true Islam is not.

He was a man consumed by hatred, he was a sadist who obtained more satisfaction and pleasure out of killing than anything else in life. His entire existence was motivated by a fierce pride in the fear he inspired in others and he had honed his body into a formidable fighting machine.

Like many of his kind, he had been content to use the Islamic Fundamentalist creed to excuse and to feed his psychotic appetites, proud to be called a Soldier of God, when in fact his master, in the terms true Islamic teachers would have recognised, was Satan himself.

He lay absolutely motionless in the long grass, just out of sight of the cable ferry which took up to eight cars and passengers from the east bank of the Essex river, broad at that point, across to the narrow country road to Old Lyme and the track leading off it to Beauregard.

In the grass beside him were three portable M racks of M-202 66mm rockets. He had earlier made a final reconnaissance of the place.

Some of the two American and Egyptian families were playing tennis at a makeshift net near the creek, rich with reeds and wild rice, providing perfect cover for a surreptitious approach.

Others were lazing on a patio at the back of the old plantation house. And the house itself would go up like a log yard, when his napalm and C-4-filled warheads struck home.

The Security detail was efficient but, from the range Hammuda had chosen, would be unable to do anything in the face of his planned attack.

He checked his watch: 12.03. Seven more minutes and he would move into position. It was only a couple of hundred yards down the bank. He had not really imagined Zina would make the rendezvous. But just in case they both made it back to Libya and Abu Nidal, he knew he had been right to go through the motions. He was too old a player to disobey orders too obviously.

The sound of birds and crickets was relaxing. The sun was warm. A helicopter had droned lazily past, maybe twenty minutes before. But that was not unusual, and, from its straight flight, it was clearly not interested in anything near where he was lying up.

12.04.

Six minutes.

Then an open-top Saab 900 appeared, coming down a narrow track from the direction of the cable ferry.

Zafir Hammuda eased the switch on his M-16 to automatic.

But it was Zina Farouche. He was impressed. She must have driven from Manhattan like a bat out of hell.

He remained hidden as the Saab stopped and she stood up, sitting on the back of the driver's seat, gazing around. She was wearing a loose sweat shirt, with her right arm in a sling.

Pretty woman, he thought, and contemplated having some fun with her, before the attack, and reporting when he got back to Libya that she had died in the operation.

A good plan, he decided, and felt his loins respond.

Heart beating slightly faster, he got to his knees and raised a hand. Over here, you dumb bitch, he thought.

But Zina did not seem to notice him. Damn it! He was in exactly the agreed rendezvous location. He waved again, but still she did not see him. It was like trying to get a waiter's attention in a Paris restaurant.

He climbed to his feet, and, as he took a step forward sixty-four full-metal-jacketed 7.62 slugs, the entire contents of two M-16 magazines, turned his head and upper body into a nightmare sight. The kind of sight he had so enjoyed creating.

As the metallic clack-clack of silenced gunfire died rapidly away, two men, faces streaked with green and black paint, hessian sack-strips wound round their rifles and their clothing, rose from the long grass, only thirty yards from the raggedy, bloody scarecrow that had been the maniac Zafir Hammuda.

They walked carefully through the grass towards the shattered corpse and Joe Cleary said, 'If this was some guy out birdwatching we say nothin', OK?'

James Gant grinned. 'You got it . . .'

Then they saw the rocket launchers and the artillery.

'Aw, Jesus . . .' gasped a relieved Cleary. 'Thank the Lord for that . . .'

And overhead, a big navy blue and white Sikorsky helicopter clattered, descending, importantly, oblivious to the drama below. Inside the Sikorsky, Al Wiscynsky listened to his men on the ground, and gave the thumbs-up to the pilot.

On the front porch of Beauregard, Annabel Curtis and Ambassador Mike Curtis watched, side by side with their good friends Ramses and Sohair Selim, families and servants behind them, flanked by the CIA and DSS security detail, as the splendidly prepared big helicopter, US 3, settled on the neat lawn, scattering grass and leaves.

The side-door opened and a set of steps dropped down.

Al Wiscynsky hurried down, and spoke briefly to the Special Agent in charge of the Beauregard detail.

Then, grinning and pushing a hand through his rotor wind-blown hair, came the President of the United States.

He was ushered out from beneath the swishing rotors by Wiscynsky and across to the pillared portico, where Mike Curtis gripped his hand.

'Mister President, welcome to Beauregard, this is a most pleasant surprise . . .'

And the President laughed and said, 'Well, it's wonderful to come and pay tribute to such a shining example of two nations' ambassadors working and relaxing in harmony. Besides,' he added, 'Al tells me New York is experiencing some excitement right now . . .'

He shook hands with everybody and they all strolled inside, followed by a White House camera crew, who kept a respectful distance.

16

The Ceremony of Innocence

David Jardine sat in the library of Roly Benedict's pleasant apartment on Fifth Avenue, looking across Central Park to the impressively Gothic Dakota Building on the other side.

It was six in the evening and the news programme on television was showing a brief report on the President's surprise visit to Beauregard. With every foot of film, Jardine's blood chilled. He felt almost sick at the thought of what could have happened if Alan Clair, not to mention the President himself, had ever learned how close it had come to an error of judgement so great it would have split the two nations asunder, for a thousand years . . .

That'll teach you, he thought to himself, not to play at God, ever again.

And just then there was a knock at the door and Roly poked his head round. 'I have James Gant, David . . .'

Jardine nodded, and switched off the television sound. He stood up and a very nervous and shame-faced James Gant entered the room, hesitantly. As well he might.

'I suppose you think you're a bloody hero,' said Jardine.

'No, sir. I think I've acted like a bloody fool.'

David Jardine stared at Gant. He forced into a corner the little voice that kept nagging him that the young man would not have gone off on his ill-conceived and potentially explosive quest if he himself had resisted his Foreign Secretary's incitement to find something to 'jolt' Washington into seeing things Patrick Orde's way.

'Yes,' he replied, 'you have.' He crossed to a bureau and opened a crystal decanter. 'You like Scotch?'

'I would kill for one, sir.'

Jardine frowned. 'Choose your words carefully, young James.' And he poured two very stiff Macallan's single malt, and handed one to Gant.

'Sorry about Edith,' he said.

'Thank you.' James toyed with his glass.

'Siddown . . .'

Gant obeyed, settling into a deep leather winged armchair.

'Part of me wants to hear every detail,' remarked Jardine, 'and part of me does not really want to know. I'm not sure if my constitution could stand it . . .'

'Sir.'

A clock ticked on the mantelpiece. Jardine realised he had not moped about Dorothy for about a week. 'Look. Give me a report. But unofficially. I'll shred it afterwards.'

Of course you will, thought James Gant, uncharitably.

'Yes, sir.'

'This Farouche girl. We have prised her out of the clutches of NYPD, thanks to certain contacts of Roly's.'

'Excellent . . .' Gant actually was pleased.

'Well, I'm not convinced of that, but we certainly could not leave her to do a deal with the Cousins. Now the legend, which you will be briefed upon, is that it was all part of an official SIS operation to stop Dante, without overshadowing the United Nations accord on nuclear proliferation. To deny Tehran the oxygen of publicity, as former Prime Minister Thatcher put it, by quietly removing Dante from the picture. Don't look so damned sceptical.'

'No, sir.'

Jardine sipped his Scotch and seemed to be contemplating his leather boots.

'I spoke to your sister,' he said, apropos of nothing very much. Merely punctuating the silence.

Gant almost choked on his drink. He wondered if he was blushing, his cheeks certainly felt warm. 'Really? How is she?'

'She says you can be dangerous . . .'

Gant glanced at the older man, slightly surprised. 'She said that?'

'Well, she knows her brother. Very well indeed. Are you quite close?'

What the hell is he getting at, wondered Gant.

'Ever since our mother died. Dad sort of . . . peeled off, emotionally. Sure. We are pretty close.'

Jardine nodded. 'Zina Farouche . . .' he said, changing the subject, to James Gant's relief. 'What the hell benefit could she be to us? I mean, why should I not simply throw her back into the water?'

Gant frowned. He had assumed the Firm would be thrilled to get a genuine, all-singing, all-dancing Abu Nidal team leader to debrief.

'Well,' he replied, 'she can fill us in on all kinds of stuff we would like to know about Abu Nidal. And Tehran, which was behind Dante from the start . . .'

Jardine buried his neck into his shoulders, and turned his baleful eye on the young man. 'Dear boy, I have the most comprehensive lines into both Abu Nidal, *and* Tehran.'

'Oh.' Gant felt guilty about letting Zina down. All right, of course she had murdered and maimed all over Europe and the Middle East. But he had made a deal with her and he did not want to rat on it.

'Until yesterday, actually. Then my prize asset inside Abu Nidal's organisation was found skinned alive.'

'Jesus . . .'

'Amen. So, James,' David Jardine gazed at Gant over the rim of his crystal tumbler, 'you don't suppose you could persuade Ma'mselle Farouche to play herself back into the field.'

'I think they'd kill her.'

'Come, come, nobody knows the part she played in trapping the surviving member of the gang. Zafir Hammuda. And Ronnie and Marietta will come up with a story sufficiently convincing to persuade Nidal to take her back.' Jardine's eyes were dark and amused, and cruel. 'But it's you she trusts. Did you and she, um . . .?'

'No.'

'Ah, well, maybe you should. She trusts you, and you are the very man to sell her the deal. We slot her back, arrange for her to receive large sums of money paid into a Swiss account, or wherever. And she makes regular – we are talking at least once every twenty-four hours – reports on every conceivable angle. So that poor Albatross might, at least in part, become less of a loss . . .'

The room was becoming dimmer, with dark alleyways of shadow in the lightless spaces between bookcases and furniture. Outside, far below, the throaty bellow of a fire engine forced its way down Fifth Avenue. James remembered the town house his grandparents used to have, just a few blocks east of here. The laughter of Charlie as they played hide and seek in pools of darkness, just like these. And his mother, in that soft, North Carolina voice of hers would call, 'Come on, children, time for bed . . .'

And James Gant felt a tightness in his throat, for all that innocence was long, long gone.

Jesus, how he wished the clock would turn back, and that fucking great car transporter had somehow missed his mother's car.

'She wouldn't last more than a fortnight,' he found himself saying, bitterly, to Jardine, 'and well you know it.'

The Director of Operations nodded. 'Even five days would be a bonus. Just until we can set up something more . . . substantial.' And he watched his flawed recruit very closely.

Gant met his gaze and examined the older man for what seemed a long time.

'How do you live with yourself?' he asked, quietly.

Jardine smiled, an infinitely tired smile. 'With very great difficulty,' he replied.

They sat in silence. Sipping and listening to the ticking of the clock.

Then Jardine said, 'You know you can't remain in SIS, James?'

He forced himself to be merciless in the face of Gant's look of utter misery.

'Yes, sir. I can completely appreciate that.'

Jardine waited for a moment, then went on, 'How many men did you kill . . .? Between ourselves.'

'Five,' Gant replied, without hesitating. 'I missed Morteza, apparently, and I shared Zafir Hammuda with Joe. That's the cop I persuaded to help us.'

Hell's teeth, reflected Jardine, you would think it was pheasants he was talking about. And talking a hard-bitten

New York cop into commandeering a helicopter and ambushing Hammuda? The youth was a natural.

'OK, Jimmy. Can I call you that?'

James Gant sensed the change of gear. 'My closest friends do.'

'When you get back, tell those close friends that the Foreign Office just was not for you. Too many stuffed shirts. No room for initiative, all that sort of thing. Will you do that?'

Gant inclined his head, and David Jardine noted the smooth move, which he would have expected from this man, from underling to . . . equal.

'Then relax for a few weeks, take a proper holiday. No adventures, please. Set about getting work as a cameraman for foreign assignments. Current affairs. News. Can you do that?'

James felt a twinge of understanding. Maybe just wishful thinking. 'Suppose I'll have to. Not much else I'm good at.'

'Good. Well, when you've done that. And not before. Report to this address.' He handed Gant a business card. It was for a car-stereo and paint shop in Brixton.

'What will I be doing?'

David Jardine liked that. Not, I don't understand, or how much will it pay? But what will he be doing . . .?

'My dear young man,' he said, 'don't be naive . . .'